AF538893

The Upaniṣads

The Upaniṣads

~

Translated by

NACHIKETA JHA

ALEPH

ALEPH BOOK COMPANY
An independent publishing firm
promoted by ***Rupa Publications India***

First published in India in 2026
by Aleph Book Company
161-B/4, Gulmohar House
Yusuf Sarai Community Centre
New Delhi 110049

ISBN: 978-93-6523-519-7

1 3 5 7 9 10 8 6 4 2

Printed in India.

Contents

List of Abbreviations

Aitareya Upaniṣad	Ai
Bhagavad Gītā	B.G.
Bṛhadāraṇyaka Upaniṣad	Br
Brahma Sūtra	Br.S
Chāndogya Upaniṣad	Ch
Īśa Upaniṣad	Īśa
Kaṭha Upaniṣad	Ka.
Kena Upaniṣad	Ke
Māṇḍūkya Upaniṣad	Mā
Muṇḍaka Upaniṣad	Mu
Praśna Upaniṣad	Pr
Ṛg Veda	R.V.
Taittirīya Upaniṣad	Ta

Guide to Pronunciation and Transliteration

In the following table, the first column on the left contains letters with diacritics which are used in Sanskrit words in the book. The second column contains their equivalent in the Devanāgrī script. The third column contains the sounds as they are pronounced in English.

	Devanāgrī	As pronounced in English
a	अ	u in hut
ā	आ	a in car
i	ई	i in bit
ī	ई	e in she
u	उ	u in pull
ū	ऊ	oo in root
ṛ	ऋ	ri in risk
e	ए	a in pervade
ai	ऐ	y in my
o	ओ	o in scope
au	औ	ou in sound
ka	क	k in karma
kha	ख	kh in khaki

ga	ग	g in garage
gha	घ	gh in yoghurt
ṅ	ङ	ng
ca	च	ch in chirp
cha	छ	chh in achha
ja	ज	j in jump
jha	झ	dheh in hedgehog
ñ	ञ	n in fringe
ṭa	ट	t in tar
ṭha	ठ	th in ant-hill
ḍa	ड	d in data
ḍha	ढ	dh in dhow
ṇ	ण	n in asunder
ta	त	t in Tirupati
tha	थ	th in thistle
da	द	th in they
dha	ध	dh in dharma
na	न	n in nursery
pa	प	p in particular
pha	फ	ph in shepherd
ba	ब	b in barfi
bha	भ	bh in abhor
ma	म	m in mother
ya	य	y in yamaraja
ra	र	r in Ranchi
la	ल	l in late
va	व	v in advert

śa	श	sh in shirt
ṣa	ष	sh in show
sa	स	s in sir
h	ह	h in harp

Preface

The wisdom of the Upaniṣads is timeless yet ever relevant. As we shall see, they are rich in spiritual content and also discuss the fundamental questions of philosophy. They have significantly impacted Indic and global thought and culture over millennia, often more than is usually acknowledged.

In today's constantly evolving society with its numerous materialistic pressures, the eternal Upaniṣads have an important message to give. They discuss and throw light upon a wide-ranging set of topics which will always be significant to humanity. The Upaniṣads strongly encourage ethical living. Values such as compassion, faith, and austerity are emphasized. Time and again in various Upaniṣads it is stated that hatred and attachment are based on ultimately false notions of the world and ourselves, and should therefore be avoided. The Upaniṣads encourage kindness, moderation, and tolerance in our dealings with each other.

The profound content of the Upaniṣads has something for every genuine spiritual aspirant. Numerous meditational techniques and practices are outlined. Their benefits are explained. The ultimate aim of the spiritual path—liberation—is explained in great detail. For the student of philosphy, it has a richness of arguments, insights, and the repeated use of reasoning and other philosphical methods. Upaniṣadic propositions and positions have impacted Indian philosophy for ages. Metaphysical questions concerning the world we inhabit and the nature of Being are asked and answered. Epistemological issues relating to valid knowledge and error are also explored. The self and Brahman, two of the central concepts of the Upaniṣads, are of course discussed in great detail.

While there exist several prior translations of some of these texts, what follows is a new, faithful, and accessible rendition of ten major Upaniṣads that are widely believed to represent the core of Vedāntic thought. Furthermore, the vast majority of the verses translated are, crucially, accompanied by my commentary based on Śaṅkarācārya's exegesis. This brings nuance, context, and clarity to the reading of the original. Verses that are self-explanatory have, however, been left as is. The book begins with a critical introduction to the Upaniṣads, summarizing not only their main themes like the self, Brahman, the relation between the self and Brahman, māyā, prāṇa, and so on, but also meditation and other spiritual practices laid out in the texts. The introduction also locates the Upaniṣads in various modern-day contexts and debates such as relating to their nature, chronology, and resonances with consciousness studies, on the one hand, and quantum physics, on the other.

I have been reading and re-reading the Upaniṣads for the last thirty years, ever since I obtained of these texts in St. Stephen's College where I was pursuing a bachelors and masters in philosophy then. But my relationship with these texts goes back much further and may even have been foretold by my naming at birth. 'Nachiketa' is a major protagonist and seeker of truth in the Kaṭha Upaniṣad whose many enquiries of Yama, the lord of death, initiate one of the most memorable discourses on the self in this corpus.

Anyone interested in Indian philosophy and thought will benefit from reading the Upaniṣads. Not only do they showcase the most important spiritual and intellectual concepts known to humankind, but a rigorous study of these texts is also an excellent means to develop greater self awareness, self control, and discipline. A study of the Upaniṣads affords a priceless opportunity to interact with thousands of years of Indic wisdom and genius.

Introduction

There can be no doubt that the Upaniṣads have played a profound role in the history of Indic thought. Sarvepalli Radhakrishnan states that the Upaniṣads 'represent a great chapter in the history of the human spirit and have dominated Indian philosophy, religion and life for three thousand years' (Radhakrishnan 2019: 17). According to Patrick Olivelle, the Upaniṣads mark the emergence of the central religious concepts of Hinduism. (Olivelle 1996: xxiii). Though modern academics have sought to date them to this or that era, they are popularly believed to be eternal. And indeed, they do provide timeless wisdom, spiritual guidance, and philosophical insights. Despite their esoteric contents, it is important to bring the message of the Upaniṣads to a wider audience. Though translating and explicating them is a monumental and daunting task, it is necessary to rediscover these great texts for every generation.

The word Upaniṣad is derived from a combination of the syllables 'upa' meaning nearness or contiguity as well as instruction by a teacher; 'ni' meaning down, under; and 'ṣad' meaning to sit down, settle, reside. Thus implying groups of students sitting respectfully near a teacher and learning. The texts themselves often refer to themselves as 'secret teachings'. They constitute a key part of Śruti (that which is heard), that is, the Vedas—sacred, eternal, aurally received knowledge. They are said to be beyond the ordinary means of comprehension such as perception, and are instead cognized by the wise with clear discerning abilities.

When did the Upaniṣads come into being? Traditionally, the Śruti which is not of human creation (apauruṣeya), and as such cannot be dated in terms of anthropic timelines. Most modern scholars have also agreed that it is difficult to pinpoint their exact chronology because, like much of early Sanskrit literature, they were orally transmitted for the longest time and so there is a difference between when they may have been composed and when they were committed to writing in the form of manuscripts much later. These difficulties are reflected in the different dates attributed to the Upaniṣads by different scholars. Radhakrishnan is of the view that, 'the ancient prose Upaniṣads, Aitareya, Kauṣītaki, Chāndogya, Kena, Taittirīya, and Bṛhadāraṇyaka, together with Īśa and Kaṭha belong to the eighth and seventh centuries BC.' (Radhakrishnan 2019: 22) Olivelle ascribes the Chāndogya and Bṛhadāraṇyaka Upaniṣads to the seventh and sixth centuries BCE; the Taittirīya, Aitareya, and Kauṣītaki to the sixth and fifth centuries BCE; and the Kena, Īśa, Śvetāśvatara, and Muṇḍaka Upaniṣads to the last centuries BCE. (Olivelle 1998: 12–13) Johannes Bronkhorst attributes a still later date of the second century BCE to the Upaniṣads. (Bronkhorst 2007: 258–59)

The system of philosophy based largely on Upaniṣadic thinking is referred to as Vedānta (the end of the Vedas) since the texts are believed to belong to the last strata of the Vedic corpus. The Upaniṣads contain the central teachings of the Vedas and also state their aims and ends. The Jñāna kāṇḍa or knowledge portion of the Vedas is contained in the Upaniṣads. The orthodox schools of Indian thought accept the authority of the Vedas and the Upaniṣads. They however differ with each other at times on the interpretation of these texts. The summary of the teachings of the Upaniṣads, in turn, is contained in the later Brahma Sūtra (attributed between 500 BCE and 200 BCE by most scholars). The commentaries on the Brahma Sūtra such as by Śaṅkarācārya in the eighth century, are very significant since it is here that the great thinkers and teachers of the Upaniṣads develop and state their views.

The number of known Upaniṣads is said to be more than two hundred. The Muktikā Canon lists 108 Upaniṣads. (Tripathy 2010, *Indian Religions: Tradition, History and Culture*, Axis Publications) According to Radhakrishnan there are ten principal Upaniṣads. (Radhakrishnan 2019: 21) These are: Īśa, Kena, Kaṭha, Praśna, Muṇḍaka, Māṇḍūkya, Taittirīya, Aitareya, Chāndogya, and Bṛhadāraṇyaka. To these some scholars add the Śvetāśvatara, Kauṣītaki, and Maitrāyaṇīya Upaniṣads. Different Upaniṣads are associated with the different Vedas: the Aitareya and Kauṣītaki with the Ṛg Veda; the Chāndogya and Kena with the Sāma Veda; the Taittirīya, Kaṭha, Śvetāśvatara and Maitrāyaṇi, Bṛhadāraṇyaka, and Īśa with the Yajur Veda; and the Muṇḍaka, Māṇḍūkya and Praśna with the Atharva Veda.

~

The Upaniṣads cover a wide range of topics. They deliberate on questions regarding the ultimate reality (Brahman), the self (ātman), the relationship between the self and the ultimate reality; the concept of māyā (cosmic illusion) along with the relative nature of the phenomenal world; the levels of reality; the states of consciousness; the journey of the soul after death; the role and implications of rituals; and karma and rebirth. The Upaniṣads reflect a world view that, as Śaṅkarācārya so brilliantly showed us, is remarkably logical: if one starts with the premises of the Upaniṣads, one is inexorably drawn to their conclusions.

Their seminality notwithstanding, some critics including Patrick Olivelle claim that the Upaniṣads do not hold a unified position on the various themes they propound. Olivelle states, 'These documents were composed over several centuries and in various regions, and it is futile to discover a sigle doctrine or philosophy in them.' (Olivelle 1996: xliv) However, while there are indeed a number of different Upaniṣads with somewhat different focus, there is also evident among them significant consistency in the treatment of their main themes such as the nature of Brahman, the self, the importance of knowledge, the need to strive for liberation, and much more (discussed in detail below). They all attempt to come to terms with some of life's most basic questions such as the nature of reality, of being, of consciousness, life and death, and self-realization. The Upaniṣads are truly philosophical in nature, attempting to answer these perennial questions in a reasoned, nuanced, and logical manner.

In the Upaniṣads we find a marked endeavour to establish an ontological basis for the diverse aspects of reality as we experience it. Thus these texts are often stated to be metaphysical in nature. By metaphysics is meant the branch of philosophy that is 'about reality'. Certainly, the Upaniṣads strive to know the nature of the real and the underlying principle behind all phenomena. But beyond the metaphysical too, the Upaniṣads also have a significant ethical content and enjoin virtues such as humility, self control, charity, faith, austerity, and compassion. An ethical life is a crucial prerequisite on the path to liberation. So is correct knowledge. Hence the Upaniṣads contain a detailed epistemology or theory of knowledge. The ways of knowing the self, the role and functioning of the sense organs, the knowledge of the phenomenal world are some of the topics on which the Upaniṣads declaim.

The ultimate aim in the Upaniṣads is the attainment of mukti or liberation. The paths to liberation and the ending of bondage are discussed in great detail, as are the necessary conditions that the spiritual aspirant has to fulfil in order to attain liberation. These texts can thus be termed soteriological. According to the Upaniṣads, the path to liberation is open to all without any discrimination on the basis of gender, caste, age, and so on.

In fact, as per this world view, all distinctions are themselves illusory and meant to be transcended.

Let us now acquaint ourselves in greater detail with the core themes and teachings of the Upaniṣads.

Māyā

Throughout the Upaniṣads it is asserted that the true nature of reality (Brahman) is beyond form and description. At the same time, we also find numerous accounts of the origin and creation of the world in all its multiplicity of form in these texts. Śaṅkarācārya reconciles these two aspects through the concept of māyā. Māyā may be termed as cosmic illusion or a magical power of God by which the world is created. This power of God is indistinguishable from God. Those who are beset by ignorance view the world as real. However, with the dawn of right knowledge, the world is seen to be nothing but an illusion, temporary and unreal, while the only reality is Brahman. The ignorance that enables illusion is twofold in its nature. It conceals the true nature of reality and it also distorts this reality into something else. Māyā does not affect Brahman. But ignorant people are misled by māyā into believing that the perceived multiplicity is real. In this aspect of concealment of reality, māyā has been termed as ajñāna or avidyā. Māyā also positively imposes an illusion on reality. In this aspect it is known as positive ignorance or bhāva rūpam ajñānam. For the ignorant, there is no beginning or end to māyā.

The Bṛhadāraṇyaka Upaniṣad states that, 'By means of māyā, Indra (the lord) goes about in multiple forms, since to him are yoked organs, ten and hundreds. Surely this is the organs, surely this is tens and thousands, numerous and countless. This Brahman is without any prior and without any subsequent, without interior and without exterior. This self which experiences all is Brahman.'

(Br. 2.v.19) The verse highlights that the different forms of the self are meant to make it known. Brahman on account of māyā is perceived as diverse yet Brahman is the same being.

In his commentary Śaṅkarācārya states that all distinctions including those of caste are destroyed by the realization of the self. In the Bṛhadāraṇyaka Upaniṣad (Section IV of Book 2) renunciation is enjoined as a means to reach immortality. An aversion to everything else that is māyā is sought to be inculcated leading to immortality.

The Taittirīya Upaniṣad (Ta. 2.vi.1) affirms that Brahman is all that there is. All modifications of name and form, all empirical truths, are in the ultimate analysis temporary and unreal. There is no reality, no existence apart from Brahman.

There is a distinction in the views of different Vedāntins regarding māyā. According to Rāmānujācārya, māyā is a real power of creation of God. Primal matter is actually transformed into the world. But for Śaṅkarācārya, māyā is not a permanent feature of Brahman. It is a creative power of the world illusion. That is, for Śaṅkarācārya, the apparent world we see is not ultimately real.

Brahman

Among the key concerns being addressed in the Upaniṣads are the basis of the world, the cause of the world, what constitutes the truly real, and that by grasping which the entire world is known. The Chāndogya Upaniṣad (Ch. 3.xiv.1) asks 'From where do all things arise and into what are they resolved and in what do they have their being?' The answer is Brahman, the supreme reality.

The word Brahman is taken from the root 'bṛh' which means to grow, increase, expand, and this is the sense in which Śaṅkarācārya also treats the word. As Radhakrishnan points out, the word is found in the Ṛg Veda where it is used to denote 'sacred knowledge' and 'the concrete expression of spiritual wisdom'. (Radhakrishnan 2019: 52) In later thought too, the word Brahman means wisdom.

Though the world may appear in diverse forms, existence itself persists through all forms and all states. Śaṅkarācārya thus comes to the conclusion, based on the authority of revealed texts and rigorous logical reasoning, that pure existence is the common cause of the entire world. He arrives at the concept of the absolute, undefinable, infinite material cause of the world which is Brahman. This Brahman is absolute existence and consciousness and 'has the power of manifesting itself in diverse apparent forms, without really undergoing any modification' (Chatterjee and Datta 2008: 377).

It is possible to discuss Brahman from two points of view, the worldly and the transcendent. From the vyāvahārika dṛṣṭi or the practical standpoint wherein the world is perceived to be real, Brahman is said to be saguna or endowed with many qualities such as omnipotence, omniscience, etc. Saguṇa Brahman or Īśvara (God) is that which is worshipped. However, from the ultimate point of view or pāramārthika dṛṣṭi, Brahman is nirguna or without attributes, devoid of qualities or distinctions, and cannot be categorized.

The Upaniṣads contain numerous accounts of the creation of the world. In the school of Advaita Vedānta, which Śaṅkarācārya represents, the world is said to gradually evolve from Brahman by means of māyā. This change is not real and is only apparent. It proceeds from that which is subtle to that which is gross. In the Vedāntasāra of Sadānanda, which is attributed to the fifteenth century, three stages are mentioned. These are the causal or seed stage, the stage of subtle differentiation or the germinating stage, and the fully developed stage. As mentioned earlier, all these changes are only apparent and reflect the creative power of māyā.

There are four aspects of Brahman with regard to the evolution of the world. The state of pure consciousness and existence is Parabrahman. Brahman viewed as associated with undifferentiated māyā is called Īśvara and is described as having attributes of being all knowing, omnipotent, etc. This is the apparent state of Brahman before creation yet possessed of the power of creation. Next is the Brahman associated with subtly differentiated māyā named Hiraṇyagarbha. This is the subtle stage. Brahman apparently associated with māyā differentiated into corporeal and perceptible objects is known as Vaiśvānara or Virāt.

The Kena Upaniṣad (Ke. 1.i.2) in its invocation states: 'Everything is the Brahman of the Upaniṣad. May I never repudiate Brahman, may Brahman never repudiate me. Let there be no rejection. Let there be no rejection of me by Brahman.' It further states: 'It [Brahman] is the ear of the ear, the mind of the mind, the speech of speech, the vital breath of vital breath, the eye of the eye, the wise after giving up (erroneous views of self identification with sense organs) and having departed from this world become immortal.' Again, 'There the eye does not go, speech does not go nor the mind. We do not know nor can we discern about how this can be taught.' (Ke. 1.i.3) Tantalizingly, Brahman is also described as that which is 'indeed different from the known, so also it is above the unknown.' (Ke. 1.i.4) The Kena goes on to describe Brahman as that which one cannot cognize through the senses yet that upon which the senses depend.

The Muṇḍaka Upaniṣad states that the entire universe emanates from Brahman (Mu. 1.i.7). 'That which is not seen, not grasped, without root, without features, with no eyes or ears, which does not have hands or feet, perpetual, pervading all material things, omnipresent, extremely subtle, that which is the undecaying origin of all elements which the discerning perceive everywhere' (Mu. 1.i.6). It is indestructible and perceived to be everywhere by the wise.

The Chāndogya Upaniṣad reiterates the point that the universe and everything in it originates from Brahman. 'Surely this entire world is Brahman. From this does everything originate, into this do they dissolve and it is by this that they are perceived. In tranquillity one ought to meditate on this.' (Ch. 3.xiv.1) In his commentary to this verse, Śaṅkarācārya says that the origin, preservation, and dissolution of the universe is all Brahman. Since all is Brahman, in the ultimate analysis, there is no scope for hatred or attachment.

Again: 'All that is created, all desires, all smells, all tastes, pervading all this, who is without speech, without concern, this is my self residing in the heart; this is Brahman' (Ch. 3.xiv.4). Both by reasoning and scriptural authority, 'Śaṅkarācārya in his commentary to Section XII of Chapter 6 of the Chāndogya Upaniṣad shows that 'that being which is subtle nameless and formless, from it arises the universe with name and form'.

The Taittirīya Upaniṣad reiterates the point that it is from Brahman that all beings are born and live and into it they merge after departing. (Ta. 3.i.1) This Upaniṣad also lays down that meditation and austerity are means by which one can attain Brahman, and they who know Brahman attain the supreme. 'Who knows Brahman as true, as knowledge, as unending, situated in the secret cavity of the heart and in the highest sky, obtains all desires together with Brahman, the learned'. (Ta. 2.i.1) Śaṅkarācārya clarifies this verse by saying that a knower of Brahman becomes all and thus obtains all desires. Further, according to Śaṅkarācārya, the truth of Brahman is affirmed by speaking of its existence.

Various arguments to prove the existence of Brahman are stated. The Kaṭha Upaniṣad points out that Brahman is not attained by means of the senses. It is the source of the universe. The world exists and so the source of the universe exists. (Ka. 2.iii.12)

The Bṛhadāraṇyaka Upaniṣad extensively deals with the subject of Brahman. It states clearly that one of the main aims of the Upaniṣads is to impart knowledge of Brahman. A qualified teacher is compared to a boat on the ocean of worldly troubles. (Br. 1.iv.9) They who know that they are Brahman become all there is. This Upaniṣad reiterates that everything emanates from Brahman. It describes Brahman as the truth of the truth. Further, it is in this Upaniṣad (Br. 2.iii.6) that the crucial, cryptic, and well-known phrase 'neti, neti' (not this, not this) is to be found. It means: Brahman is not this nor that.

Yet there is nothing other than Brahman. The term, 'not this, not this' is used to describe that which is the truth of truth. These words aim to state the elimination of all differences due to limiting adjuncts and the reference to that which does not have anything to distinguish it such as name, form, action, attribute, species, etc. Brahman has no distinguishing marks. It cannot be described as 'so and so' or 'such and such'. When Brahman is described by categories superimposed on it such as name, form, and action, then words like knowledge, bliss, pure, intelligence, etc., are used. However, when we want to describe its true nature, it can only be described as, 'not this, not this'. By eliminating all adjuncts, the desire to know space, time, and all else, one realizes one's identity with Brahman, the truth of truth.

In Section VIII of Chapter 3 of the Bṛhadāraṇyaka Upaniṣad, Yājñavalkya refers to the 'knowers of Brahman'. He goes on to describe Brahman as being devoid of any attribute, as one with no second. The text seeks to negate the attributes of Brahman and indicate its existence. It brings forth inferential evidence in favour of the existence of Brahman: the existence of Brahman can be inferred from the fixed order of the world. The consistent theme of the four chapters of this Upaniṣad is that the self is the supreme Brahman. The means to attaining the self are diverse. It is to be arrived at by the process of 'not this, not this', and the renunciation of all.

Ātman

The ātman is the self. It is taken up and discussed thoroughly in the Upaniṣads, often through dialogues, like between students and their teacher, in the form of questions and answers wherein the student is eventually led to the correct conclusions.

At the heart of the Upaniṣadic quest lies the focus on our self. What actually constitutes the self? Is it the body, the external manifestation of a person? Is it the mind, the senses, the intellect? Do the feelings of pleasure and pain constitute the self? Is the self subject to change? Is it made of what is impermanent? The Upaniṣads arrive at the conclusion that the self is permanent, it is pure consciousness (prājña). It is not subject to change or limitations. The self is infinite indeed. The self of a person is stated to be the same as the self of all beings. Later, we will discuss the identity of the self and Brahman.

Since the self is the same as the ultimate reality, people are encouraged to strive to realize the self. The highest form of knowledge is said to be knowledge concerning the self. Ātmavidyā is termed as parāvidyā or supreme knowledge. Different aspects of the path to self-realization are emphasized including repeated meditation, self-control over one's instincts and impulses, overcoming entrenched habits, desires, feelings such as attachment and hatred, and so on. Also enjoined are reasoning, study of revealed scriptures, and a balanced lifestyle. Instructive for our consumerist times, there is a strong distinction made between what is pleasant and what is good. It is the good which needs to be striven for in order to realize the self.

In the ultimate analysis, the body (śarira) is not real. It is an illusion. When one realizes this, the sole remaining reality is the self (ātman) which is the same as Brahman. The Vedāntin's conception of the body is not limited to the mere physical body. In addition to this physical body, there is the subtle body which comprises the indriyas (the sense organs), prāṇas (vital breaths) and the antaḥkaraṇa (internal organ). While the physical body is extinguished at death, the subtle body continues with the self and gets attached to the next physical body. However, both these bodies are the effects of māyā. How does the self associate itself with these limited bodies? This is due to ignorance. This state of ignorance is also the state of bondage. In this state, the self due to error mistakenly identifies with the finite body.

Śaṅkarācārya states that the ātman is self-evident in all (Brahma Sūtra 1.1.1) and puts forward numerous arguments in support of this view. An analysis of the words used in everyday language reveals that the word 'I' appears to be used in different senses, sometimes to refer to the body, sometimes to the mind, at times it refers to a feeling and so on. But what is common to all these, which remains through all states? That is consciousness. Thus, consciousness is the essence of the self.

Furthermore, it is consciousness again that is common to the three states of waking, dreaming, and deep sleep. This consciousness is not dependent on any object. From this it follows that if consciousness is independent of any object, then it is only due to an obstruction that it cannot be cognized. This obstruction or obstacle is ignorance. In the absence of ignorance or on the dawn of right knowledge, the ātman is revealed.

The ātman according to the Ṛg Veda is the 'breath of life'. (R.V. VII.87.2) Śaṅkarācārya states that the root of the word ātman is āp meaning to obtain or pervade or reach (Apte 2020: 122). It has also been derived from the root 'an' meaning to breathe or to live (Apte 2020: 23).

The Bṛhadāraṇyaka Upaniṣad speaks at length about the ātman. It is described as Brahman, immortal, consisting of light (Br. 2.v.1) The self is said to be in all including the earth, water, fire, air, the directions, truth, righteousness, etc. 'Surely, this self is the lord of all beings; the king of all beings. Just in the manner that the spokes are attached to the nave and fellow of a chariot wheel, thus only in this self are attached all beings, all deities, all worlds, all creatures and all these selves' (Br. 2.v.15). Chapter III, Section VII of this Upaniṣad also describes the self. It is said to be the inner controller, present in all, and immortal.

While it is in all, almost nothing knows the self.

> Who resides in the seed, yet is within the seed, whom the seed does not know, whose body is the seed, who is the inner controller of the seed, this is your self, the inner controller and immortal. Unseen yet the seer, unheard yet the hearer, unthought yet the thinker, unknown yet the knower. There is no seer other than this, there is no hearer other than this, there is no thinker other than this, there is no knower other than this. This is your self, the inner controller and immortal. Now anything else is afflicted. (Br. 3.xvii.23)

Again, the self is said to be 'one, alone, immeasurable, perpetual and free from any taint. The self is superior from ether, unborn, infinite and permanent'. (Br. 4.iv.20) 'It, surely this infinite, unborn self who is undecaying, imperishable, immortal, fearless is Brahman. Certainly, Brahman is fearless. He who knows thus surely becomes the fearless Brahman. (Br. 4.iv.25) The self is 'neti, neti—not this, not this'. 'It is ungraspable for it is not grasped. It is incognizable since it cannot be cognized. This self is unyoked since it is not yoken. It is untrammelled, it does not suffer, it is not injured.' (Br. 3.ix.26)

The Kaṭha Upaniṣad describes the self as that which is neither born nor dies. The self originated from nothing and nothing originated from it. It is perpetual and eternal. It is not destroyed when the body is destroyed (Ka. 1.ii.18). The famous chariot analogy is stated in this Upaniṣad. The self is compared to the owner of the chariot, the intellect to the charioteer, and the mind to the reins (Ka. 1.iii.3), the senses to the horses, and the sense objects to the pastures and roads traversed (Ka. 1.iii.4). The self, yoked with the body, sense organs, and mind, is the enjoyer or experiencer. For he who is unintelligent, whose mind is uncontrolled, his senses wander amok like the untamed horses yoked to a chariot (Ka. 1.iii.5). The intelligent person's mind is calm and restrained and his sense organs remain under control like that of good horses of a chariot (Ka. 1.iii.6). They whose intellect is not discriminating, whose mind is uncontrolled, they keep being born and reborn (Ka. 1.iii.7). The one with a discriminating intellect and unsullied mind attains the goal and is not reborn (Ka. 1.iii.8). The Upaniṣads repeatedly state that one attains liberation and eternal peace by realizing the self. There is just one self inside all beings but the self appears to assume a form in accordance with the various shapes of beings (Ka. 2.ii.1). The self itself is not stained by the sorrows of this world. It is blemishless and transcends all.

The Praśna Upaniṣad describes the self as supreme, indestructible, shadowless, bodiless, colourless, pure. 'He who realizes the self becomes omniscient. He becomes all' (Pr. 4.10). The Īśa Upaniṣad describes the self as unmoving and swifter than the mind. It is beyond the senses and all pervading (Īśa. 4). 'He who realizes the self sees the oneness in all and therefore never feels hatred and sorrow' (Īśa. 6 and Īśa. 7).

The relationship between Ātman and Brahman: the four mahāvākyas

One of the central questions that the Upaniṣads seeks to address is the relationship between ātman, the self, and Brahman, the ultimate reality, the supreme being. The Upaniṣads assert the identity of ātman and Brahman. The four mahāvākyas (great sentences) seek to proclaim the identity of the ātman and Brahman and are interrelated and mutually reinforcing statements. They are:

Tat Tvam Asi

This mahāvākya is found in in the Chāndogya Upaniṣad (Ch. 6.viii.7). It is translated as 'That thou art' or 'You are that'.

It conveys the underlying unity of the ātman and Brahman. In this Upaniṣad, Āruṇi says to Śvetaketu: 'The entire phenomenal universe is traced to the universal, all-pervasive principle of Being. This is the basis of all including humankind.' The self without any limiting adjuncts is the same as the underlying universal principle. This is one of the central pillars of the Advaita system of thought. This vākya is said to have the foremost place among all vākyas.

According to Vedānta, the body is, in the ultimate analysis, an illusion. Once a person understands this then it becomes clear that there is nothing other than Brahman left. In this mahāvākya, the word 'thou' (tvam) does not mean the physical body. It stands for the pure consciousness that is the nature of the self. 'That' (tat) stands for pure consciousness which is the nature of Brahman. This identity is not a tautology. It aims to show that, that which due to error and illusion is viewed as distinct, is actually one and the same. In reality, the self and Brahman are the same. The self, due to our erroneous identification with the body stemming from ignorance, appears as finite, mortal, and limited. But it is in fact infinite, immortal, and all encompassing, like the Brahman.

Aham Brahmāsmi

Translated as 'I am Brahman', this mahāvākya is found in the Bṛhadāraṇyaka Upaniṣad (Br. 1.iv.10). The verse states that all who realized this, such as the gods, saints, and other humans, became this (Brahman). Indeed, whoever realizes this mahāvākya attains Brahman. Once again here the unity of the self and Brahman is stressed. The knower and the known are the same. Thus, in the Bhagavad Gītā, Sri Krishna says: 'I am the self O Arjuna (dwelling in the mind of all beings).' (B.G. X.20)

Ayam Ātmā Brahma

Translated as 'This self is Brahman', this vākya is found in the Māṇḍūkya Upaniṣad (Verse 2). This verse states that all is Brahman including the self. The unity of the self and the universal principle is reiterated.

Prajñānam Brahma

This mahāvākya found in the Aitareya Upaniṣad is translated as 'Consciousness is Brahman'. (Ai. 3.i.4) All creatures are driven by consciousness. This consciousness is Brahman. The word prājña in this verse has variously been understood as consciousness, intelligence or knowledge.

> The underlying reality, when freed of all distinctions, is taintless, beyond words, thoughts and attributes. Brahman, when associated with pure intelligence, is called antaryāmī, inner controller. When associated with cosmic intelligence, it is known as Hiraṇyagarbha, the seed of the manifested world. When associated with the cosmic body, it is called Prajāpati, Virāt. It is Brahman which is given various names and forms when conditioned by divergent bodies.

Mukti

Liberation or mukti is the ultimate aim of the Upaniṣads. It is attained when there is a realization that the self is Brahman and the illusory distinction between the self and Brahman ceases. Bondage (bandhana) consists in the erroneous distinction between the self and Brahman.

Karma, which can be defined as actions, works, or deeds and their consequences, play a crucial role in causing bondage. Three types of karma are distinguished. Prārabdha karma is that type of karma the effects of which have started manifesting; sañcita karma is that type of karma whose effects are not yet manifested and lie dormant; and sañcīyamāna or āgāmi karma is that karma that we gather in the present life.

True knowledge extinguishes sañcita karma and prevents āgāmi karma. But those karmic effects that have manifested cannot be undone. Thus, the body, which is a product of prārabdha karma, persists through the present life of even the liberated soul.

This is why the word for liberation in this tradition is jīvan mukti. However, the jīvan mukta is not affected by the world. He is beyond pleasure and grief. The jīvan-mukta may undertake activities for the emancipation of those still stuck in the mire of saṁsāra. The Upaniṣads provides us with different examples of liberated souls who chose to renounce the world or engage with the world as per their personalities and temperament. Thus, Janaka was a king while Yājñavalkya chose the life of a renouncer.

Liberation as conceived of in Vedānta is not a new state. It is the realization of what always existed. Liberation is nothing but the realization of the identity of the self and Brahman. With the dawn of true knowledge is dispelled the illusion of the distinction between the self and Brahman. As the Bṛhadāraṇyaka Upaniṣad and the Muṇḍaka Upaniṣad tell us, they who know Brahman become Brahman. The jīvan-mukta at the end of this lifespan attains the disembodied state of liberation or videha-mukti.

Liberation in the Upaniṣads is a state that is not merely limited to the absence of suffering or grief. It is also the positive state of bliss (ānanda). Actions performed by the liberated soul do not bind him. In fact, people are encouraged towards the performance of selfless action (niṣkāma karma) to escape from the clutches of the ego.

The Vedas and the Upaniṣads mention characteristics associated with the state of liberation. It is said to be beyond the scope of time. It entails freedom from the cycle of birth and death. On attaining this state, one is released from the laws of karma. In fact, it is stated that the laws of karma prevail in the realm of saṁsāra. Once the self is realized, we are beyond the purview of our deeds. Thus, all and any deeds or acts, good or bad, have no effect on a liberated person. There is a complete end of bondage (bandhana). Bondage is itself the product of ignorance. With knowledge is ignorance dispelled. Knowledge also leads to the extinguishing of all desires.

To attain liberation, the Upaniṣads emphasize the correct study of Vedānta. This study consists of three practices, namely, śravaṇa or listening to the teacher's instruction; manana or understanding these instructions and clearing all doubts through correct reasoning; and nididhyāsana or repeated meditation on these truths. After proper and repeated meditation as well as a life led according to these principles, the spiritual aspirant begins to realize truth. When they realize that 'I am Brahman', mukti is attained.

Avidyā and Vidyā

The role of knowledge in the pursuit of enlightenment as well as the spiritual journey is emphasized throughout the Upaniṣads. Knowledge is said to dispel illusions both at the individual level as well as the cosmic level. It also leads to the cessation of an egoistic world view. The terms vidyā and avidyā occur frequently in the texts. Vidyā means knowledge or learning. In the context of the Upaniṣads, it is used to refer to spiritual knowledge. Avidyā refers to ignorance and in this context, spiritual ignorance or illusion or māyā. This illusion is the reason why the world and its diversity are perceived as such. But as per Vedānta, Brahman alone exists (Apte 2020: 94).

Different kinds of knowledge are also mentioned. The Muṇḍaka Upaniṣad (Mu. 1.i.4) points out that there are two kinds, the higher which concerns the supreme self and the lower the sphere of which is knowledge of virtue and vice and their means and ends. 'The supreme is attained by means of the higher knowledge' (Mu. 1.i.5). The individual self can be reached only when a set of conditions has been fulfilled including being purified by knowledge (Mu. 3.i.8). The Bṛhadāraṇyaka Upaniṣad repeatedly emphasizes that the great reality is the supreme self. This consists of permanent knowledge (Br. 2.iv.12). 'Individual existence is based on ignorance.' (Br. 2.iv.13) But the self has its own light.

The role of a teacher in attaining vidyā is crucial. The Chāndogya Upaniṣad highlights this. The importance of humility in this endeavour is also repeatedly stressed. One must not get conceited due to one's intellectual attainments. In fact, the Upaniṣads perceptively observe that delighting in knowledge leads to great darkness. 'Those who worship ignorance enter into blinding darkness and those who take delight in knowledge enter into still greater darkness' (Īśa. 9).

However, the path to immortality is through vidyā. 'He who knows both vidyā (knowledge) and avidyā (ignorance) together, crosses over death through ignorance and attains immortality.' (Īśa. 10) True knowledge of all beings leads to the self. In the Īśa Upaniṣad's rousing words, 'For one who knows all beings become the self only, what delusion, what sorrow can there be for one who has seen the oneness?' (Īśa. 7)

Further, Śaṅkarācārya states that there are two kinds of karma, that which is operative and that which has not yet fructified. The second type of karma is extinguished when one attains knowledge. Prārabdha karma, the first one, is not extinguished but has to be experienced in this lifetime. The prārabdha karma of a knower ceases at the end of their body. They then attains Brahman (Ch. 6.xiv.2).

The Kaṭha Upaniṣad states that the self cannot be attained by the senses but it reveals itself to one who is wise and without desires. The path required to attain the knowledge of reality is compared to the sharp edge of a razor (Ka. 1.iii.14). This is a difficult path to tread and only very few can do so. The importance of knowledge is stressed throughout the Upaniṣads. The results of right knowledge are permanent. That which is temporary is shunned. The attainment of right knowledge also puts one beyond the effects of evil.

Aum

The sacred syllable Aum is discussed in the Upaniṣads including its meaning and significance, its relation to the self and to Brahman as well as the elements of this sacred word. The tweleve verses of the Māṇḍūkya Upaniṣad are dedicated to Aum. For the Upaniṣads, everything is Aum. 'The past, present and future, all this is Aum. And whatever else is beyond the three periods of time is also Aum.' (Mā. 1). The Māṇḍūkya Upaniṣad goes on to say that the self is denoted by the syllable Aum. 'That is the self which with reference to the syllable (denoting it) is Aum. With reference to its elements [letters constituting Aum], the qualities are the elements and the elements are the qualities, namely a, u and m' (Mā. 8). In fact, the Māṇḍūkya Upaniṣad goes on to state that the three elements of Aum mentioned above are associated with the three states of waking, dream, and deep sleep. The waking state, Vaiśvānara, is the letter 'a', the first element; Taijasa, whose domain is the dream state, is the letter 'u', the second element; Prājña whose domain is the state of deep sleep, is the letter 'm', the third element.

Aum is supremely powerful. They who know this enter the self with their self. The Kaṭha Upaniṣad (Ka. 1.ii.16) says:

> Indeed, this syllable (Aum) is the everlasting spirit. Verily, this syllable is the supreme. Having known this syllable, whatever anybody desires, surely that will be theirs.

The vast benefits of meditating on Aum are emphasized time and again. The Praśna Upaniṣad states that by even meditating on one letter of Aum, one attains great results. Meditating on Aum leads to release from sins and attainment of realization of the all-pervading Puruṣa or self. The Chāndogya Upaniṣad enjoins meditation on Aum as a symbol of Brahman as does the Taittirīya Upaniṣad. Aum is everything and Aum pervades all. The meditation on Aum is a path to attaining Brahman. (Ta. 1.viii.1)

Meditation

The Upaniṣads repeatedly and emphatically enjoin meditation. Its role in attaining spiritual progress is highlighted over and over again. Numerous meditation practices are spoken of and described. Their benefits are also enumerated. The Chāndogya Upaniṣad begins by stating that 'one should meditate on Aum' (Ch. 1.i.1). The wise who meditate on Aum become a fulfiller of all desires' (Ch. 1.i.7). 'If anything is done with meditation, faith, and knowledge, it becomes more efficacious' (Ch. 1.i.10). 'The meditator becomes the greatest, the most excellent in this world and the next' (Ch. 1.ix.4).

Chapter 3 of the Chāndogya Upaniṣad states various benefits of different types of meditations. The benefits mentioned include becoming brilliant, wealthy, glorious, famous, and so on. Specifically, it is said that the meditator on Brahman attains radiant worlds (Ch. 4.v.3). A meditator on the Gārhapatya fire attains the full length of life, is glorious, and his descendants do not perish. And, of course, 'he who meditates on the name Brahman attains all desires and wishes' (Ch. 7.i.5). Continuing in this manner, Chapter 7 enjoins the meditation on speech, mind, will, intellect, reflection, understanding, strength, food, water, heat, ether, memory, hope, prāṇa (life force), one after the other, leading to the self. The self is omnipresent, omniscient, and everything springs from the self. At the time of departing the body, the meditator on Aum rises upwards (Ch. 8.vi.5). Even deities in Brahmaloka are said to meditate on the self (Ch. 8.xii.6).

The Bṛhadāraṇyaka Upaniṣad also calls on one to meditate on the self since here all becomes one (Br. 1.iv.7). The meditator on the self attains all desires (Br. 1.iv.15). This Upaniṣad also emphasizes meditating on the truth (Br. 5.v.1, 6.ii.15). The Taittirīya Upaniṣad mentions that all deities meditate on Brahman (Ta. 2.v.1). The person who does this, becomes supreme and his rivals perish. On leaving the world, such a person attains the self (Ta. iii.10). The Praśna Upaniṣad states that the meditator on Aum attains that which is ageless, tranquil, beyond fear, immortal, and supreme (Pr. V.7).

Prāṇa

Prāṇa is dealt with extensively in the Upaniṣads. The word refers to breath, life breath, or vital breath. Most commentators interpret prāṇa as life force. Five types of breath are identified: prāṇa, apāna, samāna, vyāna, and udāna. Prāṇa is shown to hold primacy among the sense organs. This is clearly illustrated in various verses. The pre-eminent prāṇa said '...it is I only by dividing myself five-fold, who supports and holds together this body'. (Pr. II.3) Again:

> When it [prāṇa] rose through the body, indeed all the others [parts] rose. When he rested, all the others rested too. Just as all the bees rise when the king of bees rises and as they rest when the king of bees rests, thus speech, mind, eye, ear, etc., [follow prāṇa]. Pleased, they praise prāna. (Pr. II.4).

It is stated that just as spokes are established in the centre of a chariot wheel, everything is established on prāṇa; the rks (verses), yajus (formulae), and sāmans (chants) as well as sacrifice, power, and wisdom. Prāṇa is also said to be immortal, being and non-being.

This prāṇa is born of the self. It presides over and allots all the other vital breaths to their places. Whatever one is thinking (at the moment of death), with this one enters into prāṇa. The prāṇa joined with light along with the self takes one to the world as determined by it. However, one who knows prāṇa attains immortality.

The Chāndogya Upaniṣad also extensively deals with the topic of prāṇa. In Chapter XV of verse 7, it is stated that life moves by means of prāṇa. The ātman is bound to the body by means of prāṇa. Prāṇa is Brahman and the body is respected as long as it has prāṇa.

The Five Types of Prāṇa

The Upaniṣads describe in detail the five breaths. They are the prāṇa, apāna, vyāna, udāna, and samāna. The commentary dwells on the function of each of these. Prāṇa is connected to the heart and can move to the mouth and nostrils. Apāna functions below the heart and extends to the navel; it helps excretion. The regulator and nexus between prāṇa and apāna is vyāna, which is also the cause of the actions requiring strength. Rising up of breath in the body and nutrition is due to udāna. Samāna assimilates that which we eat and drink. It is situated in the belly and helps the digestion of food.

The idea here is that the body, mind, and the prāṇa work in a coordinated manner, are interdependent towards the aim of maintaining the individual self. The relation between each of these breaths is also mentioned. In the Bṛhadāraṇyaka Upaniṣad, Śākalya asked, 'In what are you and your self established?' Yājñavalkya replied, 'In prāṇa (vital breath, in breath).' 'In what is prāṇa established?' 'In apāna (outbreath).' 'And in what is apāna established?' 'In vyāna (diffused breath).' 'And in what is vyāna established?' 'In samāna (equalizing or middle breath).' (Br. 3.ix.26)

~

There is no doubt that the Upaniṣads touch upon a very broad range of subjects and enjoin so many principles, methods, and values. While some may see their contents as largely metaphysical it is my belief that the lessons and discussions of the Upaniṣads are ever relevant. They offer much to their reader today as they did millennia ago. In fact, it may be stated that modern science, as it progresses on its journey of discovering the secrets of the world we inhabit, for example quantum mechanics and consciousness studies is moving in directions not very different from the conclusions of these timeless texts.

The Upaniṣads are in fact closely connected to our daily lives since they provide a path beyond the materialist and dross ways of life. They help us bring us back to our selves and rescue us from a lifestyle that has seen so many mental health crises and physical ailments. Out of the morass of our splintered selves, Vedānta urges us to turn inwards and shows the way toward recuperating the whole.

The Aitareya Upaniṣad

CHAPTER 1

I

1. In the beginning, indeed, there was only this self. No other being or thing even stirred. That self thought let me create there the worlds.

    The commentary of Śaṅkarācārya states that the word ātman or self is derived from a sense of pervading, knowing or engulfing. It is the foremost, most senior, all knowing and without worldly adjustment. It is permanent, immutable, pure, immortal. This, the self, was all that there was initially. The diverse manifestations seen in the world is only the self viewed from the prism of differences in name and form and action.

2. That self created these worlds—ambhas, marīci, mara, āpah. Ambhas (cloud) is located beyond heaven. Ambhas has heaven for its support. Marīci (light rays) are the atmosphere. The earth is mara (death). The worlds that are beneath they are āpaḥ (water).

    The self created these worlds. The self first created the cosmic egg, then the worlds as described in the verse. The world called ambhas is so called since it holds water. The earth is referred to as maraḥ since there is death here. The worlds below the earth are called āpaḥ. Water is predominant in them.

3. He reflected: 'These now are the worlds. Let me create the protectors of the world.' From water itself he gathered up a human form and gave shape to it.

The four worlds constitute the material for the fruits of action. For the preservation of the worlds, he created its protectors. A human form was created from the five elements.

4. He thought about him. Of him, who was being thought of, the mouth parted like an egg. Speech emerged from the mouth and from speech, fire. The nostrils parted. The sense of smell emerged from the nostrils and from the sense of smell emerged air (vāyu). The eyes parted. The sense of sight emerged from the eyes and the sun came from the sense of sight. The ears parted. Hearing came from the ears and the quarters of space from hearing. The skin parted, hairs arose from the skin and plants and trees arose from the hair. The heart parted. The mind from the heart and the moon from the mind. The navel parted. From the navel emerged the organ of ejection from which emerged death. The procreational organ parted. Semen emerged from it; and water from semen.

The human form undertook tapas (penance), constituted by knowledge. Then followed the process of creation.

II

1. These deities which were created dropped into the mighty ocean. (The self) made him endure hunger and thirst. To him (the creator) they pleaded: 'Provide us a shelter, where residing we can eat food.'

The deities, fire, and others fell into the great ocean. The world is compared to a vast ocean filled with sorrow due to ignorance, desire, and action. There is much suffering in this world, many evils and only limited respite. The raft of knowledge leads to the shore of emancipation. The point of this verse is that for the liberation from the suffering of the world, one should attain the supreme Brahman as the self.

2. He gave them a cow. They said: 'Surely this is insufficient for us.' He gave them a horse. They said: 'Surely this is insufficient for us.'

   He brought a cow and then a horse for the deities. They rejected both.

3. He then got them a person. They said: 'This is well-made; this person is indeed well-made.' He said: 'Join your own abodes.'
   For them a person was brought. Having seen this, they were freed from misery. God created man by means of his own māyā.
4. Fire entered the mouth having assumed the form of the organ of speech. Air entered the nostrils after having assumed the form of the sense of smell. The sun entered the eyes after having assumed the form of the sense of sight. The directions entered the ears after having assumed the form of the sense of hearing. The herbs and trees entered the skin having assumed the form of hair. The moon entered the heart having assumed the form of the mind. Death entered the navel having assumed the form of out-breath. Water entered the organ of generation having assumed the form of semen.
5. Hunger and thirst said to him: 'Think towards providing us a shelter.' He told them: 'Among these deities only I provide for your livelihood. I made you sharers with them. Therefore, for whichever deity a sacrifice is offered, hunger and thirst become sharers with that deity.'
   The deities found their respective abodes. Then to hunger and thirst were provided their livelihood. In any oblation, hunger

and thirst become sharers in the oblation along with the deity to whom the oblation is dedicated.

III

1. He reflected: 'These then are the worlds and the guardians of the world; let me create food for these.'

   For the sake of subsistence of all beings, food was created.

2. He deliberated about the waters and from these waters which had been deliberated upon, was generated a form. Verily, that generated form was food.

   From water was evolved a form, a solid form. This was able to support the others, both mobile and immobile. This formed thing is food.

3. This, that (food) was so created, turned back waiting to escape that which wanted to destroy it. He tried to seize it with speech. He was not able to seize it with speech. Indeed, if he had been able to seize it with speech, then one would be satisfied merely by speaking of food.

   Food was created in the presence of the senses and their deities. The aggregate of organs and their deities are the body and senses. It realized that food wanted to escape. It attempted by means of an act of speech to seize food. This attempt was not successful.

4. He tried to seize it with the sense of smell. He was not able to seize it with the sense of smell. Indeed, if he was able to seize it with the sense of smell then one would be satisfied merely by smelling food.

   The attempt to seize food through smell was unsuccessful.

5. He tried to seize it with the sense of sight. He was not able to seize it with the sense of sight. Indeed, if he had been able to seize it with the sense of sight, then one would be satisfied merely by having the sight of food.

   The attempt to seize food by the eye was unsuccessful.

6. He tried to seize it with the ear. He was not able to seize it with the ear. Indeed, if he had not been able to seize it with the ear, then one would be satisfied merely by the sound of food.

   The attempt to seize food by means of hearing was unsuccessful.

7. He tried to seize it with the sense of touch. He was not able to seize it with the sense of touch. Indeed, if he had been able to seize it with the sense of touch, then one would be satisfied merely by contact with food.

   The attempt to seize food by touching was unsuccessful.

8. He tried to seize it with the mind. He was not able to seize it with the mind. Indeed, if he had been able to seize it with the mind, then one would be satisfied merely by the thought of food.

   The attempt to seize food by thinking was unsuccessful.

9. He tried to seize it with the procreative organ. He was not able to seize it with the procreative organ. Indeed, if he had been able to seize it with the procreative organ, then one would be satisfied merely by emitting food.

   The attempt to seize food by generation was unsuccessful.

10. He tried to seize it with the apāna (out-breath). He was able to thus. This vital air is the seizer of food. Indeed, vital air is dependent on food.

After being unable to seize food by above-mentioned organs, he attempted to seize food by means of the apāna. He ate the food. Apāna is thus that which devours food. Apāna is that vital energy which is dependant on food.

11. He reflected: 'Indeed, how can this be without me?' He considered: 'By means of which way shall I enter?' He reflected: 'If utterances are through speech, if the sense of smell is through breath, seeing by the eyes, hearing by means of the ears, feeling by means of the skin, thinking by means of the mind, breathing out by means of apāna, emission by means of the procreative organ, then what am I?'

It is stated that logically just as a city is for a king, he thought that there should be a supreme lord, the witness of actions and their fruits. The body and organs should function form something else. How is he to enter? There are two ways. Prāṇa enters by the tips of the feet and he enters the crown of the head.

12. After splitting this very end (of the head), he entered through that gate. This entrance is named vidṛti (the cleft entrance). This is gladdening. Of him, there are three dwelling places, three types of dreams. This is a dwelling place, this is a dwelling place, this is a dwelling place.

He made a hole at the farthest point, where one's hair is parted. At this gate he entered. This is the passage of the supreme lord. Of him who enters as an individual soul there are three indwelling places. During the state when one is awake, it is the right eye, the place of the sense of vision, during the state of dream it is inside the mind and during the state of deep sleep it is within the heart. The three dwelling places are also enumerated as the father's body, the mother's womb, and one's very own body.

13. Having taken birth, he beheld all creation. Would there be anything else here that one would want to mention? He beheld this very Puruṣa (person) as Brahman, the all pervading and uttered thus: 'This I have seen.'

On hearing the notes of the great Upaniṣads, which awakens knowledge of the self, then it is realized that this Puruṣam, the Puruṣa is being spoken of as the lord of creation. It is known as Puruṣa since it resides in the city (pura) of the heart. He was realized as the great Brahman, the most pervasive.

14. His name therefore is Idandra. He is certainly named Idandra. Him, who is Idandra, they refer indirectly as Indra; indeed, the gods are fond of (this) the indirect.

CHAPTER 2

1. Surely in a person this one is first conceived. Semen is said to be that which is the vigour of elements together from all the limbs. Surely, one bears a self, in the self when he gives this semen into a woman, he causes its birth. It is its first birth.

   A man performs various acts such as sacrifices. Due to ignorance, desire, etc., he reaches the lunar world. In due course, he returns to this world and he is poured as an offering in the fire that is man. Vigour is the product of food. This verse illustrates the path of a person who is under the veil of desire and ignorance.

2. That becomes one with the woman, like her own limbs. Thus it (the foetus) does not cause her pain. The woman nourishes this self of his which has entered her.
3. She, the nourisher ought to become nourished. Him, the woman, bears as an embryo, before the birth. He (the father) nourishes the child at the start, shortly after the birth. While the father nourishes the child from the beginning, starting soon after the birth, he nourishes thus his own self for the sake of the continuity of all these worlds. The continuity of all these worlds is thus ensured. This constitutes the second birth.

The idea expressed in this verse is that the worlds are sustained by acts of procreation. However, such acts are not done for the sake of emancipation.

4. He deputes this self of his (the child) for the performance of virtuous actions. Then the other self of his (the father) having performed his duties and being advanced in age, departs. Indeed, as soon as he departs from here, he is born again. That constitutes his third birth. The wise seer has declared this.

   The son is deputed by the father to continue performing virtuous deeds. The father having ensured the fulfilment of all duties, being subject to old age passes on and is then reborn.

5. 'While still in the womb, I knew all the births of the gods. A hundred fortresses made of iron protected me. I burst through it by force like a hawk.' This was said by Vāmadeva while he was still in the womb.

   If someone during any of the states of transmigration, realizes the self as revealed in the Vedas, he is then liberated from all bondage.

6. He who knew thus, and rising upwards, after the dissolution of the body, obtained all desireable things in the world of heaven and attained immortality. Yes, attained immortality.

   For one who knows the self as described above, on the destruction of the body (which is a product of ignorance) having been identified with the supreme self ascends to the state of the pure, all-pervasive self. This is beyond age, death, fear, and immortality. He becomes immortal in the self.

CHAPTER 3

1. What is that we worship as the self? Which is the self? Is it that whereby one sees, whereby one hears, whereby one perceives odour, also whereby speech is uttered and whereby one tastes the sweet and non-sweet?
2. That which is this heart and mind, that which is understanding, worldly knowledge, intelligence, retentiveness, insight, steadiness, thought, genius, mental distress, memory, ascertainment, resolution, life-activity, desire, passion, etc. Indeed, all of these are names of consciousness.

   The verse concerns prājña which has been translated variously as consciousness or intelligence or knowledge. The word jñāna means knowledge. The prefix 'pra' means forward, forth, excessively. (Apte 2020: 508) *The author has chosen to interpret the word as meaning consciousness. What is single becomes multiformed. The various sense organs are able to perform their functions when the one internal organ is transformed into the many sense organs. Thus, it is the intellect which acts in order for the perceived to be perceived. Thus, the entity which is called heart and mind is the agent producing the perceptions. The functions of the inner mind are described in this verse.*

3. This is Bramhā, this is Indra, this is Prajāpati; this is all these gods and this is these five primary elements, namely earth, air, ether, water, fire and this is all these (large creatures) together with small creatures, these are seeds of one type and another, those born of eggs, those born of wombs, those born of moisture, those born of earth, namely horses, cattle, men, elephants, and all creatures which whether breathing or moving, or flying or which are immobile. These are all driven by consciousness. These are all established in consciousness. Consciousness is the eye of the universe. These are all established in consciousness. Consciousness is Brahman.

This verse contains one of the four mahāvākyas namely 'prajñam Brahman'. This is translated as 'Consciousness is Brahman'. All creatures are driven by consciousness. This consciousness is Brahman. 'The underlying reality when freed of all distinctions is taintless, beyond words, thoughts, and attributes. Brahman when associated with pure intelligence, it is called antaryāmi, inner controller. When associated with cosmic intelligence. It is known as Hiraṇyagarbha, the seed of the manifested world. When associated with the cosmic body it is called Prajāpati, Virāt. It is Brahman which is given various names and forms when conditioned by divergent bodies.'

4. He who knows Brahman as described above, by means of the self that is consciousness ascended higher up from this world, obtained all desires and attained immortality. Yes, attained immortality.

The Īśa Upaniṣad

1. Everything, all that moves in the world is covered by the lord; so through renunciation find enjoyment. Do not desire (the wealth of another) for whose is wealth?

One who lords (rules) is known as Īt, whose true form is Īśā. The lord of all, the supreme lord, is the supreme self. Being the self of all creatures, he rules all by being the inner controller. In its own form it covers all. What is this? This is all that moves on the planet earth. The fragrance of sandalwood or incense is corrupted by contact with moisture. Just as this corrupted fragrance is overcome by rubbing the pieces of wood together, thus all duality, the effect of ignorance such as whatever moves, the ideas of doership, enjoyership, modifications such as name, form, and actions will break down and be cast away by means of contemplation of the supreme, true form of the self.

There is no point hankering after wealth since wealth belongs only to the self. In the ultimate analysis wealth is unreal. The intent of this text is that so far as the knower of the supreme self is concerned the self is to be guarded by means of resolute devotion to the self and and renunciation of the threefold desire (for sons, wealth, and worlds). The next verse is directed at those unable to cognize their self due to mental attachment to the non self.

2. By doing works (karma) here one ought to wish to live a hundred years. For a person who wants to live thus, there is no other way but this, through which karma may not attach to you.

If one wishes to live to be a hundred years old then one ought to do so by means of performing karma such as the Agnihotra sacrifice which are recommended by the scriptures. By following this method inauspicious karma will not cling to a person.

3. Indeed, the worlds where devils reside are covered in blinding darkness. To them go those people, after death, who kill the self.

   Those who are covered in ignorance go to worlds of blinding darkness after death. How do such people kill the eternal self? Due to the defect of ignorance such persons conceal the true eternal nature of self which is free from death and decay. Due to this ignorance, they are subject to birth and death.

4. It is one unmoving and swifter than the mind. The senses cannot reach it since it is always ahead of them. Though standing yet it outruns those who run. In it the all-pervading air enables all activities (water stands for all activities).

   In his commentary, Śaṅkarācārya points out that there is no contradiction in saying it is unmoving, yet swifter than the mind. This is so since this is possible from the viewpoint of conditioned and unconditioned states of being. In its own unconditional aspect, it is unmoving. In its conditional aspect as apparently limited by the mind, the reflection of self, consciousness is said to be swifter than even the mind. The self is beyond the senses.

5. That moves and is stationary, that is far away and close, that is internal to all of this and that is external to all of this.

   While the self is in itself unmoving, it appears to move. It seems to be far away since it is unattainable by the ignorant, even in a million years. It is very close to those with knowledge. It is inside of all this. The commentary mentions the Bṛhadāraṇyaka Upaniṣad that states that 'Self is within all' meaning the self is within this entire world comprising name, form, and various activities. (Br. III.IV.I) It is also outside of all this since it is all pervasive.

6. The person who sees all and every being in the self only and who sees the self in all beings, he therefore does not feel any hatred.

   The seeker of liberation who sees all beings, from those that are unmanifested to those that are immobile, in the self, as not different from the self, and who sees the self in all beings, such a person feels no hatred. This is so since a person feels hatred only if the person sees something as evil and other than oneself. However, where a person sees only the self as an unending entity, then there is no other and hence no other to hate or be averse to.

7. To one who knows all beings become the self only, to such a person who has seen the oneness, what delusion, what sorrow can there be?

   Similarly, the person who knows the supreme reality and who thus sees all beings in the self, then what delusion, what sorrow can there be? For delusion and sorrow occurs only to those who do not know the seed of desires and actions. Delusion and sorrow are the result of ignorance.

8. He is all pervasive, resplendent without body, invincible, sinewless, untainted by sin and pure. He is all-knowing, wise, self existent, who exceeds all existence (and) who has duly allotted objects, through the eternal years.

   The self is all pervasive like ether. The words used in this verse, invincible and sinewless, imply the negation of the gross body with respect to the self; similarly untainted by sin, all knowing implies a negation of the causal body for the self. The self is the seer of all.

Śaṅkarācārya in his commentary points out that the Īśa Upaniṣad spells out the Vedic paths. The first verse outlines devotion to knowledge after forsaking desire. In the second verse emphasizes the importance of the path of duty.

9. Those who worship (follow the path of) ignorance enter into blinding darkness and those who take delight in knowledge enter into greater darkness than that.

The worshippers of ignorance enter into great darkness. Śaṅkarācārya in his commentary explains the second line as pertaining to those who give up performing rites and good deeds, etc., and only pursue knowledge. The aim of this verse seems to be to enjoin humility in the pursuit of knowledge.

10. It is said that surely different is the result of vidyā and different indeed is the consequence of avidyā. So has been heard from the wise men who have explained this to us.
11. He who knows both vidyā and avidyā together, crosses over death through ignorance and attains immortality through vidyā.

Śaṅkarācārya in his commentary says that by means of knowledge one attains divine realms while by means of karma, one attains the world of the ancestors.

In this verse vidyā is used to refer to meditation on deities. The import of this verse is that one who meditates on deities and performs rites, crosses over death and becomes one with the deities, that is he becomes immortal.

12. The worshippers of the unmanifest enter into great darkness, but those who delight in the manifest, enter into darkness greater than that.

Those who worship the primal unmanifested cause (Prakṛti) enter into great darkness. Yet those who delight in the manifested Brahman (Hiraṇyagarbha) enter into even greater darkness.

13. It is said that surely different is the result of the manifest and different indeed is the consequence of the unmanifest. So has been heard from the wise men who have explained this to us.

    The results of worshipping the manifested and unmanifested forms of Brahman are different, yet they are meant to lead to the same goal. Thus, says Śaṅkarācārya that it is proper to combine the worship of both.

14. He who knows both the unmanifest and the destruction together, crossed death by destruction and attains immortality through the manifest.

    The person who knows these two together obtains immortality. Śaṅkarācārya points out that the letter 'a', has been omitted from the word Asambhūti and therefore that which is unmanifested is being spoken of here. The knower of the unmanifested and destruction reaches the state of immortality which is in this case absorption in Prakṛti by means of worshiping the unmanifest. As per the scriptures absorption in Prakṛti is the highest state attainable by means of divine and human wealth. Surpassing this is the realization of the self in all.

15. Truth's face is covered by means of a vessel made of gold. O Pūṣan (sun), unveil it, so that it may be seen by I who is truthful and righteous.

    The word Hiraṇmaya means made of gold. By such a vessel, appearing to be made of gold is covered the face or gateway to the truth of Brahman. The aspirant who has attained the quality of truth by worshipping Brahman as truth beseeched Pūṣan to remove the obstacle to realizing the truth, i.e., Brahman.

The last four verses of this Upaniṣad are meant to be recited at the time of death.

16. O Pūṣan, the only seer, ruler, sun, son of Prajāpati, please remove your rays and withdraw your radiant light so that I may see your most graceful form, the person who is there. I too am that (person).

The world is nourished by the sun and the sun is known as the nourisher. He controls all and is the ruler. He acquires within himself all rays and vital forces and is therefore known as Sūrya. Śaṅkarācārya points out that the person making the entreaty is the same person as the person in the solar orb.

17. May (my) life force enter into immortal breath, and now this body may be reduced to ashes. May intelligence recall whatever deeds have been done, remember. May intelligence recall whatever deeds have been done, remember.

The seeker at the time of death prays that his vital force attain its divine all-pervading nature. The body is offered as an oblate on to fire.

Repeatedly a prayer is made to fire to remember the (good) works done since childhood.

18. O Agni, guide us by the noble path for the sake of our well-being. O God who knows all our actions free us from deceitful sins. We offer many salutations to thee.

The seeker entreats Agni to lead him via the noble path. He wishes to avoid the southern path since via the southern path there is coming and going. Further there is also the prayer to remove sin so that the desired aim may be achieved.

The Kaṭha Upaniṣad

Invocation

May he defend us together. May he be happy with us together; let us strive together with enthusiasm. May what we study be illuminating. May there be no enmity between us both. Aum, peace, peace, peace.

CHAPTER 1

I

1. Wishing indeed (for the benefits of conducting the Viśvajit sacrifice) Vājaśravasa gave away all his wealth. His son was named Naciketā.

   Wishing for the fruit of the sacrifice, Vājaśravasa conducted the Viśvajit sacrifice, wherein all is given away. He had a son whose name was Naciketā.

2. Though indeed still a youth, a sense of faith came to him when the presents were being offered to the priests. He reflected:

   Though still a boy, Naciketā was imbued with a sense of faith and he desires the well being of his father. When the cows which were being gifted were being led away, Naciketā thought:

3. He who presents (cows) that have drunk water, have eaten grass, have had their milk milked, are without their sense organs, indeed goes to those worlds that are known as joyless.

   Those that give to performers of sacrifices cows that are barren and diseased go to worlds devoid of bliss.

4. To his father he said: 'O Father, to whom will you offer me?' For a second and third time he addressed these words to him. The father said to him: 'I offer you to death.'

Naciketā wanted to spare his father from the harmful implications of the imperfect sacrifice. He asked his father repeatedly to whom he will offer him. The father replied 'to death'.

5. 'Of many, I go as the foremost; of many I rank in the middle. Today what obligation to Yama (death) can there be which (my father) will fulfil through me?'

Naciketā wonders what purpose can be attained by sending him, a son of many good qualities to death.

6. Behold, how your forefathers acted successively, consider how others act (now). A man matures like corn and is born again like corn.

Emulating ancestors and holy persons is enjoined. One ought to avoid evil conduct and prevarication. In the manner of corn, man too matures, then decays and dies and then disappears. Evil conduct in a temporary world leads to no real gain.

Naciketā asks his father to send him to the abode of death. Having gone there, Naciketā lived there for three nights, since Yamrāj was not there.

7. Like a fire a Brāhmaṇa guest enters houses. For him this propitiation is done. O Yama, bring water.

The text states that a Brāhmaṇa entering a house should be propitiated to avoid harmful consequences.

8. A man of limited intelligence in whose home a Brāhmaṇa stays unfed abandons all these, viz. hope and expectation, good association and auspiciousness, sacrifices and charitable works, sons and cattle.

The śloka aims to illustrate the point that a guest should never be neglected.

9. Since for three nights you have lived in my house without food, a guest and who is worthy of salutation, my obeisance to you O Brāhmaṇa. Let good fortune be mine. Therefore, choose three boons, in respect of three nights.
10. 'O death, may (my father) Gautama become calm minded, benevolent, without anger towards me and acknowledging me, may he talk to me, when freed by you; and this I request as the first of the three boons.'
11. (Yama said): 'As before he Auddālaki Aruni (your father), the son of Aruna, will recognize you; through my permission, he will sleep happily through the nights, having overcome his anger, seeing you free from the clutches of death.
12. (Naciketā said): 'There is no fear at all in the world of heaven, you are not there; no one shudders due to fear of old age. Having crossed both hunger and thirst and transcending sorrow one delights in the world of heaven.'

The distinction between the heavenly world and the mortal is being made here.

13. O death, thou knows the fire that leads to the attainment of heaven. Speak of it to me who am full of faith, how the deities of heaven obtain immortality. This I seek by means of the second boon.

Naciketā as his second boon seeks the knowledge of fire that leads to heaven.

14. (Yama said): 'O Naciketā knowing well the fire that leads to the attainment of heaven, I shall speak of it to you. Understand that with attention. That fire is the means to obtain the infinite world, it is also the foundation of the world, know this to be situated in the hidden place (of the heart).'

Yamarāj grants Naciketā the second boon he had requested. Fire is praised as the means to attain the infinite world as well as that which supports the world. It is located in the hidden place of the heart.

15. (Yama) told him about that fire which is the primary cause of the world, what type of bricks and their number as also the manner (for constructing the sacrificial altar). And he (Naciketā) with understanding repeated all that had been said. Being satisfied with this Yama spoke again.

Death speaks to Naciketā. That fire (in the form of Virāt) preceded the world. Other arrangements such as the type of bricks, place of sacrificial wood is stated.

16. Feeling very pleased the exalted soul said to him (Naciketā) 'I grant you another boon now. Verily, this fire will become known by thine own name. And accept this many formed garland as well.'

Being pleased with Naciketā, Yamarāj grants him another boon.

17. One who has performed the Naciketā fire thrice, gets associated with the three, does the three acts and transcends birth and death. Having known the omniscient, praiseworthy one born of Brahmā and meditating on him one attains unending peace.

The three referred to as per the commentary, are the mother, the father, and the teacher. Proper instruction from the three is regarded as a source of valid knowledge. A person who performs the Naciketā sacrifice thrice and does three kinds of acts, sacrifices, giving (of charity), and study (of scriptures) transcends birth and death. The main idea in this verse is that a person by means of meditation and correct rites attains unending peace, the state of Virāt.

18. The enlightened man who thrice performs the Naciketā sacrifice having known these three and knowing thus performs the Naciketā sacrifice throws off the noose of death even earlier and being free of sorrow delights in heaven.

A performer of the Naciketā sacrifice escapes (vice), hatred, desire, ignorance, those that are the traps of death much earlier and is freed from grief and attains heaven becoming identified with Virāt.

19. O Naciketā this for you is the fire (sacrifice) which leads to heaven that you sought by means of the second boon. People will refer to this fire (sacrifice) by your name only. O Naciketā choose the third boon.

The second boon regarding the fire has been granted to Naciketā and the boon is known by Naciketā. However, the first two boons do not lead to a true knowledge of reality. To end ignorance, which is of the nature of superimposing activity, an erroneous sense of agentship and apparent enjoyment by the self, there is a need for knowledge regarding the oneness of the self and Brahman. Without the knowledge of the self contentment in any real sense is impossible. This will be the subject of the third boon.

20. This uncertainty arises regarding a departed man, some (say) he exists and some that he does not exist. I wish to be taught by you regarding this knowledge. This is the third boon of these boons.

For the third boon, Naciketā asks whether the self exists after death or not. This question cannot be answered by means of perception or inference. Yet it is a crucial question since the ultimate goal is dependent on this.

21. (Yama said): 'In respect of this even the gods were uncertain in former times. Surely, this is not easy to comprehend, this truth being so subtle. O Naciketā select another boon. Do not press me. Let go of this (boon) that is asked of me.'

Yamaraja decides to test Naciketā. He tries to dissuade Naciketā from asking for this boon.

22. (Naciketā said): 'Verily, even the gods were uncertain in respect of this; and since you too O Death say that it is not easy to comprehend and since any other teacher regarding this is not to be obtained, there is no boon that compares, whatsoever to this one.'

Naciketā continues to request for the third boon since there is no boon comparable to this. All other boons lead to transitory results.

23. (Yama said): 'Wish for sons and grandsons who will live a hundred years. Wish for numerous animals, horses, elephants and gold, and a great expanse of land and life for yourself for as many years as you wish.'

In this and the next two verses Death continues to dissuade Naciketā from asking about the self. He puts before him all kinds of temptations.

24. If you think any boon is comparable to this, (then) choose (that). Ask for wealth and long life. O Naciketā, lord over this vast region. I will let you have the enjoyment of all desirable things.
25. All things that one may desire but are difficult to obtain in the human world, request for all those desires as you wish. Here are (celestial) women along with musical instruments, such as surely cannot be won by mortals. Let these attendants whom I offer serve you. O Naciketā, of death do not enquire.

26. (Naciketā said): 'O Death, these are temporary and they wither away the vigour of the sense organs of a man. Verily all life is short. Let the chariots be yours only; let the song and dance be yours alone.'

Regarding the temptations offered to Naciketā, he says that desirable things are transient. There is no guarantee that they will exist in the future. Further desirable things drain virtue, strength, etc.

27. A person is not to be contented by means of wealth. Is wealth to be obtained when we have seen you? We shall live as long as you are the ruler. But that only is the boon worth requesting for.

People are never contented with wealth. The boon worth aspiring for is that which regards the knowledge of the self.

28. Having come near the undecaying immortals, which decaying mortal, who resides below on earth, yet knowing (higher attainments) and meditates on (the transitory nature of) the pleasures of music and love, will rejoice in a very long life?

The lack of genuine non-transient worth of desirable things is being highlighted. When the real nature of the desirable things we encounter in life, such as wealth, attachment, music is known one will not hanker for them. Nor will one rejoice in a long lifespan.

29. O Death speak to us of this, about which there is uncertainty in relation to the world and which knowledge leads to greatness. Other than this boon which enters into what is concealed, Naciketā does not request for another.

The importance of the boon regarding the self is reiterated. All other boons can be acquired even by those that are senseless. Knowledge regarding the self appears inscrutable.

II

1. That which is preferable is different and indeed the pleasurable is also different. Serving distinct purposes these two bind mortals. Good accrues to him who selects the preferable of these two. However, he who selects the pleasurable falls short of the aim.

   The distinction between the preferable, the ultimate goal and the pleasant is emphasised. All are bound by these two. These two are opposed to each other since the preferable is the nature of knowledge and the pleasurable is the nature of ignorance. A person can only accept one of the two. He who discards the pleasurable attains well being. But he who seeks the pleasurable deviates from the supreme goal.

2. These both, the preferable and the pleasant approach this person. The person of intellect after considering them distinguishes between them. The person of intellect selects the good over the pleasant. The dull-witted selects the pleasant in pursuit of worldly well-being.

   Continuing the discourse on the distinction between the preferable and the pleasant the commentary uses the analogy of a swan separating milk from water. Just as the swan, a dhīraḥ—a man of intellect—distinguishes between the two and chooses the preferable. The dull-witted chooses the pleasurable.

3. O Naciketā, after duly considering, you have described what is pleasant and its various forms. Thou has not taken the path of obtaining wealth in which many people drown.

   The path of pleasure causes a person to ultimately come to grief.

4. Far apart, contradicting and following divergent courses are these (which constitute) ignorance and what is known as

knowledge. I think Naciketā to be keen for knowledge. Since the many desirable things are not coveted by you.

Knowledge and ignorance are stated to be contradictory like light and darkness. Knowledge has for its object the preferable, ignorance the pleasurable. Knowledge leads to liberation; ignorance leads to birth and rebirth in the worldly plane.

5. Residing amidst ignorance, learned in their own estimation, considering themselves intelligent, bewildered people follow a tortuous path, going round and round just like blind persons being led by the blind.

   Ignorant people find themselves bound by hundreds of chains (attachments). These include the desire for sons, wealth, etc. They erroneously consider themselves as intelligent and wise. Such people go round and round, being tormented all the while.

6. The means of attaining the future world is not known to the infant-minded, negligent person who is deluded due to the lure of wealth. One who thinks that there is (only) this world and nothing beyond, he comes under my control again and again.

   The other world is not revealed nor attainable to the man of ignorance. Such people cling to temporary objects and aims such as cattle and wealth. Such people keep getting born and reborn in this world and remain under the control of death.

7. Of that (self) which for many is not obtainable even for just hearing and even is not understood by many even while hearing, marvellous is the expounder and able is the receiver, marvellous is he who understands under the guidance of the proficient.

   An expounder of the self is described as marvellous. The hearer whose mind is not pure will not know the self. Yet an able receiver after hearing about the self from a truly qualified teacher attains the self since he becomes a knower.

8. This (self) when taught by a lesser (qualified) person cannot be truly known since it is thought of in diverse ways. Only taught by one who realizes he is non-different from it, there is no going (to it) here since it is beyond reasoning and is minute than even the atomic.

   The self when spoken of by a person whose understanding is limited to only the worldly realm cannot be properly known. The self is thought of in diverse ways. When properly taught there is nothing different. The culmination of knowledge is knowing the unity of the self. Then there is no birth and rebirth. The self is realized when the instructor is well-versed in sacred texts and teaches the self as non different from what is taught.

9. This understanding is not to be attained through reasoning, but dear one, when spoken of by another it is well learnt. Being resolute for truth you have attained it. Let there be an enquirer similar to you, O Naciketā.

   Realization of the self is not attained by reasoning. Realization occurs when the self is expounded on by someone who is one with it. The source of this wisdom is the Vedas. Not a logician. Naciketā's steadfast quest for true knowledge is hailed.

10. Wealth I know to be transitory. That which is eternal cannot be obtained by means of that which is transitory. Therefore, I have gathered the Naciketā fire with temporary things and by means of that I have attained the permanent.

    Commonly people strive for the fruits of action. These are transient. But by means of the transient, the permanent cannot be achieved. Thus, by the Naciketā sacrifice Naciketā attains the Nitya, the permanent.

11. Having witnessed the end of all desire, the foundation of the world, the unending results of rites, the opposite shore where there is absence of fear, the excessiveness of praise, the extensive way, the basis, O intelligent Naciketā, you have patiently renounced (them all).

Naciketā has seen Hiraṇyagarbha as the basis of all, the end of desires, infinite. The state of Hiraṇyagarbha is majestic, infinite, and most excellent.

12. Through self contemplation and meditation on the primal deity which is difficult to view, lodged in a cavity of the heart, hidden in the depths, inaccessible, the intelligent man renounces both joy and sorrow.

The self is extremely subtle, situated in an impossible place and is hence difficult to view. The self is perceived to exist in the body and the senses, the place of much grief. By meditating on the self the wise man transcends joy and grief.

13. Upon hearing this, understanding (it), a mortal separating the virtuous, attains this subtle thing, delights having obtained what leads to joy. I consider that such a place is displayed to Naciketā.

A mortal who hears of the self in a proper manner is fit for liberation. Naciketā has reached this state.

14. (Naciketā requests): 'Speak to me of that which you view as distinct from virtue, distinct from vice, distinct from what is made and unmade and distinct from the past and future.'
15. (Yama says): 'Which word that all the Vedas proclaim, which all the penances speak of, for which a person practises Brahmacarya, I shall speak of it in brief. It is this, Aum.'

The goal to be achieved is Aum. Its symbol is Aum.

16. Indeed, this word (Aum) is the everlasting spirit. Verily, this word is the supreme. Having known this word, whatever a person wishes for, surely that will be his.

The word Aum is Hiraṇyagarbha. It is also the supreme Brahman. A person who worships Aum, whatever he desires, becomes his.

17. This abode is most excellent. This abode is supreme. Having known this abode, one becomes honoured in the world of Bramhā.

This abode is the best path for the attainment of Brahman. By meditating on Aum aspirants can achieve liberation.

18. The wise one (self) is neither born and nor does it die. It originated from nothing and nothing originated from it. It is without birth, eternal, perpetual, and ancient. It is not destroyed even when the body is destroyed.

The self is intelligent since its nature is consciousness. It is not subject to modifications including birth and death. The self is not produced. Thus, it is ancient, eternal, and perpetual. Destruction of the body does not lead to destruction of the self.

19. If the killer is of the belief that he has killed it, and if the killed considers (it) as killed, both of them do not comprehend. It neither kills nor is it killed.

The self is unchanging. It cannot be killed. Worldly existence which is of the nature of virtue and vice, pertains to he who is ignorant. It does not affect a knower of Brahman.

20. Subtler than the subtle, mightier than the mighty, the self is situated in the heart of every living being. The person who has no wants sees the majesty of the self through the tranquillity of the organs and is exempt from sorrow.

All objects, subtle or mighty owe their reality to the self. The self is situated in the heart of all living beings. A person who has no wants, whose intellect has withdrawn from external objects, seen or unseen, his organs attain serenity. Such a person realizes the self and becomes free from sorrow.

21. While stationary, it travels far; while sleeping it goes to all places. Who other than I deserve to know the deity that delights and delights not?

The self is difficult to know and can only be known by a wise man. Due to being apparently conditioned by limiting adjuncts, the self appears diversely. This again makes it difficult to be known.

22. Having contemplated the self as unembodied among the embodied, as unchanging in the midst of the changing and as great, pervading all things, the discerning man does not grieve.

The wise man who knows he is the self does not grieve.

23. This self cannot be obtained through teaching, nor through intelligence and nor through hearing. Verily, this self is to be attained only by that whom the self selects. This self reveals itself to such a seeker.

The self cannot be known by intellect or hearing alone. To a person of no desires who seeks the self in a single-minded manner, the self reveals itself to such a person.

24. Not one who has not ceased from bad conduct, not one whose passions are not under control, not one whose mind is not absorbed, not even he whose mind is not calm can attain the self through knowledge.

The self cannot be achieved by one whose mind is not concentrated, whose conduct is bad, whose senses are not controlled. A man whose mind is concentrated, has good conduct, senses controlled, has a qualified teacher, attains the self through knowledge.

25. For whom both the priests and warriors are as food and for whom death is its sprinkling, who can thus know where it (the self) is?

Both by means of worldly existence and by death, neither is where the self exists.

III

1. The two partakers of the result of work, in the world of virtuous deeds are situated in the hidden place (of the heart) which is the abode of the supreme. Those who know Brahman talk of them as shadow and light and also (householders) who worship the five fires and those who perform the Naciketā sacrifice three times.

The two partakers of the truth, i.e., the result of work are discussed here. The two are located in the supreme abode in the heart. This space is supreme compared to what is outside it, that is the space occupied by the human body.

2. The bridge of those who conduct sacrifices, which is the supreme, indestructible Brahman, for they who want to go over to the distant shore beyond fear, the supreme Naciketā fire, may we be able to know.

The Naciketā fire is a bridge that leads beyond sorrow for those that perform rites. Further the lesser Brahman which is the refuge of those that perform rites and the transcendental Brahman are both worthy of realization.

3. Know the self as the owner of the chariot. As to the body know it as the chariot only. As regards the intellect know it as the charioteer and surely know the mind to be the reins.

The famous chariot analogy starts here. The self is the owner of the chariot, its master, its rider. The mortal body is the chariot itself since like the chariot is pulled by horses, the body is pulled by sense organs. The intellect is the charioteer since it guides the body. The mind are the reins, for just as horses act as directed and controlled by the reins so do the organs act when directed and controlled by the mind.

4. The sense organs are spoken of as horses. The sense objects are their pastures. The wise say that the self yoked with the body, sense organs and mind is the enjoyer.

   The sense organs are the horses. The objects of the organs such as colour, etc., are the pastures, roads. The self limited by the body, mind, and organs is the enjoyer. The absolute self can have no enjoyership.

5. As regards one who is unintelligent, whose mind is ever unyoked, his sense organs are untamable like the vicious horses of a charioteer.

   Just in the manner of an unskilled charioteer and indisciplined horses, so do the mind and sense organs of a person lacking in discrimination run wild.

6. As regards he who is intelligent, whose mind is calm, his sense organs are disciplined like good horses are for a charioteer.

   For a person who has an intellect possessed of discrimination, associated with a focused mind, his sense organs can be reined in.

7. As regards he who does not have a discriminating intellect, whose mind is uncontrolled, is ever sullied, attains not the goal but returns to this transitory existence.

   The soul that is not associated with a discriminating intellect, whose mind is not focused, such a person is sullied and does not attain the ultimate goal. He is subject to worldly existence and repeated birth and death.

8. As regards he who has a discriminating intellect, whose mind is controlled, is ever unsullied attains that state from which such a person is not reborn again.

The one with the discriminating intellect, focused mind is pure and attains the ultimate goal. He is not reborn.

9. As regards the man who has a discriminating intellect as his charioteer and the reins of whose mind are under control, he obtains the end of the journey, the supreme place of Viṣṇu.

Such a holy man, a man of knowledge, attains the end of the journey. He is released from all bondage. He attains the most exalted place, the supreme place of Viṣṇu, of the all-pervading Brahman.

10. The sense objects are superior to the sense organs and superior to the sense objects is the mind, superior to the mind is the intellect and superior to the intellect is the great self.

Sense organs are gross. Sense objects are considered to be higher since they are subtler and more pervasive. The mind being more subtle and pervasive than sense objects is higher. By mind is meant the elements in their rudimentary form which form the cause of the mind. The intellect is more subtle and pervasive than the mind and thus higher than it. The great self is the inner most principle of all and is the most pervasive as well. Hiraṇyagarbha born from (unmanifested) māyā which is made up of intelligence and activity is known as the great self.

11. The unmanifest is beyond the Mahat (great self). The Puruṣa (self) is beyond the unmanifest. There is nothing beyond the Puruṣa. That is the culmination that is the supreme goal.

The unmanifested, the origin of the universe, the yet to be manifested name and form is subtle and higher. The Puruṣa is higher than the unmanifested being the inner most self and that which is the cause of all causes. There is nothing higher than the Puruṣa. This is the ultimate goal of all those souls subject to birth and rebirth.

12. Kept secret from all living beings this self does not manifest itself. However, he is seen by the seers of subtle things by means of their sharp and subtle intellect.

    In all creatures, the Puruṣa remains hidden, it is concealed by avidyā. Due to māyā, every creature though actually one with the supreme does not grasp this. Due to this delusion a person accepts the non self i.e., the body and the senses as the self. This leads to birth and rebirth.

13. The discerning person ought to merge his speech in the mind, he ought to merge that (mind) in the knowing self, he ought to merge the knowing self in the great soul, he ought to merge the great soul in the tranquil self.

    Everyday illusions like water seen in a mirage, a snake in a rope, and dirt in the sky are dispersed by knowledge of the real nature of the mirage, the rope, and the sky. Similarly, by means of the true knowledge of one's self is dissolved all that is is projected by ignorance, action, instrument, and result which constitutes name, form and action. This leads to the ultimate goal being achieved.

14. Ascend, be attentive, having obtained your boons, learn. The enlightened ones speak of the path to be as sharp as the edge of a razor, impassable and difficult to traverse.

    Awake from ignorance, the seed of all evil, go to well-qualified teachers. Understand the all-pervading self as taught by the

Upaniṣads. The fine intellect needed is compared to a razor's edge. The path consisting in the knowledge of reality is as difficult to pass as is walking on a razor's edge.

15. One becomes liberated from the face of death by realizing that (self) which is devoid of sound, devoid of touch, devoid of form, immutable, devoid of taste, eternal, devoid of smell, without beginning and end, constant and surpassing that which is great.

    That which possesses qualities like sound, etc., is diminished, reduced. The self is not reduced, or does it decay, it is eternal. It is the cause of all, the self is not an effect. The self is eternal. Brahman is eternal. The self never changes.

16. Having heard and related to this ancient episode of Naciketā as stated by death, the man of intellect attains greatness in the world of Bramhā.
17. Whoever, after being purified, causes the supreme secret to be heard before an assemblage of Brāhmaṇas or during the time of ceremonies for the dead, that will make possible for him the eternal life that will make possible the eternal life.

    The recital of the text in the right circumstances is eulogized.

CHAPTER II

I

1. The self-existent Lord pierced the sense organs outwards. Therefore, one sees outward things and not the inner self. A rare person of intellect wishing for immortality, covered his eyes and then viewed the self.
2. The childlike persons chase external desires. They get entangled in the trap of extensive death. The discerning having known immortality in the midst of the transient, do not pray for anything here, in this world.

The true correct vision of the self is obstructed by ignorance and the thirst to enjoy external things. This leads to entanglement in the snares of worldly existence. Such persons are subject to disease, old age, death, rebirth, etc. The wise discerning people know that immortality consists in continuing in the true state of the indwelling self. Thus, the knowers of Brahman do not pray for anything here in this world. They rise above worldly goals like riches, offspring, enjoyment, etc.

3. By means of which (a person perceives) colour, taste, smell, sound, touch, sexual pleasure, by this only one perceives. What is here that is left? This surely is that.

It is by means of the self, which by its nature is consciousness, do all persons perceive colour, taste, smell, sound, touch as well as pleasure.

4. Having meditated on the great and all-pervading self, by which one perceives the dream and waking states both, the discerning man does not grieve.

   It is by the self of the nature of consciousness that a person perceives objects in the dream as well as waking state. One who realizes the self, has no need to grieve.

5. The person who knows closely this self, as the experiencer of the fruits of work, the principle of life, the ruler of the past and future, one does not withdraw from him. This surely is that.

   One who knows the self as the principle of life, the ruler of time, he does not conceal himself from the self.

6. The person who was born in ancient times from penance, who was born in ancient times from the waters, who exists having entered the secret cavity of the heart and who saw through the elements. This surely is that.

   Who sees the firstborn (Hiraṇyagarbha), who was born earlier than water, earlier than the five elements, who created the deities and resides in the cavity of the heart, sees Brahman.

7. She who originates with vital-breath, Aditi, consisting of the deities, who exists having entered the secret cavity of the heart, who is manifested with the elements. This surely is that.

   Similarly, he who sees Aditi, who enjoys all as sound, who consists of the deities, who takes birth as Hiraṇyagarbha, sees Brahman.

8. Agni situated in the fire producing wood, like the well borne embryo by pregnant women, should be lauded every day by men that are aware and who perform oblations. This surely is that.

   Sacrificial fire is here discussed. Just as the foetus is well protected so should a sacrificial fire be protected and lauded. This too is that (Brahman).

9. From which the sun rises and where it goes to set are placed all the gods and not anyone transcends that. This surely is that.
10. Verily, what is here is there; similarly, that which is there is here. Whoever views as if there is diversity here, he suffers death after death.

    The ignorant erroneously feel or associate limiting adjuncts such as the body and the senses with the self. The self in its causal condition is Brahman, which is of the nature of consciousness with no worldly qualities. Any ignorant person who feels the limiting adjuncts are real and part of the self is subject to this world being born and reborn time and again.

11. This is to be obtained only through the mind. Here, there is nothing of diversity. Whoever, views as if there is diversity here, he goes from death to death.

    Brahman is one with the self. There is nothing else. This knowledge is attained by means of the mind, daily purified by a competent teacher and sacred scriptures. The person who does not shed his ignorance transits from death to death.

12. The Puruṣa, the measure of a thumb stays in the centre of the body. Knowing him as the ruler of the past and future one does not withdraw from him. This surely is that.

13. The Puruṣa, the measure of a thumb, is like the light of a blazing fire. He is the ruler of the past and future. He exists now and he will exist in the future. This surely is that.

    The Puruṣa is being spoken of. The size of a thumb, the ruler of time, eternal and not subject to change. The Puruṣa is without equal.

14. Just as water (which has) rained on a height disperses amongst the hills, so in this manner, one who sees things separately, chases after them only.

    Just as water flowing from a height dissipates into different streams, one who sees self as different in different bodies, chases after different bodies and desires again and again.

15. O Gautama, just as pure water poured on the pure becomes like that only, thus also becomes the self of the sage of knowledge.

    Pure water poured on pure water, merges in the pure water. Similarly, the self of one who knows is also merged in Brahman.

II

1. Of the eternal person, whose consciousness is uncrooked, (there is) a city with eleven gates. By contemplating it one does not grieve and being free gets release. This surely is that.

   Here the city is used as a reference to the body. The body has the paraphernalia of a city such as gates, gate commanders; and it exists for the sake of an owner. The body has eleven gates, seven in the head, three in the lower parts, and one on top of the head. It is possessed by the birthless self. A person whose consciousness is not crooked i.e., straight, by meditating on the supreme lord, and becoming free from desire, such a person has no need to grieve. He is free from both desire and duty. He is not reborn.

2. He is the swan who resides in heaven, he resides in space, he is the sacrifice with fire, he exists as a guest in the sacrificial jar (the house). He exists in men, among the gods, in what is true and in the sky. He is born from water, he is born from the earth, he is born from truth, he is born from the mountains, he is constant and he is vast.

   The word hamsaḥ is used in the text and is a very important word in the context of meditation. It is derived from the root ham which means to go; the self is pure and resides in the intermediate space. He is permanent, great and unchanging. This verse is meant to assert that the entire world has one self only which pervades all.

3. He propels upwards the vital breath, prāṇa, he impels the in-breath inwards, the dwarf seated at the middle, whom all deities worship.

   This verse is used to point out that all the sense organs and the prāṇa exist for the self yet the self is different from them.

4. Of this embodied self that resides in the body, when it becomes untied and set free from the body, what is left remaining here? This surely is that.

   On the departure of the self, the body is as good as destroyed, completely powerless.

5. Neither by prāṇa nor apāna does any mortal live; but they live by means of another by which these two live.

   It may be argued that one lives by prāṇa or apāna. This is strongly refuted by this verse. Prāṇa and apāna themselves exist for the self.

6. Well O Gautama, I shall expound to you the mystery of the eternal Brahman and also the state of the self after attaining death.
7. Some souls attain a womb to acquire a body, others (enter) the stationary, this is as per their actions and as per their knowledge.

   Creatures take birth according to their karma and knowledge. Some enter a womb. Others after death take birth as stationary beings like trees.

8. That Puruṣa who remains awake amongst those that are asleep producing desire after desire, that verily is pure. That is Brahman and that is called immortal. On it all the worlds are supported and not anyone can transcend that. This surely is that.

   The Puruṣa is always awake. The Puruṣa is pure. It is Brahman. In all scriptures it is referred to that which cannot be destroyed. It is the support of all the worlds.

9. Just as the one fire after entering this world assumes many shapes in accordance to the form (it takes), similarly the one self who is within all beings, assumes a (different) form in accordance to each shape and it also exists outside.

   By nature, fire is luminous and single, yet when it comes into contact with different substances it appears to be of different forms. Similarly, the self is one yet it assumes different forms in accordance to the different bodies it enters. The next verse too makes this point.

10. Just as the one air after entering this world assumes many shapes in accordance to the form (it takes), similarly the one self which is within all beings, assumes a (different) form in accordance to each shape and it also exists outside.

11. Just as the sun, the eye of all the world is not stained by the external blemishes seen by the eye, similarly the one self which is within all beings is not stained by the sufferings of the world, as it is transcendent.

The sun illumines all things on earth, yet it is not tainted by external blemishes seen by the eye. Similarly, the all-pervasive self is transcendental and is not tainted by the afflictions of the world. Suffering is caused by ignorance superimposed on the self. People experience the misery of death, old age, disease due to superimposing false notions of actions, agents, fruit of action on the self, etc.

12. The one, the ruler, the self within all beings, who makes his single form diverse, to the discerning who realize him as abiding in the self, they attain eternal happiness and not for others.

He is the ruler of the universe. The self in all beings. The wise who desist from external activity, follow the instructions of the teacher, realize that God is the self. The self is homogenous and is of the nature of consciousness. It is seen as diverse due to differences in the superimposed conditions of name and form. The wise who become identified with the supreme lord attain eternal happiness. This is not so for the unwise who are attached to external objetcts.

13. The eternal amidst the temporary, consciousness amidst the conscious, the one amongst the many, who fulfils desires; to the discerning who realize him as abiding in the self, they attain eternal peace and not for others.

He is eternal, indestructible, consciousness and it is due to him that others are able to manifest consciousness. The wise who are able to realize him in their hearts attain everlasting peace.

14. That is this and therefore they realize the indefinable supreme bliss. How possibly shall I come to know this? Is its lustre of itself or is its lustre due to reflection?

The knowledge of the self is bliss, cannot be explained and supreme. The wise people who do not desire consider 'this' as something that can be directly known.

15. The sun does not shine there, neither do the moon and stars nor do lightning flashes shine. Then in what manner can this fire be? When he shines only, everything shines. By his splendours all these diverse things are illuminated.

All that is luminous is luminous as due to him the supreme lord. It is Brahman that is luminous and illuminates all that is luminous.

III

1. This is the everlasting fig tree that has its roots above and branches below. That only is pure. That is Brahman. That only is called immortal. In it are supported all the worlds and no one transcends that. This indeed is that.

The root mentioned here is the state of supreme Viṣnu. the tree of the world is known as Vṛkṣa and is subject to numerous changes. Its reality is known by seekers of the truth. Its essence lies in Brahman, it grows from ignorance. The sprout is Hiraṇyagarbha, its trunk is the subtle bodies of all creatures. The Vedas, Smṛtis, logic, learning are its leaves. Noble deeds are its flavours. The tree is felled by knowledge and detachment.

The root is Brahman, indestructible, pure, consciousness, true. Everything else is transitory and false.

2. The whole world and anything which exists here emerges and stirs due to the supreme spirit. (Like) an upraised thunderbolt it is greatly terrifying. Those who know this become immortal.

Brahman is the cause of the world. Like a thunderbolt it is greatly terrifying. The universe and its constituents function properly because of this cause. Who knows this, that Brahman is the witness of all, attains immortality.

3. From fear of this fire burns, from fear the sun blazes; from this Indra and Air and Death the fifth run on their way.

The activities of fire, the sun, Indra, air, and death are regulated by him. Since death is mentioned after fire, sun, Indra, and air, that is fifth in this sequence, it is referred to as death the fifth.

4. If, here one is able to know before the disintegration of the body (one is freed), (otherwise) from that (failing) one becomes fit for embodiment in the world of the created.

If before the dissolution of the body, one knows Brahman, while still living, one is liberated. If one does not know this one is fit for assuming a body, is reborn. Thus, the self ought to be realized in this world.

5. Just as (one sees) in a mirror so in the self; just as in a dream so in the world of ancestors; just as (one sees) in water so in the world of shade and light. So in the world of Bramhā.

When one's intellect is without blemish the self can be distinctly viewed. The vision of the self is indistinct in the world of the ancestors. Similarly in the world of the gandharvas. Only in the world of Brahmā is this vision distinct. But this world is very difficult to attain. Thus, we ought to strive to attain the self in this world.

6. Having known the different nature of the senses which are produced separately and their rising and setting, the discerning do not grieve.

The wise person does not grieve since the self is unchanging and thus cannot be the cause of sorrow. The senses do not belong to and are different from the self.

7. The mind is superior to the sense organs; superior to the mind is its essence, the intellect; superior to the intellect is the great self; superior to the great self is the unmanifest. [This verse is similar to verse I.iii.10 of this Upaniṣad.]
8. However, superior to the unmanifest is Puruṣa, all pervasive and attributeless. By knowing whom a man is emancipated and obtains immortality.

The Puruṣa supersedes the unmanifest. Being the source of all the pervasive things, it is all pervasive. He is without worldly attributes. A person who knows this from his teacher and the scriptures attains liberation.

9. His form does not stand within the range of vision. Not anyone sees him by the eyes. Through the heart, through wisdom, through the mind apprehended. They who know this attain immortality.

The self is not seen by anyone since its form is not an object of perception. The self is seen by that which is in the heart, the intellect. When the intellect is free from objects and desires, then the self can be attained. Those who know this become immortal.

10. When together with the mind, the five senses of knowledge are in a state of rest and the intellect does not make any effort that it is said is the supreme state.

When the senses renounce their objects, they are at rest in the self. This is the highest state.

11. They think this, the steady control of the senses to be yoga. Then one becomes attentive for yoga is subject to origin and disappearance.

This verse points in the direction of Sūtra 1.2 of the Yogasūtra. Yoga in this sūtra is stated to be the state where there is cessation of the modifications of consciousness. In the commentary it is mentioned that disjunction from the senses and the consequent severance of contact from evils that leads to the self being established in its own state. There is no superimposition of ignorance in this state.

12. Not through speech, not through the mind, not through the eyes can it be attained. How can it be comprehended by anyone else except he who speaks of it as existing?

Brahman is not to be attained through the senses. It is the source of the universe. The world exists and thus the self the source of the universe exists.

13. This self should be understood only as existing and then its true nature. Of both these (aspects) when the self is understood as existent then its true nature becomes clear.

This verse reiterates that the self exists. The person who realizes the self as existing, for him all limiting adjuncts disappear and the true nature of the self is revealed.

14. When all desires clinging to the heart are renounced, then a mortal attains immortality and here (he) attains Brahman.

After all desires are overcome, then the supreme reality can be realized. For such a person there is the end of bondage, immortality and the realization of Brahman.

15. When all the knots of the heart here are severed, then a mortal person attains immortality. The instruction is so much only.

The knots of the heart refer to various concepts which arise due to ignorance that leads to bondage of the intellect. When his bondage die to ignorance ceases due to knowledge of the identity of the self and Brahman, all desires related to ignorance are extinguished. Such a person becomes immortal.

16. The arteries of the heart are a hundred and one. Of these one goes to the crown of the head. One attains immortality by going up through that. The others that branch out on all sides become (the cause) of death.

The arteries issuing out of the heart are known as suṣumnā. At the point of death one ought to bring one's mind under one's control by means of this suṣumnā nerve. By this nerve if one goes up the path of the sun he attains immortality. The other nerves lead to the worldly state and rebirth.

17. The Puruṣa, the measure of a thumb, the inner self, is situated in the hearts of all men. One should steadfastly separate him from the body like a reed from the wind. One should know him as pure and immortal. Thus, one should know him as pure and immortal.

The pure consciousness of the self is to be separated from the body. It is pure and immortal.

18. Naciketā having now obtained this knowledge spoken by death and the entire way of yoga, obtained Brahman and became free from ignorance and death. So, in this manner, anyone else who knows this regarding the self.

The Kena Upaniṣad

Invocation

Let my limbs, speech, vital breath, eyes, ears as also strength and sense organs become robust. The entire universe is the Brahman of the Upaniṣad. May I never repudiate Brahman, may Brahman never repudiate me. Let there be no rejection. Let there be no rejection of me by Brahman. Let these virtues that are in the Upaniṣad be in me who are devoted to the self.

I

1. Desired and directed by whom does the mind go towards its object? Wished by whom does the first vital breath move? By means of what is speech uttered? Who is the deity that directs the eyes and ears?

   In his commentary, Śaṅkarācārya highlights the importance of the words 'desiring' and 'directing'. He points out that this question is raised by one who wishes to turn away from this phenomenal, ephemeral world and its effects, and seeks the eternal, permanent reality.

2. Since it is the ear of the ear, the mind of the mind, the speech of speech, the vital breath of vital breath, the eye of the eye, the discerning after giving up (erroneous views of self identification with sense organs) and having departed from this world attain immortality.

   In commentary, Śaṅkarācārya takes up various objections to this śloka. Just as the activities of a composite thing such as volition and cognition are for the benefit of someone; just as in the example of a house which exists for the sake of someone else, here also there is an entity outside for whose necessity the ears etc. exist. Thus, there needs to be a director of the ear that is the ear of the ear.

   The ear, eye, etc., can only reveal their objects when there is the eternal light of the self and not without it. Other Vedic texts and the Bhagavad Gītā also state this. The śloka terms those who give up self identification with the ear, eye, etc., as discerning because only those with exceptional wisdom can give up this identification. Such a person having renounced all desires attains immortality.

3. There the eye does not go, speech does not go, not even the mind. We do not know, nor can we discern about how this can be taught.

   Brahman cannot be known by means of sense organs and the mind. This is because Brahman is the self of these organs. The example of fire is given, i.e., while fire burns, it does not burn itself. Further we are unaware of Brahman since Brahman as mentioned above is not an object of perception of the organs. For this reason, Brahman needs to be taught to disciples by putting in tremendous effort.

4. That (Brahman) is indeed different from the known, so also it is beyond the unknown. This utterance we have heard from the ancients who illustrated that to us.

   The manifested world is known. Brahman is different from that. Further, that which is known is limited and miserable and ought to be rejected. By stating that Brahman is different from the known it is also meant that Brahman ought not to be rejected.

   Śaṅkarācārya interprets the known and unknown to mean the expressed (manifested) and unexpressed (unmanifested) or the effect and the cause. Brahman is different from both. Only the self is different from the known and unknown. Thus, the purport of this line is that the self is Brahman.

5. Which is not stated by means of speech but that through which speech is stated. Know that only to be Brahman, not this, which (people) here admire.

Its essence is consciousness and it is not expressed by speech. Śaṅkarācārya points out that the word 'vāk', is used to refer to the organ of speech, the letters and the sound expressed by them. Speech is expressed by consciousness, by Brahman and thus the expression 'speech of speech'. What people normally meditate on is not Brahman since objects are possessed of distinctions due to limiting adjuncts. The non-self is not Brahman. The self only is Brahman.

6. Which is not thought through the mind but by means of which the mind is thought. Know that only to be Brahman, not this, which (people) here admire.

   That which by means of the mind cannot be thought of. Here manas refers to the mind, intellect, and internal organs as one. Manas is that by which one thinks and is common to all organs. The essence of all things is the self. Thus, the mind cannot act in respect of its own self. Significantly the mind is able to think only when it is illuminated by the light of consciousness.

7. Which the eye does not see but by which the activities of the eye are seen. Know that only to be Brahman, not this, which (people) here admire.

   It (Brahman) is that which the eye along with the internal organ cannot make an object of perception, yet it is that which by means of the light of consciousness enables a person to see.

8. Which the ear cannot hear, but that due to which the ears are able to hear. Know that only to be Brahman, not this, which (people) here admire.

   It (Brahman) is that which a person does not hear by means of the ear, which is connected to the internal organ and whose realm is ether. Yet the ear is able to function by this (Brahman) by means of the light of consciousness.

9. Which cannot be smelled by the organ of smell, but that by which the organ of smell is able to smell. Know that only to be Brahman, not this, which (people) here admire.

The organ of smell is associated with the internal organ and vital breath. It is made of the element of earth and is located in the nostrils. It (Brahman) is that which a person does not smell by means of the organ of smell. Yet the organ of smell is able to attain its object by this (Brahman) by means of the light of consciousness.

II

1. If you believe you know Brahman excellently, (then) surely you know only a small aspect of it, whether relating to you or with reference to the gods. Therefore indeed, Brahman still has to be deliberated upon by you (the student). (Though the student is of the view) 'I think Brahman is known.'

This śloka, especially the first lines are meant to deter the student from erroneously concluding that he knows Brahman since the student may think that he knows himself well and the self is Brahman.

Śaṅkarācārya further says that only an object that can be cognized can be known thoroughly. Just as fire itself cannot be burnt by fire, thus the knower cannot be known by the knower. Yet, he who is genuinely wise, is free of defects may comprehend it. When viewed from the point of view of adjuncts like name and form it appears that Brahman has aspects. Yet this is not the case from the standpoint of Brahman itself.

2. I do not believe that I know this well, no, I do not know this (Brahman) and I know it. Who amongst us knows that I do not know and I know, knows that (Brahman).

This śloka also continues the dialogue between student and teacher regarding Brahman. The line, 'I do not know this and I know it' has the same import as the line, 'That (Brahman) is indeed different from the known, so also it is beyond the unknown.'

3. To him it is known, to whom it is not known, to whoever it is known, he does not know. It is not comprehended by those who comprehend it; it is comprehended by those who do not comprehend it.

The purport of this śloka is to point out that the person whose view is that Brahman is unknown to him, knows Brahman. Yet whose view is that Brahman is known to him, such a person does not know Brahman. The person who thinks he knows Brahman erroneously fails to discriminate between Brahman and its limiting adjuncts such as the senses, mind and the intellect and the self.

But if Brahman is completely unknown then what is the difference between those who know Brahman and ordinary people? The answer is in the next śloka.

4. When it (Brahman) is known through each state of cognition then it is (truly) known, because (through this) one obtains immortality. By means of one's self is obtained vitality, through wisdom one obtains immortality.

The word 'bodha' used in the verse here denotes cognitions obtained by means of the intellect. The self is the witness of all cognitions. The self by nature is consciousness and pervades all cognitions. Thus when Brahman is known as the innermost self then it is known and there is true realization. Brahman is pure, permanent and not subject to growth and decay.

5. Here if (one) realizes, then there is truth; If here (one) does not know then there is great destruction. The wise seeking

(Brahman) in all beings, having departed from this world become immortal.

If any person who is competent, capable and knows the self as described here, then here there is truth, indestructibility, and the supreme reality. However, if such a person has not realized then there is unending destruction, birth and rebirth, old age and suffering. Thus the wise having realized the one reality of the self in all beings, desist from the world of ignorance and attain the non dual state becoming one with the state of all. Such a person becomes immortal, becomes Brahman.

III

1. Verily it was Brahman that attained victory for the gods. The gods became elated in the victory which was indeed Brahman's.

In the commentary it is stated that it is well known that Para-Brahman obtained a victory for the devas. In the victory of Brahman, the deities such as fire became elated. Śaṅkarācārya says that the differences in views are only on account of ignorance. While ignorance is removed there is no difference. All beings have a self which is subtle, has consciousness in its nature and is omnipresent.

In this section a story is told. It has various objectives. Someone reading the previous verses may wrongly conclude that Brahman is non-existent. This story seeks to end this delusion. It asserts that Brahman is the ruler, the supreme lord and cause of victory of the gods. By knowledge of Brahman the gods attained preeminence. Further Brahman is inscrutable. Since it is with great difficulty that deities such as fire know Brahman.

2. They thought: 'Indeed this victory is ours, this glory is ours.' Brahman verily knew this (pretension) of theirs. To the gods

indeed it appeared. They could not comprehend what this yakṣa (venerable being) was.

Due to the ego, the seeds of ignorance manifest and the body, senses, mind, and intellect are seen as different from the eternal self. Due to knowledge ignorance is dispelled and one attains liberation.

The deities due to ignorance did not realize that this victory and glory belonged to Brahman. They thought that it belonged to them limited by their personalities. Brahman being omniscient wanted to dispel this false notion. Brahman appeared in the form of a venerable being (yakṣa) in front of them. Yet the deities were unable to comprehend the yakṣa.

3. They told Agni (fire): 'O Jāta-veda, omniscient one, find out thoroughly what this yakṣa is.' He assented.
   The deities who did not know the yakṣa, were apprehensive within, and asked Agni who is foremost of all the deities, and who is omniscient to find out what this yakṣa is since Agni was the most brilliant amongst them.
4. Agni moved towards it and to him it said: 'Who are you?' Agni said: 'Verily I am Agni, I am Jāta-veda.'
   Fire said: 'Very well' and went near the yakṣa. Fire being in the presence of the yakṣa, in the absence of arrogance remained quiet. The yakṣa asked him: 'Who are you?' Praising himself, fire stated that he was known by two names—Agni and Jāta-veda.
5. (It asked): 'What is the power in you, as you are?' (Agni replied): 'I can scorch all that which is on the earth.'
   To him, Brahman in the form of the yakṣa asked him, who had such renowned qualities and names, what his power was. Fire replied that he could burn whatever was on earth.
6. (Yakṣa) placed a blade of grass before him and said: 'Burn this.' He went to it with due swiftness. He was not able to

burn it. He retreated from that yakṣa (and said to the gods): 'I could not know fully what that yakṣa is.'

In this way the yakṣa placed a blade of grass in front of fire who was filled with pride. Brahman asked him to burn it and told him that if he could not burn it, he should give up the pride of thinking he could burn anything, anywhere. Fire could not burn the blade of grass. Fire then withdrew.

7. They then told Vāyu (Air): 'O Vāyu, find out thoroughly what this yakṣa is.' He assented.

The next few verses are similar to the preceding ones. They describe the interaction of the air deity with the yakṣa.

8. He moved towards it and to him it said: 'Who are you?' Vāyu said: 'Verily I am Vāyu, or I am called Mātariśvan.'
9. (It asked): 'What is the power in you as you are?' (Vāyu replied): 'I can blow everything away that is placed on the earth.'
10. (Yakṣa) placed a blade of grass before him and said: 'Blow (this) away.' He went to it with due swiftness. He was not able to blow it. He retreated from that yakṣa (and said to the gods): 'I could not know fully what that yakṣa is.'
11. They told Indra: 'O Maghavā find out what this yakṣa is. He assented. He moved towards it. (But) it vanished from him. Brahman in the form of the yakṣa vanished from sight as Indra approached. The yakṣa did not even grant Indra an interview. This was to break his pride.
12. In that very region of the sky, Indra approached a most graceful lady, Umā, daughter of Himavat and asked her: 'What is this yakṣa?'

Indra did not return after the yakṣa disappeared but stayed in the same area. Knowledge in the form of a very graceful woman Umā appeared. Knowledge being the most graceful, very graceful is the correct attribute. Indra asked Umā about the yakṣa.

IV

1. She said: 'This is Brahman indeed and in the victory of Brahman you have become so elated. From that (utterance of Umā) did he (Indra) realize that it was Brahman.

   It is from this statement of Umā did Indra learn that it was indeed Brahman. The Devtas, Agni, Vāyu, and Indra first came into contact with Brahman and they are therefore accorded primacy.

2. Therefore, surely these gods—Agni, Vāyu, and Indra—greatly surpassed the other gods, for it was they that verily touched it (Brahman) the nearest and they realized first that it was Brahman.

   Thus, surely due to this good fortune, their qualities and powers did Indra and these Devtas were able to converse with Brahman and came in contact with Brahman. They were able to know this is Brahman.

3. Thus did Indra exceed the other gods. For he touched it (Brahman) most closely. Verily he realized first that it was Brahman.

   Thus, do Indra and these Devtas excel the other Devtas.

4. There is this instruction of this Brahman; it is like the flash of lightning or the wink of an eye. This regards the foremost divinity.

   The above is an instruction regarding Brahman by means of analogy. This is termed as ādeśaḥ since Brahman manifested itself once and disappeared. It is compared to the flash of lightning or the winking of an eye.

5. Now the instruction concerning the individual self; apparently the mind proceeds to this; it (Brahman) is remembered by means of this mind; similar is the case regarding volition (the mind has regarding Brahman).

The analogical instruction continues, this time regarding the self. Previously in the divine context, the analogy of lightning and winking were maintained. With respect to the self the mind goes to Brahman and that mind by this means remembers Brahman.

6. That Brahman indeed, is known as that which is worshipped; and as that which is worshipped it should be meditated upon. Anyone who knows Brahman thus, him indeed, all creatures seek.

The commentary states that Brahman is tadvanam, meaning that Brahman is praiseworthy to all creatures. By means of determination and memory one ought to meditate on Brahman. Such a meditator is prayed to by all kings.

7. Disciple: 'Sir, answer regarding the secret (Upaniṣad).' (The teacher): 'The secret has been spoken of (to you); the secret knowledge regarding Brahman has been taught to you.'

The student asks the teacher about the secret teaching, the Upaniṣad. The teacher replies that since the previous discourse regarded the supreme self, the student has been instructed in the secret teaching regarding the supreme self.

8. Penance, control of the senses, and work (karma) are its foundation, the Vedas are its limbs and its abode is truth.

Concentration, penance, control of the senses, and virtuous acts are necessary so that a person is purified. Only such a purified person may obtain knowledge of Brahman. A person who is not purged of impurities will be unable to comprehend Brahman. The Vedas are the limbs, since through the Vedas are knowledge and rites revealed. Satya (truth) is its abode, since knowledge dwells in those who are free from deceit and evil.

9. Who knows this, indeed destroying sin, remains firmly established in the higher world of heaven, indeed he remains firmly established there.

   This verse states the conclusion of this Upaniṣad. The person who knows the teachings of the Upaniṣad does not return to the mortal world.

The Chāndogya Upaniṣad

Invocation

Aum. May there be growth in my limbs, speech, prāṇa (vital breath), sight, hearing, vigour, all the senses and everything. All is the Brahman of the Upaniṣads. May I never repudiate Brahman, may Brahman never repudiate me. May there be no repudiation at all. May there be no repudiation from me. May there be in me, who is devoted to that self, the virtues of the Upaniṣads. May they be in one.

Aum! Peace! Peace! Peace!

Prāṇa can be differently translated as vital breath, life breath, and life force. It is extensively dealt with in the Bṛhadāraṇyaka Upaniṣad. The point being made here is that since all is Brahman, nothing is rejected by Brahman. However, an ignorant person may erroneously deny Brahman. The word shāntiḥ is used thrice to protect against the three kinds of trouble—internal, external, and supernatural.

CHAPTER 1

I

1. Aum, on this syllable one ought to meditate, the Udgītha, because one sings the Udgītha beginning with Aum. Of this, the supplementary explanation (follows).

   Meditating on Aum as the symbol of Brahman is enjoined upon. Aum ought to be chanted at the beginning and end of a hymn. Udgītha constitutes a part of a Vedic ritual.

   Regarding the meaning of sāman (chant) it refers to the number of stanzas of the Sāmveda which are chanted melodiously. Later on, the division of sāman will be discussed.

2. Of all these beings the essence is the earth; of the earth, the essence is water. Of water the essence is vegetation; of vegetation the essence is a person. Of a person the essence is speech. Of speech the essence is the Ṛk (hymn). Of Ṛk the essence is the sāman. Of sāman the essence is Udgītha.

   The commentary explains various lines in the verse. The word essence is used in different senses in different lines of each statement. The earth is said to be the essence since it is the abode of all beings. Sāman is said in the commentary to be at a higher level than Udgītha since it brings more joy to the listener. Aum is the essence of all essences.

3. That syllable Aum, of the essences is the quintessence, the foremost, the highest, the eighth, called Udgītha.

Aum is the symbol that represents Brahman, the supreme self. It is eighth in the order of essences mentioned previously. Aum is an object of meditation.

4. Which of many is the Ṛk? Which of many is the sāman? Which of many is the Udgītha? This is being reflected upon (now).

The aim of this verse is to highlight the great importance of Ṛk, sāman, and Udgītha.

5. Speech only is Ṛk, vital breath is sāman. The syllable Aum is Udgītha. Indeed this is a couple, namely speech and vital breath and also Ṛk and sāman.

Speech expresses the Ṛk and is said to be its cause. The singing of sāman requires strength so strength is the cause. Thus, whatever is desirable may be attained by means of speech and strength. Speech and prāṇa are the sources of Ṛk and sāman.

6. This couple is combined together in the syllable Aum. Indeed, whenever a couple comes together, they fulfil each other's wishes.

This syllable is uttered by means of prāṇa and consists of speech as per the commentary.

7. Indeed, the wise who meditate on this syllable thus as the Udgītha, becomes a fulfiller of all desires.

This is so since a meditator attains the qualities on which he meditates.

8. Indeed, this syllable is of consent, for whenever one consents to a thing, one simply says Aum. Consent alone is fulfilment.

Indeed, the wise who meditate on this syllable as Udgītha thus (as endowed with prosperity) becomes a fulfiller of all desires.

9. By means of this does the threefold knowledge proceed. With Aum one causes to obey, with Aum one recites, with Aum one sings aloud for the worship of this syllable with its glory and essence.

   Worship of Aum is worship of the supreme self since Aum is the symbol of the supreme self. The importance of uttering of praṇava is also highlighted.

10. Who knows this thus and who knows not, both perform by means of it. Nevertheless, knowledge and ignorance are different (in consequences). Verily, what is done with knowledge, faith, and meditation, that indeed becomes more efficacious. Indeed, this is the elucidation of this syllable.

    The importance of knowing the true nature of Aum is stressed. The true result is produced by means of knowledge. Aum ought to be meditated upon just as one meditates on Brahman.

II

1. Verily, when the gods and demons, both descended from Prajāpati, were engaged in war, the gods performed the Udgītha, thinking by means of this we will overpower them.

   The commentary compares the devas to light and the asuras to the nature of darkness. The implication is that devas refer to purified senses and the asuras to senses afflicted by worldly attachments and objects. The story contained here seeks to show that uncontrolled sense organs lead to destruction and unrighteousness and purified inward sense organs lead to the path of righteousness. The struggle between these two is referred to as a struggle between the devas and the asuras.

2. Indeed, they meditated on Udgītha as prāṇa (vital breath) connected with the nose. The demons penetrated it with evil. Thus, with it one smells both the fragrant and foul smelling, since it has been penetrated with evil.

Aum was meditated upon as breath. That is the deity associated with olfaction. Due to penetration of evil are fouls smells perceived.

3. Then indeed they meditated on Udgītha as speech. The demons penetrated it with evil. Thus with it (a person) speaks both truth and untruth, since it has been penetrated with evil.
4. Then indeed they meditated on Udgītha as the eye. The demons penetrated it with evil. Thus with it (a person) sees both what is good looking and what is not good looking, since it has been penetrated with evil.
5. Then indeed they meditated on Udgītha as the ear. The demons penetrated it with evil. Thus with it (a person) hears both what should be heard and what should not be heard, since it has been penetrated with evil.
6. Then indeed they meditated on Udgītha as the mind. The demons penetrated it with evil. Thus with it (a person) thinks both what should be thought and what should not be thought since it has been penetrated with evil.
7. Then indeed they meditated on Udgītha as the prāṇa in the mouth. The demons struck against it and were destroyed just as a (lump of clay) striking against a hard stone is destroyed.

   Prāṇa in the nose was afflicted with evil. Yet prāṇa in the mouth was not penetrated by evil due to the strength of its deity.
8. Thus just as (a lump of clay) striking a hard stone is destroyed, thus indeed will he be destroyed who desires harm towards

one who knows thus and who also attacks him, for he is like a hard stone.

9. Indeed with this (prāṇa) one does not discern the fragrant or the foul smelling for this is removed from evil. What one eats, what one drinks with this, he defends the other vital breaths. Verily, at the time of death, not finding this in the mouth, one departs. Indeed, at the time of death one opens the mouth.

   The mouth is opened at the time of death. This is so that prāṇa may get nourishment which the mouth fails to provide at this stage.

10. Aṅgiras meditated on that (prāṇa) as the Udgītha. Indeed they (people) think this is aṅgiras which is the essence of the limbs.

    This verse emphasizes identity with prāṇa.

11. Bṛhaspati meditated on that (prāṇa) as the Udgītha. Indeed they (people) think this is Bṛhaspati since speech is great and it (prāṇa) is its ruler.
12. Ayāsya meditated on that (prāṇa) as the Udgītha. Indeed they (people) think this is Ayāsya, since it goes out from the mouth.
13. The sun of Dalbha, Baka, knew that. He became the udgātṛ—singer of the people dwelling in Naimiṣa. He sang for them to comply with their desires.
14. The singer who knows this thus (as explained in the preceeding ślokas) and meditates on Udgītha as the syllable Aum, becomes the obtainer of desired objects. This is with reference to the self.

    Meditation has two types of results, visible and invisible. The visible results are being described here. The visible result is identity with prāṇa.

III

1. Now with regards to the gods. Him who gives heat (the sun) one ought to meditate on as Udgītha. Indeed, when he rises, for all creatures' sake, he sings aloud. On rising, he repels darkness and fear. Indeed, a person who knows thus, becomes the repeller of fear and darkness.

   It is the same prāṇa that exists as divine and as physical.

2. Indeed this (prāṇa) in the mouth and that (sun) are similar. This has heat and that has heat. This people call svara (sound) and that people call svara and pratyāsvara (reflecting sound). Indeed, on this and on that one ought to meditate as the Udgītha.

   The body remains warm due to the presence of prāṇa. Prāṇa and the sun are similar in that they both leave, or the sun sets, but prāṇa does not come back once it leaves the body.

3. Now, indeed one ought to meditate on vyāna (diffused breath) as Udgītha. That which one breathes in, it is prāṇa; that which one breathed out it is apāna. The union of prāṇa and apāna is vyāna. That which is vyāna, it is speech. Thus when one utters speech one neither breathes in or breathes out.

   This verse seeks to show another way to meditate on Udgītha. The meaning of vyāna given here seems to be different from the meaning of vyāna in the Sānkhya system, namely the air pervading the entire body. Vyāna enables speech.

4. That which is speech it is Ṛk. Thus, one pronounces the Ṛk without in-breath or out-breath. That which is Ṛk, it is sāman. Thus, one sings the sāman without in-breath or out-breath. That which is sāman it is Udgītha. Thus, one chants the Udgītha without in-breath or out-breath.

Sāman is the Ṛk-mantra sung in a melody. Udgītha is a part of sāman. They are said to be equal and they are performed due to the activity of vyāna.

5. Thus, whichever other actions require vigour, like the starting of a fire by friction, running a race, the stretching of a strong bow, one does them without in-breath or out-breath. For this reason, one should meditate on vyāna as Udgītha.
6. Now verily one should meditate on the syllables of Udgītha—ut, gī, tha. 'Ut' is prāṇa, since by means of prāṇa one rises. 'Gī' is said to be speech, since speech is called giras (word). 'Tha' is said to be food, since on food is everything based.

The commentary states the equivalence of meditation on the syllables of a name and meditation on a name. 'Gī' is speed, 'ut' is prāṇa, and 'tha' is food.

7. Heaven itself is ut, the sky itself is gī, the earth itself is tha. The sun itself is ut, the air is gī, and the fire tha. The Sāma Veda itself is ut, the Yajur Veda gī, and the Ṛg Veda tha. For him speech gives rise to milk and which milk is said to be speech. The wise who knows thus and meditates on the syllables of Udgītha namely ut, gī, and tha becomes richly endowed with abundant food and an eater of food.

Heaven is highly placed and is 'ut', the sky is all pervading and is 'gī', the earth is where creatures reside. Fire is the abode of sacrifices.

8. Now verily, the fulfilment of desires. One ought to meditate on the objects contemplated. One should reflect on the sāman with which one is about to sing the stotra (a hymn of praise).

This verse seeks to show the path leading to realization of wishes. One ought to reflect on the origin of metre, etc., of the hymns one is about to sing.

9. On the Ṛk in which the sāman occurs, on the sage by which it was seen, on the deity to whom he is about to sing praises of, should one reflect upon.
10. One ought to reflect on that metre by means of which one is about to sing a stotra. One ought to reflect on the hymn form by means of which one is about to sing a hymn of praise.

The commentary describes stoma as collections of sāmans as per particular orders chanted during the soma sacrifice. Stomas are groups of Ṛg Vedic verses.

11. One ought to reflect on the quarter of the sky in honour of which he is about to sing a stotra.

Heaven and the presiding deity ought to be reflected upon.

12. Ultimately, one should think about oneself and sing a hymn of praise, meditating attentively on one's desire. For him, quickly indeed will the desire be fulfilled, desiring which he may sing the hymn of praise, indeed desiring which he may sing the hymn of praise.

This should be done after reflecting upon the sāman. By faults are meant faults of pronunciation, accent, etc.

IV

1. Aum, on this syllable one ought to meditate, the Udgītha, because one sings the Udgītha beginning with Aum. Of this, the supplementary explanation (follows).
2. Indeed, the gods being afraid of death, entered into threefold knowledge. They surrounded themselves with metrical hymns. Since they surrounded themselves with these, therefore the metrical hymns are called chandas.

By threefold knowledge is meant the three Vedas. During a sacrifice certain mantras are chanted. The rest constitute japa standing for repetition in the absence of sacrifice. This is intended to protect a person against evil.

3. As one may see a fish in water, death saw them (the gods) there in the Ṛk, Sāman, and Yajus. Having learnt this, they too arose out of the Ṛk, Sāman, and Yajus and entered the svara (sound, the syllable Aum).

Svara denotes sound, the syllable Aum. Death felt that the deities could be ensnared if they did not perform their rites properly. The deities had by means of Vedic rites purified themselves. They realized the thinking of death.

4. Indeed, when a person learns the Ṛk, one loudly pronounces Aum. Thus with Sāman and thus with Yajus. This Svara is indeed this syllable, which is immortal, fearless. Having entered that sound, the gods attained immortality and became fearless.

It is reiterated that Aum may be called Svara.

5. He who knowing this (syllable) thus, pays obeisance to this syllable, enters this syllable, the sound, which is immortal and fearless. Having entered that he attains immortality just as the gods are immortal.

V

1. Now indeed what is Udgītha is Pranava. What is Pranava is Udgītha. Thus indeed the yonder sun is Udgītha and this Pranava; since this (sun) continuously sounds Aum.

The identity of Udgītha and Pranava is stated. Meditation on this identity is enjoined. Benefits of meditation on the sun are also explained.

2. 'To him alone (the sun) I sang; thus you are my only (sun).' Thus Kauṣītaki told his son: 'Reflect on the many rays (as

Udgītha), indeed you will have many sons.' Thus with regard to the gods.

3. Now with regard to the self. Indeed, one ought to meditate on this who is prāṇa in the mouth, as Udgītha for it continually sounds Aum.

Aum can only be pronounced by a person by the permission of prāṇa. At the time of death, prāṇa in the mouth does not allow this, since it ceases its activity. We can only pronounce Aum due to prāṇa.

4. 'To him alone (the sun) I sang; thus, you are my only (sun).' Thus, Kauṣītaki told his son.' Sing praises to the vital breaths as manifold, surely you will have many sons.'

Prāṇa is adored in different ways, in the mouth and other organs. The unity of Udgītha and prāṇa is again discussed.

5. Now indeed what is Udgītha is Pranava; and what is Pranava is Udgītha. (If one knows this) indeed, by the acts from the seat of the Hotṛ priest, even if one chants wrongly it is rectified, it is rectified.

VI

1. Indeed this (earth) is the Ṛk and fire is Sāman. This Sāman rests upon that Ṛk. Thus, Sāman is sung and praised as resting upon the Ṛk. Indeed, this earth it is 'sā', fire is 'ama', and that (results in) 'Sāma'.

earth and fire are connected. Fire is dependent on the earth. earth is said to stand for the first half of Sāma and fire its second half. Together they are Sāma.

2. Indeed, the sky is Ṛk, the air is Sāman. This Sāman rests upon that Ṛk. Thus, Sāman is sung and praised as resting upon the Ṛk. Indeed, the sky it is 'sā', the air is 'ama', and

that (results in) 'Sāma'.

3. Indeed, paradise is Ṛk, the sun is Sāman. This Sāman rests upon that Ṛk. Thus, Sāman is sung and praised as resting upon the Ṛk. Indeed, paradise is 'sā', the sun is 'ama', and that (results in) 'Sāma'.
4. Indeed, the stars are Ṛk, the moon is Sāman. This Sāman rests upon that Ṛk. Thus, Sāman is sung and praised as resting upon the Ṛk. Indeed, the stars are 'sā', the moon is 'ama', and that (results in) 'Sāma'.
5. Now this white light of the sun is indeed that Ṛk; the blue that is extremely dark that is Sāman. This Sāman rests upon that Ṛk. Thus, Sāman is sung and praised as resting upon the Ṛk.
6. Then indeed the white light of the sun is Sā, the blue that is extremely dark is ama. That (results in) Sāma. Now, that person, made of gold, who is seen inside the sun, that person is endowed with golden beard and golden hair. Indeed, everything is golden even the tips of his nails.

This verse describes the divine person in the sun. This is to encourage meditation on him. The commentary states that Hiraṇyagarbha here refers to he who consists of brilliance. The Puruṣa resides in the Buddhi or who pervades the universe. The Puruṣa is perceived by those who have turned their focus within and follow correct practices.

7. His eyes are just as a red lotus. His name is ut. Above all evil he has risen. Indeed, he who knows thus rises above all evil.
8. His two joints are Ṛk and Sāman. Thus (they are called) Udgītha. Thus since the priest is the singer of 'ut' he is udgātā. He is the lord of such worlds which are beyond that (sun) and the desires of the gods. Thus, with regard to the gods.

He is the essence of all, the source of all. Ṛk and Sāman in the form of earth and fire are his joints.

VII

1. Now with regard to the self. Speech indeed is Ṛk, prāṇa is Sāman. This Sāman rests upon that Ṛk. Thus, Sāman is sung and praised as resting upon the Ṛk. Speech indeed is 'Sā', prāṇa is 'ama', and that (results in) Sāma.
2. The eye indeed is Ṛk, the self is Sāman. This Sāman rests upon that Ṛk. Thus, Sāman is sung and praised as resting upon the Ṛk. The eye indeed is 'Sā', the self is 'ama' and that (results in) Sāma.
3. The ear indeed is Ṛk, the mind is Sāman. This Sāman rests upon that Ṛk. Thus, Sāman is sung as resting upon the Ṛk. The ear indeed is 'Sā', the mind is 'ama' and that (makes) Sāma.
4. Now the white light of the eye is indeed Ṛk, and the extremely dark blue light is Sāman. This Sāman rests upon that Ṛk. Thus, Sāman is sung and praised as resting upon the Ṛk. The eye's white light is 'Sā', the extremely dark blue light is 'ama' and that (results in) Sāma.

This verse contains a meditation with respect to the body.

5. Now indeed this person seen inside the eye, he is Ṛk (hymn), he is Sāman (chant), he is uktha (recitation), he is Yajus (sacrificial formula), he is Brahman. The form of this one (person inside the eye) is the same as the form of that one (person inside the sun). His two joints are the same as the other two joints. The name of one and the name of the other are the same.

The verse relates to the object of the chief meditation. All mentioned in this verse are the person since he is the essence and source of all.

6. He (the person in the eye) is the ruler of the worlds which are beneath this one and also of the desires of men. Thus,

those persons who sing accompanied by the vīna, sing of him. Thus, they are endowed with wealth.

7. Now he who sings the Sāman after knowing this thus, sings of both. By means of that (the person in the sun) he attains the worlds which are beyond that (the sun) and also what the gods desire.

The verse seeks to describe the result achieved by a knower.

8. Now by means of this (the person in the eye) he attains the worlds which are below that (the sun) and also what men desire. Thus as Udgātṛ priest, who knows thus should utter (the following):
9. 'For you, which desires may I attain by singing this Sāman?' Surely, he only becomes capable of attaining desires by singing, who thus knowing sings the Sāman—surely sings the glorious Sāman.

VIII

1. In prior times, there were three persons skilful in the Udgītha (namely) Silaka, son of Sālāvat, Caikitāyana of the Dālbhaya clan and Pravāhaṇa, son of Jīvala. They said: 'Verily, since we are skilful in the Udgītha, if you agree, let us initiate a conversation on the Udgītha.'
   This verse introduces another way of meditating on Aum.
2. They said: 'Let it be so', and settled down. Then said Pravāhara Jaivali: 'You two illustrious sirs speak first, I will hear the words of two Brāhmaṇas speaking.'
3. Indeed, he Śilaka Śālāvatya said to Caikitāyana of the Dalbha clan:' If you agree, may I question you?'
   'Question indeed,' he said.
4. (Śilaka asked): 'What is the origin of Sāman?' 'It is sound indeed,' said (Dālbhaya). 'What is the origin of sound?' 'Prāṇa indeed,' said (Dālbhaya). 'What is the origin of prāṇa?' 'Food

indeed,' said (Dālbhaya). 'What is the origin of food?' 'Water indeed,' said (Dālbhaya).

Udgītha is being discussed as a theme of meditation here. Sound is the origin of Sāman which in turn is accompanied by prāṇa as per Dālbhaya.

5. 'What is the origin of water?' 'That world,' said (Dālbhaya). 'Of that world what is the origin?' 'One ought not to carry beyond the heavenly world,' said (Dālbhaya). We have established Sāman in the heavenly world, since Sāman is celebrated in heaven.
6. Then indeed Śilaka Śālāvatya said to Caikitāyana Dālbhaya 'O Dālbhaya, indeed, assuredly your Sāman is unestablished. And now if at present someone were to say to you, 'your head will fall down', indeed your head would fall down.
Dālbhaya's views of Sāman are countered. Śilaka says they are erroneous.
7. (Dālbhaya) said: 'Will you permit me illustrious sir to know this from you?' 'Know thus.' (Śilaka) said. 'Of that (heavenly) world what is the origin?' He replied: 'One ought not to carry beyond the world as its support.' In this world we establish the Sāman as it's support since the Sāman is celebrated as the support.
8. To him indeed Pravāhaṇa Jaivali said: 'O Śālāvatya, your Sāman assuredly has an end. Now, if at present someone were to say to you, "your head will fall down", indeed your head would fall down.' (Śālāvatya) said: 'Will you permit me illustrious sir to know this from you?' 'Know thus,' (Jaivali) said.

IX

1. (Śālāvatya) said: 'Of this world what is the origin?' (Pravāhaṇa) said: 'Ether since all these beings arise from ether only and

finally dissolve into ether. For indeed ether is more excellent than these and is what they depend on.'

Here the supreme reality is termed as Ākāśa. But it is not the elemental ether, since it (Bhūtākāśa) cannot be the abode of the infinite. Further elemental ether is not all encompassing. In other texts as well Ākāśa is used to refer to the Paramātman.

2. It is this Udgītha, greatest and most excellent. It is without end. He who knows it thus, meditates upon the Udgītha, the greatest and most excellent, becomes the greatest and most excellent and attains the greatest and most excellent worlds.

The Udgītha mentioned in this verse refers to Paramātman and nothing else. The results mentioned here are attained sequentially by the meditator since he meditates progressively on the greater and more excellent Udgītha.

3. Indeed Atidhanavan, the son of Śunaka having taught this (Udgītha) to Udaraśaṇḍilya stated: 'Among your descendants as far as this knowledge of Udgītha continues, so far will their life in this world and the next be the greatest and most excellent.'
4. And such will their state be in that other world. He who knows thus and meditates—in this world his life becomes the greatest and most excellent and such will be his state in that different world, indeed in that different world.

X

1. In the land of the Kurus when (crops) perished by hail, there lived in the village of elephant drivers a very poor man Uṣasti, the son of Cakra with his young wife Ātibi.
This section seeks to explain that along with meditation upon Udgītha one should meditate on the prastāva and

pratihāra. There is difference of opinion regarding meaning of the word Ātikī. Here it has been interpreted as a name.

2. He begged (for food) from an elephant driver while he was eating gruel. The elephant driver said to him: 'Other than these which are set beside me, I have no other.'
3. Uṣasti said: 'Give me some of them.' The elephant driver gave them to him and said: 'If you please here's water.' Uṣasti replied: 'Then I will be drinking what is rejected.'
4. 'Are these not rejected? If I did not eat these, surely, I could not have survived,' said he. 'Drinking of water is as per my wish.'
5. After eating Uṣasti brought the remainder to his wife. She, by alms, had already obtained her food. After accepting them she kept them securely.
6. Indeed, he arose the next morning and stated: 'Alas if I could obtain some food. I may obtain a small amount of wealth. There a king is having a sacrifice performed. He may select me to all the various priestly offices.'
7. To him his wife said: 'Here are the grains my lord.' After he had eaten the grains, he went off to the sacrifice which was being conducted.
8. He sat down there close to the Udgātṛ priests in the assigned place for singing the hymns. He then spoke aloud to the Prastotṛ priest:
9. 'O Prastotṛ, if you sing the commencement praise without properly knowing the deity that belongs to it, your head will indeed fall down.'

Both the knowledge and form of a rite should be known. If a rite is done without proper knowledge it leads to the southern path.

10. Thus, indeed he spoke to the Udgātṛ priest: 'O Udgātṛ, if you sing the Udgītha not properly knowing which deity that belongs to it your head will indeed fall down.'

11. Thus, indeed he spoke to the Pratihartṛ priest: 'O Pratihartṛ, if you sing the Pratihāra not properly knowing which deity that belongs to it, your head will indeed fall down.' They halted and quietly sat down.

XI

1. Then the person performing the sacrifice said to him: 'Indeed illustrious sir, I would like to know you.' He introduced himself and said: 'I am Uṣasti Cākrāyaṇa.'
2. He said: 'Indeed illustrious sir, I enquired for you for all these various priestly offices, however not being able to locate you I have selected others.'
3. 'Illustrious sir, you only take up all the priestly offices for me.' 'Then in that case let these priests only sing the hymns with my permission. However, you should give me the same amount of wealth as you give them.' 'So be it,' said the person performing the sacrifice.
4. Then the Prastotṛ priest went near him (and said): 'Illustrious sir, to me you had said, "O Prastotṛ if you sing the commencement praise not knowing the deity that belongs to it, your head will be destroyed. Can you please tell me about that deity?"'
5. 'Vital breath,' said Uṣasti, 'surely all these beings merge in vital breath (during dissolution) and rise up with vital breath (at the time of creation). This is the deity that is associated with the prastāva. If you had sung the prastāva not knowing him, after you had been so cautioned by me, your head would have been destroyed.'

   In this case, this particular deity has been chosen since 'pra' is common to both prāṇa and prastāva.

6. Then the Udgātṛ priest went near him (and said): 'Illustrious sir to me you have said "O Udgātṛ priest, if you sing the

commencement praise without knowing the deity that belongs to it, your head will be destroyed." Can you please tell me about that deity?'

7. 'The Sun,' said Uṣasti, 'surely all these beings here sing (praises) of the sun when he rises up. This is the deity connected with the Udgītha. If you had chanted the Udgītha not knowing him, after you had been so cautioned by me, your head would have been destroyed.'

Deity is chosen due to similarities. 'Ut' the deity of Udgītha is the sun.

8. Then the Pratihartṛ priest went near him (and said): 'Illustrious sir to me you have said "O Pratihartṛ, if you take up the pratihāra not knowing the deity associated with it, your head will be destroyed." Can you please tell me about that deity?'
9. 'Food,' said Uṣasti, 'surely all these beings here live by consuming food indeed. This is the deity associated with the pratihāra. If you had taken up the pratihāra not knowing him, after you had been so cautioned by me, your head would have been destroyed.'

In this and the preceding section is enjoined the duty to mediate on the deities of iprastāva, Udgītha, and pratihāra as prāṇa, the sun, and anna. These meditations lead to identity with what is meditated upon.

XII

1. Now for this reason the Udgītha relating to dogs. He, Baka Dālbhaya (also known as) Glāva Maitreya set out to study the Vedas.
2. A white dog became visible to him. Other dogs went near it and said: 'By singing get food for us. Indeed, we are hungry.'

The above verse may be interpreted in various ways. As per the commentary, a higher being impressed with his penance took the form of a dog and appeared in front of him. Alternatively, the sense organs such as speech, due to or āṇa were able to partake in food and and came to the mouth.

3. To them (the white dog) said: 'Come to me here in the morning only.' There only Baka Dālbhaya or Glāva Maitreya kept observing them.

   The importance of the morning is highlighted due to the location of the sun in the morning. The sun is the provider of food.

4. Thus, just as those who chant the Bahiṣpavamāna Stotra glide along, hand in hand, so did they (the dogs) move along. Then they settled down together and began to utter the noise 'hiṁ'.

   The commentary highlights the importance and process for singing of the Bahiṣpavamāna hymn.

5. (They chanted): 'Aum may we eat, Aum may we drink, may the (sun who is) God, Varuṇa, Prajā-pato, Savitṛ provide food here. O master of food, provide food here, indeed provide it here, Aum.'

   Now is being described the nature of 'hiṁ'. The sun shines, Varuna rains, Prajāpati protects and is the lord of people. The sun is responsible for nourishment and the production of food.

XIII

1. Indeed, this world is the syllable 'Hau', the air is the sound 'Hai', the moon is the sound 'atha', the self is the sound 'iha', and fire is the sound 'ī'.

Now will be discussed the meditation centred on topics related to the Sāman. The stobha is a part of Sāman. It may be defined as a 'technical term referring to a changed interjection.' (Swāmi Swāhānanda 1956:91) The singing of Sāmans along with stobhas has utility. The stobhas are to be meditated upon as earth, air, etc., since they are related to these. The stobhas and what they are, are to be meditated upon such as hai, atah, iha. This is explained here.

2. The sun is the sound 'U'. Invocation is the sound 'e'. The Viśvedevas is the sound 'au-ho-i', Prajāpati is the sound 'hiṁ'. Vital breath is sound. Virāj is speech.

   The sun is the syllable 'ū', and is to be meditated as 'ū'. In the relevant Sāman connected to the sun the stobhas is 'ū'.

3. The unexplained and changing thirteenth stobha is the sound 'huṁ'.

   This is unexplained or undefinable since it is indistinct and cannot be said to be this or that. Also, it is variable since it only has an assumed shape, as per the different sections of the Vedas. The word undefinable is also used to refer to Brahman. It is manifested as the entire universe; thus, it is variable. Huṁ ought also to be meditated upon as the cause.

4. Speech yields for him the milk, which is the gain from speech. He becomes abundant in food and an eater of food, who knows thus this esoteric doctrine of the Sāmans, indeed who knows the esoteric doctrine.

   The verse outlines what is attained by one who meditated on the syllables of the stobha.

CHAPTER 2

I

1. Aum, certainly meditation of the whole Sāman is excellent. Anything that is excellent people call Sāman and what is not excellent as a-sāman.

   Now will be taken up the meditation upon the entire Sāman, with all its parts, fivefold and sevenfold.

2. Thus, people also say: 'He approached with Sāman.' (By) that they say: 'We approached in a virtuous manner.' And they say: 'He approached with a-sāman.' By that they say he approached in a non virtuous manner.

   Sāma is virtuous behaviour. Out of Sāma (virtuous behaviour), dāna (gifts), daṇḍa (punitive action), bheda (division) which are the four means to attain an end, Sāma is the best.

3. Again, people say: 'This indeed is Sāman for us', when it is something virtuous; then they say this only. 'This indeed is virtuous for us.' Again, people say: 'This is a-sāman for us' when it is not virtuous. Then they say this only, 'This is not virtuous.'

   The equivalence of Sāman and Sādhu or that which is virtuous is clearly stated.

4. He who knows this thus and meditates on the Sāman as virtuous, all virtues swiftly come to him and serve him.

II

1. Now amongst the worlds, one ought to meditate on Sāman as fivefold; the earth (Pṛithvi) is the sound 'hiṁ', fire (Agniḥ) is the prastāva, the intermediate space between heaven and earth is the Udgītha, the sun (Āditya) is the pratihāra and heaven is nidhana (the conclusion). This is as regards the higher (ascending) worlds.

Sāman is virtuous and Dharma is the cause of the worlds. The analogy of a jar of clay is used. The jar is always seen in the context of clay, similarly the idea of the worlds is always followed by the idea of Dharma. Connecting to verse 1.1.1 of this Upaniṣad, the whole Sāman is divided into five parts according as per five meditations. In this section, there will be a series of meditations where numerous varied objects are offered as parallels of Sāman, the parts of the two being identified. The identification is usually based on similarity. Here the similarity between Sāman and the worlds is considered. These meditations are enjoined as per the order in which beings proceed to heaven.

2. Now in the retreating order: heaven is the sound 'hiṁ', the sun is the prastāva, the intermediate space between heaven and earth is Udgītha, the fire is pratihāra and the earth is nidhana.

Now is being enumerated Sāman in its fivefold aspect and meditation in this respect, regarding the lower worlds. In descending order, heaven is the first syllable, only after the sun rises do creatures come to life.

3. The worlds in rising and retreating orders belong to him who

knows this thus (having the quality of virtuousness), and in the worlds meditates upon the fivefold Sāman.

III

1. One ought to meditate on the fivefold Sāman as rain. The forewind is the sound 'hiṁ', the cloud that is born is prastāva, what rains is Udgītha, lightning and roaring thunder are pratihāra.

This section follows from the preceding just as the preservation of the worlds follows from rain.

2. The cessation is nidhana. It rains for him surely, rain is caused by him who knows this thus, meditates upon the fivefold Sāman as rain.

IV

1. One ought to meditate on the fivefold Sāman in all the waters. When a cloud is formed, it is the sound 'hiṁ', when the cloud rains it is the prastāva, when (the waters) flow eastwards they are Udgītha. When they flow westwards, they are pratihāra. The ocean is nidhana.

All water bodies are sustained due to rain. So meditation on these follows the meditation on rain.

2. He who knows this thus, meditates on the fivefold Sāman in all the waters does not perish in water and enjoys an abundance of water.

V

1. One ought to meditate on the fivefold Sāman among the seasons. Spring is the sound 'hiṁ', summer is the prastāva, the season of rain is Udgītha. Autumn is pratihāra and the winter indeed is nidhana.

The meditation on seasons succeeds the meditation on rain. The notion of season here is based on what is dry and what is wet, (dryness and wetness).

2. He who knows this thus, meditates on the fivefold Sāman among the seasons, to him the seasons belong and he enjoys an abundance of seasons.

VI

1. One ought to meditate on the fivefold Sāman among the animals. The goats are the sound 'hiṁ', the sheep are the prastāva, cattle are Udgītha. Horses are pratihāra and people are indeed nidhana.

Following the meditation on seasons are the meditation on animals. Animals flourish when seasons proceed as per their natural order.

2. He who knows this thus, meditates on the fivefold Sāman among the animals, to him belong animals and he enjoys an abundance of animals.

VII

1. One ought to meditate on the most preferable fivefold Sāman among the organs of the senses. The organ of smell is the sound 'hiṁ', the organ of speech is the prastāva, the eye is Udgītha. The ear is pratihāra and the mind is indeed nidhana. Surely these are most preferable.

The senses are sustained by milk, butter, etc. So now is being taken up meditation on the senses.

The commentary points out that these are progressively better. Speech is greater than smell since speech can describe what is imperceptible. The eye illumines more objects than speech and is thus superior to speech. The ear is better than the eye since it is able to hear on all sides and is not confined to one side like speech. The mind is greater than the ear since it can dwell on objects of all senses as well as those that transcend the senses.

2. He who knows this thus, meditates on the fivefold Sāman among the senses, to him belongs the most preferable and he wins the most preferable worlds.

VIII

1. Now regarding the sevenfold. One ought to meditate on the sevenfold Sāman in speech. Whatever of speech is 'huṃ', that is the sound 'hiṁ'. Whatever is 'pra', that is prastāva, whatever is 'ā', that is the (foremost) Ādi.

   This and the next verse take up the meditation on the sevenfold Sāman. One ought to meditate on the entire Sāman visualizing it as speech. The seven stages of the Sāman chant are initial vocalizing, praise, commencement, chanting, antiphony, and approaching the end conclusion.

2. That which is 'ut', that is Udgītha, that which is prati, that is pratihāra, that which is 'upa' that is upadrava, and that which is 'ni', that is nidhana.
3. He who knows this thus, meditates on the sevenfold Sāman in speech, for him speech brings milk which is the gain from speech and he enjoys an abundance in food and is also an eater of food.

IX

1. Now one ought to meditate on the sevenfold Sāman in the sun from above. He is Sāman since he is always identical. He is Sāman since he is identical for all since people think 'he is towards me', 'he is towards me'.

In this verse it is stated one ought to think of the sun as the complete Sāman, with respect to its members and that one ought to meditate on the sevenfold Sāman.

2. One ought to know that on him are all these beings dependent. What he is before rising is the sound 'him̐'. On that are animals dependent. Thus, they make the sound 'him̐'. Indeed, they are experiencers in the sound 'him̐' of the Sāman.

   All are dependant on the sun, whether they be movable or immovable. In this verse the Sāman seen as the sun is Him̐kāra.

3. Now when it has risen that is prastāva. People are dependent on this. Thus, they desire praise, desire, applause. Indeed, they are experiencers in the prastāva of this Sāman.
4. Now the form of the sun at the time of Saṅgava (gathering of cows), this is Ādi. On this, birds depend. Thus, they hold themselves supportless in the sky and fly. Indeed, they are experiencers of the Ādi part of the Sāman.
   This is related to the Ādi part of the Sāman since there is 'ā' in both—ātmānam and ādi.
5. Now when at this time of midday (the form of the sun) that is Udgītha. The gods depend on this. Thus, they are the best amongst Prajāpati's progeny. Indeed, they are experiencers of the Udgītha of this Sāman.
6. Now after midday and prior to the afternoon, (the form of the sun) that is pratihāra. All the foetuses depend on this. Thus, they are held up (in the womb) and do not drop down. Indeed, they are experiencers of the pratihāra of this Sāman.
7. Now subsequent to the afternoon and prior to sunset, (the form of the sun) that is upadrava. The forest born depend on this. Thus, when having seen a man, they run towards a hiding place as their shelter. Indeed, they are experiencers in the pratihāra of this Sāman.

The sun proceeds towards the horizon. 'Upa' the syllable is found in 'upadravaṇa' and 'upadrava'.

8. Now when it is just subsequent to sunset this is nidhana. The ancestors depend on this. Thus, people lay aside the ancestors. Indeed, they are experiencers of the nidhana of this Sāman. Thus, indeed does one meditate on the sevenfold Sāman in that sun.

Here the day is divided into five parts of equal duration namely, the rising of the sun, forenoon, midday, afternoon, and the setting of the sun. Each is said to be of three Muhūrtas (2 hours 24 minutes). A person who meditates here as prescribed achieves the sun.

X

1. Now indeed one ought to meditate on the sevenfold Sāman which is similar in its parts and which transcends death. The sound 'hiṁ' has three syllables. Prastāva has three syllables. (Thus) that is equal.

Here is being enjoined a meditation to transcend death. In this meditation the names of those that compare Sāman are to be divided into three equal parts. Death is surmounted by this meditation done properly as well as by knowledge of the self.

2. Ādi is of two syllables. Pratihāra is of four syllables. From that (Pratihāra) if we take one syllable here (Ādi) they are the same.
3. Udgītha is of three syllables, upadrava is of four syllables. Three and three, that is equal, with one syllable remaining. Being of three syllables that is equal.
4. Nidhana is of three syllables. This is equal too. Verily these are the twenty-two syllables.
5. By means of the twenty-first one attains the sun. Certainly,

from here, the sun is the twenty-first. By the twenty-second he wins what is beyond the sun. That is heaven, that is freedom from grief.

This verse and the next make the point that the twenty-one are composed of the twelve months, the five seasons, the three worlds. The twenty-first is the sun. By bliss is meant complete bliss, the absence of pleasure. Here there is no torment, pain or mental tension.

6. He attains victory over the sun, verily a victory even greater becomes his, who knows this thus, meditates on the sevenfold Sāman, which is similar in its parts, transcends death, indeed meditates on the Sāman.

XI

1. The mind is the sound 'hiṁ', speech is prastāva, the eye is Udgītha, the ear is pratihāra. Prāṇa is nidhana. This is the Gāyatrī chant set in the vital breaths.

Now will be taken up meditation on certain names to attain certain results. The eye is eulogized as the greatest sense organ. Meditation on Gāyatrā as prāṇa is prescribed in the commencement since it is said that 'prāṇa is Gāyatrī'. Prāṇa makes sacrificial rites and meditation possible.

2. A person who knows this Gāyatrī chant thus as set in the vital breath becomes the possessor of vital breaths, attains the entire lifespan, has a glorious life, becomes abundantly endowed with progeny and cattle and (enjoys) tremendous fame. One ought to be high minded. This is the holy vow.

The entire lifespan of a man is said to be of a hundred years.

XII

1. One rubs, that is the sound 'hiṁ'. The smoke that is caused that is prastāva. It intensely burns, that is Udgītha. Charcoal is produced, that is pratihāra. It falls down, that is nidhana. It becomes extinct, that is nidhana. This is the Ratantara set in fire.

   Once again, the importance of prāṇa is highlighted. Since only a person who is strong in prāṇa is able to properly rub the fire-sticks together.

2. A person who knows this Ratantara chant set in fire, becomes with sacred wisdom an eater of food, attains the full lifespan, has a glorious life, becomes abundantly endowed with progeny and cattle and (enjoys) tremendous fame. Before the fire he should neither spit nor sip. That is the holy vow.

XIII

1. He addresses, that is the sound 'hiṁ'. He makes known that is prastāva. With the woman he lies down, that is Udgītha. He goes to the end, that is nidhana. He goes to the opposite side that is nidhana. This is the Vāmdeva chant as set in a couple.

   Vāmadevya is formed from the union of air and water. It is combined like a couple like two fire sticks. This meditation is stated as fire.

2. A person who knows this Vāmadeva chant as set in a couple becomes of the couple and he procreates, attains the full lifespan, has a glorious life, becomes abundantly endowed with progeny and cattle and (enjoys) tremendous fame. He should not shun any woman. That is the holy vow.

XIV

1. The rising sun is the hiṁ sound, the sun as risen is prastātava, at midday it is Udgītha; at afternoon the sun is pratihāra. When the sun sets it is nidhana. This is the Bṛhat chant as set in the sun.

   Now is taken up the meditation on the sun. The sun sustains all creation.

2. A person who knows this Bṛhat chant thus as set in the sun becomes brilliant, an eater of food, attains the full lifespan, has a glorious life, becomes abundantly endowed with progeny and cattle and (enjoys) tremendous fame. He should not criticize the blazing sun. This is the holy vow.

   Here the word Tejasvī is used in a broad sense. Brahmavarcasī refers to tremendous fame, resplendent resulting from virtuous conduct and study of the scriptures.

XV

1. The mists surge, that is the sound 'hiṁ'. A cloud is born, that is prastātava. Rain is the Udgītha. It illuminates and roars (lightning and thunder), that is pratihāra. It ceases. That is nidhana. This is the Vairūpya chant set in rain.

   Rain is said to be produced by the agency of the sun. So now is prescribed the meditation on the rain.

2. A person who knows this Vairūpya chant thus as set in rain acquires well-formed and diverse forms of cattle, attains the full lifespan, has a glorious life, becomes abundantly endowed with progeny and cattle and (enjoys) tremendous fame. He should not criticize the rain. This is the holy vow.

XVI

1. Spring is the sound 'hiṁ', the summer is the prastātava, the

season of rains is Udgītha, autumn is pratihāra, winter is nidhana. This is the Vairājya chant set in the seasons.

Seasons change as per rain patterns. So now is taken up the meditation on Sāman as rain.

2. A person who knows this Vairājya chant thus as set in the seasons is illuminated with progeny and cattle, attains the full lifespan, has a glorious life, becomes abundantly endowed with progeny and cattle and (enjoys) tremendous fame. He should not criticize the seasons. That is the holy vow.

XVII

1. The earth is the sound 'hiṁ'. The intermediate region between heaven and earth is prastātava. Heaven is Udgītha, the quarters of the sky are pratihāra, and the ocean is nidhana. This is the Śakvari chant set in the worlds.

Regular seasons lead to a stable world. Now is taken up Sāman as meditation.

2. A person who knows these Śakvari chants thus as set in the worlds becomes a possessor of the worlds, attains the full lifespan, has a glorious life, becomes abundantly endowed with progeny and cattle and (enjoys) tremendous fame. He should not criticize the worlds. That is the holy vow.

XVIII

1. The goats are the sound 'hiṁ'. Sheep are the prastātava. Cows are Udgītha. Horses are pratihāra. Man is nidhana. These are the Revatī chants set in animals.

As a result of Vedic sacrifice are animals enabled in the world. Now meditation in this regard is taken up.

2. A person who knows these Revatī chants thus as set in animals becomes a possessor of animals, attains the full lifespan, has a glorious life, becomes abundantly endowed with progeny and cattle and (enjoys) tremendous fame. He should not criticize animals. That is the holy vow.

XIX

1. Hair is the sound 'hiṁ'. Skin is prastātava. Flesh is Udgītha. Bone is pratihāra. Marrow is nidhana. This is the Yajñāyajñīya chant as set in the limbs of the body.

Limbs are strengthened by produce obtained from animals such as milk. So now is enjoined the meditation on Sāman in respect of limbs. It is said elsewhere that the body is transformed food.

2. A person who knows this Yajñāyajñīya chant thus as set in the limbs of the body becomes well-endowed with all limbs and does not (suffer) defective limbs; attains the full lifespan, has a glorious life, becomes abundantly endowed with progeny and cattle and (enjoys) tremendous fame. He should not eat marrow (figuratively meat and fish) for a year. That is the holy vow. Rather such a person should completely avoid eating marrow at all.

XX

1. Fire is the sound 'hiṁ'. Air is prastātava. Sun is Udgītha. The stars are pratihāra amd moon is nidhana. This is the Rājana chant set in the deities.

Fire is the presiding deity for the limbs. Now will be taken up the meditation on Sāman in respect of deities.

2. A person who knows this Rājana chant thus as set in the deities goes to reside in the same world, gets the same powers and attains union with these very deities, attains the full

lifespan, has a glorious life, becomes abundantly endowed with progeny and cattle and (enjoys) tremendous fame. He should not criticize the Brāhmaṇas. That is the holy vow.

XXI

1. Threefold knowledge are the sound 'hiṁ'. The three worlds are the prastātava. The Sun, fire, and air are Udgītha. The stars, the birds, the rays of light are pratihāra, the snakes, celestial musicians and ancestors are nidhana. This is the Sāman set in all.

In Śruti it is stated that the Ṛg Veda comes from fire, the Yajurveda from air, etc. So now is being described the meditation on Sāman in respect to the Vedas. All are within the purview of the knowledge of the three Vedas. In this verse meditation on the entire Sāman is taken up. Previously meditations on different Sāmans were discussed. The present verse does not nullify the previous verses.

2. Indeed, a person who knows this Sāman thus as set in all becomes all.
3. Regarding that is this verse: those which are fivefold in groups of three, more worthy, superior than these there is nothing else.
4. A person who knows that knows all. For him all directions bring offerings. He should meditate 'I am all'. That is the holy vow. That is the holy vow.

Such a person attains the state of omniscience.

XXII

1. Of the Sāmans I select the high sounding one as beneficial to cattle, this singing aloud is sacred to Agni, the unexplained one to Prajāpati, the explained one to Soma, the delicate and

the gentle to Vāyu, the gentle and strong to Indra, the heron like to Bṛhaspati, the dull sounding to Varuṇa. (A person) may employ all these but should exclude the one attributed to Varuṇa.

Instructions regarding the meditation are being given here concerning the tune, proper singing, etc. The undefined one has as its deity Prajāpati since he himself is undefined in form.

2. Let me obtain immortality for the gods by singing, so (in this manner) one ought to sing. Let me obtain by singing offerings for the ancestors, hope for men, grass and water for animals, for the sacrificer the heavenly world and for myself food. Thus mediating in his mind on all these, one ought to sing the hymns of praise attentively.

Offerings to the ancestors are made accompanied by the utterances of Svadhā. The attaining of all things to be offered to the ancestors is prescribed in this verse.

3. The entire set of vowels are the manifestations of Indra; all the sibilants are manifestations of Prajāpati; all the Sparśa consonants are manifestations of death. If someone curses a person for his pronunciation of vowels, he should say to him 'I have sought protection in the refuge of Indra. He will reply to you.'

The correct knowledge of deities is presented here to cure defects that may occur during singing.

4. If someone censures a person for his sibilants he should say to him: 'I have sought protection in the refuge of Prajāpati. He will decimate you.' And if someone censures a person for his Sparśa consonants he should say to him, 'I have sought protection in the refuge of death; he will burn you to ashes.'
5. All vowels ought to be stated resonant and strong (with

the thought): 'May I give strength to Indra.' All sibilants should be stated articulately, distinctly and not neglecting the elements of sound, (with the thought): 'May I offer myself to Prajāpati.' All Sparśa consonants ought to be stated without merging them (with the thought): 'From death, may I withdraw myself.'

A person who thinks thus, attains results including the acquisition of tremendous strength, self surrender, and the surpassing of death.

XXIII

1. Righteous conduct has three branches—sacrifice, learning, and charity. The first indeed is religious austerity. The second is the celebate student, pursuing sacred knowledge who resides in the house of the teacher. The third is he who resides in the teacher's house till the end, mortifying his body. All these become possessors of virtuous worlds; but he who is firmly established in Brahman attains the eternal life.

   The importance of meditation on Aum is stressed here. The attainment of immortality can only be attained by meditating on Aum. Meditation on Sāman, sacrifices and rites will not lead to immortality. Here Adhyayana is used to refer to what has been learnt from a teacher by recitation and the continuation of this by declaring it to others. The result of meditation on Brahman far exceeds the attainment of meritorious worlds which are achieved by the performance of duties associated with the stages of one's life.

2. Prajāpati concentrated his thoughts on the worlds. From them thus concentrated upon emerged the threefold knowledge. He concentrated his thoughts upon this, thus

concentrated upon emerged the syllables bhūḥ, bhuvaḥ, svaḥ.

The symbols of Brahman are being thrown light upon.

3. He concentrated his thoughts on them and from them thus concentrated upon emerged the syllable, Aum. Just as all the parts of the leaf are permeated by fibres of the leaf, so indeed are all worlds permeated by Aum. Indeed, Aum is all this, surely Aum is all this.

Meditation on Aum is not to be considered subsidiary to a sacrificial rite, indeed it is meditation on Brahman as its symbol Praṇava. Elsewhere 'A' in Aum is said to pervade all the worlds and all speech. Brahman pervades all, manifests as all and is the greatest. Objects have no real existence apart from the supreme self since it is a manifestation of the supreme self.

XXIV

1. Teachers of sacred knowledge state that the morning offering is for the Vasus, the midday offering is for the Rudras, and the third offering is for the Ādityas and the Viśve-devas.

This and the next verse discuss the knowledge of Sāman, etc. A day has three periods called the three Savanas. The Vasus, Rudras, and Viśvadevas govern the earth, sky, and heaven respectively. Sacrifice is for the sake of the world.

2. So where is the sacrificer's world? How can he perform (sacrifices) who does not know this? So a person who knows should perform (sacrifices) only.
3. Prior to the begining of the morning chant, he (the sacrificer) sits down to the rear of the Gārhapatya fire, his face towards the north and sings the Sāman sacred to the Vasus.

Those Ṛks that are uttered in the morning not accompanied by singing are called Śastra.

4. 'Open the door of the world, so we may see you for (attaining) the sovereignty of the kingdom.'
5. Then he makes the oblation reciting: 'Salutation to fire, who resides on earth, who resides in the world. Obtain the world for me, the sacrificer. Verily to the world of the sacrificer will I go.'
6. After the duration of this life, I the sacrificer will come here. Svāhā (hail). Remove the obstacle (to the world). Having said this, he stands up. To him the Vasus bestow the morning offering.

Svāhā indicates the end of the mantra and after its repetition is the offering poured. It is an invocation to the deity while making the offerings of the sacrifice.

7. Prior to the beginning of the midday offering, he (the sacrificer) sits down to the rear of the Agnīdhrīya fire, his face towards the north and sings the Sāman which is sacred for the Rudras.

The means to conquer the earth is described. The means to conquer the sky will be shown.

8. 'Open the door of the world, so we may see you for (attaining) the sovereignty of the kingdom.'
9. Then he offers (the oblation) reciting: 'Salutation to air, who resides in the atmosphere, who resides in the world. Obtain the world for me, the sacrificer. Verily to the world of the sacrificer will I go.'
10. After the duration of this life, I the sacrificer will come here. Svāhā (hail). 'Remove the obstacle (to the world). Having said this, he stands up. To him the Rudras bestow the midday offering.

11. Prior to the beginning of the third offering, he (the sacrificer) sits down to the rear of the Āhavanīya fire, his face towards the north and sings the Sāman which is sacred for both the Ādityas and Viśvadevas.

The path for achieving heaven will now be discussed.

12. 'Open the door of the world, so we may see you for (attaining) the sovereignty of the kingdom.'
13. Thus, the Sāman sacred to the Ādityas. Now the Sāman sacred to the Viśvadevas. 'Open the door of the world, so we may see you for (attaining) the sovereignty of the kingdom.'
14. Then he offers (the oblation) reciting 'Salutation to the Ādityas and to the Viśvadevas, who resides in heaven, and who resides in the world. Obtain the world for me, the sacrificer.'

Here what is to be performed and done by the sacrificer is outlined such as singing the Sāmans, offering various oblations and recitation of the correct mantras.

15. 'Verily to the world of the sacrificer will I go. After the duration of this life, I the sacrificer will come here. Svāhā (hail). Remove the obstacle (to the region).' Having said this, he stands up.
16. For him the Ādityas and the Viśvadevas bestow the third offering. Surely, he alone knows this real nature of the sacrifice, who knows thus, Indeed, who knows thus.

CHAPTER 3

I

1. Surely, the distant sun is the honey of the gods. Of this honey heaven is the traverse; the atmosphere is the honeycomb; and the rays of light are the children.

   The central importance of the sun is stated. All beings benefit from the sun as per their karma and so the sun may be said to be the result of all sacrifices. Now will be discussed meditation on the sun with a view to the pursuit of liberation. The whole aim of the similes used in this verse is to aid meditation. This, i.e., such similes are repeated in the following verses.

2. Its (the sun's) eastern rays are indeed its eastern honey-cells; the Ṛks are the makers of honey(bees). The Ṛg Veda indeed is the flower and those waters are the nectar and verily those Ṛks (are the bees).

   The first seen rays which are reddish and viewed at sunrise are produced by the Ṛks. The rites correctly done along with Ṛks produce the due results.

3. These concentrated their thoughts on the Ṛg Veda; from it thus concentrated upon emerged as its essence glory, brilliance, (acuteness of) the senses, heroism, and food.

4. That flowed forth; that went near the sun. Surely this is that which is the red form of the sun.

The rites and sacrifices are performed with a view to attaining certain results. How these results settle in the sun are being considered. The sacrificer is of the belief that the results of the sacrifice will be stored in the sun and will fructify in due course.

II

1. Now its (the sun's) southern rays are indeed its southern honey-cells; the verses of the Yajur Veda are the makers of honey(bees). The Yajur Veda indeed is the flower and those waters constitute the nectar.
2. Surely these Yajus formulae concentrated their thoughts on the Yajur Veda; from it thus concentrated upon emerged as it's essence glory, brilliance, (acuteness of) the senses, heroism, and food.
3. That flowed forth; that went near the sun. Surely this is that which is the white form of the sun.

III

1. Now its (the sun's) western rays are indeed its western honey-cells; the verses of the Sāman chants are the makers of honey(bees). The Sāma Veda indeed is the flower and those waters constitute the nectar.
2. Surely these Sāman chants concentrated their thoughts on the Sāma Veda; from it thus concentrated upon emerged as its essence glory, brilliance, (acuteness of) the senses, heroism, and food.
3. That flowed forth; that went near the sun. Surely this is that which is the black form of the sun.

IV

1. Now its (the sun's) northern rays are indeed its northern honey-cells; the hymns of the Atharvans and Aṇgirasas are the makers of honey(bees). The history and sacred lore indeed are the flower and those waters constitute the nectar.

The rites enjoined in the Ātharvaṇa Brāhmaṇa are being prescribed in this verse. They may also refer to Pāriplavq, which are told as narrated tales to be spoken during intervals between the performance of rites during a given sacrifice.

2. Surely these hymns of the Atharvans and Aṇgirasas concentrated upon that history and sacred lore; from it thus concentrated upon emerged as its essence glory, brilliance, (acuteness of) the senses, heroism, and food.
3. That flowed forth; that went near the sun. Surely this is that which is the highly black form of the sun.

V

1. Now its (the sun's) upper rays are indeed its upper honey-cells; the hidden instructions are the makers of honey(bees). Brahman indeed is the flower and those waters constitute the nectar.

This verse indicates Brahman as Praṇava.

2. Surely these hidden instructions concentrated upon Brahman; from it thus concentrated upon emerged as its essence glory, brilliance, (acuteness of) the senses, heroism, and food.
3. That flowed forth; that went near the sun. Surely this is that which is the shaking in the centre of the sun.

This appears to one whose mind is properly focused due to spiritual practices.

4. They, surely these are the essences of the essences, because the Vedas are the essences and these are their (the Vedas) essences. They, surely these are the nectars of the nectars because the Vedas are the nectars and these are their (the Vedas) nectar.

The essence of the worlds are the Vedas. In the form of rites correctly performed their final essences are hues of different colours. So, these can be termed the essence of essences.

VI

1. That which is the foremost nectar, on that subsist the Vasus with Agni (fire) as their leader. Indeed, the gods do not eat or drink this nectar. Only having seen it they become content.

Now is being described the meditation on the deities that feed on honey. Seeing here refers to enjoying by means of the senses.

2. They enter this form only and from this form they arise.
3. Thus, a person who knows this nectar, becomes one of the Vasus and by means of Agni as his leader is content merely by seeing this nectar. He enters this form and from this form he arises.

Now is being taken up the method and result of these meditations.

4. As much as the sun rises in the east and sets in the west, so much does he attain the power and rulership of the heavenly kingdom of the Vasus.

The commentary once again emphasizes true knowledge. The knower is independent and free. On the other hand, one who only does rites goes to the world of the moon.

VII

1. Now that which is the second nectar, on that subsist the Rudras with Indra as their leader. Indeed, the gods do not eat or drink this nectar. Merely having seen it they become content.
2. They enter this form only and from this form they arise.
3. Thus, a person who knows this nectar, becomes one of the Rudras and with Indra as his leader is content merely by seeing this nectar. He enters this form and from this form he arises.
4. As much as the sun rises in the east and sets in the west, twice as much does it rise in the south and set in the north and just that much does he attain the power and sovereignty of the heavenly kingdom of the Rudras.

This verse is similar to verse 3.10.4. It is underlined that the period of bliss of the Rudras is double that of Vasus. This is also the case of the meditator of the second duration.

VIII

1. Now that which is the third nectar, on that subsist the Ādityas with Varuna as their leader. Indeed, the gods do not eat or drink this nectar. Merely having seen it they become content.
2. They enter this form only and from this form they arise.
3. Thus, he who knows this nectar, becomes one of the Ādityas and with Varuna as his leader is content merely by seeing this nectar. He enters this form and from this form he arises.
4. As much as the sun rises in the east and sets in the west, twice as much does it rise in the west and set in the east and just that much does he attain the power and sovereignty of the heavenly kingdom of the Ādityas.

The duration of the bliss of the Ādityas and of the knower is double that of the Rudras.

IX

1. Now that which is the fourth nectar, on that subsist the Maruts with Soma as their leader. Indeed, the gods do not eat or drink this nectar. Merely having seen it they become content.
2. They enter this form only and from this form they arise.
3. Thus, he who knows this nectar, becomes one of the Maruts and with Soma as his leader is content merely by seeing this nectar. He enters this form and from this form he arises.
4. As much as the sun rises in the east and sets in the west, twice as much does it rise in the north and set in the south and just that much does he attain the power and sovereignty of the heavenly kingdom of the Maruts.

The duration of the bliss of Maruts and the knower is double of that of the Ādityas.

X

1. Now that which is the fifth nectar, on that subsist the Sādhyas with Brahmā as their leader. Indeed, the gods do not eat or drink this nectar. Merely having seen it they become content.
2. They enter this form only and from this form they arise.
3. Thus, he who knows this nectar, becomes one of the Sādhyas and with Brahmā as his leader is content merely by seeing this nectar. He enters this form and from this form he arises.
4. As much as the sun rises in the north and sets in the south, twice as much does it rise overhead and set in the nadir and just that much does he attain the power and sovereignty of the heavenly kingdom of the Maruts.

The rising and setting of the sun are discussed here. The period of the rising and setting are discussed from the viewpoint of the beings in each region who perceive the rising and setting. In this section descriptions are given from the standpoint of the inhabitants of the earth.

XI

1. Then having risen from there upwards he will not rise nor will he set. He will abide alone in the centre. Regarding that is this verse:

   Here is an elucidation of how the doctrine of honey acts and how it leads to various results. By rising and setting the sun enables the enjoyment of the fruit of rites. Then the creatures are dissolved in himself. The sun also remains in its own brilliance as Brahman. This verse is meant to contain the reply of a yogi who was asked about the effect of the sun on the lifespan of creatures.

2. Verily it is not there. The sun did not set there nor there did it ever rise. O gods! by means of this truth from Brahman may I not be deprived.

   The truth of the above assertions is beyond doubt since the listeners are the witnesses.

3. Indeed for him who knows thus knows, this secret teaching of Brahmā, the sun does not rise nor does it set. For him it is always day.

   What is meant here is that the knower becomes Brahman, perpetual, unending and unborn. He transcends time as defined by the rising and setting of the sun. Such a person is also self-luminous.

4. Indeed, Bramhā imparted this (doctrine of honey) to Prajāpati, Prajāpati to Manu, Manu to his offspring. The father declared this (knowledge of) Brahman to his first son, Uddālaka Āruṇi.
5. Indeed, a father may expound this knowledge of Brahmā to his first son or any deserving student.
6. And not to any other person. Even if he should be offered this (earth) entirely, surrounded by water and filled with wealth, (he ought to state): 'This indeed surpasses that, yes surpasses that.'

XII

1. Indeed, the Gāyatrī is all this, whatever beings that are. Surely Gāyatrī is speech. Surely, speech sings and protects all the beings that are.

Above has been stated the doctrine of Brahman. Now will be explained the meditation on Brahman as Gāyatrī. Gāyatrī is spoken of here as speech which is the source of the Gāyatrī meter. The Gāyatrī is called Gāyatrī since it sings (Gāyati) and protects (trāyate). Gāyatrī is the name of a Vedic metre. The commentary calls it the greatest of all metres. The gods obtained Soma by means of this. The Gitā also recognizes it to be the greatest. Brahman may be expounded and meditated upon by Gāyatrī. In all the commentary it is stated to have four feet and each having six syllables.

2. Indeed that which this Gāyatrī is, indeed that is what this earth is; since all beings are established on this earth and they do not exceed it.

Gāyatrī is connected to all creatures by means of singing and protecting. Since creatures rest on the earth, the earth is also connected to all creatures. Gāyatrī is thus identified with the earth.

3. Indeed that which this earth is, indeed that is what the body in a person is; since these vital breaths are established in this body and they do not exceed it.

The body has a preponderance of the element earth. The body is said to be identical with Gāyatrī since both are related to prāṇa.

4. Indeed that which this body in a person is, indeed that is what the heart within a person is; since these vital breaths are established in this body and they do not exceed it.
5. This Gāyatrī has four parts and is sixfold. This is also expressed in a Ṛk verse.

Gāyatrī is said to be sixfold. It's four parts are beings, the earth, the body and the heart. Speech and prāṇa are also related to Gāyatrī and also considered a form of Gāyatrī. From the viewpoint of meditation, this is a significant verse.

6. Its glory is so much. Yet the Puruṣa is more worthy than this. All beings are a quarter of him. The remaining three quarters (constitute) the state of immortality in the sky (heaven).

The commentary clarifies that Brahman has no parts. It is eternal, unchanging, and immortal.

7. Indeed that which is called Brahman, even that is what the ether outside the person is. Indeed what the ether outside a person is.
8. Even this is that ether which is inside a person, indeed that ether which is inside a person.
9. Even this is that which is the ether within the heart. That is complete and unchanging. He who knows thus obtains complete and unmodifiable prosperity.

Brahman as Gāyatrī ought to be meditated upon as the Ākāśa in the heart. This is discussed here. There are three aspects of Ākāśa in the waking, dream and deep sleep states. Ākāśa within the heart is the supreme aspect. Thus the mind ought to concentrate on the Ākāśa in the heart. Brahman is omnipresent and not limited to any one place or location.

XIII

1. Surely, indeed, of this heart there are five entrances for the gods. That which is the eastern entrance of this is the prāṇa. That is the eye, that is the sun. One ought to meditate on this as light and as the source of food. A person who knows this thus becomes brilliant and an eater of food.

   Now is being described the meditation of the doorkeepers. The sun is the deity of the eye. The sun is said to be identical with prāṇa. This prāṇa resides in the eye and in the external forms and is thus known as the sun and the eye.

2. Now that which is the southern entrance of this is vyāna. That is the ear, he is the moon. This should be meditated on as wealth and glory. A person who knows this thus becomes wealthy and glorious.

   Vyāna is said to be related to both the ear and the moon. The ear and the moon are said to be the source of knowledge and food respectively. Knowledge and food cause prosperity and fame. So vyāna is associated with both of these.

3. Now that which is the western entrance of this is apāna. That is speech, he is fire. One should meditate on it as the splendour born of sacred knowledge and as a source of food. A person who knows this thus becomes possessed of the splendour born of sacred knowledge and also an eater of food.
4. Now that which is the northern entrance of this is samāna. That is mind, he is rain. One ought to meditate on it as fame

and propriety. A person who knows this thus becomes well known and prosperous.

In the scriptures samāna and Varuṇa are said to be related to the mind. One should meditate on them connected to the mind. From the mind arises knowledge and fame.

5. Now that which is the upper entrance of this is udāna. That is air, he is ether. One ought to meditate on it as strength and greatness. A person who knows this thus becomes possessed of strength and greatness.
   Ākāśa is the substratum of air. Air is also said to be the same as Ākāśa. Both are the source of strength and are great.
6. Indeed there are five Brahma-persons, the wardens of the heavenly world. He who knows thus the five Brahma-persons, the wardens of the heavenly world, a hero is born in his family. He who knows thus the five Brahma-persons, the wardens of the heavenly world, attains the heavenly world.

   The doorkeepers of Brahman, five in number are also known as Brahma–Puruṣa or ministers of Brahman. They are the gatekeepers of Brahman in the heart. They can block or open the path to the attainment of Brahman. The doorkeepers i.e. the sense organs if not controlled makes the mind unable to rest, in the Brahman of the heart, due to attachment to various objects. When the sense organs are controlled and there is stability then they become an aid in achieving the knowledge of Brahman. All this is contained in the Kaṭha Upaniṣad.

7. Now the light which shines above heaven, above the world, above all, in the highest worlds which are unsurpassed, indeed even this is the light within a person.

   Now is being described the way to meditate on Brahman in his own glory. The regions which are most proximate to Brahman are the most exalted such as the region of Satya, the abode of

Hiraṇyagarbha. The light in the body causes the body to be warm. At the time of death this light departs leaving the body cold. Light is said to merge with the supreme deity.

8. This can be seen like when in this body one discerns warmth by touch. This can be heard like when one shuts the ears one hears a sound like the bellowing of a bull or a brightly blazing fire. One ought to meditate on this that is seen and heard. One who knows this thus becomes beautiful to behold and heard of highly, indeed one who knows this thus.

XIV

1. Surely this entire world is Brahman. From him does everything originate, into him do they dissolve and it is by him that they are preserved. In tranquillity one ought to meditate on him. Now surely a person has intent as is a person's intent in this world, thus does the person become when departing. Thus let him cultivate the (right) intent.

   Now is being described the meditation on Brahman with attributes. The importance of sincere meditation and worship continues to be emphasized upon. In this meditation the mind ought to be concentrated upon the ultimate. This is the source, abode, and aim of the universe. The syllables 'ja', 'ca', and 'an' stand for origination, dissolution, and preservation. All this is Brahman only. If all is Brahman how can there possibly be either hatred or attachment.

2. He who is constituted by mind, whose body is vital breath, whose form is consciousness, whose residue is truth, whose self is ether, containing all creation, containing all desires, possessing all (pleasant) smells and tastes, pervading all this, who is without speech and who is without worry.
3. This is my self dwelling in the heart, more minute than a grain of rice, than a barley corn, than a mustard seed, than a

grain of millet or than the kernel of a grain of millet. This is my self dwelling in the heart surpassing the earth, surpassing the sky, surpassing heaven, surpassing all these worlds.

The mind is described as an adjunct of the ātman. The mind can only function when permeated by the light of ātman. When this is the case, the mind operates when it is contacted by objects by means of the senses. The ātman is said to be Chaitanya–Jyoti, the supreme intelligence which illuminates all and dispels darkness. The ātman is responsible for the universe's existence and the functioning of the mind. In metaphorical terms, sometimes ether is compared to the ātman since it is formless, odourless, cloudless subtle and omnipresent. Ātman is extremely subtle, it is not minute. In fact, it surpasses all that exists.

4. All that is created, all desires, all smells, all tastes, pervading all this, who is without speech, without worry, this is my self dwelling in the heart; this is Brahman. On departing from this world I shall enter into him. Surely, a person who understands this shall have no further doubts. Thus stated Śāndilya, yes Śāndilya.

Śaṅkarācārya states that the aim of the meditation here is the ultimate reality implied by the qualities and not the qualities themselves. The Paramātman the supreme self is the object of this meditation.

The knowledge of Brahman is to be thought of at the time of death. Then one attains Brahmalok and gradually progresses towards liberation.

XV

1. The chest, having the atmosphere for its hollow, and the earth for its place of rest does not waste away. Verily, the

quarters are its corners and the sky its upper lid. This chest contains wealth and on this everything here rests.

The following meditation is aimed at ensuring a long lifespan for the son. This is to ensure the well-being of the father in the afterlife since the son can conduct the necessary cermonies and rites for the benefit of his ancestors. By 'everything' is meant all creatures and the results of their acts.

2. Of this the eastern quarter is named Juhū; the southern quarter is named Sahmānā, the western is named Rājñi, and the northern is named Subhūta. Of these the child is air. He who knows this air as the child of the quarters thus, never weeps in mourning for his son. I who know this air thus as the child of the quarter of air, let me never weep for my son.

   The southern quarter Sahamānā is the region where people bear the consequences of evil deeds, it is the abode of Yama. Rājnī is red and ruled by Varuṇa. Subhūtāis presided over by prosperous deities such as Kubera.

3. I take shelter in the perfect chest of such a one, of such a one, of such a one. I take shelter in the vital breath of such a one, of such a one, of such a one. I take shelter in the Bhūḥ of such a one, of such a one, of such a one. I take shelter in the Bhuvaḥ of such a one, of such a one, of such a one. I take shelter in Svaḥ of such a one, of such a one, of such a one.
4. When I said: 'I take shelter in vital breath', surely, all these beings whatsoever that exist, are vital breath. So it was in this only that I took shelter.
5. Now when I said: 'I take shelter in Bhūḥ', that what I only said was: 'I take shelter in earth, I take shelter in the intermediate region between heaven and earth, I take shelter in heaven.'
6. Now when I said: 'I take shelter in Bhuvaḥ', that what I only

said was: 'I take shelter in fire, I take shelter air, I take shelter in the sun.'

7. Now when I said: 'I take shelter in Svaḥ', that what I only said was: 'I take shelter in the Ṛg Veda, I take shelter in the Yajur Veda, I take shelter in the Sāma Veda.' Indeed that I said.

XVI

1. Surely, a human being is a sacrifice. The morning libation is said to be His (first) twenty-four years, since the Gāyatrī (metre) is constituted of twenty-four syllables and the morning libation is connected with a Gāyatrī hymn. With this the Vasus are associated. Indeed the vital breaths are the Vasus, since they make everything firm.

This is a meditation to ensure one's own longevity. Here 'prāṇa' stands for both the senses and vital breath. Creatures live only when prāṇa remains in the body.

2. If in this period of life any distress should befall him, he should say: 'O prāṇas, Vasus may the morning libation be united with the midday libation. May I, the sacrificer not be destroyed in the midst of the vital breaths of the Vasus. From that he recovers and becomes free from disease.'

The entire lifespan is viewed as a sacrifice. A man is referred to therefore as a sacrifice.

3. Now his next forty-four years is that which is the midday libation since the Triṣṭubh (metre) is constituted of forty-four syllables and the midday libation is connected with a Triṣṭubh hymn. With this the Rudras are associated. Indeed the prāṇas are the Rudras since they make everything weep.
4. If in this period of life any distress should befall him, he should say: 'O prāṇas, Rudras may the midday libation of mine be united with the third libation. May I, the sacrificer not be

destroyed in the midst of the Rudras who are the prāṇas.' From that he recovers and becomes free from disease.

5. Now the third libation is that which are his next forty-eight years. The Jagatī metre is made of forty-eight syllables and the third libation is connected with the Jagatī metre. With this the Ādityas are connected. Indeed the prāṇas are the Ādityas since they accept everything.

The prāṇas are compared to the Ādityās since these senses and prāṇa accept sound, etc.

6. If in this period of life any distress should befall him, he should say: 'O prāṇas, Ādityas let this third libation of mine extend to a full lifespan. May I, the sacrificer not be destroyed in the midst of the Ādityas who are the prāṇas.' From that he recovers and becomes free from disease.
7. Indeed knowing this Aitareya Mahidāsa used to say: 'Why do you inflict this distress on me who cannot be killed by it?' His life duration was of 116 years. Indeed a person who knows this lives for 116 years.

XVII

1. He who feels hunger, who feels thirst, who does not enjoy, these are the initiatory rights.

The initiatory rites of the Soma sacrifice involve certain restraints and suffering of the sacrificer. It is pointed out that the pains of life are similar to the pains of initiation

2. And who eats, who drinks, who enjoys such persons join the Upasada ceremonies.

One ought to realize the cause of pain and their remedies. The sacrifice itself gives far more happiness than the initiation. This is compared to food and drink which leads to the cessation of the pain of hunger and thirst in our daily lives.

3. And who laughs, who eats, who experiences the pleasures of a couple, these all join Stotra (chant) and Śastra (recitation).

Śaṁsana refers to praise or Stuti. Śastra refers to those mantras containing Śaṁsana. Ṛk mantras sung in the appropriate tune become Sāmans. They are called Stotras.

4. And religious austerity, charity, upright conduct, non-violence, truthful speech—these are the gifts of this sacrifice.

Austerity, etc., are mentioned in this verse and should be looked upon as gifts for the priest since the two have similarities. It is said that dakṣiṇā leads to righteousness as does austerity. The underlying principle is that a person ought to look upon himself as a sacrifice.

5. From that people say: 'He will procreate and he has procreated. Again of this, that is the procreation, death only is the Avabhṛta bath.'

At the conclusion of the sacrifice takes place the Avabhṛta, the bath taken at the conclusion of the sacrifice to signify the completion of the sacrifice.

6. Indeed this was expounded by Ghora Āṅgirasa to Krṣṇa the sun of Devakī. He said having become free from desire, 'at the final moment, one ought to seek refuge in this triad—Thou art undecaying, Thou art unchanging, thou art the essence of prāṇa.' With regard to this there are the two Ṛk stanzas.

Śaṅkarācārya states in his commentary that the reference to Kṛṣna highlights the excellence of this vidyā. In this passage historians find an early reference to Kṛṣna.

7. From the primary seed, may we too having perceived the most excellent light, which transcends darkness, reach it. Having perceived the most excellent light in ourselves we

attain the Sun God among the gods, the most excellent light, indeed the most excellent light.

This is a part of the Ṛk (Ṛg Veda 8.6.30) and contains similar ideas.

XVIII

1. One ought to meditate on the mind as Brahman. This is with regard to the self. Then with regard to the deities one ought to meditate on ether as Brahman. This is the twofold rule which refers to the self and to the deities.

   Both the mind and Ākāśa are appropriate symbols of Brahman since both are subtle. Ākāśa is all pervasive. A person who cannot meditate on Brahman as such can consider meditating on these two as Brahman.

2. This Brahman has four quarters. The organ of speech is one quarter, prāṇa is one quarter, the eye is one quarter and the ear is one quarter. This is with regard to the self. Then with regard to the deities. Agni is one quarter, Vāyu is one quarter, Āditya is one quarter and the directions are one quarter. This is the twofold rule which refers to the self and to the deities.

   The four-footed aspect of Adhidaivata Brahman is known as Ākāśa.

3. Speech indeed is one of the four quarters of Brahman. With the light of fire it is bright and warm. He who knows thus sparkles and warms with fame and glory and with the brilliance of sacred knowledge.

   The fourth foot is related to the other three. The mind by means of the other organs is able to express its thoughts. The visible effect of this meditation is mentioned in the verse. The non-apparent result of this meditation is the attainment of Brahman.

4. Vital breath indeed is one of the four quarters of Brahman. With the light of air it is bright and warm. He who knows thus sparkles and warms with fame and glory and with the brilliance of sacred wisdom.
5. The eye indeed is one of the four quarters of Brahman. With the light of the sun it is bright and warm. He who knows thus sparkles and warms with fame and glory and with the brilliance of sacred knowledge.
6. The ear indeed is one of the four quarters of Brahman. Aided by the light which reveals directions it is bright and warm. He who knows thus sparkles and warms with fame and glory and with the brilliance of sacred knowledge.

XIX

1. The sun is Brahman. This is the precept of this, the further exposition (is as follows). At first this (world) was non-existent. Then it came into being. It grew; it became an egg. For a period of one year it (the world) lay. It burst open. Of the two halves of the eggshell one was silver and one was of gold.

   This verse enjoins viewing the sun as Brahman. Only that which is differentiated into name and form is known as existent or sat. This differentiation is mainly caused by the sun. In the absence of the sun, there would be no light.

2. That earth is what was silver. That heaven is what was golden. The mountains was the outer membrane. The clouds were the inner membrane. The rivers were the veins. That ocean was water in the lower belly.
3. Now that which was born from it is the distant sun. When he was born sounds of loud shouts arose as also all beings and all wishes. Thus at his rise and at his every return sounds of loud shouts arise as do all beings and wishes.

A person who knows this thus, meditates on the sun as Brahman, auspicious sounds will come to him and please him, indeed please him.

CHAPTER 4

I

1. Aum, there lived a descendant of Janaśruta, his great grandson, a faithful giver, a liberal donor, who had much food cooked for others. He made dwelling places everywhere thinking: 'Of my food will people eat everywhere.'

   Now will be taken up direct meditation on vāyu and prāṇa. The story which follows also seeks to show the correct method for imparting knowledge. The method emphasizes due reverence for the teacher as well as faith in what is being taught.

2. And once at night the swans flew past. One swan spoke to another thus: 'Hey, Ho, O Bhallākṣa, Bhallākṣa, the splendour of Jānaśruti, the great grandson (of Jānaśruta) has expanded like daylight. Do not touch it so it may not burn you.'

   It was a group of sages and deities who were impressed with the king's virtues and took the shape of swans.

3. To him the other swan replied: 'Who is this whom you describe as if he were Raikva with the cart? Indeed, what type is this Raikva, the person with the cart?'
4. In the manner that the lower throws of the dice go to the victor, that whatsoever virtuous men do, all goes to him. He

(also) who knows that what Raikva knows, this is spoken by me.

The side of the dice with the number four is referred to as kṛta. Tretā refers to the side with three, Dvāpara the side with two, and Kali is one. The higher numbers include the lower.

5. Now Jānaśruti Pautrāyana overheard this. Just as he rose, he declared to the attendant: 'O friend, did you describe me in the same way as Raikva with the cart? Indeed, what type of man is this Raikva with the cart?'
6. Just as the lower throws of the dice go to the victor, that whatsoever virtuous men do, all goes to him. He (also) who knows that what Raikva knows, this is spoken by me.
7. The attendant after enquiring after him returned stating: 'I could not find him.' He said to him: 'O where a knower of Brahman is to be enquired for, there look for him.'
8. He went to a man scratching a scab under a cart, sat near him and asked, 'Illustrious sir, are you Raikva with the cart?' 'Yes, I am,' he stated. 'I have indeed found him.' The attendant returned.

II

1. Then Jānaśruti Pautrāyana took hold of six hundred cows, a gold ornament, a chariot drawn by mules and spoke to him thus:
2. 'O Raikva, these six hundred cows, this gold ornament, the chariot drawn by mules (are for you). Now illustrious sir please teach me about the deity, the deity whom you worship.'
3. The other replied: 'O let the gold ornament together with the chariot and cows remain with you.' Then again Jānaśruti Pautrāyana took hold of one thousand cows, a gold ornament, a chariot drawn by mules, and his daughter, and approached Raikva.

4. To him Jānaśruti said: 'O Raikva these are one thousand cows, this gold ornament, this chariot drawn by mules, this wife, this village in which you dwell (are for you). Now illustrious sir, please enlighten me.'
5. Then holding up her face towards himself he (Raikva) stated: 'You have brought all these along; just by means of this face you will make me speak. There are these villages in the Mahāvṛṣa country called Raikvaparṇa where Raikva lived. Then Raikva said to him:

The verses reflect the rules for those qualified to impart and receive knowledge such as those who were intelligent, had knowledge of the Vedas, etc.

III

1. Surely air is the absorber. Indeed, when fire goes out, it enters into air; when the sun sets it is in air that it enters into, when the moon sets it is in air that it enters into.

Air ought to be meditated upon in its respect of absorption since the air absorbs fire, etc. Air is also viewed as that which causes movement. At the time of dissolution the sun, etc., merge into air which is their casual form. Air is therefore said to be the absorber.

2. When water dries up, indeed it enters into air. Indeed, air absorbs all these. Thus it is with regards to the gods.
3. Then with regard to the self: Vital breath surely is the absorber. When one sleeps, speech enters into vital breath, the eye enters into vital breath, the ear enters into vital breath, the mind enters into vital breath for vital breath indeed absorbs all these.
4. Indeed, these two are the two absorbers; air with regard to the gods and vital breath with regard to the sense organs.

5. Now when Kāpeya Śaunaka and Kākṣaseni Abhipratāriṇ were waiting at a meal a Brahmacāri begged of them. To him they did not give anything.

It was believed that the student was conceited. So they decided to put him to the test.

6. He (the Brahmacārin) said: 'The one God has swallowed up four great selves, he who is the world's protector. O Kāpeya, O Abhipratāriṇ, him mortals do not perceive, even though he abides in diverse forms. Indeed, this food has not been given for whom this food is meant.'

Fire and others were swallowed in the form of air and speech and others in the form of prāṇa.

7. Indeed, after reflecting on all this Kāpeya Śaunaka approached him (and said) he who is the self of the gods, the producer of all beings, with teeth of gold, the devourer, the wise one, indeed his glory is spoken of as very great, since he devours even what is not food, without being eaten. Verily, O Brahmacārin, do we thus meditate on this Brahman. Then he told his attendants: 'Provide him food.'

During dissolution all is destroyed by means of assuming the form of air. During creation fire and other deities are created. During sleep he destroys speech and regenerates all this during waking.

8. Then to him they provided (food). And these five and the other five combine to make ten and constitute the kṛta (dice cast). From that in all directions these ten are food and the highest throw. This Virāt of the form of ten gods is the eater of food. By him this whole world is perceived. He sees all this and becomes an eater of food who knows thus, indeed who knows thus.

The kṛta is the eater, the rest is food. Food and the eater of food are said to be ten. Air, fire, the sun, the moon, and water are five; the five sense organs are five. Together they make ten. Both groups of ten are identical due to similarity of number.

IV

1. At one ancient point of time, Satyakāma Jābāla asked his mother, Jābāla: 'Mother, I wish to live the life of a Brahmacāri. Of what descent am I?
2. She said to him: 'I do not know of what descent you are my child. In the days of my youth, I did many works and attended to others, I begot you. Thus I do not know of what descent you are. But I am by name Jābāla and you are by name Satyakāma. So you may speak of yourself as Satyakāma Jābāla only.
3. Then he approached Hāridrumata Gautama and said: 'I wish to live under you, Illustrious sir, as a Brahmacārin, may I become your student, illustrious sir?
4. To him he said: 'Of what descent are you, dear boy?' He replied: 'I do not know of what descent I am, sir. I asked my mother, and she said: "In the days of my youth I did many works and attended to others. I begot you. Thus I do not know of what descent you are. But I am by name Jābāla and you by name are Satyakāma." So, I am Satyakāma Jābāla, sir'.
5. Then he said to him: 'No one who is not a Brahmin can explain thus. Fetch the sacrificial fuel, dear boy, I shall initiate you as a Brahmacārin, you have not veered from the truth.' Having initiated him, he sorted four hundred emaciated and feeble cows and said, 'Dear boy, go with these.' While taking them away Satyakāma said: 'I will not return without a thousand.' He resided away for a considerable period of time, till when the cows grew to one thousand.

V

1. Then indeed the bull addressed him thus: 'Satyakāma' He replied: 'Illustrious sir.' 'We have attained a thousand, dear boy. Proceed with us to the teacher's house.'

The diety of the quarters, Air was happy with the efforts of Satyakāma, especially his true faith and penance. The deity entered the form of a bull to help him.

2. 'And let me speak to you about a quarter of Brahman.' 'Speak to me illustrious sir.' To him (the bull) said: 'The eastern quarter is one part, the western quarter is one part, the southern quarter is one part, the northern quarter is one part. Dear boy, this surely is one foot of Brahman consisting of four quarters named the splendid.'
3. He who knows this thus as one foot of Brahman consisting of four parts and meditates on it as splendid becomes splendid in this world. Indeed, he wins splendid worlds, who knows this thus as one foot of Brahman consisting of four parts and meditates on it as splendid.

VI

1. 'Fire will state to you a foot of Brahman.' He indeed the next morning drove the cows on. Where the cows gathered towards evening, he heaped together the firewood, penned the cows, laid on the fuel and sat down close to them, behind the fire facing east.
2. To him the fire said: 'Satyakāma.' He answered: 'Illustrious sir.'
3. 'Dear boy, let me speak to you about a quarter of Brahman.' 'Speak to me, illustrious sir.' Indeed to him he said: 'The earth is a part, the atmosphere is a part and the ocean is a part. Dear boy, this verily is a foot of Brahman consisting of four parts named the unending.'

Fire in itself exists as the earth. Thus it instructed Satyakāma about itself.

4. He who knows this thus as one foot of Brahman consisting of four parts and meditates on it as unending becomes unending in the world. Indeed, he wins unending worlds, who knows this thus as one foot of Brahman consisting of four parts and meditates on it as unending.

VII

1. 'The swan will state to you a foot of Brahman.' He indeed the next morning drove the cows on. Where the cows gathered towards evening, he heaped together the firewood, penned the cows, laid on the fuel and sat down close to them, behind the fire facing east.

   This meditation is related to effulgence. The swan here refers to the sun. Like the sun, the swan moves in the sky and has the attribute of whiteness.

2. To him the swan flew and said: 'Satyakāma!' He answered: 'Illustrious sir.'
3. 'Dear boy, let me speak to you about a quarter of Brahman.' 'Speak to me, illustrious sir.' Indeed, to him he said: 'Fire is a part, the sun is a part and the moon is a part and lightning is a part. Dear boy, this verily is a foot of Brahman consisting of four parts named the resplendent.'
4. He who knows this thus as one foot of Brahman consisting of four parts and meditates on it as resplendent becomes resplendent in the world. Indeed, he wins resplendent worlds, who knows this thus as one foot of Brahman consisting of four parts and meditates on it as resplendent.

VIII

1. 'A driver-bird will state to you a foot of Brahman.' He indeed

the next morning drove the cows on. Where the cows gathered towards evening, he heaped together the firewood, penned the cows, laid on the fuel and sat down close to them, behind the fire facing east.

The magdu is a type of bird. It is connected to water and is used here to refer to prāṇa, since the existence of prāṇa in the body depends on water.

2. To him a driver-bird flew and said: 'Satyakāma!' He answered: 'Illustrious sir.'
3. 'Dear boy, let me speak to you about a quarter of Brahman.' 'Speak to me, illustrious sir.' Indeed to him he said, 'Prāṇa is a part, the eye is a part and the ear is a part and mind is a part. Dear boy, this verily is a foot of Brahman consisting of four parts named the sanctuary.'

The abode here is the mind. The mind is the support for all the experiences which are had by means of the sense organs.

4. He who knows this thus as one foot of Brahman consisting of four parts and meditates on it as the sanctuary comes to possess a sanctuary in the world. Indeed, he wins worlds possessing a sanctuary, who knows this thus as one foot of Brahman consisting of four parts and meditates on it as the sanctuary.

IX

1. Then indeed he arrived at the teacher's house. To him the teacher said: 'Satyakāma!' He answered: 'Yes, illustrious sir.'
2. 'Indeed, dear boy, you are lustrous like a knower of Brahman. Who is it that has taught you?' Satyakāma declared: '... (these) different from men. But I desire, illustrious sir, that you explain it to me.'

The commentary describes the qualities of a knower of

Brahman. These include clear perception, positive outlook, freedom from worry, and a bearing of contentment.

3. For I have heard from illustrious persons like yourself only, that knowledge learnt from a teacher is the means to attain the most excellent. To him indeed he expounded it. In this nothing was missing. Indeed, nothing was missing.

X

1. Now indeed Upakosala Kāmalāyana resided with Satyakāma Jābāla leading the life of a Brahmacārin. For twelve years he tended to his fires. Satyakāma permitted other disciples to return home (after completing their studies) but did not allow him (Upakosala) to depart.
2. To him his wife said: 'The Brahmacārin has performed severe austerities and attended properly to the fires, you should instruct him so the fires do not blame you.' But the teacher journeyed away without instructing him.

Satyakāma was confident that Upakosala would be directly instructed by the fire.

3. Then by due to grief (sickness) he resolved to fast. The wife of the teacher spoke to him: 'O Brahmacārin, please eat, why are you not eating?' He answered: 'In this person there are manifold desires running in different directions; I am full of sickness. I will not eat.'

Sorrow is always caused by unfulfilled desires. People are conscious about ways to fulfil desires and disappointed when they are not able to.

4. Then the fires discussed among themselves: 'This Brahmacārin has performed his austerities and attended to us properly. Let us instruct him. Then for him they said: 'Prāṇa is Brahman, bliss is Brahman, ether is Brahman.'

5. Indeed, he said: 'I discern that prāṇa is Brahman; but I do not discern that bliss and ether.' They replied to him: 'What indeed is bliss that is ether, what indeed is ether that is bliss.' Then they expounded to him about prāṇa and ether.

Life depends on prāṇa. Brahman and prāṇa are the same. The commentary points out the method of meditating on the pleasure centres in the Ākāśa and the non-physical Ākāśa. This unworldly happiness due to causal Brahman is to be meditated upon. So the Ākāśa which is in the heart is related to prāṇa and has the attribute of happiness that is Brahman in its causal form. This is connected to Brahman as the effect and is to be meditated upon.

XI

1. Then indeed the Gārhapatya fire instructed him: 'earth, fire, food, and the sun (are my forms), the person who is seen in the sun, I am he, surely, I am he.'

The householder's fire is being described. It is to burn during day and night. During its performance the wife has a seat, and it is known as Iṣṭi.

2. A person who knows this thus and meditates on it (fire) destroys sinful acts, becomes the possessor of (this) world, attains the full lifespan, leads a glorious life, and his descendants do not diminish. Of such a one we protect him in this world and the yonder one who knowing this (fire) thus meditates on it (the fire).

XII

1. Then the Anvāhāreyapacana fire expounded to him: 'Water, the directions, the stars, the moon (are my forms). The person who is viewed on the moon, I am he, surely, I am he.'

Both the moon and fire are said to be luminous. They are related to food. Thus they are equivalent. The stars are referred to as the objects of enjoyment of the moon. Water is said to create food. So, both the water and the stars are food.

2. He who knows this thus and meditates on it (fire) destroys sinful acts, becomes the possessor of (this) world, attains the full lifespan, leads a glorious life and his descendants do not diminish. Of such a one we protect him in this world and the yonder one who knowing this (fire) thus meditates on it (the fire).

XIII

1. Then the Āhavanīya fire expounded to him: 'Prāṇa, ether, heaven, and lightning (are my forms). The person who is viewed in lightning I am he, surely I am he.

   The equivalence of lightning and the Āhavanīya fire is being set out here. Both are stated to be of the nature of luminosity. Both are enjoyed by heaven and Ākāśa. Āhavanīya is the fire of the deities.

2. He who knows this thus and meditates on it (fire) destroys sinful acts, becomes the possessor of (this) world, attains the full lifespan, leads a glorious life and his descendants do not diminish. Of such a one we protect him in this world and the yonder one who knowing this (fire) thus meditates on it (the fire).

XIV

1. The fire then said: 'Upakosala, dear boy, you have this knowledge of us (the fire) and knowledge of the self; but the teacher will show you the path.' Then his teacher came back to him and said to him: 'Upakosala.'
2. 'Illustrious sir,' he replied. 'Your face is lustrous as one who

knows Brahman. Who has expounded to you?' 'Who ought to instruct me, illustrious sir?' said he. Here as it were he obscured the truth. And he said (indicating the fires), they are now of this form, but they were (previously) a different form. The teacher said: 'Dear boy, verily what did they state to you?'

3. 'This indeed,' he affirmed. 'Dear boy, they have verily spoken about the worlds only. However, I will speak to you regarding that which just as water does not cling to the lotus leaf, so evil sin does not cling to one who knows this thus.' 'Please instruct me, illustrious sir,' to him he said.

The next few verses will discuss the ātman in a more elaborate way.

XV

1. He (the teacher) said: 'This person who is viewed in the eye, this is the self. This is immortal, without fear, this is Brahman. Thus even if one sprinkles water or clarified butter on this (the eye) it slides away to the side (of the eye).

Throughout the Upaniṣads, Brahman is stated to be that which is the sight of sight, the seer which sight presupposes. This verse seeks to point out the unblemished nature of the person residing in the eye. The eye is free from blemish, so the person residing there is all the more so.

2. This is called Samyad-Vāma, for all blessings are united in him. All blessings accrue to him who knows thus.

Brahman ought to be meditated upon as that on which all blessings are based.

3. This only is Vāmāni, the vehicle of blessings, since he brings all blessings. He who knows this thus brings all blessings.

It is due to him that the results of righteous deeds accrue to all beings.

4. This only is Bhāmānī, the vehicle of light since he is lustrous in all the worlds. He who knows this thus is lustrous in all the worlds.
5. Now, verily for such persons, whether the cremation rites are done or not, they go to light, from light to day, from the day to the fortnight of the waxing moon; from the fortnight of the waxing moon to the six months when the sun rises towards the north, from these months to the year, from the year to the sun, from sun to moon, from moon into lightning. Indeed, a person, different from human, he causes them to realize Brahman. This is the path of the gods and the path to Brahman. Those who go by this path do not come back again to the human whirlpool, indeed, they do not come back again.

The path that an aspirant dedicated to meditation takes, is described and enjoined. The crucial significance of meditation is highlighted here and the aim is not to deprecate rites. In its quest for perfection, the point is that the self is not assisted nor retarded by rites.

The word 'this' is used. It indicates that such a person will not return in this cycle. Those who meditate on Brahman never return. Those who do not meditate on God, but perform spiritual disciplines return in the next cycle.

XVI

1. Surely this which here (the wind) purifies is the sacrifices since blowing along purifies all. And since moving along this purifies all, this is the sacrifice of this. Of this the mind and speech are the parts.

In this verse is described the means to get the desired results from sacrifices. The importance of silence at the right times is stressed. Success in a sacrifice is said to depend on mind and speech. Prāṇa is also said to become the sacrifice, that which ensures purification.

2. One of these two, the Brahmā priest conducts by means of his mind. By means of speech the Hotṛ, Adhvarya, and Udgātṛ conduct the other. After the morning litany has commenced and prior to the concluding recitation the Brahmā priest ought to speak.

The Soma sacrifice has four types of priests associated with it. The commentary states that the Brahmā priest may be compared to a physician since he treats the wounds of the sacrifice.

3. (When) only one of the paths is proceeded upon (that by words) the other is harmed. Just as a one-footed man on a single-wheeled chariot is harmed so his sacrifice is harmed when the sacrificer is harmed. By having conducted such a (defective) sacrifice he becomes more of a sinner.
4. Now when the morning litany has commenced and prior to the concluding recitation if the Brahmā priest does not utter anything then both parts are embellished and neither is harmed.

Here is clearly stated that a sacrifice which is completed and not defective is far superior to one which is defective in any way. The means to cure this defect is also shown.

5. Just as a man with two feet walking or a chariot with two wheels moving is well established, thus is his sacrifice well established. When the sacrifice is well established, the sacrificer is well established. By concluding the sacrifice, he is better off.

XVII

1. Prajāpati cogitated on the worlds. From them thus cogitated upon he drew out their essences, fire from the earth, air from atmosphere, and from heaven the sun.
2. He cogitated on these three deities. From them thus cogitated upon he drew out their essences, the Ṛg verses from the fire, from the air the Yajus mantras, and from the sun the Sāman chants.

They received the three Vedas.

3. He cogitated on these three Vedas. From them thus cogitated upon he drew out their essences; Bhūḥ from the Ṛg verses, Bhuvas from the Yajus mantra; Svaḥ from the Sāman chants.

So it is emphasized that the three Vyāhṛtis (syllables)—Bhūḥ, Bhuvaḥ, Svaḥ—are the essence of the Vedas, the deities, and the regions.

4. Thus if the sacrifice is made defective due to (a mistake in rendering) the Ṛg verses, one ought to make an offering in the Gaārhapatya fire (the householder's fire) with the mantra 'Bhūḥ Svāhā'. Thus of the Ṛg verses only by means of the essence of the Ṛg verses and by power of the Ṛg verses he binds together (cures) the defect of the sacrifice.

Rectification of defects of numerous mistakes are explained here.

5. Also if the sacrifice is made defective due to (a mistake in rendering) the Yajus mantras, one ought to make an offering in the Southern fire with the mantra 'Bhūḥ Svāhā'. Thus of the Yajus mantras only by means of the essence of the Yajus mantras and by power of the Yajus mantras he binds together (cures) the defect of the sacrifice.

6. Now if the sacrifice is made defective due to (a mistake in rendering) the Sāma chants, one ought to make an offering in the Āhavanīya fire with the mantra 'Svaḥ Svāhā'. Thus of the Sāma chants only by means of the essence of the Sāma chants and by power of the Sāma chants he binds together (cures) the defect of the sacrifice.
7. Just as one would join gold by means of salt, silver by means of gold, tin by means of silver, lead by means of tin, iron by means of lead, wood by means of iron, or wood by means of leather.

These verses deal with curing of defects and restoration to health. Just as experts restore persons to health, so does a qualified priest remove defects of a sacrifice not performed properly.

8. Thus does (the priest) cure the defect of the sacrifice through the strength of these worlds, of these deities, of the three Vedas, surely that sacrifice is healed where there is a priest who knows this.
9. Surely, that sacrifice is inclined northwards where there is a Brahmā-knowing priest who knows thus. Also with respect to the Brahmā-knowing priest there is this song. Wherever the sacrifice comes back there indeed he goes.
10. In the manner that the mare defends the soldiers, does the Brahmā priest only protect persons engaged in sacrifices. The Brahmā priest who knows thus, surely protects the sacrifice, the sacrifice, and all priests. Thus, one should only make he who knows thus a Brahmā priest and not one who is ignorant of this, indeed not one who is ignorant of this.

CHAPTER 5

I

1. Surely, he who knows the eldest and most excellent becomes himself the eldest and most excellent. Prāṇa is surely the eldest and most excellent.

   This chapter explains how the northern paths can also be achieved by householders by means of the five fires and by celibates following the correct austerities and faith. The southern path for those who only perform rites and the path for ordinary worldly people will also be described. The aim of this is to reduce attachment to the world so as to attain Brahman.

2. Surely, he who knows the wealthiest, becomes the wealthiest amongst his own people. Speech surely is the wealthiest.
3. Surely, he who knows (what is) firmly established becomes firmly established in this world and in the next. The eye verily is firmly established.
4. Surely, he who knows prosperity, his desires, human and divine are fulfilled. Verily the ear is prosperity.
5. Surely, he who knows the sanctuary becomes the sanctuary of his people. Verily the mind is the sanctuary.

   By sanctuary is meant the sanctuary of organs and objects. The mind is the sanctuary. All objects are presented in the form of perception by the sense organs to be experienced by the Jīva.

6. Now the five senses argued between themselves about who was most excellent (saying): 'I am most excellent, I am most excellent.'
7. These five senses approached the father Prajāpati and said to him: 'Illustrious sir, who is the most excellent amongst us?' In reply he said: 'He who on departing the body appears the worst, he is the most excellent amongst you.'
8. Indeed, speech departed for a year and stayed out. It returned and said: 'How have you managed to live without me?' (The others replied): 'In the manner of the dumb, not being able to speak, but breathing by means of breath, seeing with the eye, hearing by means of the ear, thinking by means of the mind.' Speech entered (the body).
9. The eye departed for a year and stayed out. It returned and said: 'How have you managed to live without me?' (The others replied): 'In the manner of the blind, not being able to see, but breathing by means of breath, speaking by means of the organ of speech, hearing by means of the ear, thinking by means of the mind.' The eye entered (the body).
10. The ear departed for a year and stayed out. It returned and said: 'How have you managed to live without me?' (The others replied): 'In the manner of the deaf not hearing, but breathing by means of breath, speaking by means of the organ of speech, seeing by means of the eye, thinking by means of the mind.' The ear entered (the body).
11. The mind departed for a year and stayed out. It returned and said: 'How have you managed to live without me?' (The others replied): 'In the manner of children without (mature) minds, not being able to see, but breathing by means of breath, speaking by means of the organ of speech, seeing by means of the eye, hearing by means of the ear.' The mind entered (the body).

12. Then when prāṇa was about to depart, dislodging the other senses just as a spirited horse would dislodge the pegs on which it is tethered. They all came near him and said: 'Illustrious sir, remain, you are the most excellent amongst us; do not depart (from our body).

This is an allegory to show that from the viewpoint of meditation which is the most excellent organ. Physically the senses do not leave the body as above.

13. Then indeed speech said to that one: 'Just as I am the wealthiest in the same manner you are also the wealthiest.' Then to that one the eye said: 'Just as I am the firm support, you are the firm support.'

The word 'tat' meaning that is used in the Sanskrit verse. This word is an adverb. The implication is that the quality of wealthiest and other qualities belongs to prāṇa. In ignorance it was thought to belong to the various sense organs.

14. Then to that one the ear said: 'In the manner in which I am prosperous, in that manner are you prosperous.' Then to that one the mind said: 'In the manner in which I am the sanctuary, in that manner are you the sanctuary.'
15. Surely people do not refer to them as speech, nor as eyes, nor as ears, nor as minds. But they refer to them as prāṇa, since surely the prāṇa is all of these.

Prāṇa in its aspect as Hiraṇyagarbha or the cosmic being is manifested in three forms, the Adhyātma, Adhibhūta, and Adhidaiva. Prāṇa presides over the sense organs of perception, the ear as direction, the skin as air, the eye as the sun, the tongue as Varuṇa and the nose as the Aśvins.

II

1. He (prāṇa) said: 'What will constitute my food?' They (the senses) said: 'Whatever, which is here even (the food) of dogs and birds! Indeed, this is the food of "ana" (breath). Surely the name "ana" is obvious. For he who knows thus there is nothing at all that is not food.'

In prāṇa-vidyā is enjoined that food belongs to prāṇa. The root 'an' indicates movement. Prāṇa the word is derived from this source. Prāṇa consists of movement. Prāṇa ought to be meditated upon with the view that everything is the food of prāṇa and prāṇa is the enjoyer of all.

2. He said: 'What will constitute my garments?' They (the senses) said: 'Water! From that surely those who are going to start to eat cover, twice before eating and after eating by means of water. He who knows thus becomes the obtainer of clothes and does not remain naked.'

Now is being enjoined the meditation on prāṇa as the garment. The sipping of water is seen symbolically as garment since it covers prāṇa. The sipping of water is viewed as a purification and is ought to be done before and after the meditation.

3. Satyakāma Jābāla conveyed this (doctrine of prāṇa) to Gośruti, the son of Vijāghrapāda, and stated: 'If anyone speaks of this, even to a shrivelled-up stump, then on it branches would be produced and leaves would grow.'
4. Then if one wishes to attain greatness, then having initiated himself on a new moon day and on the night of the full moon let him stir up curds and honey with a mash of all kinds of herbs and then make an offering to the fire, on the spot prescribed for offerings, saying: 'Svāhā (hail) to the oldest and most excellent.' Then let him throw the rest into the mash.

Here is contained a description of the Martha rite. These sections may be compared to sections of the Bṛhadāraṇyaka Upaniṣad. (Br. 6.3.1 to Br. 6.3.3)

5. Accompanied by the mantra, 'Svāhā to the wealthiest', he ought to offer an oblation to the fire at the place prescribed for offerings and throw the rest into the mash accompanied by the mantra, 'Svāhā to what is firmly established.' He ought to offer an oblation to the fire at the place prescribed for offerings and throw the rest into the mash accompanied by the mantra, 'Svāhā to success'. He ought to offer an oblation to the fire at the place prescribed for offerings and throw the rest into the mash accompanied by the mantra, 'Svāhā to the dwelling place'. He ought to offer an oblation to the fire at the place prescribed for offerings and throw the rest into the mash.
6. Then moving out carrying the mash in his hands, he ought to recite the mantra, 'Thou art Ama by name since all this (universe) rests with you. He is the oldest, most excellent, the ruler and sovereign. May he cause one to attain to the oldest age, to the most excellent position, to rulership and sovereignty. Indeed, I desire to be all this.'

   'Ama' is a name of prāṇa. Prāṇa functions by means of food in the body.

7. Then, verily he takes a sip reciting the Ṛk mantra step by step. 'We ask for that food pertaining to Savitṛ the progenitor.' Saying this line he ought to sip. 'The most excellent and all sustaining.' Saying this he ought to sip. 'We promptly meditate on the deity Bhaga,' saying this and raising the pot shaped like a goblet or a cup, he ought to drink the whole. Then he should sit down behind the fire either on a skin or on the ground while restraining his mind and speech. If at

this point, he perceives a woman (in a dream) let him know that his rite has attained fruition.

The full Ṛk mantra is contained in Ṛg Veda (5.82.1). It means that a prayer is made for food to the effulgence saints.

8. Regarding this, there is this verse:
'When during the performance of rites for the attainment of wishes, there is perceived (by the performers of the rite) a woman in a dream, then he ought to recognize completion in such a vision in a dream, indeed in such a vision in a dream.

III

1. Once upon a time Śvetaketu Āruṇeya approached an assembly of Paṇcālas. Then Pravāhaṇa Jaivali asked of him: 'My boy, has your father counselled you?' 'Illustrious sir, indeed he has.'

As per the commentary of Śaṅkarācārya, the paths of souls are enumerated in the following verses. The aim of this is to instil in the minds of seekers the need for dispassion and the absence of attachment.

2. 'Do you know to which place created beings go from this place?' 'No, illustrious sir.' 'Do you know the means by which they again return?' 'No, illustrious sir.' 'Do you know the place where the two paths, the path leading to the gods and the path leading to the fathers separate?' 'No, illustrious sir.'

Both those with the knowledge of this meditation and those without, together go up to a certain point and then separate.

3. 'Do you know just how the distant world never gets filled?' 'No, illustrious sir.' 'Do you know how the fifth offering, the

liquid offering, comes to be called a person?' 'No, indeed illustrious sir.'

4. 'Then why did you state that you had been instructed?' Since how can anyone who does not know these (referred to above) say: 'I have been instructed.' He was pained, proceeded to his father's residence and to him he said, 'Illustrious sir, verily without properly instructing me you said, "I have properly instructed you".'
5. 'That member of the princely class asked five questions of me, and I was unable to comprehend even a single one.' He (the father) said: 'Just as you have spoken to me regarding them, in that manner even I do not comprehend a single one of them. Had I known them, how could I not have instructed you?'
6. Then, he, Gautama went to the king's location. When he reached he was shown due respect by the king. The king said to him: 'O illustrious Gautama, ask for a wish of human wealth.' He answered: 'O king, yours be the wealth of men, tell me which words you spoke to my young boy.' The king was troubled.

   The king is showed as perturbed here. He did not want to turn down a request.
7. 'Reside for a long time.' He (the king) commanded him. To him he said: 'Just as you said to me, O Gautama, before you this knowledge never reached the Brāhmaṇas. Thus in all the worlds this teaching belonged to the Kṣatriyas.' Then he explained this to him.

   Realizing that Gautama was a worthy recipient he instructed him.

IV

1. 'Indeed, the distant world is a (sacrificial) fire, O Gautama. Of this the sun is the fuel, the rays of light are the smoke,

the day the flame, the moon is the embers, and the stars are surely the sparks.'

The meditation in this verse is centred on the commonalities in fire and heaven. The sun in this is the sacrificial fuel. The aim of this is to enjoin meditation.

2. Into this fire the gods make (the offering) of faith. Of this offering originates Soma the king.

The meaning of faith is taken up. Offerings made, accompanied by faith lead to the attainment of non-visible effects. Thus it is faith on which a sacrifice is supported.

V

1. 'O Gautam, surely the god of rain is the (sacrificial) fire, air only is the fuel, the cloud indeed is the smoke, lightning is the flame, thunder is the embers and the loud roar of thunder are the sparks.'

In this verse it is mentioned that lightning is the flame. Their similarity is that both are bright. Thunder and the embers are hard.

2. Into this fire the gods make (the offering) of Soma the king. Of this offering originates rain.

VI

1. 'O Gautam, the earth indeed is the (sacrificial) fire, of this the year is surely the fuel, ether is indeed the smoke, the night is the flame, the quarters are the embers and the in-between quarters constitute the sparks.'

earth's productivity is galvanized by time in the form of the year. Also, since the year energizes the earth it is referred to as fuel.

2. Into this fire the gods make (the offering) of rain. Of this offering originates food.

VII

1. 'O Gautam, man certainly is the (sacrificial) fire, of this speech indeed is the fuel, vital breath is the smoke, the tongue constitutes the flame, the eye is the embers and the ears surely constitute the sparks.'

A person excels in gatherings by means of speech. A person is glorified by speech just as fire is brightened by fuel. Prāṇa is said here to be smoke since it goes out of the mouth in a manner similar to smoke going out of the fire.

2. Into this fire the gods make (the offering) of food. Of this offering originates semen.

VIII

1. 'O Gautam, the woman indeed is the (sacrificial) fire, of this the organ of generation is the fuel, the act of inviting is the smoke, the female organ of generation is the flame, what is inside are the the embers and the sparks are joy.'
2. Into this fire the gods make (the offering) of semen. Of this offering originates the foetus.

IX

1. Thus in the fifth oblation, water comes to be known as man. That foetus covered in a thick membrane, lies in the mother's womb for as much as nine or ten months and then it emerges to be born.
Again, the objective of these verses is to highlight the pain and grief associated with death, rebirth, etc. It shows the transitory nature of these events. This in turn is expected to inculcate an attitude of dispassion.

2. He being born, lives as much as his due length of his life. When he departs, as destined, they carry him from this place to fire itself, from whence only he came and from whence he originated.

X

1. Those who know hence (the knowledge of the five fires) and those who dwell in the forest and meditate on faith as austerity, they progress to light, from light to day, from the day to the fortnight of the waxing moon; from the fortnight of the waxing moon to the six months when the sun rises towards the north

These verses are similar to the verses found in Chapter 4.

2. From these months they proceed to the year, from the year they proceed to the sun, from the sun they proceed to the moon, from the moon they proceed into lightning. Indeed, a person, different from human, he causes them to realize Brahman. This indeed is the path which leads to the gods.

From the point of view of meditation, the universe can be divided into five sections. Each section is viewed as a fire. Consequently, the worshipper by means of the northern path reaches Brahmaloka.

3. In the case of those who live in villages and perform sacrifices, donate gifts and carry out works of public utility, they proceed into smoke, from smoke they proceed to night, from night they proceed to the dark half of the month, from the dark half of the month they proceed to the six months in which the sun moves southwards. From there they are not able to attain the year.

The word Iṣṭa refers to sacrifice such as the Agnihotra and other ceremonies referred to in the Vedas. Pūrta stands for acts of public utility and Datta the giving of gifts. Once again, the paths of the meditators and those who only perform rites are shown to be different. Meditators gradually attain the world of Brahmaloka and the performers of action proceed to the world of the fathers and then the world of the moon.

4. From the months they proceed to the fathers' world, from the fathers' world they proceed to ether, from ether they proceed to the moon. That is the king Soma. That constitutes the food of the gods. This indeed the gods eat.

   The performer of acts enjoys himself in the world of the moon and also becomes an instrument of enjoyment. To enjoy himself he needs a body. This body is created by water particles and smoke arising from his cremation.

5. Having resided in that region to the extent that they have exhausted (the results of action) they then again return by the way by which they came. They proceed to Ākāśa, from Ākāśa they proceed to air. Having become air, they then become the smoke; after having become smoke they form clouds.

   After exhausting the karma which leads to the attainment of the lunar world, such a soul returns for rebirth. The nature of rebirth depends on the residual karma. It is not necessary that the ascending and descending paths be the same.

6. Having become white clouds, they become clouds, after becoming clouds he pours down as rain. Then in this world they are born as rice and barely, herbs and trees, as sesamum plants and beans. However, indeed the escape from these is very arduous since whoever eats this as food and sows such a seed, they become like that only.
7. Those who here have been of good conduct will quickly get a good birth (womb), the womb of a Brāhmin, the womb of

a Kṣatriya or the womb of a Vaiśya. However, they who here have been of bad conduct will quickly get a bad womb, the womb of a dog or the womb of a hog.

8. Then on neither of these ways do they go. They continually keep revolving, being born as small creatures, (of whom it is said) 'Be born and die'. This is the third state. Thus the world (of the moon) is never filled. Thus one should abhor (this state). Regarding that is this verse.

As per the commentary, the process and lives of small creatures are often marked by suffering and the absence of pleasant experiences.

9. A person who steals gold, who indulges in wine, who defiles the teacher's bed, and who harms a Brāhmaṇa, these four fall as does the fifth, who joins with them.
10. And he who knows thus these five fires is not defiled by evil, even though he may associate with these sinners. He who knows these thus becomes pure and attains the virtuous worlds, he who knows this thus, indeed he who knows this thus.

The verse here is meant to evoke an admiration of the power of true knowledge.

XI

1. Prācīnaśāla, the son of Upamanyu; Satyayajña, the son of Pulusa; Indrayumna, the son of Bhāllavi; Jana, the son of Sarkarākṣa; and Budila, the son of Aśvatarāśva, the renowned householders, these celebrated vedic scholars, having come to the same place deeply reflected as to 'What is the Ātman in us? What indeed is Brahman?'

This verse seeks to address a key question of the Upaniṣads. In the commentary, it is stated that the two terms qualify each other. The term Brahman does not refer to the limited ātman in the body and the ātman does not refer to Brahman as manifested in the form of the sun, etc. However, there is no distinction between the two. Ātman is Brahman and Brahman is ātman.

2. Then they deeply discussed amongst themselves: 'Illustrious sirs, at present Uddālaka Āruni is learning about this Vaiśvānara ātman (universal self). Indeed, may we go to him.' Then they approached him.

The commentary explains why ātman is known as Vaiśvānarah. This is so since he causes men to their respective states as per karma. He is the self of all.

3. He (Uddālaka) thought: 'These renowned householders and celebrated Vedic scholars are going to ask questions of me. I will not be able to explain everything to them. However, I shall introduce them to another (qualified) teacher.'
4. To them he said: 'Illustrious sirs, Aśvapati Kaikeya, at this time studies this universal self. Indeed, may we go to him.' They approached him.
5. When they reached, he (the king) arranged separately for each of them a welcome with appropriate rites. On rising the next morning, the king said to them: 'In my territory there is no robber, no miser, no drunkard, no man who has not installed the sacrificial fire, no uneducated person, no adulterer and hence how can there be an adulteress? Illustrious sirs, I am going to conduct a sacrifice. Illustrious sirs, as much wealth as I give to each single priest, that much I shall give you. Please remain, illustrious sirs.'

The king thought they wanted wealth but hesitated to directly request for it.

6. Then they said: 'Indeed the end for which a person goes, regarding that only he ought to speak to him. At this time, you are studying the universal self. Indeed, tell us about that.'

They clearly stated that it was knowledge they wanted and not wealth.

7. He (the king) then said to them: 'I will give you an answer in the morning.' Thus the next morning they went to him with sacrificail fuel in their hands. Then the king without first receiving them as pupils spoke to them as follows:

The verse mentions the Upanayana ceremony. The word literally means, 'falling at the feet (of the teacher)'. The aim of the story is to show that householders and scholars who were duly humble renouncing pride, desirous of knowledge went to a competent teacher to seek knowledge. They were duly instructed.

XII

1. 'O Aupamanyava, what is it you meditate on as the self?' He said: 'Heaven alone, O illustrious king.' The king said: 'This self that you meditate upon is the universal self known as "the very bright". From that in your family are seen the Suta, Prasuta, and Āsuta libations (of Soma juice).'
The Soma sacrifice is mentioned to be of three forms—Jyotiṣṭoma, Ahīna, and Satra. Suta is said to be the Soma juice in the Jyotiṣṭoma; Prasuta is extracted from the Ahīna sacrifice; Āsuta is extracted from Ahargaṇa.
2. 'You eat food, behold what is dear. One who thus meditates on this universal self, eats food and also beholds what is dear and in his family, there is the brilliance born of sacred knowledge. Yet this is only the head of the self. Had you not come to me your head would have fallen down.'

XIII

1. Then he (the king) said to Satyayajña Pauluṣi: 'O Prācīnayogya, what is it you meditate on as the self?' (He said): 'The sun alone, illustrious king.' The king said: 'This self that you meditate upon is the universal self known as "possessed of all forms". From that in your family are seen much and manifold desirable things.'
2. 'Provided for you is a mule-drawn chariot, maidservants and gold necklaces, you eat food, behold what is dear. One who thus meditates on this universal self, eats food, and also beholds what is dear and in his family, there is the brilliance born of sacred knowledge. Yet this is only the eye of the self. Had you not come to me your head would have fallen down.'

XIV

1. Then the king said to Indra-dyumna Bhāllaveya: 'O Vaiyāghrapada, what is it you meditate upon as the self?' He said: 'Air alone, illustrious king.' The king said: 'This self that you meditate upon is the universal self known as "diverse ways". From that offerings come to you in diverse ways and diverse rows of chariots proceed along your path.'
2. You eat food, behold what is dear. One who thus meditates on this universal self, eats food and also beholds what is dear and in his family, there is the brilliance born of sacred knowledge. Yet this is only the prāṇa of the self. Had you not come to me your prāṇa would have left you.'

XV

1. Then he (the king) said to Janam Śārkarākṣya: 'What is it you meditate upon as the self?' He said: 'Ether alone, illustrious king.' The king said: 'This self that you meditate upon is the universal self known as "the abundant". From that you are abundant of offspring and wealth.

2. You eat food, behold what is dear. One who thus meditates on this universal self, eats food and also beholds what is dear and in his family, there is the brilliance born of sacred knowledge. Yet this is only the body of the self. Had you not come to me your body would have been smashed.'

XVI

1. Then he (the king) said to Budila Aśvatarāśvi: 'O Vaiyāghrapadya, what is it you meditate upon as the self?' He said: 'Water alone, illustrious king.' The king said: 'This self that you meditate upon is the universal self known as "wealth". From that you are endowed with wealth and nourishment of body.'
2. 'You eat food, behold what is dear. One who thus meditates on this universal self, eats food and also beholds what is dear and in his family, there is the brilliance born of sacred knowledge. Yet this is only the lower belly of the self. Had you not come to me your lower belly would have split open.'

XVII

1. Then he (the king) said to Uddālaka Āruni: 'O Gautam, what is it you meditate upon as the self?' He said: 'earth alone, illustrious king.' The king said: 'This self that you meditate upon is the universal self known as "the basis". From that you are well supported in progeny and cattle.'
2. 'You eat food, behold what is dear. One who thus meditates on this universal self, eats food and also beholds what is dear and in his family, there is the brilliance born of sacred knowledge. Yet this is only the feet of the self. Had you not come to me your feet would have disintegrated.'

XVIII

1. To them the king said: 'Surely, indeed you all eat food

knowing this universal self as if it were diverse. But he who meditates on the universal self as a whole consisting of parts and self conscious, consumes food in every world, in every being and in every self.'

The term Prādeśamātra has been used in the Sanskrit text. It is interpreted differently. These include whose area is from heaven to earth as well as who is the enjoyer or witness in the body. Abhivimāna is also diversely interpreted as self conscious, the individual self that is subtle and cannot be measured.

2. Now surely of this universal self the head is 'very bright', the eye is 'possessed of all forms', the trunk is 'abundant', the lower belly is'wealth', the feet are the 'earth', the chest is the 'altar', the hair is the 'sacred grass', the heart is the 'Gārhapatya fire', the mind 'Anvāhārya-pacana fire', and the mouth is indeed the 'Āhavanīya fire'.

The verse states that Vaiśvānarah is the eater of all as it is the self in all. This verse also introduces the Agnihotra in prāṇa.

XIX

1. Thus, the food which comes first ought to be an offering. The eater when he offers the first offering, ought to offer it saying: 'Svāhā to prāṇa.' Thus prāṇa is contented.

The verse calls upon to view the act of eating as Agnihotra, etc.

2. Prāṇa being contented the eye is contented. The eye being contented the sun is contented. The sun being contented heaven is contented. Heaven being contented, whatsoever is under heaven and under the sun is contented. Along with this contentment he is contented with progeny, cattle, food, brightness, and the brilliance born of sacred wisdom.

XX

1. Then he ought to offer the second offering saying: 'Svāhā to vyāna.' (By this) vyāna is contented.
2. Vyāna being contented, the ear is contented. The ear being contented, the moon is contented. The moon being contented the quarters are contented. The quarters being contented whatsoever is under the moon and quarters are contented. Along with this contentment he is contented with progeny, cattle, food, brightness, and the brilliance born of sacred wisdom.

XXI

1. Then he ought to offer the third offering saying: 'Svāhā to apāna.' (By this) apāna is contented.
2. Apāna being contented, speech is contented. Speech being contented, fire is contented. Fire being contented earth is contented. earth being contented whatsoever is under the earth and fire are contented. Along with this contentment he is contented with progeny, cattle, food, brightness, and the brilliance born of sacred wisdom.

XXII

1. Then he ought to offer the fourth offering saying: 'Svāhā to samāna.' (By this) samāna is contented.
2. Samāna being contented, the mind is contented. The mind being contented, the god of rain is contented. The god of rain being contented lightning is contented. Lightning being contented whatsoever is under lightning and the god of rain are contented. Along with this contentment he is contented with progeny, cattle, food, brightness, and the brilliance born of sacred wisdom.

XXIII

1. Then he ought to offer the fourth offering saying: 'Svāhā to udāna.' (By this) udāna is contented.
2. Udāna being contented, the skin is contented. The skin being contented, air is contented. Air being contented ether is contented. Ether being contented whatsoever is under air and the ether are contented. Along with this contentment he is contented with progeny, cattle, food, brightness, and the brilliance born of sacred wisdom.

XXIV

1. He who without knowing this offers the Agnihotram sacrifice, that would be akin to the situation where someone would remove the live embers and throw the offerings on the ashes.

   This verse aims to eulogize the Prāṇāgnihotra sacrifice. But this is not at the cost of the Agnihotra. One of the duties of the householder is to offer oblations twice a day in the prescribed fire.
2. Moreover, who knowing this thus offers the Agnihotra sacrifice to prāṇa, his offering is poured into every world, every being and every self.

   Being one with all he enjoys and they also enjoy through him.
3. Just as when cotton fibres are burnt when placed on fire, so are all the sins extinguished of a person who knowing this thus offers the Agnihotra sacrifice.

   The results of actions are viewed as sins here; both favourable and unfavourable.
4. From that, if he who knows this thus offers the food to a person it would be an offering to the universal self. Regarding that there is this verse.

5. Just as hungry boys gather near the mother, thus do all beings assemble near the Agnihotra sacrifice, indeed they assemble near the Agnihotra sacrifice.

The entire world benefits from the eating of a knower of Vaiśvānara.

CHAPTER 6

I

1. Aum. Once upon a time there lived Śvetaketu Āruṇeya. To him his father said: 'O Śvetaketu, live as a Brahmacārin. Indeed, dear boy there has never been anyone in our family who is not learned, who is only notionally a Brāhmaṇa.'

   The primary teaching of this chapter is that there is only one single self in all beings.

2. He, having gone to the (teacher's house) when he was twelve years, returned aged twenty-four years having studied all the Vedas. He was haughty, obstinate, and considered himself full of knowledge. To him his father then said: 'Śvetaketu dear boy, I see that you are haughty, obstinate, and consider yourself full of knowledge, did you ask for that teaching?'

   The word 'ādeśa', appears in the sanskrit verse. It here refers to the teaching regarding Brahman which is to be learnt on the basis of the scriptures or the instructions of a qualified teacher.

3. 'By means of which the unheard becomes heard, the unthought becomes thought of, the unknown becomes known?' 'How possibly illustrious sir can there be such teaching?'

4. 'Dear boy, just as by means of a single lump of clay, all which is constituted of clay is known, for the transformation is only in name, arising from words, while the clay only is real.'

Replying to a doubt expressed by Śvetaketu, the father states that here the cause and effect are not different. Thus if the cause is known so is the effect known. The clay evidently pervades the objects made of clay and is real. The different names and forms are ultimately unreal.

5. 'Dear boy, just as by means of a single ingot of gold all which is constituted of gold is known, for the transformation is only in name, arising from words, while the gold only is real.'
6. 'Dear boy, just as by means of a single pair of nail scissors made of iron, all which is constituted of iron is known, for the transformation is only in name, arising from words, while the iron only is real, this dear boy is that teaching.'
7. 'Surely those illustrious teachers did not know it since had they known it why they not have spoken of it to me? Illustrious sir, please teach it to me.' 'So be it, dear boy.' Said he.

In this verse the motive of Śvetaketu is not disrespect to his teacher but the apprehension that he may be sent again to the residence of the teacher.

II

1. 'Dear boy, in the beginning this was being only, single only without a second. It is said by some that in the beginning, this was non-being only, single only, without a second. From that non-being being arose.'

The important concept of 'sat', is taken up here. What is real, what exists is sat. It is existent, subtle, pervades all, one, without any defect. It is pure consciousness. This is stated in the various texts of Vedānta. It is not different form its effects and is free of bhedas both svajātīya (generic) and svagata (intrinsic). Here the term being is used in a positive sense. Non-being does not imply a negation of being. Rather it is meant to convey denial of wrong notions.

2. He said: 'Dear boy, but from where verily can it be thus? How could being arise from non-being? Dear boy, in reality in the beginning was being alone, single only, and without a second.'
3. That being thought: 'May I become abundant, may I generate forth.' That created fire. Fire thought: 'May I become abundant, may I generate forth.' That created water. From that whenever a person grieves or perspires, then water arises from fire.

The purport of this verse is not a listing of all products but to show that everything is a product of that which is sat.

4. That water thought: 'May I become abundant, may I generate forth. That created food. From that whenever it rains anywhere there is much food. It is from water only that food for eating is produced.'

Food is said to be of the nature of earth. It is the product of water.

III

1. Surely, of these above-mentioned beings, there are three sources alone, those born from eggs, those born from living beings, and those born from a sprout.

All elements are created due to Brahman. So all effects, gross and subtle are due to Brahman. This is being described here. The commentary further explains that all creatures are covered in the three sources mentioned here.

2. That deity thought: 'Indeed let me enter into these three deities by means of this living self and then classify names and forms.'

The jīva is an aspect of Brahman conditioned by adjuncts. Thus it is not different from Brahman. By means of knowledge of Brahman one can know the jīva. Thus by means of knowledge of one one can know all. After this follows the allocation of name and form. The jīva is itself unaffected by the experiences of the body such as pleasure and pain.

3. Of these may I make each one threefold. This deity entered into these three deities by means of the living self and then classified names and forms.

By implication is meant that in each of these, one element is primary and the other secondary. For example, gross fire is compared to one half of subtle fire and a quarter of water and a quarter of earth. This triplication process occurs in different ways; triplication of those elements which constitute the body and triplication of those universal elements (outside the body).

4. 'Each of these it made threefold. However, dear boy, how these three indeed became each of them threefold, that learn from me.'

IV

1. 'In fire whatever is of red form is of the form of fire; whatever (is) white, that (is the form) of water, whatever (is) black that (is the form) of food (earth). Thus vanishes (the idea of) the quality of fire from fire; for the transformation is only in name arising from words while the three forms alone are real.

It is stressed that when modifications are analysed it becomes clear that the effect and cause are not really different. Fire, water, earth, and the elements that constitute the visible universe are on analysis shown to be only a means of apprehending the original, untriplicated element in a threefold manner.

2. 'In the sun, whatever is of red form is of the form of fire; whatever (is) white, that (is the form) of water, whatever (is) black that (is the form) of food (earth). Thus vanishes (the idea of) the quality of the sun from the sun; for the transformation is only in name arising from words while the three forms alone are real.
3. 'In the moon whatever is of red form is of the form of fire; whatever (is) white, that (is the form) of water, whatever (is) black that (is the form) of food (earth). Thus vanishes (the idea of) the quality of the moon from the moon; for the transformation is only in name arising from words while the three forms alone are real.
4. 'In lightning whatever is of red form is of the form of fire; whatever (is) white, that (is the form) of water, whatever (is) black that (is the form) of food (earth). Thus vanishes (the idea of) the quality of lightning from lightning; for the transformation is only in name arising from words while the three forms alone are real.

Again, it is reiterated that the cause is real only. Thus fire, water, and earth are created by being and have no real existence apart from this. Other objects such as the sun, moon, and lightning can be further analysed into their constituent elements. Phenomenal objects are not ultimately real.

5. Surely it was knowing this that the great householders and great Vedic scholars of ancient times uttered: 'There is nothing at all at present that can be told to us that we have not heard, that we have not thought of or which is unknown.' For from these (three forms) they understood everything.

Again, it is stated that all gross elements are ultimately unreal. The subtle cause is only real. He who knows this 'being', knows all.

6. 'Whatever it was that appeared as if it was red, they know to be the form of fire, whatever it was that appeared as if it was white they know to be the form of water, whatever it was that appeared as if it was black they know to be the form of earth.'
7. 'Whatever it was that appeared as if unknown they knew to be a combination of these three deities. Yet, dear boy, surely learn from me how on reaching (a) person, these three deities each become threefold.'

Even what is perceptible is an aggregate of these three deities. All objects can be analysed as composed of three elements or three primary elements namely fire, water, and earth.

V

1. Food when consumed gets divided threefold; its grossest constituent that becomes the faeces; its middle (constituent) flesh, and its smallest (constituent) mind.

The three constituents of food are taken up here, the nutritive, the subtle, and what is ejected. The subtle element sustains the senses and sustains the mind. In Vedānta, the concept of Chaitanya holds that the material mind becomes capable of knowledge due to its proximity to the self.

2. Water when drunk gets divided threefold; its grossest constituent that becomes urine; its middle (constituent) blood, and its smallest (constituent) prāṇa.

To continue in the body prāṇa needs water. It is however not a modification of water.

3. Fire when consumed gets divided threefold; its grossest constituent that becomes bone; its middle (constituent) marrow, and its smallest (constituent) speech.
4. ‘Dear boy, thus mind consists of food, prāṇa consists of water, and speech consists of heat.’ ‘Illustrious sir, please expound it to me further.’ ‘So be it, dear boy.’ Said he.

The mind, prāṇa, and speech are by nature subject to change and destruction since they are composed of three elements of which they are aggregates. ‘Being’, only is permanent and indestructible. Further prāṇa, speech, and mind is each an aggregate of these three elements.

VI

1. ‘Dear boy, regarding curd when churned, that what constitutes the smallest part, rises upwards; this indeed becomes clarified butter.’

This section seeks to show that in a gross compound, its subtle component can lead to the causation of other products.

2. ‘Dear boy, thus indeed regarding the food that is eaten, the smallest part rises upwards; that indeed becomes mind.’

Food by the process of digestion is assimilated. From this develops the mind and its parts.

3. ‘Dear boy, regarding the water that is drunk, the smallest part rises upwards; that indeed becomes prāṇa.’
4. ‘Dear boy, regarding the fire that is consumed, the smallest part rises upwards; that becomes speech.’
5. ‘Dear boy, thus mind consists of food, prāṇa consists of water, and speech consists of fire.’ ‘Illustrious sir please expound it to me further.’ ‘So be it, dear boy.’ Said he.

VII

1. 'Dear boy, a person consists of sixteen parts. Do not eat (any food) for fifteen days, drink water as as much you desire. Prāṇa which consists of water will not be severed from one who drinks water.'

It is stated that mind depends on food. By means of food is the mind sustained. Also, mental strength is divided into sixteen components.

2. For fifteen days he (Śvetaketu) did not eat. Then he went to him and said: 'What shall I say, sir?' The father said: 'The Ṛk verses, the Yajus mantras, and the Sāman chants, dear boy.' 'Sir, they do not occur to me.'
3. To him he said: 'Dear boy, just as a single coal, the measure of a firefly remaining from a great blazing (fire) cannot burn much, thus, dear boy, of your sixteen parts only a single part remains by means of which you cannot apprehend the Vedas. Eat, so that you may understand me.
4. He ate and then went to his father. All the questions he put to him, the father answered them all.
5. Then to him, he (the father) said: 'Dear boy, just as a single coal, the measure of a firefly, remaining from a great blazing fire is made to blaze (intensely) by heaping straw on it and by means of it the fire burns much more.'
6. 'Dear boy, thus of your sixteen parts, only a single part remained and that when nourished by food blazed up by means of it. You now understand the Vedas. For dear boy, the mind consists of food, prāṇa consists of water and speech consists of heat. From these words of his (Śvetaketu) grasped it, indeed he grasped it.

The verses here seek to show by means of agreement and distinction that the mind is dependant on food.

VIII

1. Uddālaka Āruni said to his son Śvetaketu: 'Dear boy, understand from me the true nature of sleep. Dear boy, when a person here sleeps, as it is called, he has attained pure being. He has attained his own nature. From that people speak of him as sleeping, for he has reached his own nature.'

   Here is discussed 'being', and the jivā as Brahman during the course of deep sleep. It is said that during deep sleep the jivā attains its true nature. Here the mind is compared to a mirror. The mind reflects the light of the self. The jivā in deep sleep due to karma still remaining in a subtle form. So this state is not considered the ultimate cessation of birth and rebirth.

2. Just as (in the manner of) a bird tied to a string having flown in different directions without obtaining a resting place elsewhere, takes refuge at the place where it is bound, thus indeed, dear boy, the mind after having flown in different directions without obtaining a resting place anywhere else takes refuge in prāṇa only; since dear boy the mind is bound to prāṇa.

   The commentary points out that here prāṇa refers to the supreme principle, the sat. Just as a bird tied to a string returns to a branch, the jivā too returns to its original source. The soul eventually gets tired of transmigration existence and returns to its original state.

3. 'Dear boy, understand from me (the real nature of) hunger and thirst. When a person is said to be hungry (it may be understood that) water only is leading away what has been consumed. Just as they speak of the leader of cows, the leader of horses, the leader of men, thus similarly people speak of water as the leader (or carrier) of food. From this, dear boy,

understand that the body is an offshoot that has arisen since it cannot survive in the absence of a root.'

Everything including the jivā has as its one source Brahman.

4. 'What else can its root be distinct than food? Similarly, dear boy, with food as the sprout search for water as the root; dear boy, with fire as the sprout search for being as the root. Dear boy, all these creatures have being as their root, have being as their sanctuary, have being as their basis.'
5. Now when a person is said to be thirsty, then (it may be understood that) fire only is leading away what has been drunk; just as they speak of the leader of cows, the leader of horses, the leader of men, thus similarly people speak of fire as the leader (or carrier) of water. From this, dear boy, understand that this (water) is an offshoot that has arisen, since it cannot survive in the absence of a root.'

Here once again 'being' is discussed.

6. 'What else can its root be other than water? Dear boy, with water as the sprout search for fire as the root; dear boy with fire as the sprout search for being as the root. Dear boy, each of these creatures have being as their root, have being as their sanctuary, have being as their basis. Yet, how indeed, dear boy, each of these deities on reaching the human becomes threefold has already been spoken of. Dear boy, when a person is about to leave from this world, his speech amalgamates in the mind, mind amalgamates in prāṇa, prāṇa amalgamates in fire, and fire amalgamates in the supreme deity.'

The death experience is detailed here. By speaking of death the doctrine of being is further explained. This verse speaks about the last stages leading to death. At the last stage fire withdraws and merges into Brahman. The commentary states that just as when a mirror is shattered the face in the mirror is withdrawn and merges into the real face, so also at death the living self withdraws and remains as Brahman. A person with the knowledge of Brahman does not return. But the ignorant without this knowledge are reborn again and again.

7. 'That which is this subtle essence, this is the self of all this (the whole world). That is truth. That is the self. That thou art, O Śvetaketu.' 'Illustrious sir, please expound it further to me.' 'Dear boy, so be it,' said he (the father).

This verse contains the great mahāvākya, saying, 'Tat tvam asi' or 'That thou art'. This is said to have the supreme place amongst all the vākyas. Here it is stated by Āruṇi to Śvetaketu. The phenomenal universe in its entirety is traced to the universal principle of being which is subtle in nature. This is the basis of all including man. A man without his limiting adjuncts is the same as the underlying reality. This is one of the central tenets of the Advaita system.

IX

1. 'Dear boy, just as the bees produce honey by gathering the essences (juices) of many trees and condensing them all to a single essence.'
2. 'Just as these juices have no cognition that "I am the essence of this tree, I am the essence of that tree", dear boy, similarly indeed all creatures having entered into being are unable to realize that they have entered into being.'

The creatures referred to above enter into being at death, at the time of deep sleep and during pralay or cosmic dissolution.

3. 'Here in this world, whatever these creatures are, tiger or lion or wolf or boar or worm or fly or goat or mosquito, they take that form again.'

Due to ignorance at dissolution, the jivā remains unconscious. They do not know their identity with Brahman. Thus as per their karma they are reborn.

4. 'That which is this subtle essence, this is the self of all this (the whole world). That is truth. That is the self. That thou art, O Śvetaketu.' 'Illustrious sir, please expound it further to me.' 'Dear boy, so be it,' said he (the father).

Śvetaketu's query or doubt is explained. If creatures have come from being, why are they not aware of it?

X

1. 'Dear boy, these rivers pour forth, the eastern ones towards the eastern direction and the western ones towards the western direction. They (originate) from the ocean and join in the ocean, they become the ocean only. Just as these rivers while they are there, do not know themselves as 'I am this river, I am that river.'
2. 'Dear boy, similarly indeed all creatures having come from being are unable to realize that they have come from being. Here in this world, whatever these creatures are, tiger or lion or wolf or boar or worm or fly or goat or mosquito, they take that form again.'

Such creatures rise as clouds and vapour. They return as rain and merge in the oceans.

3. 'That which is this subtle essence, this is the self of all this (the whole world). That is truth. That is the self. That thou art, O Śvetaketu.' 'Illustrious sir, please expound it further to me.' 'Dear boy, so be it,' said he (the father).

Śvetaketu wishes to know why the jivā is not destroyed when it merges in Brahman.

XI

1. 'Dear boy, of this great tree, if anyone were to injure it at the root, it would bleed yet remain living. If anyone were to injure it in the middle it would bleed yet remain alive. If anyone were to strike at it at the top, it would bleed yet remain alive. Since the tree is pervaded by the living self, it stands firm drinking constantly filled with joy.'

   This verse seeks to point to the all-pervasive nature of life.

2. 'Of this, if life abandons a single branch, then that branch shrivels up, if it abandons a second, then that shrivels up, if it abandons a third then that shrivels up. If it abandons the whole then the whole shrivels up. Thus, indeed, dear boy, know this,' he said.

   At death the jivā and prāṇa withdraw. The jivā as per the commentary obtains food and drink as per its unfulfilled karma.

3. The father spoke: 'Dear boy, indeed understand thus that, certainly this body dies when the living self departs, yet the living self does not die. That which is the subtle essence this is the self of all this (the whole world). That is truth. That is the self. That thou art, O Śvetaketu.' 'Illustrious sir, please expound it further to me.' 'Dear boy, so be it,' said he (the father).

   The tree with jivā is living. In the absence of it, it dies. The commentary gives examples of behaviour patterns which indicate the remembering of experiences from prior births. Further it is repeated that the jivā is immortal. The body is what undergoes death and destruction. Śvetaketu's query here pertains to how the varied gross universe can be produced by the self.

XII

1. 'Bring here a fruit of this fig tree.' 'Illustrious sir, here it is.' 'Break it.' 'Illustrious sir, it is broken.' 'What do you view here?' 'Illustrious sir, these seeds like very fine particles.' 'My child, of these, break one.' 'Illustrious sir, it is broken.' 'What do you view here?' 'Illustrious sir, nothing.'
2. To him (the father said): 'Dear boy, this subtle essence which you do not see, indeed of this very essence, dear boy, the great fig tree stands thus. Dear boy, have faith.'

The purport of these verses is to show both by means of reasoning and scriptural authority that from being which is subtle, nameless, and formless arises the universe with name and form. The importance of true faith is also emphasized.

3. 'That which is this subtle essence, this is the self of all this (the whole world). That is truth. That is the self. That thou art, O Śvetaketu.' 'Illustrious sir, please expound it further to me.' 'Dear boy, so be it,' said he (the father).

The query of Śvetaketu's here is that if being is what causes the universe then why can we not perceive it?

XIII

1. 'Place the salt in water and approach me in the morning.' He did as asked. To him (the father) said: 'My child, bring the salt you had placed in water at night.' He searched for it but was unable to locate it since it had fully dissolved.
2. 'My child, please take a sip from this end.' 'How is it?' 'It is salty.' 'Please take a sip from the centre.' 'How is it?' 'It is salty.' 'Please take a sip from that end.' 'How is it?' 'It is salty.' 'Throw the water away and approach me.' He did as asked. It is perpetually the same. Then he (the father) said to him:

'Dear boy, surely even here you do not perceive being. Surely certainly it is here.'

Śvetaketu's queries continue to be addressed. The example of salt dissolving in water is given. Brahman the subtle essence is not perceived by the senses just as the salt is not perceived. Yet it is present and there are other means to perceive it.

3. 'That which is this subtle essence, this is the self of all this (the whole world). That is truth. That is the self. That thou art, O Śvetaketu.' 'Illustrious sir, please expound it further to me.' 'Dear boy, so be it,' said he (the father).

Śvetaketu enquires as to the other means to know being.

XIV

1. 'Dear boy, just as a person brought from Gandhāra region with his eyes bound and covered abandoned in a lonely and uninhabited place, and just as that person would shout in the direction of the east, or in the direction of the north, or in the direction of the south, or in the direction of the west (declaring): 'I have been led here with my eyes bound, I have been abandoned here with my eyes bound and covered.
2. 'Just as if someone might loosen his bindings and tell him: "In this direction is the Gandhāra region, go in this direction." And he asking his way from village to village, being instructed and capable of judgement, he would thus arrive at Gandhāra only. Thus does a person in this world who has a teacher, know that his delay will be only so much as he is not freed (from ignorance) and then he will merge with being.'

The commentary states that there are two kinds of karma, that which is operative and that which has not yet fructified. The second type of karma is extinguished when one attains knowledge. Prārabdha karma the first one is not extinguished but has to be experienced. The prārabdha karma of a knower ceases at the end of his body. He then attains Brahman.

3. 'That which is this subtle essence, this is the self of all this (the whole world). That is truth. That is the self. That thou art, O Śvetaketu.' 'Illustrious sir, please expound it further to me.' 'Dear boy, so be it,' said he (the father).

Śvetaketu's query here pertains to if the knower of Brahman gets liberated in the body itself or he traverses through the path of the sun and other deities.

XV

1. 'Dear boy, the family members of a sick person gather around him (and ask): "Do you recognize me? Do you recognize me?" Just as long as his speech is not amalgamated in the mind, the mind amalgamated in prāṇa, prāṇa amalgamated in fire and fire amalgamated in the supreme deity, thus far does he still recognize them.'
2. 'And when his speech enters in mind, mind enters in prāṇa, prāṇa enters in fire, and fire enters in the supreme deity, then he does not recognize them.'

The man of knowledge and an ordinary person merge in being in the same way yet the man of knowledge is not subjected to rebirth. He is liberated in this birth and does not traverse the path of the sun, etc. The ordinary person is reborn again and again.

3. 'That which is this subtle essence, this is the self of all this (the whole world). That is truth. That is the self. That thou art, O Śvetaketu.' 'Illustrious sir, please expound it further to me.' 'Dear boy, so be it,' said he (the father).

Śvetaketu's query is if both merge in being in the same way then why the difference in outcomes? Why is one subject to rebirth and not the other?

XVI

1. 'Dear boy, they (the king's officers) lead a man holding his hand stating: "He has carried away something, he has committed the crime of theft, for him, warm the axe." If he has performed that (the act of theft), then he makes himself false only. Being habitually prone to falsehood, concealing himself through falsehood, he seizes the warmed axe and is burnt. He is then punished.'
2. 'If he is not the performer of that (the act of theft), then he makes himself true only. Being habituated to truth, covering himself with truth he seizes the warmed axe and is not burnt. He is then, at this point, released.'

The verse seeks to answer Śvetaketu's query by comparing it to a heated axe.

3. 'Just as there (in the case of a truthful man) he is not burnt, this is the self of all this (the whole world). That is truth. That is the self. That thou art, O Śvetaketu.' Then of this he knew; indeed he knew.

CHAPTER 7

I

1. Aum. 'Illustrious sir teach me.' Stating thus Nārada went to Santakumāra. He (Santakumāra) said: 'By means of that which you already know, approach me. Then I shall speak to you about what is subsequent.'

The last chapter dealt with Sat Vidya or knowledge of reality, i.e., Brahman. The present chapter aims to throw light on the modifications of reality. Also, a step-by-step analysis from the gross to the subtle to the highest is undertaken to help the spiritual aspirant.

2. 'Illustrious sir, I know the Ṛg Veda, the Yajur Veda, the Sāma Veda, Atharvaṇa as the fourth, Itihāsa-Purāṇa as the fifth, the Veda of the Vedas (grammar), the worship of ancestors, the science of numbers (mathematics), the science of portents, the science of chronology, logic, ethics, the knowledge of the deities, the knowledge of sacred wisdom, the knowledge of the elements, the knowledge of war, the knowledge of stars, the knowledge of serpents, the fine arts, I know all this, illustrious sir.'

The subjects mentioned here stand for the subjects of knowledge which the sage Nārada had a mastery over. Since he was restless, he approached Santakumāra.

3. 'However, illustrious sir, I am only a knower of texts and not a knower of the self. Verily, it has been heard by me, from persons such as your illustrious self, that a knower of the self crosses over grief. Illustrious sir, I am suffering such a condition of grief. Can your illustrious self take me across it (grief)?' To him Santakumāra replied: 'All that you have studied over here, is but only a name.'

The commentary discusses mantras which serve to provide instructions regarding deities and ceremonies. The knowledge of the self is also taken up and is stated as being of another level. Intellectual knowledge of Ātman presupposes a connection between an expression and what it expresses. Knowledge of the self leads one beyond pain, suffering, and sorrow.

4. 'Surely name is Ṛg Veda, Yajur Veda, Sāma Veda, Atharvaṇa as the fourth, Itihāsa-Purāṇa as the fifth, the Veda of the Vedas (grammar), the worship of ancestors, the knowledge of numbers (mathematics), the knowledge of portents, the knowledge of chronology, logic, ethics, the knowledge of the deities, the knowledge of sacred wisdom, the knowledge of the elements, the knowledge of war, the knowledge of stars, the knowledge of serpents, and fine arts. Name is this only. Meditate on the name.'

Name refers to speech and idea. The worship of texts by Nārada is enjoined as if they were Brahman itself. This is meant to instil a mindset consistent with what the text stands for. This is a method to help the spiritual aspirant in a step-by-step approach.

5. 'He who meditates on the name as Brahman so far as the name goes becomes (able) to act just as per his wishes there; he who meditates on the name as Brahman.' 'Illustrious sir, is there any entity superior than name?' 'There is some entity even superior than name.' 'Illustrious sir, speak about it to me.'

II

1. 'Certainly, speech is superior than name. Indeed speech makes known the Ṛg Veda, Yajur Veda, Sāma Veda, Atharvaṇa as the fourth, Itihāsa-Purāṇa as the fifth, the Veda of the Vedas (grammar), the worship of ancestors, the knowledge of numbers (mathematics), the knowledge of portents, the knowledge of chronology, logic, ethics, the knowledge of the deities, the knowledge of sacred wisdom, the knowledge of the elements, the knowledge of war, the knowledge of stars, the knowledge of serpents, and fine arts, along with heaven and earth, air and ether, water and fire, deities and men, cattle and birds, grass and trees, animals down to worms, flies and ants, virtuous and non-virtuous, true and false, good and bad, pleasant and unpleasant. Surely if speech did not exist neither virtue nor non-virtue would be known, neither truth nor falsity, neither good nor bad, neither pleasant nor unpleasant. Surely speech makes all this known. (Hence) on speech meditate.'

The mechanism of speech is explained in the commentary. Vaikharī refers to uttered expression which arises from its root which is known as madhyamā, this is in turn caused by paśyanti of which the origin is the supreme speech or parā vāk. This is the same as the Chaitanya of ātman. Speech has aspects such as conceiving, retaining, imagining, recalling, and expressing. The Vedas are learnt through this mechanism.

2. 'A person who meditates on speech as Brahman so far as speech goes becomes (able) to act just as per his wishes there; he who meditates on speech as Brahman.' 'Illustrious sir, is there any entity superior than speech?' 'There is some entity even superior than speech.' 'Illustrious sir, speak about it to me.'

III

1. 'Certainly mind is superior than speech. Just as the closed fist grips two āmalaka or two kola or two akṣa fruits, in the same manner does mind grasp speech and name. When by means of the mind one intends to know mantras then he knows (them). If he has the mind to do sacrificial acts, then he performs them. When in the mind he has a wish for sons and cattle, then he wishes for them. When in the mind he has a wish for this world and the next, then he wishes for them. Surely mind is Ātman, surely mind is the world. Surely mind is Brahman. (Hence) on the mind meditate.'

   Speech is said to be contained in the mind. Here mind is called ātman since the ātman permeates the mind just as a white, hot iron ball is called fire. The ātman cannot be an agent or an enjoyer.

2. 'A person who meditates on mind as Brahman so far as mind goes becomes (able) to act just as per his wishes there; he who meditates on mind as Brahman.' 'Illustrious sir, is there any entity superior than mind?' 'There is some entity even superior than mind.' 'Illustrious sir, speak about it to me.'

IV

1. 'Certainly, will is superior than mind. Indeed, when one wills, then in his mind he intends, then one utters speech, and it (speech) is uttered in name. In the name sacred formulas become one and in sacred formulas are included sacred works.'

   Will is described as an operation of the internal organ. By this one discriminates between what should and should not be done. Action is thus enabled.

As per tradition two important aspects of Vedic lore are mantras or sacred formulas and Brāhmaṇas which are liturgical books detailing procedures of sacrifices and rites. Vedic mantras are grouped in the Vedas as Ṛk, Yajur, and Sāman.

2. 'Surely all these merge in the will, are composed of will and established in will, through this will, heaven and earth were formed, through this will air and ether were formed; through this will water and heat were formed. By means of their being willed rain is willed. By means of the willing of rain food is willed. By means of the willing of food, prāṇa is willed. By means of the willing of prāṇa, sacred formulas are willed. By means of the willing of sacred formulas, sacred acts are willed. By means of the willing of sacred acts, the world is willed. By means of the willing of the world, all things are willed. Such is this will. (Hence) on will meditate.'

Food is produced by means of rain. Prāṇa is nourished by food. A person with strong prāṇa is competent to read mantras. Due to results of karma the universe is existent and sustained.

3. 'A person who meditates on will as Brahman surely he accomplishes the perpetual worlds, himself being perpetual, the well established, himself being well established, the painless, himself being painless. So far as will goes he becomes (able) to act just as per his wishes there; he who meditates on will as Brahman.' 'Illustrious sir, is there any entity superior than will?' 'There is some entit even superior than will.' 'Illustrious sir, speak about it to me.'

V

1. 'Certainly, intellect is superior than will. Indeed, when one understands then he wills, then in his mind he intends, then one utters speech, and it (speech) is uttered in name. In the

name sacred formulas become one and in sacred formulas are included sacred works.'

Intelligence is looked at from two viewpoints. First, in connection to the context of space and time it is the ability to comprehend an object therein. Secondly, from the point of view of the past and future it is the capacity to analyse connections, objects, and events.

2. 'Surely, these all merge in intelligence, have intelligence as their self and abide in intelligence. From that even if someone was possessed of much knowledge, yet without intelligence people speak of him in this manner only, he does not exist, irrespective of what he knows; since if he really knew he would not be without intelligence. On the other hand, a person possessed of intelligence, even though he may know a little, people are keen to hear him. Surely intelligence is the single centre of all these, intelligence is their self, intelligence is their basis. (Hence) on intelligence meditate.'
3. 'A person who meditates on intelligence as Brahman surely he accomplishes the perpetual worlds, himself being perpetual, the well established, himself being well established, the painless, himself being painless. So far as intelligence goes he becomes (able) to act just as per his wishes there; he who meditates on intelligence as Brahman.' 'Illustrious sir, is there any entity superior than will?' 'There is some entity even superior than intelligence.' 'Illustrious sir, speak about it to me.'

VI

1. 'Certainly, reflection is superior than intelligence. The earth reflects as it were. The atmosphere reflects as it were. Heaven reflects as it were. Water reflects as it were, the

mountains reflect as it were. Thus here, who among men attain greatness, they appear to have obtained a share of (the fruits of) reflection. Then, the small-minded persons who quarrel are abusive and slanderous. However, the great men appear to have obtained a share of (the fruits of) reflection. (Hence) on reflection meditate.'

Now is taken up reflection. The commentary describes it as the process of firmly focusing one's thoughts on an object without distraction. Perfect meditation is characterized by tranquillity and contentment.

2. 'A person who meditates on reflection as Brahman so far as reflection goes becomes (able) to act just as per his wishes there; he who meditates on reflection as Brahman.' 'Illustrious sir, is there any entity superior than reflection?' 'There is some entity even superior than reflection.' 'Illustrious sir, speak about it to me.'

VII

1. 'Certainly, understanding is superior than reflection. Indeed understanding makes known the Ṛg Veda, Yajur Veda, Sāma Veda, Atharvaṇa as the fourth, Itihāsa-Purāṇa as the fifth, the Veda of the Vedas (grammar), the worship of ancestors, the knowledge of numbers (mathematics), the knowledge of portents, the knowledge of chronology, logic, ethics, the knowledge of the deities, the knowledge of sacred wisdom, the knowledge of the elements, the knowledge of war, the knowledge of stars, the knowledge of serpents, and fine arts, along with heaven and earth, air and ether, water and fire, deities and men, cattle and birds, grass and trees, animals down to worms, flies and ants, virtuous and non-virtuous, true and false, good and bad, pleasant and unpleasant. Surely if understanding did not

exist neither virtue nor non-virtue would be known, neither truth nor falsity, neither good nor bad, neither pleasant nor unpleasant, food and drink, this world and the subsequent one—one knows by means of understanding only. (Hence) on understanding meditate.'

It is necessary to understand or appreciate the scriptures to properly do reflection or meditation.

2. 'A person who meditates on understanding as Brahman, indeed he obtains the world of understanding, of knowledge. So far as understanding goes he becomes (able) to act just as per his wishes there; he who meditates on understanding as Brahman.' 'Illustrious sir, is there any entity superior than understanding?' 'There is some entity even superior than understanding.' 'Illustrious sir, speak it to me.'

VIII

1. 'Certainly strength is superior than understanding. A single man of strength causes a hundred men of understanding to quiver. When he becomes strong then a man rises. Having risen he serves (the wise); serving he goes nearer; having gone nearer he becomes a seer, becomes a hearer, becomes a thinker, becomes wise, becomes a doer, becomes realized. Surely, by means of strength the earth stands, by means of strength the atmosphere, by means of strength heaven, by means of strength the mountains, by means of strength deities and men, by means of strength cattle and birds, grasses and trees, animals down to worms, flying insects and ants, by means of strength the world stands. (Hence) on strength meditate.'

It is stated that strength here is understood as the ability of the mind to grasp the knowledge which is presented. Mind is sustained by food.

2. 'A person who meditates on strength as Brahman, so far as strength goes he becomes (able) to act just as per his wishes there; he who meditates on strength as Brahman.' 'Illustrious sir, is there any entity superior than strength?' 'There is some entity even superior than strength.' 'Illustrious sir, speak about it to me.'

IX

1. 'Certainly, food is superior than strength. Thus if a person does not eat food for ten days, even though he may remain alive, however surely, he becomes unable to see, hear, think, understand, perform, realize. Then on the arrival of food he sees, hears, reflects, understands, performs, and realizes. (Hence) on food meditate.'

Food sustains strength. So it is said to surpass strength.

2. 'A person who meditates on food as Brahman, surely he obtains the worlds of food and drink. So far as food goes, he becomes (able) to act just as per his wishes there; he who meditates on food as Brahman.' 'Illustrious sir, is there any entity superior than food?' 'There is some entity even superior than food.' 'Illustrious sir, speak about it to me.'

X

1. 'Certainly, water is superior than food. Thus when there is not enough (beneficial) rain, living creatures are in immense pain (thinking): "Food will become scarce". Then when there is beneficial rain living creatures celebrate (thinking): "Food will be plenty". Verily it is water that assumes (different) forms of earth, atmosphere, sky, mountains, deities and men, cattle and birds, grass and trees, animals down to worms, flying insects and ants. Surely water is all these forms. (Hence) on water meditate.'

Water is what sustains crops and is said to surpass food.

2. 'A person who meditates on water as Brahman, attains all his wishes and becomes contented. So far as water goes, he becomes (able) to act just as per his wishes there; he who meditates on water as Brahman.' 'Illustrious sir, is there any entity superior than water?' 'There is some entity even superior than water.' 'Illustrious sir, speak it to me.'

XI

1. 'Certainly, heat is superior than water. Thus it is this that grips the air and warms the ether. Then it is said: "It is hot, it is burning hot, certainly it will rain." There only fire first manifests itself and creates water. It is due to this fire that lighting flashes across and upwards and thunder is heard. Thus people say: "There is lightning and thunder and so it will rain." There only fire first manifests itself and creates water. (Hence) on fire meditate.'

Fire in the form of heat and lightning precedes rain. So fire is called the cause of water.

2. 'A person who meditates on fire as Brahman, he indeed being brilliant himself, attains brilliant worlds filled with light, free of darkness. So far as fire goes, he becomes (able) to act just as per his wishes there; he who meditates on fire as Brahman.' 'Illustrious sir, is there any entity superior than fire?' 'There is some entity even superior than fire.' 'Illustrious sir, speak about it to me.'

XII

1. 'Certainly, ether is superior than fire. Indeed in ether exist both the sun and the moon, lightning, stars, and fire. By means of ether one calls, by means of ether one hears the reply. In ether one enjoys and in ether one does not enjoy. In ether is

one born and towards ether does it grow. (Hence) on ether meditate.'

The commentary points out that the cause is greater than the effect. Ākāśa (ether) along with air causes fire and is said to surpass fire.

2. 'A person who meditates on ether as Brahman, he indeed attains the worlds of ether and light, unobstructed and large. So far as ether goes, he becomes (able) to act just as per his wishes there; he who meditates on ether as Brahman.' 'llustrious sir, is there any entity superior than ether?' 'There is some entity even superior than ether.' 'Illustrious sir, speak about it to me.'

XIII

1. 'Certainly, memory is superior than ether. Thus if numerous people gather and if they have no memory, verily they would be unable to hear any sound, or think, or know. But certainly, if they had memory, then they would hear, think and know. By means of memory indeed (a person) recognizes sons, by means of memory one's cattle (are recognized). (Hence) on memory meditate.'

The importance of memory is being discussed now. For the mind to function it requires memory to recall ideas and remember impressions. Ākāśa, etc., are received into the mind by means of memory. So memory is said to surpass Ākāśa.

2. 'A person who meditates on memory as Brahman, so far as memory goes, he becomes (able) to act just as per his wishes there; he who meditates on memory as Brahman.' 'Illustrious sir, is there any entity superior than memory?' 'There is some entity even superior than memory.' 'Illustrious sir, speak about it to me.'

XIV

1. 'Certainly, hope is superior than memory. Kindled by hope memory becomes proficient in the sacred hymns, performs rites, wishes for sons and cattle, wishes for this world and the subsequent one. (Hence) on hope meditate.'

   Aspiration or desire is stated as surpassing memory. This is because a person is said to remember only what he desires to remember.

2. 'A person who meditates on hope as Brahman, by means of hope all his desires prosper, his prayers are fruitful. So far as hope goes, he becomes (able) to act just as per his wishes there; he who meditates on hope as Brahman.' 'Illustrious sir, is there any entity superior than hope?' 'There is some entity even superior than hope.' 'Illustrious sir, speak about it to me.'

XV

1. 'Certainly, prāṇa (life breath) is superior than hope. Just in the manner that the spokes of a wheel are fastened to the hub, so on prāṇa is all this fastened. Life moves by means of prāṇa. Prāṇa gives life and it gives to a living being. Prāṇa is the father, prāṇa is the mother, prāṇa is the brother, prāṇa is the sister, prāṇa is the teacher, prāṇa is the Brāhmaṇa.

   Prāṇa is described as the power which functions through all actions, instruments, and results. It is the universal power. The ātman is bound to the body by prāṇa. When prāṇa leaves so does the ātman. Prāṇa binds and upholds the universe based on aspirations.

2. 'If one replies in an excessive and violent manner to his father, mother, brother, sister, teacher or a Brāhmaṇa, to him people say: "Fie on you, surely you are a killer of your father, surely you are a killer of your mother, surely you are

a killer of your brother, surely you are a killer of your sister, surely you are a killer of your teacher, surely you are a killer of a Brāhmaṇa".'

3. 'Now if when this prāṇa has departed from them, even if one assembles them together with a fork and burns them completely, surely to him people will not say: "You are a killer of your father", nor "You are a killer of your mother", nor "You are a killer of your brother", nor "You are a killer of your sister", nor "You are a killer of your teacher", nor "You are a killer of a Brāhmaṇa."'

A body is respected as long as prāṇa resides there. This underlines the importance of prāṇa.

4. 'Verily prāṇa becomes all this. He surely who thus sees, thus thinks, and thus knows such a person thus becomes an eloquent speaker. Even if to him people were to say: "You are an eloquent speaker", he ought to say, "I am an eloquent speaker." He should not negate it.'

The importance of prāṇa continues to be stressed. One is encouraged to eloquently speak about prāṇa. Prāṇa is known by observation, reflection, and reasoning.

XVI

1. 'But he speaks eloquently who speaks eloquently with truth.' 'Illustrious sir, I am such (and) would speak eloquently with truth.' 'But one must desire to know clearly.' 'Illustrious sir, I desire to know clearly.'

Santakumāra encourages Nārada towards realizing the highest truth. As per Santakumāra only he who has realized the supreme truth speaks eloquently.

XVII

1. 'Surely when one knows then he speaks the truth. One who does not know does not speak the truth. A person alone who knows speaks the truth. But one must desire to clearly know knowledge.' 'Illustrious sir, I desire to clearly know knowledge.'

Śaṅkara in his commentary on this verse discusses two viewpoints to the truth. The vyāvahārika satya or truth from the practical standpoint is truth as perceived by senses in the world. It is the truth of the day-to-day world. In the ultimate analysis it is sat mediated by means of the instruments of human knowledge. There is a higher truth Parmārtha satya which is the supreme truth. In order to attain the higher truth, common perception has to be transcended. The understanding of this truth is referred to here as Vijñāna.

XVIII

1. 'Surely when one thinks, then one knows. Without thinking one does not know. A person alone who thinks, knows. But one must desire to clearly know thinking.' 'Illustrious sir, I desire to clearly know thinking.'

XIX

1. 'Surely when a person has faith then such a person thinks. Without faith a person does not think. A person alone who has faith thinks. But one must desire to clearly know faith.' 'Illustrious sir, I desire to clearly know faith.'

The word śradhā is analysed into two elements, 'śrat' and 'dhā'. The former stands for truth. It indicates firm attachment to this truth. It has also been explained as 'āstikya-Buddhi' or a firm belief in the reality of the soul, rebirth, karma, etc.

XX

1. 'Surely when a person has steadfastness then such a person has faith. Without steadfastness a person does not have faith. He alone who has steadfastness has faith. But a person must desire to clearly know steadfastness.' 'Illustrious sir, I desire to clearly know steadfastness.'

Here steadfastness is spoken about. It refers to earnest obedience of the teacher with regard to the teachings on Brahman.

XXI

1. 'Surely when a person is active he is steadfast. Without being active a person is not steadfast. He alone who is active is steadfast. But one must desire to clearly know activity.' 'Illustrious sir, I desire to clearly know activity.'

Activity is discussed in the context of realization of the truth. It consists of two aspects—sense control and concentration.

XXII

1. 'Surely when a person attains happiness then such a person is active. Without attaining happiness, a person is not active. He alone who attains happiness is active. But one must desire to clearly know happiness.' 'Illustrious sir, I desire to clearly know happiness.'

Here the yearning for supreme happiness is seen as a necessity for the attainment of the transcendent goal.

XXIII

1. 'Indeed that which is infinite is happiness only. In anything finite there is no happiness. The infinite only is happiness.

But one must desire to clearly know the infinite.' 'Illustrious sir, I desire to clearly know the infinite.'

The term bhūman is discussed here. Śaṅkarācārya employs the words mahat and niratiśayam. mahat is synonymous to bṛhat. In fact, the word Brahman is derived from the root 'bṛh' which has the meaning, 'to grow'. The terms bhūman, mahat, and Brahman refer to the same ultimate reality. This ultimate reality transcends all and includes all. Thus, Brahman is unsurpassed bliss, unparalled, and unequalled.

XXIV

1. 'Where one does not see anything else, does not hear anything else, does not know anything else, that is the infinite. However, where one sees something else, hears something else, understands something else is small. Surely that which is infinite is immortal. However, that which is finite is mortal.' 'Illustrious sir, on what is the infinite based? On its own majesty or not even on its own majesty?'

   The nature of bhūman is described here. For bhūman the threefold division of knowledge, knower, and instrument of knowledge does not apply. Bhūman transcends all attributes of mortal existence. This is not a denial of ātman. Rather bhūman is the ātman without any superimposition. The realization of bhūman is by means of vidyā. The realization of bhūman is immortality, amṛta. Bhūman is self-sufficient and self-supported. The person who has attained this attains infinite bliss.

2. 'Here in this world, cows and horses, elephants and gold, servitors and wives are called glory. Thus I do not speak.' He said: 'Since in that case one entity would be based in another.'

   This verse also highlights the fact that bhūman is self supported.

XXV

1. It (the infinite) only is below. The infinite is above, it (the infinite) is behind. It is in front. It is that which is to the south. It is that which is to the north. It only is all this. Hence now the next teaching is with regard to the self sense only. I only am above. I surely am below. I surely am behind. I surely am in front. I am that which is to the south. I am that which is to the north; Certainly, I only am all this.

   The verse rejects firmly the otherness in bhūman.

2. Hence now the teaching regarding the self. The self only is below. The self is above. The self is behind. The self is in front. The self is that which is to the south. The self is that which is to the north. The self only is all this. Surely, he who is this thus, sees thus, thinks thus, knows thus, has pleasure in the self, has play in the self, has union in the self, has bliss in the self. He becomes sovereign, he becomes free to act as he desires in all worlds. Yet those who know differently than this are ruled by others. They reside in perishable worlds. In all the worlds they do not become free to act as per their desires.

   Bhūman is not the 'I' of the body and senses. 'I' in the previous verse stands for ātman, the nature of pure being. Ātman is achieved by deep reflection and superior understanding. One who achieves bhūman is said to be svarāṭ or a supreme ruler. He is also self luminous, since it is the ātman that illuminates all.

XXVI

1. 'Surely for him only who sees thus, thinks thus, knows thus, prāṇa arises from the self, hope arises from the self, memory arises from the self, ether arises from the self, manifestation

and disappearance arise from the self, food arises from the self, might arises from the self, knowledge arises from the self, reflection arises from the self, consciousness arises from the self, will arises from the self, mind arises from the self, speech arises from the self, name arises from the self, sacred hymns arise from the self, rites arise from the self, certainly all this, the entire world is from the self only.

The principle of sadātman or the self as being is not distinct from the self.

2. Regarding that there is this verse: He does not see death who sees this, nor disease nor grief. He sees all who sees this and obtains all everywhere.
He is single, becomes threefold, becomes fivefold, sevenfold and indeed manifold. Now again he is known as the elevenfold, also a hundred and tenfold and also a thousand and twentyfold.
When nourishment is pure there is purity of nature. When there is purity of nature, memory becomes perpetual. When memory becomes perpetual there is release from all the knots of the heart. For such a person whose impurities have been removed, the illustrious Santakumāra reveals the further shore of darkness. Hence they call him Skanda. Indeed, they call him Skanda.

Along with reflection and understanding a necessary condition for the achievement of the supreme truth is purity of the internal organ or sattva-śuddhi. This can happen by purification of the mind. Śaṅkarācārya interprets the term āhāraśuddhi in terms of its ethical and psychological aspect. All that is brought to the mind by perception or imagination is food for the mind. A pure mind receives only proper impressions.

CHAPTER 8

I

1. Aum, now in this city of Brahman there is a dwelling, a small lotus, in this is a small inner ether. That which is within this ought to be sought. Surely that is what one ought to desire to clearly know.

   For a spiritual aspirant the supreme goal is liberation. For this one needs to realize the highest truth as described before such as sat, ātman, Brahman, and bhūman. The rarest, best aspirants who are of the most pure with highest order concentration and discipline realize the non-dual absolute. For the lesser able aspirants, the way is through meditation, worship, and discipline. One who worships Brahman in one's heart he will be able to realize Brahman. Such a person must be indifferent to external pleasures and must fulfil the necessary vows. Brahman manifests itself in the lotus of the heart residing as the jīva. Brahman manifests the universe and it is unending and timeless.

2. If to him (the disciples) should say: 'With regards to this city of Brahman in which there is a dwelling, a small lotus, in this is a small inner ether, what lies here that ought to be sought, or that surely one ought to desire to know clearly.'

This verse aims to clarify the concept of the ākāśa in the heart as Brahman. Ākāśa most accurately serves as an illustration to explain Brahman. In itself Brahman is unique.

3. He ought to say in reply surely as large as this ether is, so much extends the ether inside the heart. In it verily are assembled both heaven and earth, both fire and air, both the sun and the moon, lightning and the stars. Whatsoever that is here in this world and whatsoever that is not, all that is assembled in it.
4. If to him they should say: 'If within this city of Brahman is assembled everything, all beings and all desires, then what remains when age overcomes it or it is destroyed?'

The student asks as to how the content of the body can continue if the body is destroyed.

5. He ought to say: 'Of this (Brahman called inner ether) it does not age with ageing, it is not killed with killing. This is the true city of Brahman. In this are all desires assembled. This is the ātman, free from evil, free from age, free from mortality, free from grief, free from hunger, free from thirst, whose desire is truth, whose will is truth. Just as here in this world, subjects do as instructed and whatever end they desire, be it a district or part of an area, on that they live only.'

The reply to the doubt is stated here, namely that the decay of the body does not lead to the decay of the ākāśa in the heart which is Brahman. The body is not really the abode of Brahman since the body is transitory. The ātman is truly the abode of Brahman, the Brahmapura. It is only by association that the body is known as Brahmapura. Also, the disciple is encouraged to take up Daharopāsanā or meditation of one's self as the reality dwelling in the heart. This entails complete detachment and the absence of cravings.

6. In the manner as here in this world, that which is won by action perishes, thus there, that which is won by righteous acts perishes. They who depart from this world without knowing the self and the desire for truth, for them there is no freedom to act as per their wishes in all the worlds. However, for those who depart from this world, having known the self and the desire for truth they become free to act as per their wishes in all the worlds.

   Enjoyment which is dependant on external causes is transitory in nature. The aim here is to underline the importance of realizing one's own nature as Bhumā-Brahman during his life here on earth as per the scriptures and the instructions of a qualified teacher.

II

1. If such a person desires the world of the fathers, from his will only fathers arise. By means of the world of the fathers he is prosperous and mighty.

   This verse shows the freedom to do as he wants of the person who realizes the Ātman in the heart before the end of this life.

2. If such a person desires the world of the mothers, from his will only mothers arise. By means of the world of the mothers he is prosperous and mighty.
3. Then if such a person desires the world of brothers, from his will only brothers arise. By means of the world of the brothers he is prosperous and mighty.
4. Then if such a person desires the world of sisters, from his will only sisters arise. By means of the world of sisters he is prosperous and mighty.
5. Then if such a person desires the world of friends, from his will only friends arise. By means of the world of friends he is prosperous and mighty.

6. Then if such a person desires the world of perfumes and garlands, from his will only perfumes and garlands arise. By means of the world of perfumes and garlands he is prosperous and mighty.
7. Then if such a person desires he the world of food and drink, from his will only food and drink arise. By means of the world of food and drink he is prosperous and mighty.
8. Then if such a person desires the world of song and music, from his will only song and music arise. By means of the world of song and music he is prosperous and mighty.
9. Then if such a person desires the world of women, from his will only women arise. By means of the world of women he is prosperous and mighty.
10. Whatever end such a person becomes desirous of, whatever desire such a person desires, from his will only it arises. By means of it he is prosperous and mighty.

III

1. These desires are true (but) concealed by falsity. Although the desires are true they are concealed by the false. Since, whoever of his here departs, of him here in this world one is not able to obtain a sighting.

   False knowledge covers what is true. The desire for what is external and for relations is also due to false knowledge.

2. Now those of his here, whether they are living at present or departed and whatever else one desires but does not obtain, all of that one finds having gone there (into the self, the ether in the heart), since here, surely are those true desires concealed by falsity. Just as in that manner of those who do not know, walk again and again over a hidden treasure of gold yet do not find it, thus do all these creatures here in the world proceed daily into the Brahma-world, yet they are

unable to discover it, being swayed by falsity.

3. Surely this self is in the heart, of it, this only is the etymological explanation. This is in the heart, from that it is the heart. A person who knows this thus, surely on a daily basis is able to attain the world of heaven.

While it has been stated that all reach the state of Brahman in deep sleep, there is a distinction between a person of knowledge and one who is ignorant. The distinction is that the knower knows that he has realized Brahman whereas the ignorant do not. Again, after death only those who realized the identity of the jīva and Brahman transcend birth and rebirth and do not return.

4. Then that graceful being arising from this body and arriving at the supreme light manifests in its own form. This is the self said he (the teacher). This is immortal, beyond fear. This is Brahman. Surely, the name of this is the true.

The jīva in sleep attains the supreme self and gives up the false notion that the body is the self. During sleep it is happy and free.

5. Surely, these are the three syllables, 'sat', 'ti', 'yam'. That which is 'sat', that is immortal. What is 'yam', by means of it one holds two together. Since by means of it one holds the two together, from that it is 'yam'. A person who knows this thus, surely on a daily basis is able to attain the world of heaven.

The importance of Brahman as an object of meditation is stressed again.

IV

1. Now this self is the bridge, the support for the separation of these worlds. On this bridge neither day nor night cross, neither old age nor death, not grief, not merit, not demerit.

All evil returns form it since the Brahma-world is removed of evil.

The self is beyond time and is unaffected by merit and demerit.

2. Hence surely on crossing this bridge, if one is blind he stops being blind, if one is injured he stops being injured, if one is sorrowful he stops being sorrowful. Thus surely on crossing this bridge even night appears as day since this Brahma world is always luminous.

Bodily defects are only possible in a body. They arise due to karma. The man of knowledge is ever in light due to the light of consciousness.

3. But those alone who by means of Brahmacarya attain this world of Brahman, their's only is this world of Brahman. They become free to act as per their wishes in each and every world.

Practices which aid in the attainment of Brahman are emphasized.

V

1. Now what is generally referred to as sacrifice, that is Brahmacarya only since it is by means of Brahmacarya only does the knower achieves that (world). Now what is generally referred to as worship, that is Brahmacarya only since by worshipping by means of Brahmacarya does a person achieve the self.

The aim here is to encourage Brahmacarya by praising it. Brahmacarya is termed as a sacrifice. It is also termed as Iṣṭa since by means of this one worships the ultimate or develops a desire to attain the self.

2. Now what is generally referred to as the long sacrificial

session that is Brahmacarya only since it is by means of Brahmacarya does one achieve preservation of the true self. Now what is generally referred to as the vow of silence is that Brahmacarya only since by means of Brahmacarya only does one understand the self and meditate.

The verse highlights the similarity between 'sat trāyaṇam' and 'sataḥ trānam'. Mauna and manute are similar being derived from the root 'man'.

3. Now what is generally referred to as a period of fasting that is Brahmacarya only since this self which one achieves by means of Brahmacarya is not destroyed. Now what is generally referred to as the life of a renunciate is that Brahmacarya only. Indeed that 'Ara' and 'Ṇya' are the two oceans in the Brahma world in the third heaven from here and there lies that lake Airammadīya and there that tree that showers Soma, that unconquered city of Brahman and there is the hall of gold made by the lord.

The benefits of Brahmacarya in the spiritual path are being eulogized. It is called the highest auxiliary of knowledge.

4. Thus only they who obtain the two oceans, 'Ara' and 'Ṇya' in the Brahma world by means of Brahmacarya, to them only belongs the Brahma world. They become free to act as per their wishes in each and every world.

Brahmaloka and its objects are described. Being the effects of a pure mind the objects of Brahmaloka have greater vailidity than the objects of our day to day lives.

VI

1. Now with regard to heart's arteries, they consist of a minute substance that is reddish brown, white, blue, yellow, and red.

Indeed, the sun there is reddish brown, this is white, this is blue, this is yellow, this is red.

A person of spiritual practices free from cravings for external objects and who worships Brahman, at the time of death he goes out through the artery of the head. The colours of the substances mentioned are so due to the sun, its heat enters the various arteries and takes up these colours.

2. Just as in the manner an extensive highway goes between two villages, this one and the one there, thus the sun's rays reach both these worlds, this one and the one there. They spread out from the sun there and go into these arteries. And from these arteries they go into the sun there.
3. Thus when one is deeply asleep, entirely serene, knowing no dream, then into these arteries he enters, to him no evil touches, for he is possessed of light.

The functions of all organs are withdrawn at the time of sleep. Thus there is no contact with impurity and such a person is serene and calm. In sleep one reaches the state of pure being. One is untouched by daily experiences of pleasure and pain, for these presuppose the body and senses. Due to ignorance and residual karma the jīva returns from this state.

4. Now where this is reduced to a feeble state, those who sit in his presence say: 'Do you recognize me? Do you recognize me?' So long as he has not departed from the body, for that period he recognizes them.
5. Then when he in this manner leaves from this body then he rises upwards by means of these rays only or he ascends verily meditating on Aum. That much time it takes for the mind to travel in that time he goes to the sun. Surely, that is the door to the world, an entrance for those that know and a control for those that do not know.

6. Regarding that there is this verse: the heart's arteries are a hundred and one; of them one extends to the crown of the head. Rising upwards through that one attains immortality; the other (arteries) serve for departing in different directions indeed departing in different directions.

VII

1. The self that is free from vice, free from old age, free from mortality, free from grief, free from the pangs of hunger and thirst, whose desires the truth, whose resolve is the truth, he ought to be sought, him one should desire to clearly understand. He who has found out and knows that self obtains all worlds and all desires. So said Prajāpati.

Now are being taken up the questions that arise from the previous verse. Who is this serene being? How does this serene being have knowledge of the supreme self? These and other questions are answered here.

2. That was heard by both the gods and the demons. They said: 'Indeed let us search for that self, by searching for which one obtains all worlds and all what a person desires.' Then Indra only among all the gods proceeded to him and Virocana from the demons. Then without a covenant with each other, they both arrived in the presence of Prajāpati carrying fuel.

The immense value of knowledge seeks to be impressed upon. Knowledge ought to be sought with proper humility.

3. The two lived there for thirty-two years as Brahmacarya s. Prajāpati then asked them: 'Wishing for what have you been living here?' They both replied: 'The self that is free from vice, free from old age, free from mortality, free from grief, free from the pangs of hunger and thirst, whose desires the truth, whose resolve is the truth, he ought to be sought, him

one should desire to clearly understand. He who has found out and knows that self obtains all worlds and all desires. Illustrious sir, these words are known to be said by you. Wishing for this have we been living.'

Being eager for knowledge, Prajāpati, Indra, and Virocana put aside their enmity.

4. To them both Prajāpati said: 'This person which is viewed in the eye, this is the self.' He said, 'This is immortal, beyond fear. This is Brahman.' 'However, illustrious sir, this which is perceived in water and in a mirror, what is this?' 'What is perceived in all these us this only,' he replied.

The true self is neither the body nor the reflection self. The ātman is truly inside all.

VIII

1. 'See yourself in a bowl of water and whatever you do not know of the self, that tell me.' The two viewed the bowl of water. To the two Prajāpati asked: 'What is it that you perceive?' The two said: 'All this only, illustrious sir, we both perceive of the self's image, even the hair and nails.'

The reflection is not the self. Questions are asked by Prajāpati to clarify this.

2. To both Prajāpati then said: 'Having become excellently adorned, excellently attired, and excellently groomed look into the bowl of water.' Both then excellently adorned, excellently dressed, and excellently groomed themselves and looked into the bowl of water. 'What do you perceive?' Prajāpati asked the two?
3. They both replied: 'Illustrious sir, just in the manner as we are only excellently adorned, excellently attired,

and excellently groomed, thus are both these excellently adorned, excellently attired, and excellently groomed.' 'This is the self (Ātman).' He said. 'This is immortal, beyond fear, this is Brahman.' They both proceeded on their way with their hearts at ease.

Impurities in the mind are an obstacle to conceive the truth.

4. Prajāpati then looked at both of them and said: 'They proceed without having recognized, without having known the self. Whichever of the two will follow this doctrine, whether deities or demons, they will be defeated.' Then Virocana, his heart at ease approached the demons and stated this doctrine: 'Here in this world the (bodily) self only is to be worshipped, the self is to be served. He who worships the self here and serves the self, he achieves both worlds, this one and the distant world.'

Virocana misunderstood and thought that the body is the self.

5. Thus even here people say of a person who is not a giver, has no faith, does not perform sacrifices, 'He is called a demon.' Since this is the doctrine of the demons. They adorn the body of the departed with what they have asked for, with clothes and ornaments and think by means of this they will attain the other world.

IX

1. However, Indra prior to reaching the gods only perceived this misgiving. 'Just as in the manner as this (bodily) self is excellently adorned when this body is excellently adorned, excellently attired when this body is excellently attired and excellently groomed when this body is excellently groomed, thus that self will become blind when the body is blind, one-eyed when the body is one-eyed, deformed when the body is

deformed and is destroyed when the body is destroyed. I see no benefit in this.'

Indra's mind was purer than that of Virocana. So even though initially he did not fully understand his conception was better than that of Virocana.

2. Carrying fuel in hand he returned. To him Prajāpati said: 'Wishing for what have you returned, O Indra, since you went away along with Virocana with your heart at ease?' Indra replied: 'Just as in the manner as this (bodily) self is excellently adorned when this body is excellently adorned, excellently attired when this body is excellently attired and excellently groomed when this body is excellently groomed, thus that self will become blind when the body is blind, one eyed when the body is one eyed, deformed when the body is deformed and is destroyed when the body is destroyed. I see no benefit in this.'

   Since Prajāpati described the self as immortal and fearless, Indra realized that the self could not be the reflected body.

3. 'Thus is this only, O Indra,' said Prajāpati. 'Yet to you I will comment on this further. Stay with me another thirty-two years.' Again, he stayed with him for another thirty-two years. For him he said:

   Brahmacharya leads to better purity of the mind and therefore better comprehension.

X

1. Prajāpati stated: 'This one who moves about great in a dream, this is the self, immortal, beyond fear. This is Brahman.' Indra proceeded with his heart at ease. However, prior to reaching the gods only he perceived this misgiving. Even though this

(dream self) is not blind (while the body) is blind, is not one-eyed (while the body) is one-eyed, nor it it defective when the body is defective.

2. This is not injured (while the body) is injured. This is not oozing (through the eyes and nose) when the body is oozing (through the eyes and nose). Yet as if they kill this only, as if they go to it, it comes to experience it as unfavourable and even weeps. I see no benefit in this.
3. Carrying fuel in hand he returned. To him Prajāpati said: 'Wishing for what have you returned, O Indra, since you went away along with your heart at ease?' Indra replied: 'Illustrious sir, even though this (dream self) is not blind (while the body) is blind, is not one-eyed (while the body) is one-eyed, nor it it defective when the body is defective.'
4. 'This is not injured (while the body) is injured. This is not oozing (through the eyes and nose) when the body is oozing (through the eyes and nose). Yet as is they kill this only, as if they go to it, it comes to experience it as unfavorable and even weeps. I see no benefit in this.' 'Thus is this only, O Indra,' said Prajāpati. 'Yet to you I will comment on this further. Stay with me another thirty-two years.' Again he stayed with him for another thirty-two years. For him he said:

XI

1. He (Prajāpati) said: 'He who is wholly asleep, serene, knows no dream, this is the self, this is immortal, beyond fear, this is Brahman. Indra then proceeded with his heart at ease. However, prior to reaching the gods he perceived this misgiving. Certainly, this here does not know himself now as "I am this" nor as these beings. It appears as if he has entered into destruction. I see no benefit in this.'

Again, there is a confusion, due to wrong knowledge that there is something other than the self that may be known.

2. Carrying fuel in hand he returned. To him Prajāpati said: 'Wishing for what have you returned, O Indra, since you went away along with your heart at ease?' Indra replied, 'Illustrious sir, certainly, this here does not know himself now as "I am this" nor as these beings. It appears as if he has entered into destruction. I see no benefit in this.'

3. 'Thus is this only, O Indra,' said Prajāpati. 'Yet to you I will comment on this further. Stay with me another five years.' He stayed with him for another five years. That makes a hundred and one years. With regard to that it is said, 'Indeed for a hundred and one years Indra lived the life of a Brahmacāri with Prajāpati. For him Prajāpati said:

A disciplined life is necessary to acquire knowledge of the self.

XII

1. 'O Indra, mortal surely is this body gripped by death. Yet it is the basis of this immortal, bodiless self. Indeed, the embodied self is gripped by pleasure and pain. Certainly, there is no closure from pleasure and pain for one who is embodied. Surely one who is bodiless is beyond the reach of pleasure and pain.'

The self as has been said before is immortal, eternal, and bodiless.

2. Bodiless indeed is the air, the clouds, lightning, thunder. These too are bodiless. Now just as these spring from the distant ether and reach the supreme light issuing in his own form.

The self transcends the three stages of waking, dream, and deep sleep. It is due to ignorance that the true self is identified with the empirical self. With true knowledge this ignorance disappears and the true self is attained. Various examples are given to illustrate this such as the clouds and the sky.

3. Thus does this serene one arise from the body, reach the supreme light, and issue in its own form. He is the supreme person. There he wanders about eating, playing, rejoicing with women, rejoicing with relations, chariots, and having no memory of this body in which he was born. Just as a horse is joined to a chariot, thus in this body is this self joined only.
4. Now where this eye is connected to ether and it is the seeing person, the eye is for (the self's) seeing alone. And a person who knows, 'May I smell this', it is the self, the nose is for (the self's) smelling alone. And a person who knows, 'May I speak this', it is the self. The organ of speech is for (the self's) uttering alone. And a person who knows, 'May I hear this', it is the self, the ear is for (the self's) hearing alone.

The sense organs are instruments by which experience and knowledge of the external world is accessed. This is used as an argument for the existence of the self. The self is the one for whom the body and senses are instruments.

5. Then a person who knows, 'May I think this', it is the self and the mind is his divine eye. And indeed, he seeing these desired objects by means of his divine eye, the mind rejoices.

This verse seeks to describe the self or ātman. The nature of ātman is awareness. Its nature is knowledge. The agency of ātman is only in the context of the body and senses which are its tools and limiting adjuncts. The realized soul is one with the supreme lord. Such a soul sees all objects of past, present, and future and enjoys them. His enjoyment is the unlimited divine enjoyment.

6. Surely these are the deities in the Brahma world who meditate on the self. From that all the worlds and all that is desired is possessed by them. A person attains all the worlds

and all that is desired who knows the self and understands it. So stated Prajāpati, indeed so stated Prajāpati.

The commentary to the previous verse is meant to emphasize that the knower of Brahman is endowed with the attainment of all his desires.

XII

1. From the dark, I arrive at the varied, from the varied I arrive at the dark. Throwing off evil just as a horse his hairs, throwing off the body just as the moon releases itself from the mouth of Rāhu, I, a perfected self, attain the uncreated world of Brahman, indeed I attain it.

This verse is a mantra. It is meant to be repeated and meditated upon. The word dark is used to indicate the incomprehensible Brahman in the heart. Then is attained the variegated Brahmalok.

XIV

1. Surely what is named ether is the sustainer of name and form. That inside which they are is that Brahman, that is immortal, it is the self. I arrive at the assembly and abode of Prajāpati. I am the renown of the Brāhmaṇas, the renown of the Kṣatriyas, the renown of the Vaiśyas. May I attain that renown. I am the renown of the renowns. May I never go to that which is white and toothless yet devouring and slippery, indeed may I never go to that.

Here is contained the definition of Brahman for the purposes of meditation. Brahman is all-pervasive like the ākāśa, subtle, bodiless, and consciousness.

XV

1. This was explained to Prajāpati by Brahmā, Prajāpati to Manu, and Manu to his progeny. He who has studied the Vedas as per the prescribed rules, in the time after serving the gurus, he who after returning from the teacher's home and settles down as a householder, continues the study of the Vedas in a pure place and has noble sons, he who withdraws every sense of his into the self, who practises non-violence to all beings except when specifically ordained (by scriptures), he who thus behaves as long as he lives, attains the world of Brahman and does not turn back again. Indeed, he does not turn back again.

Here is being clarified that actions and rites performed by those that are wise also bring about excellent consequences. Further virtuous behaviour like non-violence is enjoined. Brahmaloka is said to continue for a kalpa, which is a unit of time equal to the duration of the present world cycle, for such a person.

The Taittirīya Upaniṣad

CHAPTER 1

I

1. Aum, may Mitra (the sun) be beneficial to us; may Varuna be beneficial to us; may Aryamān be beneficial to us; may Indra and Bṛhaspati be beneficial to us. May Viṣnu of great strides be beneficial to us. Obeisance to Bramhā. Obeisance to you, O Vāyu. You indeed are the perceivable Brahman. Of you indeed the perceivable Brahman will I speak. I will speak of righteousness, I will speak of truth; may that protect me; may that protect the expounder. May that protect me; may that protect the expounder. Aum, peace, peace, peace.

The benevolence of the gods is prayed for since only when the gods are benevolent will there be no obstacle in the hearing, retention, and utilization of knowledge. Vāyu is spoken of as the perceivable Brahman. Since it is proximate and needs no intermediary unlike outer organs such as the eye.

The word śāntiḥ is used three times for pacifying three kinds of obstacles, pertaining to the self (ādhyatmik), the natural (ādhibhautik), and the supernatural (ādhidaivik).

II

1. Aum, we shall explain pronunciation, letters, accent, measure, force, articulation, juxtaposition. Thus has been uttered the chapter on pronunciation.

Pronunciation is crucial since there should be no inaccuracy in recital of the text. Śīkṣām is the science of pronunciation.

III

1. May we both be famous, may we both attain the brilliance of Bramha-knowledge. Therefore we shall expound the sacred teaching regarding compilation under five categories, relating to the universe, relating to light, relating to knowledge, relating to offspring, relating to the self. These are spoken of as the great compilations. Concerning the universe, the earth is the prior form, heaven the subsequent form, ether is their conjunction. Vāyu (air) is their combination. Thus concerning the universe.

The commentary for this verse pertains to Section III.

Section III relates to the sacred teaching concerning samhitā (compilation) under five categories. This is a prayer of a student, since for a student these aims are not yet attained. The teacher has however attained that which is considered 'the good or great'. The five categories are the universe, light, knowledge, offspring, and the self. These categories are termed as 'great'. The person who meditates on these categories attains them.

2. Now concerning light, the prior form is fire, sun the subsequent form. Water is their conjunction lightning is their combination. Thus concerning light.
3. Now concerning knowledge, the prior form is the teacher, the student is the subsequent form, knowledge is their conjunction, teaching is their combination. Thus concerning knowledge.
4. Now concerning offspring, the prior form is the mother, the father is the subsequent form, the offspring is the conjunction, generation is their combination. Thus concerning offspring.

5. Now concerning the self, the prior form is the lower jaw, the upper jaw is the subsequent form, speech is the conjunction, the tongue is their combination. Thus concerning the self.
6. Thus these are the great compilations. Anyone who thus knows these great compilations as explained becomes conjoined with (attains) offspring, cattle, the brilliance of Bramha-knowledge, food, and the heavenly world.

IV

1. May Indra who is most excellent in the Vedas, who is omnipresent, who has emerged from the immortal Vedas, may he grant me intelligence, O lord, may I be the bearer of immortality.
   May I be bodily skilful, my tongue immensely sweet, with my ears may I hear plentifully. You are the shield of Brahman, covered by intelligence. May what I have heard be protected.
2. Bring to me that prosperity which makes and ever increases clothes, cattle, food, and drink and then for a non-transient duration bring to me prosperity in cattle and wool. Svāhā (hail). May Brahmacārins (students of sacred knowledge) approach me on all sides. Svāhā. May Brahmacārins approach me variously. Svāhā. May Brahmacārins approach me befittingly. Svāhā. May Brahmacārins be at peace. Svāhā.

These above two verses are meant for those who wish for intelligence and wealth. Indra is entreated to bring intelligence and wealth for such persons.

The worship of that which is pre-eminent in the Vedas—Aum is also enjoined here. Prajāpati performed penance with the aim of achieving the worlds, deities, Vedas, and the Vyāhṛtis (Bhūḥ, Bhuvaḥ, Suvaḥ). Then Aum appeared to him.

By bearer of immortality is implied knowledge of Brahman which leads to immortality. The passage in entirety is a prayer that one's body become proper and fit to attain knowledge of the self.

Intelligence is prayed for since like the scabbard is the seat of the sword, intelligence is the seat of realization or the shield of Brahman. This is followed by a request for prosperity for a fit person.

3. May I be famous amongst people. Svāhā. May I be superior to the exceedingly wealthy. Svāhā. O excellent one, may I enter into you, as you are. Svāhā. O excellent one, as you are, enter into me. Svāhā. O excellent one, in yourself, of a thousand branches may I purify my sins. Svāhā. Just as water runs down a slope, as months into a year, thus into me may students arrive. Svāhā. O giver of all, approach from every direction. Svāhā. You are a shelter, your light shines on me, to me do you reach.

Here the aspirant requests for fame, exceeding wealth and to enter and be entered by the venerable one who is the sheath of Brahman. There is also a prayer for prosperity. To reduce one's accumulated demerits, one needs to perform rites for which one needs to be prosperous. When demerits are exhausted one attains knowledge.

V

1. Indeed, the three Vyāhṛtis (utterances) are Bhūḥ, Bhuvaḥ, Suvaḥ. Of them, this forth one, Mahaḥ was made known by Māhācamasya. That is Brahman. It is the self. The other gods constitute its limbs. This Bhūḥ is indeed the world. Bhuvaḥ is the intermediate region. Suvaḥ is the other world. Mahaḥ is the sun. Verily by means of the sun do all the worlds attain greatness.
2. As regards this Bhūḥ it is indeed the fire. As regards this Bhuvaḥ it is the air. As regards this Suvaḥ it is the sun. As

regards this Mahaḥ it is the moon. Verily by means of the moon do all celestial bodies attain greatness.

3. As regards Bhūḥ it is indeed the Ṛg Veda; As regards Bhuvaḥ it is the Sāmā Veda. As regards Suvaḥ it is the Yajur Veda. As regards Mahaḥ it is the Brahman. The Vedas are great. Surely it is due to Brahman.

These three verses speak about the three vyāhṛtis. It is then stated that there is a fourth namely mahaḥ. Here the meditation on Brahman as embodied in the vyāhṛtis is being enjoined upon. The vyāhṛti maha is great. It is Brahman and it is the self. The other vyāhṛtis are encompassed by the self in this form (the form of mahaḥ).

4. As regards Bhūḥ it is indeed prāṇa (in-breath). As regards Bhuvaḥ it is apāna (out-breath). As regards Suvaḥ it is vyāna (diffused breath). As regards mahaḥ it is the food. Surely, by means of food do all the vital breaths attain greatness.
5. Surely these four are four kinds. The vyāhrtis are four and four. A person who knows them, he knows Brahman. For him do all the deities carry offerings.

The commentary to the above-mentioned two verses points out that these vyāhṛtis are four and each is of four kinds. These verses also strictly state a rule regarding the sequence of their meditation.

VI

1. In this space which is inside the heart is this Puruṣa (person) who is made of mind, immortal and golden. This which is in-between the palates like a nipple, that is the path of Brahman; where the ends of the hair divide, it passes out by splitting the skull of the head. (On passing through this path a person) is established in fire as Bhūḥ, in air as Bhuvaḥ.

2. In the sun Suvaḥ, in Brahman Mahaḥ. He obtains the dominion of heaven. He attains mastery over the mind, mastery of speech, mastery of sight, mastery of hearing, mastery of intelligence. Thus and more he becomes Brahman whose body is ether, whose self is truth, whose delight is the vital breath, whose mind is bliss, which is richly endowed with peace, is immortal. Thus do you meditate, O Prācīnayogya.

These two verses of Section V emphasize the importance of meditation. Within the heart is a space ākāśaḥ and within this is the Puruṣa, the person. The Puruṣa is derived as per the commentary from śayana (sleeping) within the city or puri; or who fills up—pūrṇa the worlds. The Puruṣa is manomayaḥ (consists of knowledge), immortal and golden. The verse which states 'a person is established in fire as Bhūḥ, means that an enlightened person, by means of his identity with fire pervades the world and similarly in air with Bhuvaḥ, in the sun with suvaḥ. He who identifies with the fourth vyāhṛti, mahaḥ becomes established in Brahman. He becomes a sovereign over all others.'

VII

1. The earth, atmosphere, heaven, the primary quarters and the intermediate quarter; fire, air, the sun, the moon and stars; water, plants, trees, sky, and the body these are with regard to the all-pervading natural existence. Then with regard to the personal, prāṇa, vyāna, apāna, udāna and samāna, eyes, ears, the mind, speech, touch, skin, flesh, muscles, bones, marrow. Having envisaged these the seer said: 'Indeed, all this is fivefold. Verily by means of the fivefold is one granted the fivefold.'

In this verse is being enumerated the groups of five natural things and deities which regards what is ādhibhutam. Next regarding the personal, ādhyātamam are three groups of five, vital forces, sense organs and five material constituents of the body. By 'is one granted the fivefold' is meant that a person who realizes all this as being fivefold, becomes identified with Prajāpati. Prajāpati as stated in the commentary is constituted by the five elements.

VIII

1. As regards Aum it is Brahman. As regards Aum it is all this. As regards Aum it is indeed concurrence. Moreover on uttering 'Aum recite', they recite. They sing the Sāman chants with Aum. They recite hymns while uttering the words 'Aum Śom'. The Advarya priest utters the response by means of Aum. By means of Aum does the Bramhā (priest) utter the initial accolades. By means of Aum does one assent to the performance of the Agnihotra sacrifice. A Brāhmaṇa (who) utters Aum wishing 'may I attain Brahman', indeed, he does attain.

Once again it is stated that Aum is Brahman. This, that Aum as a word is Brahman, ought to be meditated upon. Aum is 'all this'. Aum permeates everything.

IX

1. Righteousness and self study and expounding; truth and self study and expounding; religious austerity and self study and expounding; self restraint and self study and expounding; calmness and self study and expounding; the (sacrificial) fires and self study and expounding; the Agnihotra sacrifice and self study and expounding; guests and self study and

expounding; humanity and self study and expounding; progeny and self study and expounding; generating and self study and expounding; a grandson to be raised and self study and expounding. Truth as per Satyavacās, of the line of Rāthītaraḥ; religious austerity as per Taponityah, son of Puruśiṣṭi, a self study and expounding alone as per Nāka, son of Mudgala. That indeed is religious austerity. Indeed, that is religious austerity.

Here is emphasized the importance of truth, religious austerity, and self study.

X

1. I am the driving force of the tree (of the world). My glory is like the peak of a mountain. I am a result of the pure (Brahman) like the sun I am immortal. I am splendid wealth, possessed of excellent intellect, immortal, undecaying. Thus the recitation of Triśanku after realization.

Triśanku was a sage who knew Brahman and attained Brahman. Repetition of mantras of the Vedic texts leads to the acquiring of knowledge of the self as was the case with Triśanku.

XI

1. Being well versed in the Vedas the teacher instructs the students. Speak truthfully, act righteously. Ensure that there be no negligence regarding your study. Having offered wealth to the teacher that pleases (him), do not cut off the line of progeny. There should be no carelessness with regard to truth. Let there be no negligence of righteousness. Let there be no negligence of what is auspicious. Let there be no negligence of welfare. Let there be no negligence of self

study and teaching. Let there be no negligence with regard to duties for the gods and the ancestors.

After the instruction regarding texts now is enjoined scriptural duties. Truth, which is gathered by valid means of knowledge and is correct to be spoken, righteousness, sincerity in study and continuation of the family, these are emphasized. The verse calls for righteousness in conduct and action.

2. You must be one for whom the mother is a goddess. You must be one for whom the father is a god. You must be one for whom the teacher is a god. You must be one for whom the guest is a god. Whichever actions are faultless these are to be practised, not the rest. Those deeds of ours which are virtuous are to be followed by you, not the rest.
Commentary for verses 2 (i) to 6:

The commentary for verses 2 (i) to 6 of this chapter emphasizes that one ought to perform all duties sincerely in respect of ancestors and deities. Parents, teachers, guests are to be treated as gods (Atithi devo bhava). Good conduct, that which is not prohibited by the scriptures, are to be performed consistently. Further whatever is donated or given should be given with faith and humility.

Next the commentary takes up the important question of knowledge (vidya), karma, and liberation. The questions are:

(i) Whether the supreme aim, liberation can be obtained only by karma?
(ii) Or by karmas along with vidyā?
(iii) Or is it obtained by the mutual combination of karma and vidyā?
(iv) Or is it obtained by knowledge along with karma?
(v) Or only by means of knowledge?

After discussing various attempts to answer these questions and objections raised it is stated that vidyā and karma cannot be combined since they are different. From the point of view of liberation knowledge does not depend on karma. Yet on the dissipation of sins does knowledge emerge. In the commentary it is asserted that the supreme end, liberation is attainable only by means of vidyā.

3. Those who are better than us (Brāhmaṇas) you should comfort them by offering a seat. An offering should be given with respect, it should not be given without respect, the offering should be plentiful, the offering should be made with modesty, the offering should be made with awe and it should be pleasing.
4. Now if you are uncertain with respect to any actions, or with respect to any conduct, you ought to behave in these matters as the learned persons there who are capable of judging, intent on (virtuous acts), not directed by others, not harsh, desirous of merit, would behave in such cases.
5. Now regarding those who are falsely charged, you ought to behave in these matters as the learned persons, there who are capable of judging, intent on (virtuous acts), not directed by others, not harsh, desirous of merit, would behave in such cases.
6. This is the order, this is the prescription. This is the secret teaching of the Veda. This is the teaching. (All this) is to be performed thus. Indeed, this is to be performed thus.

XII

1. (Aum) May Mitra (the sun) be beneficial to us; may Varuna be beneficial to us; may Aryamān be beneficial to us; may Indra and Bṛhaspati be beneficial to us; may Viṣnu of great strides be beneficial to us. Obeisance to Bramhā. Obeisance to you, O Vāyu. You indeed are the perceivable Brahman. Of

you indeed, the perceivable Brahman have I spoken. I have spoken of righteousness. I have spoken of what is true. May that protect me, may that protect the expounder. Indeed, may that protect me. May that protect the speaker. Aum, peace, peace, peace.

CHAPTER 2

I

Invocation

May he defend us both together. May he be benign to us both together. May we both become full of vigour; may our study be splendid; may there be no dispute amongst us. Aum, peace, peace, peace.

1. Aum. (They who) know Brahman attain the supreme. With regard to this the following has been uttered: who knows Brahman as true, as knowledge, as unending, situated in the secret cavity of the heart and in the highest sky, obtains all desires together with Brahman, the learned. From this ātman (self) indeed originated ether; from ether air; from air arose fire; from fire arose water; from water arose the earth and from the earth originated medicinal plants and food, from food human beings.

   This indeed is the person whose essence is food. This verily is the head, this the southern side, this the northern side, this is the self, this the lower part, which (serves as the) foundation. As to that also is this śloka (verse).

   The knower of Brahman attains the supreme. In the

commentary it is further stated that the individual self which is Brahman, falsely identifies with the different sheaths thus limiting it. The self then accepts that which is the non-self. The first line, 'The knower of Brahman attains the supreme', is the central theme. Further it will be stated that Brahman is not different from the self.

Brahman as truth, knowledge and that which is unending is meant to be a definition of Brahman. Knowledge cannot be distinguished from the self. However, the intellect serves as a limiting adjunct. Consciousness is also inherent to Brahman. Brahman is unending, infinite.

II

1. Indeed, all creatures that exist on the earth are born from food. As also, by means of food only they live. Then into this do they go at the end. Food, indeed, is the firstborn of beings. Therefore it is called the medicine for all. Indeed, they who meditate on food as Brahman obtain all food. Indeed, food is the eldest of all beings. Thus it is called the medicine for all. Beings are born of food. After being born, they develop by food. It eats beings and is eaten, thus it is called food.
Indeed, distinct from this and inside that whose essence is food is the self that consists of prāṇa (vital breath). By means of that is this filled. Indeed, this is of human form. Indeed he (the self) which is this, is also of the human form. His human form is based on the human form of that (previous one). Of this verily, prāṇa is the head; vyāna (diffused breath) is the right side; apāna (out-breath) is the left side; ether is the self, the earth is the lower part, (which serves as) the foundation. As to that also is this śloka.

The source of all living beings is food. All beings subsist on food. One who meditates on food as Brahman attains all food. Next the text states that Brahman is the indwelling self, the blissful self, which is innermost of all selves starting form the physical sheath.

III

1. The deities breathe along with prāṇa so do those who are humans and animals. Indeed, prāṇa is the life of beings. From that it is called the life of all creatures. Those who worship vital breath as Brahman, they indeed attain a full life span, since prāṇa is the life of all beings. Thus it is called the life of all. Of the previous (physical sheath) one, this (life) is verily the embodied self. Indeed, different from that and from within this which consists of prāṇa is the self which consists of mind. By means of that this is full. Indeed, that self which is this only has the form of a human only. Thus a person's human form of this (mental body) is similar to the human form of that (vital body). The Yajur mantras are its head; the Ṛg mantras are its right side; the Sāma mantras are its left side; the teachings are its self; the hymns of the Atharvans and the Aṅgirasas are the lower part, (which serves as) the foundation. As to that also is this śloka.

The importance and role of breath and the vital force prāṇa is being discussed here. The deities become active by means of prāṇa with regard to the physical body. The senses become active by means of breathing. He who meditates on prāṇa as the self of all beings attains a full lifespan. They do not meet an untimely or accidental death. Full lifespan is interpreted to mean a hundred years.

IV

1. While having being unable to obtain it speech returns along with the mind, the wise after attaining the bliss of Brahman

does not fear anything whatsoever. Verily this is the embodied self of the prior (life). Indeed, distinct from that and from inside this which consists of the mind is the self constituted by wisdom. By means of that this is full. Indeed, that self which is this has the form of a human only. Thus a person's human form is similar to the human form of that earlier one. Its head is faith. Righteousness its right side; truth its left side; yoga (union) the self; and the principle mahat its lower part, (which serves as) the foundation. Regarding that is this śloka.

The self constituted by wisdom is discussed here. Vijñāna is wisdom regarding the contents of the Vedas. The self which is constituted by vijñāna is vijñānamayaḥ. From knowledge arises faith. Faith precedes all duties and can be termed the head. This cognitive self is supported by mahat, the firstborn.

V

1. Wisdom actualizes a sacrifice and also actualizes deeds. All the deities meditate on the firstborn Brahman which is wisdom. If a person knows Brahman as wisdom and is not negligent (about it) he lays all his sins in the body and obtains all desires. Verily this (cognitive) one is the embodied self of the prior (mental) one. Indeed, distinct from that and from inside this which consists of wisdom is the self constituted by bliss. By means of that this is full. Indeed, that self which is this has the form of a human only. Thus a person's human form is similar to the human form of that earlier one. Its head is joy. Its right side is pleasure; its left side is rejoicing; Its self is bliss; Brahman is (which serves as) the foundation. Regarding that is this śloka.

Continuing from the last verse the point is made that knowledge is the doer since knowledge actualizes a sacrifice. The cognitive self is Brahman. If a person abandons all erroneous ideas of identity with the physical self, etc., he lays aside all sins and enjoys all that is desirable. The blissful self is not the supreme self. It is more internal than the cognitive self. It is constituted by bliss.

VI

1. Indeed, he who knows Brahman as non-real, he (himself) becomes non-real. If one knows Brahman as existing, from that such a person is known as existing. Verily, of that prior (cognitive) one, this is the embodied self. Thus now these questions follow. Does any unwise person having departed after death go to the other world? Or does any wise person after departing this world obtain the other world?
He (the self) desired 'let me be many, let me take birth'. He practised austerities. Having practised austerity all this he created, whatsoever there is. That (Brahman) having created that (all this), verily he entered it. Having entered it he became the real and the formless, the explained and the unexplained; the refuge and the non-refuge, the wise and the unwise, the true and the non-true. As true he became all this that there is. That they call the truth. Regarding that is this śloka.

The person who realizes the existence of Brahman is known as worthy by all. One who denies the existence of Brahman is asat (unrighteousness). Someone may erroneously infer the non-existence of Brahman since it has no distinctions and is omnipresent. Thus various questions in this regard are taken up in the commentary. The truth of Brahman is affirmed by speaking of its existence. There is only one absolute truth, Brahman. Relative truths are found in the empirical world. The one Brahman which is truth, knowledge, and unending, became all that there is. There is no existence for all modification of name and form except that of Brahman.

VII

1. Indeed, at first this was all non-existent. From that indeed was born the existent. That created itself as a soul. Thus that is referred to as the well-made.
Indeed that which is well-made, surely its essence is existence. Indeed in obtaining this essence one is blissful. For surely who could live, who could breathe if this bliss was not there in the space (in the heart). This surely is what gives bliss. For truly whenever one gets fearlessly established in him who is unseen, bodiless, inexplicable and unsupported, then he attains the state of fearlessness. When, however, there is in this (soul) uncertainty present, created in it, then his state is one of fear. That indeed is the terror of the learned that does not deliberate. Regarding that is this śloka.

The word 'asat' is used here to refer to the unmanifested state of Brahman, that is the state where there are no distinctions in terms of name and form. It does not indicate non-existence. From this the manifested state was self-created by Brahman. Brahman is thus called the sukṛtam, self creator. The word sukṛta is also used to denote merit or virtue and from this point also Brahman is sukṛta, the cause of virtue.

Further from the fact of sukṛta it is clear that Brahman exists. Further proofs are given in the commentary for the existence of Brahman. Brahman is the source of bliss or joy. It is for the purpose of Brahman that activities of the body and senses take place. Brahman is inexpressible and also the cause of fear in the ignorant and the cause of fearlessness in the enlightened. Who reaches the state of fearlessness? Those who do not perceive anything other than the self, nor create any differences within the self.

VIII

1. The wind blows due to fear of him. Due to (this) fear does the sun rise. Due to fear of him do Agni and Indra and death the fifth run.

   This is a deep reflection regarding bliss. May there be a youth, a virtuous youth, learned, quick in action, resolute, mighty, may this entire earth be filled with wealth for him. It is one unit of human bliss.

   That which is human bliss multiplied a hundred times is one unit of bliss of the man-gandharvas, also of one proficient in the Vedas and not influenced by desire.

   That which is the bliss of man-gandharvas multiplied a hundred times is one unit of bliss of the divine-gandharvas, also of one proficient in the Vedas and not influenced by desire.

   That which is the bliss of divine-gandharvas multiplied a hundred times is one unit of bliss of the ancestors in their everlasting world, also of one proficient in the Vedas and not influenced by desire.

   That which is the bliss of ancestors in their everlasting world multiplied a hundred times is one unit of bliss of the gods who are so born by birth, also of one proficient in the Vedas and not influenced by desire.

   That which is the bliss of the gods who are so born by birth multiplied a hundred times is one unit of bliss of gods known as karma-devas, who reach the gods through work, also of one proficient in the Vedas and not influenced by desire.

   That which is the bliss of the gods known as karma-devas multiplied a hundred times is one unit of bliss of gods, also of one proficient in the Vedas and not influenced by desire.

   That which is the bliss of the gods multiplied a hundred times is one unit of bliss of Indra, also of one proficient in the Vedas and not influenced by desire.

That which is the bliss of Indra multiplied a hundred times is one unit of bliss of Bṛhaspati, also of one proficient in the Vedas and not influenced by desire.
That which is the bliss of Bṛhaspati multiplied a hundred times is one unit of bliss of Prajāpati, also of one proficient in the Vedas and not influenced by desire.
That which is the bliss of Prajāpati multiplied a hundred times is one unit of bliss of Brahmā, also of one proficient in the Vedas and not influenced by desire.
He who is in this person and who is there in the sun are one. The person who knows this after having departed from this world obtains this self consisting of food, obtains this self consisting of prāṇa, obtains this self consisting of mind, obtains this self consisting of wisdom, obtains this self consisting of bliss.
Regarding that is this śloka.

As has been already stated, Brahman is bliss. Here bliss is being discussed. Bliss may arise in two ways, firstly from contact of subject and object like the case of worldly happiness or secondly, bliss that is intrinsic. Worldly bliss is only a minute particle of the bliss that is Brahman. Worldly bliss is transient. In this verse it is shown that bliss keeps significantly increasing from that of the man-gandharvas to the bliss of Hiraṇyagarbhas per the decline of ignorance and desire.

IX

1. (While) having being unable to obtain it speech returns along with the mind, the wise after attaining the bliss of Brahman does not fear anything whatsoever. Verily he is not afflicted by the pain of 'Why have I not performed virtuous deeds? Why have I performed bad deeds?' He who knows thus extricates the self from both these (thoughts). Indeed,

he who knows thus extricates the self from both these. Such is the secret teaching.

Words cannot be applied to Brahman, it is inexpressible. It is beyond concepts and words. The wise person who knows the bliss of Brahman, that is independent of the relation of subject and object, is eternal and inherent, such a person is fearless for there is no cause of fear. For there is nothing distinct to be afraid of.

CHAPTER 3

I

1. Indeed, Bṛghu son of Varuṇa, went to Varuṇa, his father and requested: 'O illustrious sir, teach me Brahman.' For him he (Varuṇa) expounded as follows: 'Food, vital breath, the eye, the ear, mind, speech.'
   For him he expounded: 'Indeed from which all is born, having been born that through which they live, having departed that into which they merge. That, strive to know. That is Brahman.
   He practised penance. Having practised penance—

   Bṛghu son of Varuṇa requests his father to teach him about Brahman. The father speaks of food (the body), prāṇa (vital breath, the eater) and the aids to cognition, the various senses, which are the doors to Brahman's realization. Brahman is that from which all beings originate, by means of which they live and into which they merge at dissolution.

II

1. He knew this food is Brahman. Surely indeed these beings are born from food, having been born they live by means of food, and into food when departing they merge.

Having realized that verily he again went to his father Varuṇa and requested: 'O illustrious sir, teach me Brahman.' To him he (Varuṇa) expounded: 'By means of penance strive to know Brahman, Brahman is penance.'
He practised penance. Having practised penance—

Food is stated to be Brahman. Food is that from which all beings originate, by means of which they live and into which they merge at dissolution.

III

1. He knew this prāṇa is Brahman. Surely indeed these beings are born from prāṇa, having been born they live by means of prāṇa, and into prāṇa when departing they merge.
Having realized that verily he again went to his father, Varuṇa and requested: 'O illustrious sir, teach me Brahman.' To him he (Varuṇa) expounded: 'Through penance strive to know Brahman, Brahman is penance.'
He practised penance. Having practised penance—

Prāṇa is stated to be Brahman. Prāṇa is that from which all beings originate, by means of which they live and into which they merge at dissolution.

IV

1. He knew this mind is Brahman. Surely indeed these beings are born from mind, having been born they live by means of mind, and into mind when departing they merge.
Having realized that verily he again went to his father, Varuṇa, and requested: 'O illustrious sir, teach me Brahman.' To him he (Varuṇa) expounded: 'Through penance strive to know Brahman, Brahman is penance.'
He practised penance. Having practised penance—

Mind is stated to be Brahman. Mind is that from which all beings originate, by means of which they live and into which they merge at the time of dissolution.

V

1. He knew this wisdom is Brahman. Surely indeed these beings are born from wisdom, having been born they live by means of wisdom and into wisdom when departing they merge.
Having realized that verily he again went to his father Varuṇa and requested 'O illustrious sir, teach me Brahman.' To him he (Varuṇa) expounded: 'Through penance strive to know Brahman, Brahman is penance.'
He practised penance. Having practised penance—

Wisdom is stated to be Brahman. Wisdom is that from which all beings originate, by means of which they live and into which they merge at the time of dissolution.

VI

1. He knew this bliss is Brahman. Surely indeed these beings are born from bliss, having been born they live by means of bliss and into bliss when departing they merge.
This knowledge of Bṛghu and Varuṇa culminates in the supreme heaven. A person who knows this becomes firmly established. Such a person becomes a possessor and eater of food. He becomes fortunate in progeny, cattle and in the brilliance of sacred knowledge as well as in glory.

By means of penance and in stages from food, Bṛghu attained the supreme bliss which is Brahman. The preceding verses and this verse aim to convey that a person who wishes to attain Brahman ought to meditate on both internal and external organs as an excellent form of penance. A person who concentrates as recommended above attains the bliss that is Brahman, he attains Brahman.

VII

1. Do not criticize food. That is the vow. Indeed the vital breath is food. The body is established in vital breath. The vital breath is established in the body. This food is established in food. The person who realizes this that food is established in food becomes firmly established. Such a person becomes a possessor and eater of food. He becomes fortunate in progeny, cattle, and in the brilliance of sacred knowledge as well as in glory.

The purport of this verse is to emphasize the importance and praiseworthy nature of food. Food is a means for the realization of Brahman. The relationship between the body and prāṇa (vital breath) is also discussed. As per the principle that whatever is encompassed by something else, becomes food for that something else, both the body and prāṇa are mutually food and the eater. Prāṇa is lodged in the body and again the body is fixed is prāṇa. Since they are situated in each other they are both food. Since they support each other, they are both eaters.

VIII

1. Do not discard food. That is the vow. Indeed water is food. Light is said to be that which eats food. Light is based on water, water resides in light. This food is based in food. A person who knows this that food is established in food becomes firmly established. Such a person becomes a possessor and eater of food. He becomes fortunate in progeny, cattle, and in the brilliance of sacred knowledge as well as in glory.

This verse is also in praise of food. Food should not be wasted.

IX

1. Make food abundantly. That is the vow. Indeed the earth is food. Ether is said to be that which eats food. Ether is based in earth. earth is established in ether. This food is based in food. He who knows this that food is established in food becomes firmly established. Such a person becomes a possessor and eater of food. He becomes fortunate in progeny, cattle, and in the brilliance of sacred knowledge as well as in glory.

This verse relates to the previous one. The vow to make food abundant is enjoined on the person who worships fire and water as possessing the qualities of food and the eater of food.

X

1. Do not deny shelter to anyone. That is the vow. Therefore one should obtain abundant amounts of food by any means. It is said food is prepared for him. Indeed, if this food is offered at an early stage, food is given to him in the early stage. Indeed, if food is offered at the middle stage, food is given to him at the middle stage. Indeed, if food is offered at the end stage, food is given to him last.
2. Who thus knows this as beneficial in speech, as obtaining and securing the in-breath and out-breath, as action in their hands, as motion in the feet, as discharge from the anus, these are as regards human recognitions. Then with regard to the deities (Brahman may be contemplated) as contentment in rain, as might in lightning.

In both the preceeding verses, the vow is not to deny shelter to anyone. Along with shelter food is to be given. The significance of the giving of food is stated. The giver of food gets food just in the manner that he offers food.

Brahman ought to be meditated upon as that which exists in speech. Brahman ought to be meditated upon as existing in out-breath and in-breath, in the aspect of acquiring and preserving.

3. Brahman is to be meditated on as good fortune in cattle, as great luminosity in the stars, as procreation, immortality, and bliss in the organ of generation, as the entirety of space. One should meditate on that as the support, thus one is supported. One should meditate on that as great, thus one becomes great. One should meditate on that as mind, thus one is able to reflect.
4. One should meditate on that by paying obeisance, thus desirable things bow down to one. One should meditate on that as the foremost, thus one becomes possessed of the foremost. One should meditate on that as Brahman's medium of destruction, thus one's enemies perish, as do those enemies whom one dislikes.
He that is here in human form and he that is there in the sun are one.

Both the preceeding verses enjoin meditation on Brahman in different aspects. A person who meditates on Brahman as being the sustainer, such a person is himself well established. All effects are Brahman only. A person who meditates on these effects comes to possess them.

Space is Brahman's medium of destruction. One ought to meditate on this to vanquish one's enemies.

5. Thus a person who knows having departed from this world attains that self which consists of food, attains that self which consists of vital breath, attains that self which consists of mind, attains that self which consists of wisdom, attains that self which consists of bliss, traversing these

worlds eating food as he wishes and taking forms as he wishes. He sits singing this Sāma song.

Ah joy; ah joy; ah joy.

6. I am the food, I am the food, I am the food. I am the eater of food, I am the eater of food, I am the eater of food. I am the unifying force, I am the unifying force, I am the unifying force. I am the foremost of this world, prior to the gods. I am at the core of immortality. Whoever gives me thus (as food) he indeed protects me as I am. I who are food, eat he who eats food without offering. I overwhelm the whole universe. I am resplendent like the sun. He who knows thus (attains such results). This is the secret teaching.

The last two verses seek to explain part of the verse in II. I, namely, 'who knows Brahman as true, knowledge, unending, obtains all desires, together with Brahman'. How does a knower obtain all desires in the state of identity with Brahman? The answer stated in the commentary is that it is possible since he becomes the self of all.

The Praśna Upaniṣad

1. Aum O gods, let us through our ears hear what is auspicious, O who are worthy of worship, let us through our eyes see what is auspicious; while offering praise with stable limbs may we be contended with a life which is as desired by the gods.
2. May Indra of expanding fame bestow good fortune on us, may the all-knowing Pūṣan bestow good fortune upon us. May Bṛhaspati bestow good fortune upon us. Aum, peace, peace, peace.

Question 1

1. Sukeśā son of Bharadvāja, Satyakāma son of Śibi, the grandson of Sūrya, born in the line of Garga, Kausalya son of Aśvala, Bhārgava of Vidharbha, and Kabandhī descended from Kātya, all of them verily devoted to Brahman, dedicated to realizing Brahman and striving to attain the supreme Brahman, with sacrificial fuel in hand approached the revered Pippalāda believing that he would certainly tell them everything about it.

   As per the commentary the persons mentioned in this verse were focused on the lower Brahman and mistook it for the higher Brahman. They were also searching for the supreme Brahman. What is this (Brahman)? It is eternal and to be realized.

2. The sage said to them: 'Live here for a year in a proper manner with austerity, Brahmacarya (chastity), and faith. Then raise questions as desired. If we know, certainly, we

shall explain all that.'

3. Afterwards Kabandhī of the line of Kātya, went to him and asked: 'Revered sir, from what cause indeed are all these beings born?'

4. To him he said: 'Indeed, the lord of all creatures, Prajāpati desired progeny. He undertook penance. Having done penance, he generated a couple—matter and prāṇa (the breath of life or vital breath) thinking that this pair would generate creatures for him in diverse ways.'

   'The lord of creatures Prajāpati, evolved at the start of a cycle of creation as Hiraṇyagarbha, the lord of all, moving and unmoving. He performed penance regarding objects mentioned in the Vedas. He created a couple which would produce other creatures.

5. Surely the sun is prāṇa. Surely matter is the moon. Surely matter is all this, corporeal and subtle. Therefore, whatever is corporeal is itself matter.

   The sun is prāṇa, the eater, the fire. The food is the moon. The eater and eaten are one. They are Prajāpati who has created a couple.

6. Now then, the sun rises and enters the eastern direction. By this, into its rays, it absorbs all creatures in the east. When it enters the west, the south, the north, when it reaches the lowest and the highest, and it enters the in between spaces, it is that which illuminates all, thereby all living things are absorbed into its rays.

   As it rises the sun is visible to all creatures. It pervades the eastern direction and pervades all creatures by its light. Similarly with the western, southern, and northern direction. It illuminates all living things.

7. He is this, which is identified with all beings, who assumes all forms, life-breath and fire, who rises up. This which has been

spoken of is stated in the (following) mantra.

8. The possessor of all forms, golden, enlightened, that to which all are devoted, the one light, the giver of heat. It is possessed of a thousand rays and exists in a hundred forms, it is the life of all creatures, this is the sun that rises.

Those who realize Brahman, realize first as their own soul the sun as described above, as the life of all creatures.

9. Surely the year is the ruler of all creatures. Of him there are two paths, the northern and the southern. In that way, verily who worship, thinking sacrifice and acts of public good, etc., are our work, conquer indeed the world of the moon. Indeed such persons come back again. Thus the seers who desire offspring resort to the southern path. This which is the path of the ancestors is indeed food.

The year is the lord of all creatures. It is a combination of lunar days (tithi) with solar days and nights, that is the sun and moon. The commentary dwells on two paths, each of a duration of six months, the southern and northern. Those who perform rites and other actions with an aim to obtain their results, but do not follow what is eternal and uncreated, they conquer the world of the moon, enjoy the fruit of their deeds, and after this is exhausted are born again, in this world or an inferior one.

10. Now, those who search for the self, through penance, Brahmacarya, faith, and knowledge, they attain the sun by means of the northern route. This indeed is the support of all that lives; that is immortal, fearless, this is the supreme goal. From this there is no return. This is unrealizable (to the ignorant). Regarding that is this verse.

Those who strive to know the self proceed via the northern path. They strive for the self by means of penance, Brahmacharya, faith, and knowledge. This is the supreme goal for those who meditate and for those who meditate as well as perform rites. From this path one does not return. This path is unattainable for the ignorant.

11. Some speak of (this sun) as having five feet, as the father, possessed of twelve forms, in the exalted part of heaven, full of water. Then, there are others who call him omniscient and possessing (a chariot) of seven wheels and six spokes on which is set (all creation).

In the commentary it is stated that the five feet are used to mean the seasons. The seasons are that by which the sun revolves. He is known as the father since he generates all. The twelve forms are the twelve months. Others say he is possessed of seven wheels and six spokes or seasons. From either viewpoint it is the year, the embodiment of time, the lord of all, the sun and the moon, which is the cause of the world.

12. Surely the month is the ruler of all creatures. The dark fortnight is the substance, the bright fortnight is his prāṇa. Therefore the sages conduct sacrifices in the bright fortnight, the others in the other (fortnight).

Of the month, the kṛṣṇapakṣaḥ is the dark fortnight. It is food, the moon. The śukla, is the bright fortnight, the prāṇa, the eater, the fire, the sun. Sages who realize all, perform sacrifices in the bright fortnight, even though they may be conducting them in the dark fortnight, since they do not perceive anything apart from prāṇa. Those who do not see prāṇa, perform (their sacrifices) in the dark fortnight, even though they may be conducting them in the bright fortnight.

13. Surely day and night are the ruler of all creatures. Of this, day verily is prāṇa and night certainly is matter. They who indulge in passion by day exhaust their prāṇa. They that

indulge in passion by night is indeed Brahmacarya.

14. Surely food is the ruler of all creatures. From food indeed is semen generated. From that these offspring are born.

From food originates the human seed, from which originates creatures. Beings are born by means of pairs, starting with the sun and the moon and ending at day and night by means of food, blood, and semen.

15. This, those who undertake the vow of the lord of creatures produce pairs. For them only is this world of Bramhā, in which are established (the virtues) of penance, Brahmacarya, and truth.
16. For their sake is that pure world of Brahman in whom there is no dishonesty, falsehood, or deceit.

The northern course is pure, untainted. Then untainted seers, Brahmacaris, who undertake meditation and penance, for them is the world of Brahman.

Question II

1. Then Bhārgava of Vidharbha put a question to him: 'Revered sir, how many deities, indeed, sustain the creatures (of the world)? Which among them illuminate this? And who among them has primacy?'
2. To him he said: 'Ether in fact is this deity and also wind, fire, water, earth, speech, mind, eye, and ear. Having thrown light on it they say, "We are the foundation for this body and we hold it together".'

Ether is this deity, as well as wind, fire, water, earth, which are the material causes of the body. Also speech, mind, the eyes, and the ears which are the organs of knowledge and action. The deities who preside over the body and organs uphold the aggregate (body and senses).

3. To them, the pre-eminent prāṇa, said: 'Do not hold this delusion, it is I only by dividing myself five-fold, become the foundation of this body and hold it together.' They did not believe him.

   To those alluded to in the last verse, the pre-eminent prāṇa said: 'Do not hold this delusion.' It is prāṇa that upholds the aggregate of body and organs. They did not believe him.

4. Through pride he appeared to be rising up (from the body). When he rose, indeed all the others rose. When he rested all the others rested too. Just as all the bees rise when the king of bees rises and as they rest when the king of bees rests, thus speech, mind, eye, ear, etc. They being pleased praised prāṇa.

   Noticing their disbelief, prāṇa appeared to rise. All the other organs rose with him. When prāṇa was calm, the organs were calm. They realized the greatness of prāṇa.

5. This (prāṇa) as fire, burns, this is the sun. This is the cloud, this is Indra, this is air, this is the earth, substance, deities. This is being and non-being and which is immortal.
6. In the manner of a chariot wheel and the spokes in its centre, just as spokes in the centre of a chariot wheel, all is established on prāna; the Ṛks (verses), Yajus (formulas), and Sāmans (chants) as well as sacrifice, power, and wisdom.
7. As ruler of creatures it is thou that moves in the womb; it is thou only that takes birth again. O prāṇa, it is for you, who reside with the life-breaths, that these creatures bring offerings.

   The aim of this verse is to bring out that prāṇa is one with all. Food, gifts, etc., are only for prāṇa.

8. O prāṇa, thou are the foremost bearer (of gifts) for the

deities, thou are the first gift to the world of fathers, thou are the the true conduct of the seers, of the lines of Atharvan and Angiras.

Prāṇa is also the best carrier of offerings to the deities and ancestors. The conduct of prāṇa is true and right and consists in maintaining the body and eyes.

9. O prāṇa, thou are Indra, by your splendour thou are Rudra, the protector on every side. Thou moves in the sky as the sun, the lord of all that is illuminated.

   Prāṇa is splendid. The lord of all that is illuminated.

10. When thou come down as rain all these creatures are able to breathe. They remain in a blissful state (believing) that there will be as much food as they wish.

    Prāṇa pours down as rain leading to food and nourishment. Prāṇa is the nourisher of creatures.

11. O prāṇa, thou are perpetually pure, thou are always pure, O prāna, the sole seer, the eater of food, the ruler of all that exists. We are the givers of (that) food. Thou are our father, O Mātariśvā.

    As per the commentary prāṇa is pure by nature. Prāṇa is the eater of offerings, the lord of all. Prāṇa is the father of the universe.

12. That aspect of yours that is established in the organ of speech or in the ear or in the eye, this which pervades the mind, may that be a blessing. Do not rise away.

    There is an aspect of prāṇa in the sense organs. If prāṇa withdraws the sense organs become inactive.

13. All of this (in the world) is subject to the rule of prāṇa, which

is firmly established in the three worlds. Protect us like a mother protects her sons and bestow upon us intelligence and wealth.

Everything here, all that is desirable, is under the control of prāṇa. Hence prāṇa is beseeched for protection.

Question III

1. Then Kausalya, son of Aśvala, put a question to him him: 'O revered sir, from where is this prāṇa brought into existence? How does it enter the body? And how does it divide and support itself? How does it depart? How does it support that which is extended and that which is external and what concerns the self?'

   The greatness of prāṇa has been ascertained. The question now regards how prāṇa is born. How is prāṇa embodied? How does it depart?

2. To him he said: 'You are asking questions that are beyond the normal. Since you are striving (towards) Brahman, therefore I will answer you.
3. 'This prāṇa is comes into existence from the self. Just as when there is a person, there is a shadow, (similarly) on this (self) is spread this (prāṇa). It comes to the body due to the doings of the mind.'

   Prāṇa is from the self, the supreme Puruṣa. Prāṇa is compared to a shadow and arises as a result of actions of the mind such as thoughts and wishes.

4. As a king commands his officers saying: 'Preside over these villages (and) these villages', so does this prāṇa indeed assign the other organs separately to their respective functions.

Prāṇa is most senior like a king and so places the other organs in their respective places. The other organs are a manifestation of prāṇa.

5. He placed Apāna (out-breath/one of the five life winds of the body) in the organs of excretion and generation. Prāṇa itself is established in the eyes and ears and also in the mouth and nose. In the middle is Samāna (equalizing breath/one of the five life-winds). It is indeed this that distributes equally all that is eaten or drunk. From that these seven flames originate.

   This verse states the placement of the various breaths. Thus prāṇa distributes all that is drunk or eaten. By mentioning seven flames is meant that the revealing of objects which constitute it being seen, heard etc is also due to prāṇa.

6. Surely this self is in the heart. There are these hundred and one arteries. They each have a hundred (divisions). Each of these is divided into seventy-two thousand sub-branches. Vyāna (diffused breath) moves amongst them.

   The breath vyāna is taken up here. The word vyāna is derived from pervasiveness and like the sun and the rays, it pervades the entire body through the nerves. It is the performer of actions requiring strength.

7. Now when udāna (up-breath/one of the five life winds) rises up through the one (artery), it leads to a virtuous world when it is due to virtuous (actions), to an evil world when it is due to evil (actions) and to the human world when it is due to both of these.

   The breath udāna when it has an upward trend, leads to a virtuous world, as a result of virtuous deeds. When it moves as the result of evil acts, it leads to an evil world.

8. Indeed, the sun is the external prāṇa. It (the sun) rises favouring this prāṇa which exists in the eye. The deity which is in the earth supports the apāna (out-breath) of a person. That ether which is in the middle is samāna (equalizing breath). Air is vyāna (diffused breath).

The prāṇa in the external manifestation is the sun. This is the one that produces light which enables the eye to perceive. Apāna is the deity identified with the earth and by means of this the human body is controlled and kept in place. Otherwise the body might fall or fly. In the intermediate region is samāna. The pervasive air that is the air in general is vyāṇa.

9. Luminosity is indeed udāna. Therefore one whose light has ceased is born again with the sense organs that enter (his) mind.

An ordinary man, when his light is extinguished is about to die. Such an ordinary man is reborn. This luminosity is udāna.

10. Along with one's thoughts a person (at the moment of death) enters into prāṇa. The prāṇa joined with light along with the self takes one to the world as determined by him.

At the moment of death the thoughts one has, along with the organs enter into prāṇa. The prāṇa along with the udāna and the soul, leads the enjoyer to the world determined (by his karma).

11. Any wise person who knows prāṇa thus, for him there shall certainly be no lack of offspring. He attains immortality. Pertaining to that is this verse:
12. Having known the source, entrance, place, and indeed the fivefold overlordship of prāṇa one attains immortality, having known one attains immortality.

Having known the above aspects of prāṇa, as discussed in the previous verses, one attains immortality.

Question IV

1. Then the grandson of Sūrya, Gārgya, put a question to him: 'O revered sir, which are these (the organs) which go to sleep in this person? What keeps awake in him? Who is the deity which views dreams? Who experiences this happiness? On whom are all these dependent?

   The next three questions dwell on what is changeless and eternal, the Puruṣa. The previous three dwelt on the domain of lower knowledge. The question being asked in this verse is are these activities performed by a deity associated with prāṇa, the body, the senses, or the mind? To whom does the peace and calm accrue to when the waking and dream states have ceased?

2. To him he said: 'O Gārgya, just as all the rays of the sun get unified in this luminous circle and as they spread from the sun when it rises again and again, thus indeed, does all that become one in a supreme deity, the mind. Hence, at that time, this does not hear, smell, taste, touch, speak, grasp, enjoy, eject, nor move. It is said that he sleeps.'

   All the senses, their objects, all these get unified in the luminous mind. They lose their distinctions during dream and deep sleep. At the time of waking, they go to their respective functions, like the rays of the sun. Thus at the time of sleep the senses desist from their functions ie one does not see, hear, smell, taste, etc.

3. Indeed, it is the fire of prāṇa that keep awake in this city. Gārhapatya (the householder's fire) is verily apāna. Vyāna is Anvāhāryapacana (the southern sacrificial fire). The

Ahavanīya (oblation fire) confirms to prāṇa, since it is obtained from Gārhapatya.

The body has nine gates. The senses when asleep, the five divisions of vital functions, which may be compared to fire, remain awake. The resemblance of the breaths to various sacrificial fires is stated.

4. It is called samāna (the equalizing breath) since it leads to a balance between these two oblations, exhalation and inhalation. The mind is verily the sacrificer. The desired fruit of the sacrifice is udāna (up-breath). Thus it leads the sacrificer to Brahman every day.

The samāna, since it strikes a balance, is said to be similar to the Agnihotra sacrifice. The commentary also states that the enlightened person is not a performer of rites. The body and organs of an enlightened person perform sacrifices continuously, even during sleep. The mind is the sacrificer. The mind is the principal in the context of body and senses. Just as the sacrificer seeks heaven, the mind seeks Brahman.

5. Here in the dream state, this deity (mind) experiences glory. It sees again whatever has been seen, it hears again whatever has been heard, it repeatedly experiences that which has been experienced in different directions and locations. What is seen and unseen, what is heard and unheard, what is experienced and what is not experienced, what is and what is not, it sees all by becoming all.

During dream state the organs cease their normal functions and the vital forces are awake and maintain the body in the intermediate state (between waking and sleep). During dreams the mind sees dreams unified with all its various organs.

6. When it (the deity) is overwhelmed by light, here (in this state) this deity does not experience dreams. Then there is happiness here, in this body.

During sleep the tendencies affecting the mind are shut down. In this state the mind pervades the body in the form of general consciousness. In this state of deep sleep, there are no dreams. Here, the nature of the self is calm.

7. O pleasing one, just as the birds proceed to the trees for an abode, thus surely do all these find their abode in the supreme self.

This verse indicates that everything goes to the supreme self.

8. Earth and its constituents, water and its constituents, light and its constituents, air and its constituents, space and its constituents, sight and what is seen, hearing and what is heard, smell and what is smelt, taste and what is tasted, the skin and what is touched, speech and what is said, the two hands and what can be grasped, the organ of generation and enjoyment, the organ of excretion and refuse, the two feet and the area walked upon, the mind and what can be thought, the intellect and what can be understood, the ego and the acts connected to it, consciousness and its contents, light and what can be illuminated by it, prāṇa and all that is supported by prāṇa.

What are these that proceed to the supreme self? These are being enumerated here.

9. This indeed is the seer, toucher, hearer, smeller, taster, thinker, knower, doer, the knower by nature, the person. He is established in the supreme indestructible self.

The reality of the self is that which by nature knows. In the absence of ignorance, the nature of the self is realized. The individual self is then established in the supreme eternal unchanging self.

10. The supreme indestructible (self) is attained by he who verily realizes the shadowless, bodiless, colourless, pure, indestructible self. O pleasant one, he who realizes thus becomes omniscient, becomes all. (Pertaining to) that is this verse.

The characteristics of the self are being enumerated, including being without prāṇa. The realized renunciate becomes the knower of all. Nothing is unknown to him.

11. O pleasant one, he who knows the indestructible (self) in which is established that whose nature is to know, as also the vital breaths and the elements together with the gods become all knowing, indeed enters everything.

Question V

1. After that Satyakāma, son of Śibi put a question to him him: 'O revered sir, which world does he thus attain, who among various persons, intently meditates on Aum until the cessation of his present life?'

The question raised in this verse is a means of stressing the importance of meditating on Aum to attain Brahman.

The question also seeks as to which worlds are conquered by one who meditates on Aum along with observing various forms of Yama (Rules laying out restraints and self-control) and Niyama (positive duties).

2. To him he said: 'O Satyakāma, surely that what is the sound Aum, is the supreme and non-supreme Brahman. Therefore, the wise through this means alone attain either of the two.

Brahman the superior and non-superior is Aum. The superior is known as true non-eternal and the Puruṣa. The non-superior Brahman is the firstborn. The superior Brahman is devoid of all distinctions and cannot be described by words nor can the mind explore it. Brahman is favourable to one who meditates on Brahman.

3. If this person intently meditates on Aum as one letter 'a' through that alone he becomes enlightened and quickly accomplishes a birth on earth. The Ṛcas (verses) lead him to the human world. There being possessed of penance, chastity, and faith he attains a glorious life.

   By meditating on even one letter of Aum, a person attains great results. He attains an excellent human birth, blessed with self control, brahmacharya, faith, glory.

4. Then if this person (meditates on Aum) by means of the second letter 'u' he becomes identified with the mind. Through the Yajuṣ mantras he is uplifted to the intermediate space, the lunar world. Having experienced glory in the lunar world he returns again.

   One who meditates on the second letter of Aum, 'u', is led to a birth in the world of the moon, where he experiences glory. Then he comes back to the human world.

5. Again, this person who meditates on the supreme Puruṣa by means of the very syllable Aum as comprising of three letters 'a', 'u', 'm', becomes one with the sun consisting of light. Just as a snake is released from its skin, so too in this he is released from his sins. He is uplifted to the world of Bramhā by means of the Sāma mantras. From this sense mass of living beings he perceives the Puruṣa who pervades all beings and is higher than the supreme. Regarding this there are these two verses.

If one meditates on the syllable Aum as residing within the solar orb, based on knowledge of the three letters of Aum, he is unified in the sun, consisting of light. He does not return after death.

6. The three syllables (each) are within the purview of death. But if they are yoked, joined one to another, are not differently applied separately, are used in actions well-performed, external, internal or intermediate, then the knower rains unperturbed.

   The yogi, when meditating during the three courses of action, external, internal, intermediate, while performing yogic actions in meditation on the Puruṣas associated with the states of waking, dream, and sleep, he (the yogi) remains unperturbed. He sees the unity of these three states with the three syllables of Aum. He becomes the self of all and one with Aum.

7. The wise know that through the Ṛk mantras (one attains) this (world), with the Yajur mantras the intermediate space is attainable and that which is attained by the Sāma mantras. That, the wise persons attain just through Aum only; and through Aum as a support the wise reach that which is ageless, tranquil, beyond fear, immortal and supreme.

   By the aid of Aum, can be reached the three abovementioned aims and by means of Aum can the supreme Brahman, unchanging, true, called Puruṣa be attained. This is fearless, immortal, etc.

Question VI

1. Then Sukeśā, son of Bhārdvāja put a question to him, 'O revered sir, a prince from the Kosala kingdom named Hiraṇyanabha came to me and asked: 'Bhāradvāja, do you know the Puruṣa of sixteen parts?' I said to that prince: 'I do

not know him. If I happen to know him why should I conceal it from you? He who speaks falsely, indeed, withers to his roots. Thus it is improper that I utter falsehoods.' Riding his chariot in silence he went away. Regarding that, I ask you: 'Where is that Puruṣa?'

This question is stated with a view to indicate where the unchanging true Puruṣa is to be realized. By referring to the challenges involved in this quest is is intended to induce a special effort in those desiring liberation. Also the verse enjoins that one ought to impart knowledge to a student who is competent and who approaches the teacher in the correct manner. One should never utter falsities.

2. To him he said: 'O pleasant one, here only, within the body is that Puruṣa in whom is the source of these sixteen parts.'

In the space inside the lotus of the heart resides the Puruṣa. The Puruṣa is not to be sought elsewhere. The Puruṣa is partless. Yet, on account of ignorance it appears as it possesses sixteen parts as its limiting adjuncts. These apparent parts are dispersed by knowledge. By ignorance are the parts superimposed on Puruṣa. Consciousness appears diversely due to limiting adjuncts. Yet consciousness is nothing but the self. Consciousness remains changed even objects change in their essence.

3. He considered: consequent to whose departure will I also depart? And in whose being established shall I continue to be established?
4. He (the Puruṣa) created prāṇa; from prāṇa faith, sky, air, light, water, earth, sense-organs, mind and food; from food vigour, penance, mantras, works, the worlds and in these worlds, names.

The Puruṣa created prāṇa known as Hiraṇygarbha, who is the repository of all organs as well as the inner soul of all creatures.

From prāṇa, Puruṣa created faith, the elements that become the material constituents of the body, the organs, the mind. He then created food, vigour, self control. Then the mantras, the Ṛk, Yaju, Sāma, and Atharva texts. Then rites, the worlds, and name and form as well.

5. Just as the various flowing rivers (which) proceed to the sea, disappear on attaining the sea, their names and forms dissipate and they are simply called the sea, in this manner, of this all seeing Puruṣa, these sixteen parts which proceed towards the Puruṣa disappear on reaching the Puruṣa, their names and forms dissipate and they are simply called Puruṣa. He this (person) is free from parts and becomes immortal. Regarding that is this verse.

   Puruṣa is the seer of all. The sixteen parts of Puruṣa mentioned before on reaching Puruṣa is merged in Puruṣa and disappear. Their names and forms are destroyed. He who knows this, himself becomes free from parts and thus immortal. Since death is a creation of these parts originating from ignorance.

6. Just as the spokes are well placed in the centre of a wheel, you should know the Puruṣa as being worthy to be known, so that you are not afflicted by death.

   The student is enjoined to know Puruṣa so as to be free from misery and death.

7. To them Pippalāda said: 'Only to this extent do I know this supreme Brahman. There is nothing superior to this.'
   Pippalāda tells the students that there is nothing higher to be known. The students had attained their goal.
8. Worshipping him they said: 'Thou surely are our father, who has taken us across the shores of ignorance.'
   Salutation to the most excellent seers.
   Salutation to the most excellent seers.

The Bṛhadāraṇyaka Upaniṣad

CHAPTER 1

I

1. Aum, indeed the dawn is the head of the sacrificial horse, the sun is the eye (of the sacrificial horse), the wind the vital breath, the open mouth the fire named Vaiśvānara; the year is the trunk (of the sacrificial horse), the back is heaven, the intermediate region between heaven and earth is the belly, the earth the hoof, the four directions are the sides, the intermediate directions are the ribs, the limbs are the seasons, the months and half months are the joints, the days and nights are the feet, the stars are the bones, the clouds are the flesh, the half digested food are the sands, the rivers are the arteries and veins, the mountains are the liver and spleen, the herbs and trees are the hair. The rising (sun) is the front part and the setting (sun) the hind part. Its yawn is lightning, thunder is its shaking the body, when it makes water it rains, its speech certainly is speech.

Here in this verse, the different aspects of the world, i.e., the units of time, the earth, the seasons, the stars, rivers; trees, etc., are compared to the parts of a sacrificial horse, i.e., one fit for a sacrifice. The name given to Brahmamuhūrta is uṣā. The particle 'via' which is used in the Sanskrit verse is used to indicate something to be recalled.

2. The day indeed is the vessel called Mahiman which arose in front of the horse. Its origin is in the eastern sea. The night indeed is the vessel called Mahiman which arose behind the horse. Its origin is in the western sea. Indeed, these two vessels called Mahiman appeared on either side of the horse (as the two sacrificial vessels). Having become a steed it transported the deities, as a stallion the gandharvas, as a courser the demons, as a horse, men. Indeed, the sea is his relation, the sea is his origin.

This verse is a meditation regarding the two sacrificial vessels, which are called Mahiman. The horse is Prajāpati consisting of the sun, etc. The source of the horse is the supreme self. Thus the horse is pure and has a pure source.

II

1. In the beginning there was nothing at all here (in the universe). By means of death this (the universe) was enveloped only or by means of hunger, since hunger is death. He created that mind (thinking): 'May I have a self.' He moved about worshipping. From his worshipping water was born. (He thought) indeed while I was worshipping water sprang up. That only is why water is known as Arka (fire). Certainly, water comes for him who knows thus (the reason) why water is called fire.

This verse relates to the origin of the fire that is fit for the sacrifice previously described. In the beginning of the universe there were no distinctions of name and form. Everything was covered by death including the cause and effect which were both existent before the universe originated. The commentary details various objections and replies, to this view of origination.

2. Indeed water is arka (fire). That which was the froth of the water hardened. It became the earth. In this (he) was tired.

From him thus fatigued and heated (due to practice of penance) came forth his essence of splendor. That was fire.

The commentary states that fire rests on water. Water is an accessory of worship. Out of water came the embryonic state of the universe. Producing this led Prajāpati to be tired. Then his essence and lustre came from his body. This was fire, Virāj, the firstborn also known as Prajāpati. He was the first embodied being.

3. He divided himself in three ways, making the sun a third, air a third (and fire a third). His prāṇa is also appointed in three ways. The eastern direction is his head and his two arms are this and this (the right and left sides). So also his tail is the western direction and his two hip bones are this and this. The southern and northern directions are his two flanks. Heaven is his back and the intermediate space between heaven and earth is his belly. His chest is the earth. He is thus well established in water. He who knows this thus is firmly established everywhere he goes.

Virāj himself divided his body and organs in three ways as fire, air and sun. Then the verse describes the meditation on fire. The previous described origin is intended for its eulogy to stress its purity.

4. He wished: 'May a second self (form or body) be born to me.' He, hunger or death caused the union of speech with the mind. That which was the seed there became the year. Prior to that there was no year. He nurtured him for as much as one year and after that time produced him. (Death) opened his mouth (to swallow him) as he was born. Crying, he (the baby) exclaimed, 'bhāṇ'. It only became speech.

How did death manifest himself? This is dealt with here. The origin of the year, and speech are also stated here.

5. He considered: 'If indeed I kill him I shall have very little food.' He by means of that speech, by means of that self created all that there is, the (hymns of the) Ṛg Veda, the (formulae of the) Yajur Veda, the (chants of the) Sāma Veda, the metres, sacrifices, human beings, and animals. What all he created all of that he intended to devour. Indeed, he devours all, that is why he is called Aditi. Thus he who knows the significance of this name Aditi becomes the eater of all this and all this becomes food for him.

This verse also relates to creation. The manifestation of the already existing Vedas, so that they may be applied to ceremonies is stated here. The union mentioned in the previous verse was unmanifested in character, the present union mentioned in this verse is manifested. In his commentary Śaṅkarācārya quotes Śruti, the Ṛg Veda (I.Iix.10). 'Aditi is heaven, Aditi is sky, Aditi is the mother and he is the father.' The meaning of this is that he becomes identified with all. Everything is his food since everything is the food of an eater who is identified with all.

6. He wished: 'May I sacrifice again with a greater sacrifice.' He was fatigued. He performed penances. While he was thus fatigued and performing penances, glory, and vigour left. Indeed, the prāṇa (vital breath or organs) are glory and vigour. When the organs left the body began to swell. However his mind remained (attached) to the body only.

This verse and part of the next are meant to explain the derivation of the words, Aśva (horse) and Aśvamedha (the horse sacrifice). By using the word again the verse indicates that Prajāpati had performed a horse sacrifice in his previous life and was born with these thoughts at the beginning of the cycle. By means of penance was all creation effected.

7. He wished: 'May this (body) be fit for sacrifice and may I have a self through this.' Since it swelled up it became a horse and since it became fit for sacrifices thus verily the horse sacrifice came to be known as the Àsvamedha. He who knows this thus knows only the horse sacrifice. Leaving it free, he reflected. He sacrificed it to himself at the end of a year. He assigned the other animals to their respective deities. Thus (priests) sacrifice to Prajāpati the purified horse dedicated to all deities. Indeed, the sun that radiates heat is the horse sacrifice. His body is the year. This (earthly) fire is the Arka (sacrificial fire). The (three) worlds are the limbs of Arka. These two, fire and the sun are respectively Arka and the horse sacrifice. And again they become one deity only, even death. He who knows this thus conquers recurring death. Death cannot triumph over him since it becomes his self and he becomes one with the deities.

This verse contains a eulogy on the horse and a tribute to the sacrifice since it mentions Prajāpati. The aim of the verse is to encourage a collective meditation on Prajāpati in the context of the horse sacrifice. Further it states that he who knows the horse sacrifice conquers further death and is not reborn.

III

1. Indeed, the descendants of Prajāpati were of two types, the gods and the demons. There, the gods were fewer in number and the demons were larger in number. They struggled with each other for (mastery of) these worlds. The gods said: 'Well by means of the Udgītha in the sacrifice let us overcome the demons.'

The word two in this verse refers to two types or classes. These are the gods and the asuras, the organs, that of speech and the rest, of Prajāpati himself. These become gods when they function as influenced by what is taught in the scriptures. However, when acting as influenced by their natural thoughts and actions on the basis of perception and inference and directed to visible worldly ends they are known as asuras. This is so since they rejoice in their own lives (asu) or since they are different or other than the gods (sur). These are stated to be in the commentary to be more numerous than the gods since, 'the asuras are influenced by thoughts and actions directed to visible ends.' (Swāmī Mādhavānanda 2018: 29). The tendency cultivated by the scriptures are indeed a rarity.

2. To speech they said: 'Chant the Udgītha for us.' 'May it be so.' Declared speech. Speech chanted for them. What enjoyment there is due to speech, it obtained for the deities by chanting. What it spoke propitiously that was for itself. They (the demons) knew indeed that by means of this chanter they (the gods) would exceed them. They therefore rushed to it and penetrated it with evil. What evil there is in speaking that which is unfit that only is this evil.

   In this verse the organs of speech, etc., are referred to as agents of meditation and work. Later it is shown that the self does not do these. All our activities in meditation and work are done by the organ of speech, etc. The universe has three components, name, form, and action. The self is separate from these and is, 'Not this, not this.'

3. Then to the nose they said: 'Chant the Udgītha for us.' 'May it be so.' Declared the organ of smell and chanted for them. What enjoyment there is due to smell, it obtained for the deities by chanting. What it smelt propitiously that was for itself. They (the demons) knew indeed that by means of this chanter they (the gods) would exceed them. They therefore rushed to it and penetrated it with evil. What evil there is in smelling that which is unfit that only is this evil.

4. Then to the eye they said: 'Chant the Udgītha for us.' 'May it be so.' Declared the eye and chanted for them. What enjoyment there is due to the eye, it obtained for the deities by chanting.

What it saw propitiously that was for itself. They (the demons) knew indeed that by means of this chanter they (the gods) would exceed them. They therefore rushed to it and penetrated it with evil. What evil there is in seeing that which is unfit that only is this evil.

5. Then to the ear they said: 'Chant the Udgītha for us.' 'May it be so.' Declared the ear and chanted for them. What enjoyment there is due to the ear, it obtained for the deities by chanting. What it heard propitiously that was for itself. They (the demons) knew indeed that by means of this chanter they (the gods) would exceed them. They therefore rushed to it and penetrated it with evil. What evil there is in hearing that which is unfit that only is this evil.
6. Then to the mind they said: 'Chant the Udgītha for us.' 'May it be so.' Declared the mind and chanted for them. What enjoyment there is due to the mind, it obtained for the deities by chanting. What it thought propitiously that was for itself. They (the demons) knew indeed that by means of this chanter they (the gods) would exceed them. They therefore rushed to it and penetrated it with evil. What evil there is in thinking that which is unfit that only is this evil. Similarly, they also affected the other deities with evil, penetrated them with evil.

All the deities tried to chant the Udgītha. But these organs were penetrated with evil by the asuras. They were not the deities mentioned in the mantra. Due to these defects it appeared that they would be unable to transcend death.

7. Then to the prāṇa they said: 'Chant the Udgītha for us.' 'May it be so,' said the prāṇa and chanted for them. They (the demons) knew indeed that by means of this chant they (the gods) would exceed them. They therefore rushed to it and wanted to penetrate it with evil. However just as a lump of clay striking a hard stone is destroyed thus indeed were they dispersed in all directions and destroyed. From that the gods became (their true being) and the demons were defeated.

This verse is similar to a verse of the Chāndogya Upaniṣad which appears in Section II of Book 1.

Prāṇa is said to be taintless. Who identifies with prāṇa gives up limited identification with the body only and identifies with Virāj. A sacrificer who adopts this procedure, becomes his true self. Evil tendencies that oppose this are crushed.

8. They (the gods) then said: 'What was he who thus joined us (to our real being)?' 'He is here inside the mouth.' Thus the (life breath) is called Ayāsya Āṅgirasa since it is the essence of the limbs.

The organs were restored to their divinity due to prāṇa. They deliberated on who this was that restores them to their divinity. They realized that it was prāṇa which was present in the inner ether.

9. It this deity indeed is named Dūr (distant) since death is far away from it. Certainly, death is far away from him who knows this thus.

The commentary tackles various possible objections to this position and stresses that prāṇa is pure and taintless. Death is ever far away from the prāṇa, since prāṇa is unattached. Death is far from one who knows thus.

10. It, this deity, indeed warded off the evil from from these gods (and) death and made it go to where the end of the directions are. There he deposited their evils. From that no one should go to a person (of that area) or go to the end (of the directions) lest one contact evil there or even death.

The commentary states that death is due to the evil caused by attachment of the organs to contact with the sense objects, prompted by ignorance. This evil is death. Since the deities identified with prāṇa, they (the deities) were taken away from death.

11. It, this deity, indeed warded off the evil from from these gods (and) death, then carried them beyond death.
12. Indeed, it carried speech beyond (death) first. When it (speech) was released from death it became fire. This fire when it transcended beyond death, blazed away.

The prāṇa carried the organ of speech first. It is important since it is a superior instrument to chant Udgītha than the other organs. When the organ of speech got rid of death it became fire. This fire is distinguished from prior fire, since having transcended death, it shines, is luminous beyond its reach.

13. Then it carried the nose beyond (death). When it (the nose) was released from death it became air. This air when it transcended beyond death, blew.

Similarly having transcended death the nose became air which air blows beyond its reach.

14. Then it carried the eye beyond (death). When it (the eye) was released from death it became the sun. The sun when it transcended beyond death, glowered immensely.
15. Then it carried the ear beyond (death). When it (the ear)

was released from death it became the directions. These directions transcended beyond death.

16. Then it carried the mind beyond (death). When it (the mind) was released from death it became the moon. This moon when it transcended beyond death, shone in splendour. Thus indeed this deity carries beyond death him who knows thus.

17. Then for itself (prāṇa obtained) food by chanting. Since whatever food is consumed by anyone it is consumed by this only and it is established here.

Prāṇa secured food for itself by chanting hymns. The reason is: food, whatever food is eaten by creatures in the world is eaten by prāṇa only. Prāṇa also rests in that food. The food is only eaten by prāṇa so that it may live in the body.

18. The deities said: 'Indeed all this food, whatever there is, you have attained it for yourself by chanting. So in this food let us be sharers.' (Prāṇa said): 'Then sit around, facing me.' '(The deities said): 'Let it be so.' Around him they sat. From that whatever food one eats by means of this (vital breath) they (the organs) are contented by it. Thus indeed do his relatives sit around facing a person who knows this, he becomes the support of these relatives, the most excellent among them, the foremost, their chief, an eater of food. Whichever person among his dependents wishes to be equal to him who has this knowledge, he (such a person) is not competent to support his dependents. However whoever follows him and following him wishes to support his dependents, surely, he will be competent to support his dependents.

The benefits of food come from prāṇa to the other organs. The organ of speech etc have no independent relation to food. A person who knows thus becomes the refuge of his relatives.

19. He is (known as) Ayāsya Āṅgirasa since he is the essence of the limbs. Certainly, prāṇa is the essence of the limbs. Indeed, prāṇa is the essence of the limbs. From that, from which, from whom prāṇa departs, that surely dries up, since this indeed is the essence of the limbs.

This verse repeats that it is called Ayāsya Āṅgirasa. The prāṇa is the essence of the members. This is well known since from whichever part of the body the prāṇa departs that withers away or dries up. Prāṇa is thus the self of the body and organs. Prāṇa ought to be meditated upon. Śruti magnifies prāṇa as the self of all and a fit object of meditation.

20. This again is Bṛhaspati only. Speech indeed is Bṛhati and this (prāṇa) is its lord. From that this is Bṛhaspati.

Prāṇa is also called Bṛhaspati. Speech is Bṛhatī, the metre with thirty-six syllables. In Bṛhatī are all Ṛces included. Śruti states that one should know the Ṛces as prāṇa. (Ai.Ā.II.ii.2)

21. This again is Brāhmaṇaspati. Speech indeed is Brahman, this is its lord. From that this is Brāhmaṇaspati.

Speech is Brahman or Yajus. The Yajus is said to be, by the commentary a kind of speech. Since this is its lord, it is indeed Brāhmaṇaspati. Ṛk and Yajus are forms of speech.

22. This again is indeed the Sāman. Verily speech is Sāman, this is 'sā' (she), and 'ana' (he). That is why Sāman is called Sāman. (Or) since it is same as a white ant, same as a mosquito, same as an elephant, same as these three worlds, same as the universe. From that Sāman indeed, he who knows this Sāman thus, obtains union with Sāman or resides in the very same world along with it.

The commentary states that speech is sā, that which feminine words denote is speech since sā refers to all objects denoted by them. Prāṇa is ama. Ama, similarly refers to objects denoted by masculine words. Another Śruti states that masculine names are got by prāṇa and feminine names through speech. Thus the word Sāman denotes prāṇa and speech.

23. This again is indeed the Udgītha. Prāṇa (vital breath) is indeed 'ut', since by means of prāṇa all this (the universe) is upheld. Speech only is Gītha (a variety of sound). Since it is 'ut' and 'Gītha', so it is Udgītha.

Indeed prāṇa it is, since the universe is supported by prāṇa. Ut means holding aloft, which is a feature of prāṇa. Thus prāṇa is ut. Speech only is Gītha. Gīthā is derived from the root 'gai', which denotes sound.

24. (Regarding) this also Brahmadatta Caikitāyana while drinking Soma juice uttered, 'Let this Soma juice make my head fall down, If I say that Ayāsya Āṅgirasa chanted the Udgītha by means of anything other than this (prāṇa and speech) for he chanted the Udgītha by means of prāṇa and speech only.'

The term 'Ayāsya Āṅgiras' is used to refer to prāṇa in the mouth and indicates the priest who chanted in the ancient sacrifices of the sages who protected the world.

25. Of this Sāman he who knows the wealth becomes wealthy. The sweet tone is indeed its wealth. From this, he who holds the office of a priest should wish to have a sweet tone in his voice. He ought to perform his priestly duties by means of his voice enhanced by a sweet tone. From that, in a sacrifice people wish to see a priest with a sweet tone and also one possessed of wealth. He who knows this wealth of the Sāman thus, surely obtains wealth.

This verse highlights the importance of tone in order to enrich Sāman. Tone is stated to be the wealth of Sāman.

26. Of this Sāman, he who knows what is its gold (correct articulation) obtains gold. Indeed, the sweet tone is gold. He who knows this the gold of the Sāman thus, surely attains gold.

The word Suvarna means both correct sound and gold.

27. Of this Sāman, he who knows what is its support, indeed acquires a support. Indeed, speech only is its support; since surely when supported on this, the prāṇa chants. However, some state that it is (supported) on food (the body).
28. Hence now the ascending utterances of the purificatory hymns (are being urged). Indeed, he the Prastotṛ priest surely chants the Sāman. Where he chants it, the sacrificer ought to recite these (three Yajus mantras): 'Lead me from falsehood to truth, lead me from darkness to light, lead me from death to immortality.' When it (the mantra) says: 'Lead me from falsehood to truth, falsehood surely is death, truth is immortality.' 'Lead me from death to immortality', make me immortal, this only is what he says. 'Lead me from darkness to light.' Darkness surely is death, light is immortality. 'Lead me from death to immortality, make me immortal' this only is what he says. 'Lead me from death to immortality. Here there is nothing hidden as it were. Now as to the other hymns, in them one should acquire food by chanting. From that, in them the sacrificer should seek any boon, whichever desire he desires. He (the Udgātṛ priest) who thus knows this, whichever desire he desires, for himself or for the sacrificer that he attains by chanting. Indeed this (enables one) to win the worlds. He who knows this Sāman thus, for him indeed there is no occasion to be unfit for the world.

This verse prescribes the depiction of mantras for one who knows the prāṇa. The repetition of these mantras by one with the necessary knowledge leads to the elevation to divinity. The repetition of these mantras is called Abyāroha since by means of this repetition one possessed of appropriate knowledge 'advances towards' the realization of one's innate divinity.

The commentary explains the meaning of the three Yajur mantras. From falsehood to truth, here falsehood means death, our natural actions and thoughts, since they degrade us. By truth is meant actions and thoughts as regulated by the scriptures, which lead to immortality. Thus this means from ignorance and evil lead me to thought and actions as per the scriptures i.e., which lead to divinity. Now from darkness to light, darkness means death. Ignorance is the nature of a veil, is darkness which is the cause of death. Light signifies the opposite of ignorance, light means immortality, one's divine nature. Knowledge is luminous and is called light. Light is immortality being imperishable.

From death to immortality is an entreaty to realize the divine status of Virāj.

The first mantra means help me to identify myself with the means of realization, as opposed to that which is not a means of realization, the second one means an entreaty to attain identity with the result. The third gives the combined meaning of the first two. The third should be taken literally, the first two should not be taken literally.

IV

1. This (the universe) in the beginning was the self only in the form of a person. Pondering he did not see anything else other than himself. At first, he said: 'I am.' Thus came about the name 'I'. From that, even now, when a person is addressed, he first says, 'It is I', and then says whatever other name he has. (Since) he who in the beginning, from this, from all, consumed all evil, from that, he is (known) as

a person. Indeed, he who knows this thus consumes those who wish to be prior to him.

This section seeks to describe the excellent results of Vedic meditations by highlighting Hiraṇyagarbha, his powers and independence. That Hiraṇyagarbha is himself the result of his past actions is stated in the commentary.

It is however stressed that knowledge of Brahman alone can lead to liberation. It extols the self and later it is stated that: 'This self is dearer than a son.' (I.iv.8)

Virāj had been purified by Vedic knowledge in his past life, thus he said, 'I am he.' Meaning by this that he is the Virāj who is the self of all. Thus later it is said: 'His secret name is Aham.' (V.V.4) Virāj is also called Puruṣa, one who burnt first. In his past incarnations he had burnt all evils, attachment, and ignorance.

2. He was apprehensive. From that he who is alone is apprehensive. He this (one) reflected: 'Since there is not anything other than myself, what am I apprehensive of?' Hence his fear only departed, for of what should he be apprehensive? Surely fear arises from a second.

In this verse fear is said to arise from a false notion of extinction. Fear stems from the erroneous view of a second. Fear is incompatible with true knowledge of the supreme self. Fear comes from a second entity. Yet a second entity is merely the projection of ignorance.

3. Indeed he had no enjoyment. From that, when one is alone, he has no enjoyment. He wished for a second. He became just as much as a man and a woman embracing. He divided this self only into two. Therefore, husband and wife came into being. 'From that, this (body) is half of oneself, like the half of a two-celled seed.' Thus said Yājñavalka. From that,

this space surely is filled by a wife. He was united with her. Therefore, human beings were born.

4. She reflected (on) this,'How can he unite with me after having given birth to me from himself?' Indeed, let me disappear. She became a cow. The other became a bull, united with her. Therefore, cows were born. She became a mare, the other a stallion. She became a she-ass the other a he-ass and united with her. Therefore were born one-hoofed animals. She became a she goat, the other a he-goat. She became an ewe, the other a ram and united with her. Therefore goats and sheep were born. Thus whatever there is he created in pairs only, down to ants.
5. He knew: 'Truly I am this creation, verily I created all this.' Hence he became creation. (He) who knows thus becomes (a creator) of this, his creation.
6. Then he churned and created fire from its origin, from the mouth and from the hands. From that both these are hairless since internally the origin is hairless. When people state, 'Sacrifice to this, sacrifice to that one,' treating them as separate deities (then they are in error) since all of this is his creation only and he is himself all the gods. Now, this, whatever is wet, that he created from seed and that is Soma. Surely all this (the universe) is this much food and an eater of food. Indeed, Soma is food and fire an eater of food. Of Brahman this is a surpassing creation since he created the deities who (may) even surpass him. Even though he being mortal, (he) created the Immortals. Thus this is a surpassing creation. Surely, he who knows this thus becomes (a creator) in this creation.

As per the commentary, the aim of this verse is not to describe creation, but to indicate that all gods are Virāj, as stated here. It is stated that manifested objects are not at variance from that which manifests. The deities have been manifested by Virāj. The different deities are all said to be projections of Virāj. Virāj is the cosmic prāṇa.

Further regarding Hiraṇyagarbha the commentary states that, 'essentially he is the supreme self'. Yet through his relation to limiting adjuncts, he may be perceived as different. Ordinary individuals are tainted by excess impurity in their limiting adjuncts, are mostly spoken of as the transmigratory self. However the Śrutis and Smṛtis state that devoid of limiting adjuncts everyone is spoken of as the supreme self.

7. That, this (universe) was at that time unmanifested. It became manifested only by name and form. 'It has this name, it has this form.' Even at present this (universe) is manifested by name and form only. 'It has this name, it has this form.' He, this (self) has pervaded here right upto the tips of the nails, just in the manner a razor lies in the razor case; or fire lies in the source of fire. People do not see it since it is incomplete. When it breathes it is only called prāṇa; when speaking the organ of speech; when seeing the eye; when hearing the ear; when contemplating the mind. These are only its names based on functions. He who meditates on one or other of these, he does not know, since this is incomplete being one or other (of these). One should meditate on the self since here all these become one. Of all these, this the self only is to be known since one knows all these by means of it, just as in the manner one can find (what was lost) by means of footprints. He who knows this thus attains glory and praise.

This verse aims to throw light upon the state of the universe, before the manifested universe, characterized by name and form, consisting of means and ends. This verse points to an identity of the universe in these two states. The undifferentiated universe manifested into name and form.

Further, the aim of the scriptures is to teach the self. As a result of ignorance, agent and action and result are superimposed on the self. The self is the cause of the universe. Yet the self is distinct from this name and form being eternal, pure, enlightened, and free by nature. The self enters into bodies from Hiraṇyagarbha to a clump of grass.

8. That which is this self is dearer than riches, is dearer than all else and is the innermost. If anyone should say to a person who describes anything other than the self as dear that, What is dear (to you) will perish', indeed it will be so. A person ought to meditate on the self only as dear. Of him, who meditates only on the self as dear, surely what is dear to him will not perish.

The verse seeks to stress that the self should be known to the exclusion of everything else. Why is the self dearer than everything else? The self is innermost. The self is even nearer than the body and organs. One ought to strive to the utmost to attain the self.

9. That is said (by some): 'Men think, "by means of knowledge of Brahman we shall become all". What indeed was that which Brahman knew, by means of which he became all?'

This verse indicates one of the main aims of the Upaniṣads, i.e., to impart knowledge of Brahman. The commentary highlighting the necessity of this knowledge speaks of seekers of Brahman, who get a qualified teacher, which is compared to a boat on the boundless ocean of worldly struggles. The next verse addresses the issues raised in this and the last few verses.

10. This (self) was indeed Brahman in the beginning. It knew only itself. Therefore it became all. Of the gods, who all realized this, he became that only. Similarly of the sages, similarly of

the men. Indeed, seeing this the sage Vāma-deva knew, 'I am Manu and the sun.' Even at present who thus knows this that, 'I am Brahman', he becomes all this. Certainly, even the deities cannot prevent his becoming thus, since he becomes their self. Now who meditates on another deity (other than his self) thinking, 'He is different, I am different', he does not know. Just as an animal (is to man) thus he is to the gods. Indeed just as many animals serve men, thus does each man serve the gods. Even if only a single animal is taken away, it leads to unpleasantness, what indeed of many? From that it is not pleasing for them that men should realize this.
This (self) was indeed Brahman in the beginning. It knew only itself. Therefore, it became all.'

This verse contains the mahāvākya, aham Brahmāsmi. The commentary stresses the unity of the self and Brahman. It quotes other texts such as 'That thou art' (Ch.VI.viii.7), 'There's is no other knower but him' (III.vii.23). The Gītā (G.x.20) is also quoted, 'I am the self O Arjuna (dwelling in the mind of all beings).' The commentary highlights that the words are, 'I am Brahman', to stress that the entity known and the knower are the same. Otherwise it would be, 'It is Brahman', or 'That is Brahman'.

11. Surely in the beginning there was only one Brahman. That did not prosper being one. That created an excellent form the Kṣatriya, those who among the gods are Kṣatras (rulers), Indra, Varuṇa, Soma (the moon), Rudra, Parjanya, Yama, death and Īśāna. From that there is nothing surpassing the Kṣatriya. From that in the Rajasuye, the Brāhmaṇa is seated below the Kṣatriya. That glory is bestowed to the Kṣatriya alone. However it is the Brāhmaṇa who is the source of the Kṣatriya. From that even though a king goes on to become supreme, at the end the Brāhmaṇa is his source. He who

insults the Brāhmaṇa destroys his own source. He becomes very wicked since he injures one who is his better.

12. Still he did not prosper. It brought into existence those classes of deities who are described in groups namely the Vasus, Rudras, Ādityas, Viśvadevās, and Maruts.
13. Still he did not prosper. He created the other castes, as Pūṣan; for the earth nourishes what all there is.
14. Still he did not prosper. It created an excellent form of righteousness. Of the Kṣatriyas, that which is the ruler is this righteousness. From that there is nothing superior to Dharma. So even one who is weak seeks (to defeat) a stronger person through Dharma, just as one does through a king. He verily who is righteousness, that surely is true. From that people say of one speaking the truth, he speaks what is righteous, (and) indeed a man who speaks what is righteous, that he speaks what is true. For both becomes this (righteousness) only.

The commentary says that righteousness is the controller of all. Righteousness when expressed as conduct being practised by people is truth. Truth is said to be the fact of being in consonance with the scriptures. Thus they are the same since the same thing, when practised is known as righteousness and when it is said to be as per scriptures is truth.

15. (Thus) that (were created), the various castes. Within the gods, that Brahmā became fire only and within men various castes came about. From that people wish to obtain a place among gods by means of fire only, and within men as the Brāhmaṇa. For both these forms were assumed by Brahmā. Now indeed who departs this world not viewing (knowing) his own world, this not being known, does not protect him just in the manner that the Vedas unread, or any other action not performed (does not help). Here, even who does a work

of great merit, without knowing thus, that (work) of his gets extinguished at the end only. One ought to meditate on the self as the world only. He who meditates only on the self as the world, his works are not extinguished, for from that self only, whatever he desires, that all is created.

The importance of fire and its role as a receptacle for sacrificial rites is emphasized. At the same time the results desired for which a rite is conducted may also be attained by the chanting of mantras by a suitable person. Yet if a person who performs rites, dies from the transitory world without realizing the self, he is not protected by the self from evils such as fear, grief, and delusion.

16. Now surely this self of all beings is the world. He who makes offerings and sacrifices, by means of that (attains) the world of deities. Now who recites (the Vedas) (attains) the world of the sages. Now who makes the offerings to the fathers, who wishes for offspring, by means of that (attains the) fathers. Now who gives shelter and food to men by means of that (attains the world of) men. Now who provides grass and water to animals, by means of that (attains the world of) animals. Who, in his house, beasts and birds, even ants, dwell in his house, by means of that (attains) their world. Surely, just as one wishes happiness for his world, thus all beings wish happiness for him who knows thus. Certainly, that is known and analysed.
17. Surely in the beginning was only this one self. He desired, 'Let there be a wife for me, so also may offspring be born. Then let there be wealth for me, so I may perform rites.' Surely, so much is (what comprises) desire. This is why even if one wishes one cannot obtain more than this. From this, even at present one who is single desires, 'Let there be a wife for me, so also may offspring be born. Then let there be wealth

for me, so I may perform rites.' So long as he does not attain each of these, that long does he consider himself incomplete only. His completeness (can be attained like this): surely, the mind is his self, speech is his wife, prāṇa is his offspring, the eye is human wealth, for he obtains it by means of the eye, the ear is divine (wealth) for he hears it by means of the ear, the body only is its rites, for he does rites by means of the body. It, this sacrifice is fivefold, animal is fivefold, person is fivefold, all this is fivefold, whatsoever that there is. Who thus knows that, attains all this.

The text states that, 'This much indeed, that is things limited to the desire for means, namely for wife, sons, riches, and rites is desire. The three worlds, the world of the deities, of the ancestors and of men are the result of this above.' The commentary points out that how much so ever one may wish, they cannot get more than this, which consists of ends and means, either perceptible or imperceptible. Desire is the pursuit of these ends and means and is the sphere of the ignorant. The wise ought to renounce desire.

V

1. When seven kinds of food were created by the intellect and penance, the father of this one was general (to all beings), two he assigned to the deities, three he constructed for himself, to animals he gave one. On this, all is established, that which breathes and does not (breathe). From which do these not perish, since they are continually being consumed? Surely, who knows this indestructibility he eats food by means of his mouth. He goes to the deities, he lives on energy. Regarding this are the verses:

The ignorant man worships another, and by performance of rites, etc., projects all beings and the entire universe as the objects of enjoyment. Therefore all become both the enjoyer and the object of enjoyment of the universe depending upon rites performed and meditations. It follows from this that everyone is alternatively the cause and then effect of everyone else.

2. When seven kinds of food were created by the intellect and penance of the father implies that the father created them by means of the intellect and penance. 'Of this, one was general (to all beings)', implies that this food of his is indeed that which is the general food (of all). He who worships this food is never away from sin, since this is mixed.

   'Two he assigned to the deities' implies performing fire sacrifices and other offerings. From that a person performs sacrifices and makes offerings to the gods. Now some say these two mean the new moon and full moon sacrifices. From that one ought not to be (overly) preoccupied with sacrifices for material gains.

   'To animals he gave one', that is milk, since in the beginning men and animals live only in milk. From that indeed, a newborn baby is in the beginning made to lick clarified butter or suckle it. Some say regarding a newborn calf that it is not eating grass. On this all is established. That which breathes and that which does not (breathe) implies that on milk is established that which breathes and that which does not. Regarding that some say this, that by making offerings by means of milk a person overcomes recurring death. One ought to know that this is not the case. For who knows thus conquers recurring death on the day he makes the offering only, since he offers all eatable food to the gods.

   'From which these do not perish, since they are continually being consumed', implies that indeed the person is indestructible since he creates this food again and again.

   'Surely he who knows this indestructibility' implies that surely the person is the cause of the indestructibility since he creates this food by means of repeated meditation and by

means of activities. If he would not do this, his food would surely be exhausted.
He eats food by means of his mouth. The mouth is prominent, this (is eaten) by means of the mouth.
He goes to the deities. He lives on energy. Regarding this are the verses:

The words medhā and tapas are used to indicate meditation and rites. This verse seeks to explain the seven kinds of food produced by the father by meditation and rites.

The text seeks to induce an aversion to objects and the means and ends among them so as to enjoin the knowledge of Brahman. There can be no desire regarding the subject matter of knowledge of Brahman since it is the oneness of all. It goes on to state that one who primarily aims to enjoy food to sustain his existence is never very distant from evil. Such food is common food of all, any part of this that is eaten entails pain to others.

3. Three he constructed for himself implies the mind, the organ of speech and prāṇa. These he constructed for himself. (It is said): 'My mind was somewhere else, I did not see; my mind was somewhere else, I did not hear.' For it is by means of the mind only that one sees. It is by means of the mind that one hears. Desire, will power, doubt, faith, absence of faith, patience, absence of patience, modesty, absence of modesty, intellect and fear, all this is the mind only. From this, even if one were touched on the back, he discerns it by means of the mind. And whatever sound there is, it is speech only, since this is dependent on an end (yet) this is not (an end). The prāṇa, apāna, vyāna, udāna, samāna, and ana, all this is vital breath only. Surely this self is composed of these, composed of speech, composed of mind, composed of vital breath.

This verse seeks to address the doubt concerning the existence of the mind. By means of an illustration it is shown that the internal organ called mind, which joins itself to the objects of various organs in order to enable perception. The nature of the mind is then explained. The commentary also explains the organ of speech whose function is stated to be to reveal.

Prāṇa the vital breath is described. Prāṇa is connected to the heart and can move to the mouth and nostrils, apāna, functions below the heart, it extends to the navel and it helps excretion. The regulator and nexus between prāṇa and apāna is vyāna, which is also the cause of the actions requiring strength. Rising up and nutrition is due to udāna. Samāna assimilates that which we eat and drink. It is situated in the belly and helps the digestion of food. All these are the prāṇa.

4. These are the three worlds only. Indeed speech is this world (the earth). The mind is the intermediate space between heaven and earth. Prāṇa is that world (heaven).

The commentary also highlights the importance of the number three. This will continue in the following passages.

5. These are the three Vedas only. Indeed, speech is the Ṛg Veda. The mind is the Yajur Veda. Prāṇa is the Sāma Veda.
6. These are the deities, ancestors and men only. Indeed, speech is the deities. The mind is the ancestors. Prāṇa is the men.
7. These are the father, mother, and progeny. Indeed, the mind is the father. Speech is the mother. Prāṇa is the progeny.
8. These are the known, what is to be known, and the unknown only. Whatsoever is known is a form of speech, since speech is the knower. This speech by becoming that (the known) protects him (the knower).
9. Whatsoever is to be known that is a form of the mind since that mind is to be known. This mind by becoming that, protects him.

10. Whatsoever is unknown is a form of prāṇa since prāṇa is unknown. This prāṇa by becoming that protects him.

Śruti in the Chāndogya Upaniṣad (Ch.II.xxii.1) has spoken of prāṇa as undefined. The preceding verses seek to describe the manifestation of the prāṇa, mind and organs of speech regarding the elements. The next three relate to their manifestation in the context of the deities.

11. The earth is the body of this speech, (its) luminous form is this fire. As far as that speech goes, indeed that far the earth and so far goes this fire.

The commentary states that both the earth and fire are the vocal organ of Hiraṇyagarbha.

12. Then, of this mind, the body is heaven, the luminous form is that sun. Indeed, as far as the mind goes, so far heaven, so far that sun. The two were united and therefore prāṇa was born. He is the supreme lord. This (prāṇa) is without an enemy. Surely a second (being) is an enemy. There is no enemy for he who knows thus.

Regarding the deities, fire and sun are forms of the organ of speech and mind. Even though these two are different from the prāṇa, they never become its rivals since on the cosmic plane both are subordinate to prāṇa.

13. Now of this prāṇa, the body is water, the luminous form is that moon. Indeed as far as that prāṇa goes, so far water, so far the moon. They, these are all similar and all unending. Certainly, he who meditates on these as finite gains a finite world. However, he who meditates on these as infinite gains an infinite world.

The organ of speech, mind and prāṇa are the three types of food which were produced by the father through rites. The universe in its aspect of body and elements is pervaded by these. They pervade the entire universe and are therefore infinite. He who meditated on these as finite, wins a finite world. But who meditates on these as infinite, wins an infinite world.

14. This Prajāpati is the year and he has sixteen parts. Indeed, his nights have fifteen parts and his sixteenth part is immovable. (As the moon), he through the nights only, waxes and wanes. He by means of the sixteenth part, on the new moon night, pervades all that is breathing and therefore he is born in the morning. From that, in honour of this deity only, on this night, one ought not to cut off the breath of any living being, not even that of a lizard.

Prajāpati is being described as the year or time. Prajāpati pervades all living creatures through the herbs they eat and the water they drink.

Prajāpati consists of five factors: Heaven, the sun and mind are the father, the earth, fire, and organ of speech are his wife, the mother. Prāṇa is their progeny. The lunar days are wealth. The lunar days or digits which are units of time, these cause alterations in the universe and are rites.

15. Surely, he the person who knows thus is described as the year and he who has sixteen parts. His wealth only is fifteen parts, his self is the sixteenth part. He, through wealth only waxes and wanes. That which is the self corresponds to the nave of a wheel and the wealth (corresponds to) the felloe. From that even if a person loses all but lives by means of the self only, it is said that he has only been deprived of his periphery.

This verse seeks to explain how by the performance of rites with five factors along with proper meditation, the divine wealth, a man becomes Prajāpati consisting of the three kinds of food.

16. Now surely there are three worlds—the world of men, the world of the fathers, and the world of the deities. It, this world of men is attained by means of a son only, not by means of anything else such as actions (rites). The world of the fathers by means of actions (rites); the world of deities by means of knowledge. Certainly, the world of deities is the most excellent world. From that they extol knowledge.

The verse emphasizes that there are three worlds attainable by ways outlined in the scriptures.

17. Thus now (the transmission): At this time when a man considers that he is about to depart, then he tells his son: 'You are Brahman, you are the sacrifice, you are the world.' He, the son replies: 'I am Brahman, I am the sacrifice, I am the world.' Surely, whatsoever has been studied, of all this, it is one with Brahman. Surely whatever sacrifices there are, of them all is one sacrifice. Surely whatever worlds there are, of them all is one world. So much (a householder's duties) is indeed all this. He, by means of being identified with all this will save me. From that, it is said of a son who is instructed, as leading to the worlds. From that they instruct him. When he who knows thus departs from this world, he enters into his son, along with his breaths. If any duty has not been done by him, from all that he is released by his son. From that he is named a son. By means of his son a father is established in the world. Then these immortal divine breaths enter into him.

The role of a son and duties expected of a sun are being spoken about here. This verse seeks to explain how a son can help the winning of worlds. In this context the rite of entrusting, where a father entrusts his son is described. The father enjoins on the son the duties of study, sacrifice and winning of worlds. Further, if anything is left undone by the father, the son by fulfilling it himself exonerates his father from the related obstacles. Thus the derivative meaning of the word 'putra', is 'he who saves', the father by completing his mission.

18. The divine speech pervades him from the earth and from the fire. Surely that is the divine speech by means of which whatever one speaks, indeed that all comes to be.
19. The divine mind pervades him from heaven and from the sun. Surely that is the divine mind by means of which one becomes blissful indeed and does not grieve.
20. The divine prāṇa pervades him from water and the moon. Surely it is the divine prāṇa which whether in motion or not in motion, is neither perturbed nor perishes. He who thus knows, of all beings becomes the self. Just as this deity (Hiraṇyagarbha) thus he is. Just as all beings bow before this deity, thus do all beings bow before him who knows thus. Whatever grief these creatures suffer, that stays with them. Yet to him, only merit accrues. Certainly, no evil goes to the deities.

The import of this verse is to point out that the person who knows the meditation on the three types of food as same with himself, as mentioned in the preceding verses, becomes the self of all beings, their prāṇa, mind and speech. Since he is the self of all he becomes all knowing and the doer of all. So, also, Hiraṇyagarbha who attained this state first is always all knowing and all powerful.

Further it is mentioned that the self is not affected by the joys and sorrows of all beings since the understanding of the self is not limited. Grief is the result of identification with limited things.

21. Now for this reason an analysis of the vow. Indeed, Prajāpati created the organs. After being created they contended with one another. 'I will speak only,' resolved speech. 'I will see':

the eye. 'I will hear': the ear. Thus just as per their functions the other organs. Having become exhausted, death seized them. (It, death) acquired them. Having acquired them, it restrained them. From that only speech gets tired, the eye becomes tired, the ear becomes tired. Now this (death) indeed could not acquire this which is in the middle, the prāṇa. They (the other organs) resolved to know it. 'Surely this is the most excellent among us, since whether it is in motion or not in motion, is neither perturbed nor perishes. Well let us assume its form only.' Indeed of this they all became a form. From that they are called by its name, prāṇa. In whichever family there is a person who knows thus, indeed that family is designated by the name of that person. And whoever contends with he who knows thus, withers away and after withering away, in the end dies. This with regard to the self.

22. Now with regards to the deities. Fire resolved: 'I will keep on burning.' The sun: 'I will warm.' The moon: 'I will shine.' Thus also the other deities resolved just as per their divine functions. Just as prāṇa is central among the organs, just in this manner is Vāyu among the deities. For other deities may not always perform their functions but not Vāyu. He, Vāyu, is the deity that never sets.

Vāyu is the deity that never sets. The vow of a person who identifies with the prāṇa with regard to the body and with Vāyu regarding the deities is uninterrupted.

23. Now regarding that is this verse: 'From which the sun rises and where it goes to set. Surely this rises from prāṇa, in prāṇa it sets. The deities made him the law. Surely, he is today only. Indeed, he is tomorrow.'

Certainly, what these (functions) observed of old, even that only they achieve today. From that a person should perform one vow only. He ought to breathe in and breathe out wishing: 'May the evil of death not overwhelm me.' When he observes it he ought to desire to complete it. By means of this he achieves union with or residence in this world of the deity.

The verse seeks to strew the significance of the vow of air and prāṇa.

VI

1. Surely, this universe is a collection of three—name, form, and action. Of these, concerning names, the source is speech since from it do all names arise. This is their common feature, since this is common to all names. Of these, this is Brahman, since this supports all names.

   The entire universe consists of three things—name, form, and action. All these three are non-self. Thus from these should one turn away. If one is not averse to the non-self then there is no inclination to meditate on the self. This verse and the next two verses seek to show how the universe made of actions, their factors and results consists of name, form, action, and is not the self.

2. Now of forms, the eye is the source, since from the eye do all forms arise. This is their common feature since this is common to all forms. Of these, this is Brahman, since this supports all forms.
3. Now of actions, the body is the source, since from it all actions arise. This is their common feature since this is common to all actions. Of these this is Brahman since this supports all worlds. That, this collection of three are one, this self; this self though single is this collection of three. That is immortal concealed by means of the true. Certainly, prāṇa is immortal, name and form are true.

CHAPTER 2

I

1. Aum. There was a learned descendant of Garga named Dṛpta-bālāki. To Ajātśatru of Kāśi he said: 'Let me speak to you about Brahman.' He Ajātśatru said: 'For this proposal I grant you a thousand cows.' Certainly, people run saying: 'Janaka, Janaka.'

   The verse indicates that the king Janaka was wise and liked to hear about Brahman. Those who want to hear or discuss regarding Brahman or have a request rushed to King Janaka.

2. He (Gārgya) said: 'The person who indeed is in that sun, on him I meditate as Brahman.' He (Ajātśatru) said: 'Please do not converse about him to me. I meditate on him only as transcendent, as the head of all beings and splendid. He who thus meditates on him becomes transcendent, the head of all beings and splendid.'

   Here Ajātaśatru during the dialogue refutes the view of the sun as Brahman. Ajātśatru says he meditates on Brahman as transcendent, that is transcending all beings, the head of all and splendid. One who meditates on Brahman as such becomes exactly as meditated upon.

3. He (Gārgya) said: 'The person who indeed is in that moon on him I meditate as Brahman.' He, (Ajātśatru) said: 'Please do not converse about him to me. I meditate on him only as the vast, white-robed splendid king Soma. He who thus meditates on him, for him Soma is extracted and poured forth daily. His supply of food is never diminished.'

   Then Gārgya put forward the presentation of the moon as Brahman.

4. He (Gārgya) said: 'The person who indeed is in that lightning on him I meditate as Brahman.' He, (Ajātśatru) said: 'Please do not converse about him to me. I meditate on him only as the brilliant. He who thus meditates on him becomes brilliant, indeed his progeny also become brilliant.'

   Similary Gārgya presents the one God in lightning as that which he meditates upon as Brahman.

5. He (Gārgya) said: 'The person who indeed is in that ether on him I meditate as Brahman.' He, (Ajātśatru) said: 'Please do not converse about him to me. I meditate on him only as the complete and immovable. He who thus meditates on him becomes fulfilled with progeny and cattle and from this world his progeny never die out.'

   Again, Gārgya presents the person in the ether as that which he meditates upon as Brahman.

6. He (Gārgya) said: 'The person who indeed is in that air on him I meditate as Brahman.' He (Ajātśatru) said: 'Please do not converse about him to me. I meditate on him only as sovereign, triumphant and as the invincible army. He who thus meditates on him becomes triumphant, invincible and a vanquisher of enemies.'

7. He (Gārgya) said: 'The person who indeed is in that fire on him I meditate as Brahman.' He (Ajātśatru) said: 'Please do not converse about him to me. I meditate on him only as tolerant. He who thus meditates on him becomes tolerant and his progeny also become tolerant.'
8. He (Gārgya) said: 'The person who indeed is in this water on him I meditate as Brahman.' He (Ajātśatru) said: 'Please do not converse about him to me. I meditate on him only as what is similar. He who thus meditates on him, to him comes what is similar, not what is not similar, from him is born what is similar.'
9. He (Gārgya) said: 'The person who indeed is in this mirror on him I meditate as Brahman.' He (Ajātśatru) said: 'Please do not converse about him to me. I meditate on him only as what is resplendent. He who thus meditates on him becomes resplendent and his progeny also become resplendent. His radiance exceeds all those he associates with.'
10. He (Gārgya) said: 'The sound which arises here after one who walks, on him I meditate as Brahman.' He (Ajātśatru) said: 'Please do not converse about him to me. I meditate on him only as life. He who thus meditates on him achieves a full lifespan in this world. Prāṇa does not leave him before his (due) time.'
11. He (Gārgya) said: 'The person who indeed is in the directions on him I meditate as Brahman.' He (Ajātśatru) said: 'Please do not converse about him to me. I meditate on him only as the second who never parts. He who thus meditates on him becomes possessed of followers and his attendants are never cut away from him.'
12. He (Gārgya) said: 'The person who indeed is made of shadow, on him I meditate as Brahman.' He (Ajātśatru) said: 'Please do not converse about him to me. I meditate on him only as death. He who thus meditates on him achieves a full

lifespan in this world. Death does not approach him before his (due) time.'

13. He (Gārgya) said: 'The person who indeed is in the self on him I meditate as Brahman.' He (Ajātśatru said: 'Please do not converse about him to me. I meditate on him only as self-possessed. He who thus meditates on him becomes self-possessed. His progeny becomes self-possessed.' He, Gārgya became quiet.

When Gārgya's views on Brahman were refuted, he had nothing else to state, he became quiet.

14. He (Ajātśatru) said: 'Is this all?' 'This is all.' (Said Gārgya). 'By means of this much only it is not known.' (Said Ajātśatru). He, Gārgya said: 'May I approach you as a disciple?'

The preceding verses speak about the conditional Brahman spoken about by Gārgya stemming from the sphere of ignorance and the unconditional Brahman spoken about by King Janaka.

15. He (Ajātśatru) said: 'That is contrary to the accepted custom that a Brāhmaṇa should approach a Kṣatriya with the thought that he will explain to me about Brahman. Yet I will enlighten you.' Taking him by means of the hand he arose. The two came to a person who was sleeping. Calling him the following names the two addressed him: 'Great one, white-robed one, splendid one, Soma.' He did not wake up. He roused him by rubbing his hand. Then he awoke.

The commentary further distinguishes the two conceptions of Brahman that is the views regarding Brahman espoused by Gārgya and Ajātśatru. The analogy of the sleeping man is used since in the waking state both these two appear mixed up. Further it is stated that the experiencer is the subject, the seer and not an object. That what is not the experiencer is an object and not a subject.

16. He (Ajātśatru) said: 'When this person was asleep, this person who consists of intelligence, where was this then and from where did it come?' Indeed, this too Gārgya was not aware of.

It is stated that here consciousness is used to denote the mind or intellect, i.e., the instrument of knowledge. The expression, 'full of consciousness' is used to refer to what is perceived in the intellect, that which is perceived by means of it, and which perceived by means of it.

17. He (Ajātśatru) said: 'When this person was asleep, this person who consists of intelligence, by means of his intelligence that person takes up for himself the intelligence of these breaths (sense organs) and lives in the space in the heart. When he takes in these breaths then this person is said to be sleeping. When that prāṇa is withdrawn, indeed speech is withdrawn, the eye is withdrawn, the ear is withdrawn, the mind is withdrawn.'

The being full of consciousness when asleep, it during this time absorbs the functioning of the organs, their ability to perceive objects, by means of its own consciousness, the mind which is caused by ignorance and lies in the ākāśa in the heart. Ākāśa is used here to refer to the supreme self which is same as its own self. The concept is that it gives up its differentiated forms which are due to limiting adjuncts, and it remains in its undifferentiated natural, absolute self.

18. 'When it wanders in a dream these are its worlds. That as it were becomes a great king or as it were a great Brāhmaṇa or as it were enters high or low states. Just as he, a great being, takes his citizens and goes about as he wishes in his own kingdom, thus this only takes his breaths (organs) and goes about as he wishes in its own body.

The commentary refutes the objection that the self is possessed of attributes like being happy, undergoing grief, etc. It is said that these experiences are false. The self is not really connected to these various experiences such as joy and grief. Further it is reiterated that identification with the body or the organs is unreal and the consequence of the superimposition of ignorance.

19. Now when one is fast asleep, when one is not aware of anything, it returns to the body by means of the seventy-two thousand nerves named Hitā which branch of from the heart to the pericardium and lies there. Indeed, just as in the manner as a youth, a great Brāhmaṇa lives, having attained the peak of bliss, thus does he rest then.

It becomes pure in dream state. In deep sleep it attains its state of natural purity. Here it gives up impurities due to contact with other things. The process of the taking place of deep sleep is made clear in the verse.

20. Just as a spider travels along a thread, or just as small sparks issue from a fire, thus from this self only do all organs, all worlds, all gods, all beings issue. Its secret name is the truth of truth. Surely prāṇa is truth and their truth is this.

All, the organs, the worlds, the deities, all living beings emanate from the real nature of the individual self. The world, both moving and unmoving proceeds from the self like sparks from a fire.

II

1. Surely, he who knows the calf with its abode, with its special place, with its pillar and rope, restrains his seven jealous relatives. Surely this calf is that prāṇa which is the middle. Of this the place is this (body) only, the special place is this (the head), its pillar is prāṇa, its rope is food.

The seven organs, i.e., the eyes, the ears, the nostrils, and the mouth which are instruments for perception and lead to attachment to sense objects are the seven kinsmen. They are termed as envious kinsmen since they hinder a person from perceiving the inner self. The prāṇa in the body, i.e., the subtle body is the calf. The abode of the calf is the body. Food is the tether of the calf. Food is transformed into three forms. The gross for which is excreted and absorbed by the earth, the intermediate form which passes through the stages of blood, etc and nourishes the body. The finest form known as nectar, is very powerful, proceeds past the navel to the heart, penetrating the seventy-two thousand nerves, radiates generating strength, helping the subtle body. Thus like a calf's tether, food connects the prāṇa and the body.

2. These seven undecaying ones worship it. In this manner there are these red lines in the eye and by means of them. Rudra is united with it; now through the water in the eyes Parjanya; by means of the pupil, the sun; by means of the dark portion, fire; by means of the white portion, Indra; by means of the lower eyelid the earth is united to it, and by means of the upper eyelid, heaven. His stock of food is never depleted who knows thus.

   Here the seven names of deities are used to indicate mantras instrumental to prayer.

3. Regarding that is this verse:
   There is a bowl with its opening below and its bottom rising up. On this is situated the glory of manifold forms. On its side sit seven sages, speech is the eighth which converses with Brahman. 'The bowl with its opening below and its bottom rising up' is the head for it is a bowl with its opening below and its bottom rising up. 'On this is situated the glory of manifold forms' refers to the organs, which surely are where the glory of manifold forms is situated. 'On its side sit

seven sages' refers to the organs which indeed are the sages. 'Speech is the eighth which converses with Brahman' since speech as the eighth communicates with Brahman.

The bowl refers to the head whose shape resembles a bowl. Like soma juice in a bowl, different kinds of knowledge are put in the bowl. The organs in seven forms constitute various forms of knowledge since these are the cause of perception of sight, sound, etc.

4. These two (the ears) are Gotama and Bharadvāja only. This indeed is Gotama and this indeed is Bharadvāja. These two (the eyes) are Viśvāmitra and Jamadagni. This indeed is Viśvāmitra and this indeed is Jamadagni. These two (the nostrils) are Vasiṣṭha and Kaṣyapa only. This indeed is Vasiṣṭha and this indeed is Kaṣyapa. Indeed, the tongue is Atri, since by means of the tongue is food eaten. Surely Atri is not indeed this name Atti. He becomes the eater of all, everything becomes his food who knows thus.

III

1. Indeed, these are the two forms of Brahman—corporeal and subtle, mortal and immortal, the fixed and the moving, the real and the true.

Brahman though formless, by the superimposition of ignorance appears definable, conceivable and having two forms. The two forms are corporeal and subtle, their phases are mortal and immortal.

2. The corporeal form (of Brahman) is that which is different from air and the intermediate region between heaven and earth. This is mortal, this is fixed, this is true. The essence of this corporeal, of this true is the sun which radiates warmth since this is the essence of the truth.

The corporeal and subtle have four phases each. These phases are now being enumerated. Gross implies that whose parts are well defined, and solid. These are the three elements other than air and ether. These are mortal or perishable since they are limited. Since it is limited it is defined. The three elements having the four features of being corporeal, mortal, limited, and defined are the corporeal form of Brahman. The sun is the perfection of these three elements.

3. Now the subtle form. It is air and the intermediate region between heaven and earth. This is immortal, this is moving, this is true. The essence of this subtle, of this immortal, of this moving, this is real, is this person that is in the solar disc. Since he is this essence. This is with regard to the deities.

   The subtle form is air and ether, the other two elements. It is subtle, immortal, unlimited, and undefined. Its essence is Hiraṇyagarbha, the being in the sun, as the cosmic organ. From the undifferentiated these two elements emerge to form Hiraṇyagarbha.

4. Now with regard to the self. Indeed, the corporeal form is this, which is different from Prāṇa and this ether which is within the self. This is mortal, this is established, this is real. The essence of this corporeal form of this mortal, of this established, of this real is the eye, since it is the essence of the real.

   This verse sets out the distinction of corporeal and subtle with respect to the body. The corporeal from of the body are the three elements in the body other than air and ether. Its essence is the eye.

5. Now the subtle form is prāṇa and this ether which is within the self. This is immortal, this is moving, this is real. The

essence of this subtle form, of this immortal, of this moving, of this real is this which is in the right eye since this is the essence of the real.

The subtle form of the body is prāṇa (air) and ether. Its essence is the being in the right eye.

6. Of this person, its form is just as a red coloured cloth, or grey sheep's wool or just as the Indragopa insect, or just as a tongue of fire, or just as a white lotus, or just as a sudden flash of lightning. Surely, of this who knows thus becomes splendid like a sudden flash of lightning. Therefore now is the instruction (regarding Brahman): 'Not this, not this', since there is nothing other than this (Brahman) and there is not anything else greater than this. Now the sacred name of this is the truth of the truth. Surely prāṇa is truth, and this is the truth of that.

This crucial verse speaks about the nature of Brahman referred to as the truth of truth. In the commentary, initially Śaṅkarācārya refutes the positions of other schools regarding the self such as Buddhist idealists (Yogācaras), Naiyāyikas, Vaiśesikas, Saṁkhya, etc. The term, 'neti, neti' (not this, not this) is used to describe that which is the truth of truth. These words aim to state the elimination of all differences due to limiting adjuncts and the reference to that which does not have anything to distinguish it such as name, form, action, attribute, species, etc. Brahman has no distinguishing marks. It cannot be described as 'so and so' or 'such and such'.

When Brahman is described by categories superimposed on it such as name, form, and action then words like knowledge, bliss, pure, intelligence, etc. are used. However, when we want to describe its true nature it can only be described as, 'not this, not this'.

By eliminating all adjuncts, the desire to know space, time, and all else one realizes one's identity with Brahman, the truth of truth.

IV

1. Yājñavalkya said: 'Maitreyī, indeed I am about to be elevated from this place, my dear. Well let me conclude your relationship with this Kātyāyanī.'
2. She Maitreyī said: 'Illustrious sir, even if the entire earth filled with wealth be mine, how by means of this shall I be immortal?' 'No,' said Yājñavalkya, 'just as the life of those having plentiful means, so indeed would your life be. But of immortality there is no hope by means of wealth.'
3. She Maitreyī said: 'What shall I do with this by means of which I shall not become immortal? Illustrious sir, speak to me of that alone which you know.'
4. He Yājñavalkya said: 'Ah you have been dear (always) to me, so speak what is dear. Come, sit down I shall expound to you. However, while I expound, deeply meditate on it.'
5. He said: 'Surely, my dear, not for the sake of a husband does a husband become beloved, however a husband is beloved for the sake of the self. Surely, my dear, not for the sake of the wife does a wife become beloved, however a wife is beloved for the sake of the self. Surely, my dear, not for the sake of sons do sons become beloved, however sons are beloved for the sake of the self. Surely, my dear, not for the sake of wealth does wealth become beloved, however wealth is beloved for the sake of the self. Surely, my dear, not for the sake of Brāhmaṇa does a Brāhmaṇa become beloved, however a Brāhmaṇa is beloved for the sake of the self. Surely, my dear, not for the sake of a Kṣatriya does a Kṣatriya become beloved, however a Kṣatriya is beloved for the sake of the self. Surely, my dear, not for the sake of the worlds do the worlds become

beloved, however the worlds are beloved for the sake of the self. Surely, my dear, not for the sake of the gods are gods beloved, however the gods are beloved for the sake of the self. Surely, my dear, not for the sake of beings do beings become beloved, however beings are beloved for the sake of the self. Surely, my dear, not for the sake of all is all beloved, however all is beloved for the sake of the self. Certainly, O Maitreyī, it is the self that ought to be seen, ought to be heard, ought to be reflected on and ought to be meditated upon. Surely, by means of the seeing, by means of the hearing, by means of the thinking, by means of realization of the self all this is known.

This verse seeks to teach renunciation as a means to immortality. An aversion to everything else is sought to be inculcated leading to immortality. The enumeration is made in order of proximity as sources of joy. The word 'all' is then used to cover all that which has not been explicitly mentioned.

Love for the self is primary. Love for everything else is secondary since they apparently contribute to pleasures of the self. The self should be realized. The self should be heard from a qualified teacher and the scriptures be reflected on by means of reasoning and then steadily meditated upon. Thus by means of hearing, reflection and meditation only can the realization of the unity of Brahman be attained. Śaṅkarācārya states that all distinctions including those of caste are destroyed by the realization of the self.

6. The Brāhmaṇa shuns him who knows the Brāhmaṇa as other than the self. The Kṣatriya shuns him who knows the Kṣatriya as other than the self. The world shuns him who knows the world as other than the self. The deities shun him who knows the deities as other than the self. Beings shun him who knows beings as other than the self. All shun him

who knows all as other than the self. This Brāhmaṇa, this Kṣatriya, these worlds, these deities, these beings, all this is that which is the self.

7. Just as one is not able to grasp the external sounds of a drum being beaten, however by grasping the drum or the beater of the drum only are the sounds grasped.
8. Just as one is not able to grasp the external sounds of a conch being blown, however by grasping the conch or the blower of the conch only are the sounds grasped.
9. Just as one is not able to grasp the external sounds of a vīnā being played, however by grasping the vīnā or the player of the vīnā only are the sounds grasped.
10. Just as from a fire which arises from damp fuel different kinds of smoke are produced, thus my dear the Ṛg Veda, the Yajur Veda, the Sāma Veda, Ātharvāṇgirasa, history, the Purāṇas, sciences, Upaniṣads, verses, aphorisms (sūtras) elucidations, and commentaries are the breath of this great reality. From this are all these inspired.

While explaining this verse Śaṅkarācārya states that the Vedas are eternally composed and manifested without any effort on his behalf. Thus they are the authority with respect to their meaning, they do not require validation from any other means of knowledge. The authority of the Vedas is underlined.

11. Just as the ocean is the one abode of all waters, thus the skin is the one abode of all kinds of touch, the nostrils are the one abode of all odours, thus the tongue is the one abode of all tastes, thus the eye is the one abode of all forms, thus the ear is the one abode of all sounds, thus the mind is the one abode of all volitions, thus the intellect is the one abode of all knowledge, thus the hands are the one abode of all actions, thus the organ of generation is the one abode of all enjoyment, thus the organ of excretion is the one abode of

all excretions, thus the feet are the one abode of all walking, thus the organ of speech is the one abode of all the Vedas.

At the time of origin, continuance, and dissolution the universe is throughout Brahman. Just as bubbles are non-existent without water, so is the universe non-existent without Brahman. Brahman is thus homogeneous and is known as pure intelligence.

12. 'Just as a piece of rock salt thrown into the water dissolves in the water only, and there may be none to pick it up, however wherever one may take the water, it has a salty taste only, thus surely dear, this great being (reality), without end, without limit, consists of permanent knowledge. From these elements does one arise and into these does one disappear. Once it departs there is no consciousness. My dear, this is what I speak,' said Yājñavalkya.

This great reality is known as the supreme self. Due to ignorance a person gets cut off from this great reality as a separate entity connected to limiting adjuncts such as the body and organs. The person is then subject to birth and death, hunger and thirst, etc. This is a form of delusion. The supreme self is undecaying, immortal, fearless, homogeneous, infinite and unlimited and is pure intelligence.

13. She Maitreyī said: 'Here indeed, illustrious sir, you have confused me by saying, "Once it departs there is no consciousness."' He (Yājñavalkya) said: 'My dear, surely, I am not saying anything confusing. Surely, my dear, this is sufficient for knowledge.'

This verse seeks to dispel the doubt of Maitreyī. It is reiterated in the commentary that the ignorance based individual existence connected to limiting adjuncts such as the body, etc., is destroyed by knowledge along with the consciousness associated with the limiting adjuncts. Throughout Brahman which is transcendent is unchanged. Brahman is the self of the whole universe. It is eternal. Individual existence, based on ignorance is destroyed.

14. 'Since where there is duality as it were, there one smells another, one views another, one hears another, one speaks of another, one thinks of another, one knows another. However, where all has become the self only, then by means of whom and what should one smell, then by means of whom and what should one view, then by means of whom and what should one hear, then by means of whom and what should one speak, then by means of whom and what should one think, then by means of whom and what should one know? By means of which is all this known, through what should one know that? My dear, by means of what should a person know the knower?'

V

1. Of all beings this earth is honey and of this earth all beings are honey. And this person who is in this earth, (this person) consists of light, consists of immortality. With regard to oneself, the immortal person consisting of light who is in the body, he is this only, this which is the self. This is everything, this is immortal, this is Brahman.

The earth is the honey or effect of every being from Hiraṇyagarbha to grass. Likewise, all beings are the effects of the earth. Also, the immortal being possessed of intelligence, immortal in the earth and the corporeal being in the body are helpful to all beings and all beings are helpful to them.

Therefore, these four are the effect of all beings and vice versa. And thus the universe originated from one cause. This cause is Brahman. All else is a modification, a name. This is the import of this entire section.

2. Of all beings this water is honey and of this water all beings are honey. And this person who is in this water, (this person) consists of light and consists of immortality and with regard to oneself, the immortal person consisting of light who is identified with seed, he is this only, this which is the self. This is everything, this is immortal, this is Brahman.
3. Of all beings this fire is honey and of this fire all beings are honey. And, this person who is in this fire, (this person) consists of light and consists of immortality and with regard to oneself, the immortal person consisting of light, who consists of speech, he is this only, this which is the self. This is everything, this is immortal, this is Brahman.
4. Of all beings this air is honey and of this air all beings are honey. And this person who is in this air, (this person) consists of light and consists of immortality, and with regard to oneself, the immortal person consisting of light who is prāṇa, he is this only, this which is the self. This is everything, this is immortal, this is Brahman.
5. Of all beings this sun is honey and of this sun all beings are honey. And this person who is in this sun, (this person) consists of light and consists of immortality and with regard to oneself, the immortal person consisting of light who is in the eye, he is this only, this which is the self. This is everything, this is immortal, this is Brahman.
6. Of all beings these directions are honey and of these directions all beings are honey. And this person who is in these directions, (this person) consists of light and consists of immortality and with regard to oneself, the immortal person consisting of light who is in the ear and at each occasion of hearing, he is this only, this which is the self. This is everything, this is immortal, this is Brahman.
7. Of all beings this moon is honey and of this moon all beings are honey. And this person who is in this moon, (this person)

consists of light and consists of immortality, and with regard to oneself, the immortal person consisting of light who is in the mind, he is this only, this which is the self. This is everything, this is immortal, this is Brahman.

8. Of all beings this lightning is honey and of lightning all beings are honey. And this person who is in this lightning, (this person) consists of light and consists of immortality and with regard to oneself, the immortal person consisting of light who is in the light, he is this only, this which is the self. This is everything this is immortal, this is Brahman.

9. Of all beings this thunder-cloud is honey and of the thunder-cloud all beings are honey. And this person who is in this thundercloud, (this person) consists of light and consists of immortality and with regard to oneself, the immortal person consisting of light who is in the sound and the voice, he is this only, this which is the self. This is everything, this is immortal, this is Brahman.

10. Of all beings this ether is honey and of ether all beings are honey. And this person who is in this ether, (this person) consists of light and consists of immortality and with regard to oneself, the immortal person consisting of light who is in the ether in the heart, he is this only, this which is the self. This is everything, this is immortal, this is Brahman.

11. Of all beings this righteousness is honey and of this righteousness all beings are honey. And this person who is in this righteousness, (this person) consists of light and consists of immortality and with regard to oneself, the immortal person consisting of light who is righteousness, he is this only, this which is the self. This is everything, this is immortal, this is Brahman.

The effects due to righteousness are perceived. Righteousness is described as consisting of Śrutis and Smṛtis, as the power which controls the social order, which leads to the variety of the universe. Truth and righteousness are conformity with the scriptures and ethical conduct. Truth and righteousness produce their results in two forms visible and invisible. Righteousness that is invisible produces its effects generally as directing the elements of the earth and particularly directing the aggregate of the body and organs.

12. Of all beings this truth is honey and of this truth all beings are honey. And this person who is in this truth, (this person) consists of light and consists of immortality and with regard to oneself, the immortal person consisting of light who is truth, he is this only, this which is the self. This is everything, this is immortal, this is Brahman.

    Righteousness in its viable form as good conduct that is practised is known as truth. It is general and particular. The general form is inherent in the elements, the particular in the body and organs.

13. Of all beings, humankind is honey and of this humankind all beings are honey. And this person who is in this humankind, (this person) consists of light and consists of immortality and with regard to oneself, the immortal person consisting of light who is a human being, he is this only, this which is the self. This is everything, this is immortal, this is Brahman.
14. Of all beings this self is honey and of this self all beings are honey. And this person who is in this self, (this person) consists of light and consists of immortality and with regard to oneself, the immortal person consisting of light who is in this (individual) self, he is this only, this which is the self. This is everything, this is immortal, this is Brahman.
15. Surely, this self is the ruler of all beings; the king of all beings.Just in the manner that the spokes are attached to the nave and felloe of a chariot wheel, thus only in this self are attached all beings, all deities, all worlds, all creatures, and all these selves.

The self of all beings is an object of universal worship; it is the ruler of all. The knower of Brahman becomes free. One always has been Brahman. Yet due to ignorance it appears otherwise. By dissipating this ignorance by means of the knowledge of Brahman the knower of Brahman realizes Brahman, is Brahman. And since Brahman is all, becomes all. Illustrations are provided to make clear that the entire universe is fixed on the knower of Brahman who is the self of all.

16. This indeed is that honey which Dadhyac versed in the Atharva Veda expounded to the two Aśvins. Observing that this sage said: 'O Aśvins in the form of men I will reveal that fearful deed known as Daṁsa committed for the sake of acquisition just as a cloud reveals the imminent rain, even indeed which honey that Dadhyac versed in the Atharva Veda expounded to you by means of a horse's head.'

This verse by means of eulogy seeks to instruct one on the meditation on things that are mutually helpful. (The story of the horse's head is narrated in the commentary.)

17. This indeed is that honey which Dadhyac versed in the Atharva Veda expounded to the two Aśvins. Observing that this sage said: 'You place the head of a horse on Dadhyaṅ versed in the Atharva Veda. O destroyers of enemy forces, he expounded to you the honey relating to the sun, which is your secret in order to keep his promise.

This continues the train of instruction from the previous verse. It also emphasizes the importance of keeping one's word.

18. This indeed is that honey which Dadhyac versed in the Atharva Veda expounded to the two Aśvins. Observing that this sage said: 'He created persons with two feet, he created persons with four feet. That supreme being having become a

bird (subtle body) he occupied the persons. Surely this is the person that reposes in all persons. There is nothing that does not return to him, there is nothing that he does not pervade.'

The last two verses are concerned with the rite known as Pravargya. This verse aims to explain the purport of two chapters that deal with meditation on Brahman. While describing the meditation on things mutually helpful relating to Brahman it also indicates the unity of the self.

19. This indeed is that honey which Dadhyac versed in the Atharva Veda expounded to the two Aśvins. Observing that this sage said: 'He assumed many forms corresponding to the different forms. That form of his is meant for his revelation. By means of māyā, Indra (the lord) goes about in multiple forms, since to him are yoked organs, tens and hundreds. Surely this is the organs, surely this is tens and thousands, numerous and countless. This Brahman is without any prior and without any subsequent, without interior and without exterior. This self which experiences all is Brahman. This is the instruction.'

This verse highlights that the different forms of the self is meant to make him known. Brahman on account of māyā is perceived as diverse yet he is the same being. Brahman the self is without cause or effect, without interior or exterior. This homogeneous Brahman is the self. The perceiver of all and that because of which perception is possible.

VI

1. Now the lineage (of teachers): Pautimāṣya (obtained this instruction) from Gaupavana, Gaupavana from (a different) Pautimāṣya. This Pautimāṣya from (a different) Gaupavana. (This) Gaupavana from Kauśika, Kauśika from Kaundinya,

Kaundinya from Ṣāṇḍilya, Ṣāṇḍilya from Kauśika and Gautama.

2. From Āgniveśya, Āgniveśya from Śāṇḍilya and Ānabhimlāta, Ānabhimlāta from (a different) Ānabhimlāta, Ānabhimlāta from (yet another different) Ānabhimlāta. (This particular) Ānabhimlāta from Gautama. Gautama from Saitava and Prācīnayoga, Saitava and Prācīnayoga from Pārāśarya, Pārāśarya from Bhāradvāja. Bhāradvāja from Bhāradvāja and Gautama, Gautama from (a different) Bhāradvāja, Bhāradvāja from Pārāśarya, Pārāśarya from Baijavāpāyana, Baijavāpāyana from Kauṣikāyani, Kauṣikāyani.

3. From Ghṛtakauṣika, Ghṛtakauṣika from Pārāsaryāyana, Pārāsaryāyana from Pārāśarya, Pārāśarya from Jātūkarṇya. Jātūkarṇya from Āsurāyaṇa and Yāska. Āsurāyaṇa from Traivani. Traivani from Aupajandhani. Aupajandhani from Āsuri. Āsuri from Bhāradvāja. Bhāradvāja from Ātreya. Ātreya from Māñṭi. Māñṭi from Gautama. Gautama from Vātsya. Vātsya from Śāṇḍilya. Śāṇḍilya from Kaisorya kāpya. Kaisorya kāpya from Kumārahārita. Kumārahārita from Gālava. Gālava from Vidarbhīkauṇḍinya. Vidarbhīkauṇḍinya from Vatsanapāt Bābhrava. Vatsanapāt Bābhrava from Pathaḥ Saubharāt. Pathi Saubhara from Ayāsa Āṅgirasa, Ayāsa Āṅgirasa from Ābhuti Tvāṣtra, Ābhuti Tvāṣtra from Viśvarūpa Tvāṣtra. Viśvarūpa Tvāṣtra from the two Aśvins. The two Aśvins from Dadhyac Atharvaṇa. Dadhyac Atharvaṇa from Atharvan Daiva. Atharvan Daiva from Mṛtyu Prādhvaṁsana. Mṛtyu Prādhvaṁsana from Prādhvaṁsana. Prādhvaṁsana from Ekarṣi. Ekarṣi from Vipracitti. Vipracitti from Vyaṣṭi. Vyaṣṭi from Sanāru. Sanāru from Sanātana. Sanātana from Sanaga. Sanaga from Parameṣṭhin from Brahmā. Brahmā is self-generated. Salutation to Brahman.

CHAPTER 3

I

1. Janaka (emperor) of Videha conducted a sacrifice by means of which many gifts were offered. There were assembled Brāhmaṇas from Kuru and Pañcāla. Of this Janaka of Videha arose a desire to know which of these Brāhmaṇas were most devoted to the study of the Vedas. He confined a thousand cows. And to the horns of each cow was attached gold weighing ten Pādas.

   The emperor of Videha named Janaka, performed a sacrifice in which many scholars were assembled. He wished to know who was the greatest Vedic scholar among them.

2. To them he said: 'Illustrious Brāhmaṇas let him, who is the greatest scholar of the Vedas, conduct these cows away. Indeed those Brāhmaṇas did not dare. Then Yājñavalkya said to his own disciple: 'Dear Sāmaśravas, conduct them away.' He conducted them away. The Brāhmaṇas grew angry and thought: 'How amongst us can he state that he is the greatest Vedic scholar?' Now Janaka of Videha had a Hotṛ (invoking) priest, Aśvala. To him (Yājñavalkya) he asked: 'Yājñavalkya are you indeed the greatest Vedic scholar amongst us?' He said: 'We perform obeisance to the greatest Vedic Scholar

amongst us, however we are desirous of the cows only.' Thus the Hotṛ priest Aśvalu resolved to ask him questions.

3. (He) said: 'Yājñavalkya, all this what (there is) is acquired by death, all is subdued by death, by means of what does the sacrificer transcend death's reach?' (Yājñavalkya said): 'By means of the Hotṛ priest, by means of fire, by speech. Surely of the sacrifice speech is the Hotṛ. That which is this speech, it is this fire. This is Hotṛ. This is liberation, liberation is transcendence.'

Here various questions are directed at Yājñavalkya. He answers them convincingly.

4. (He) said: 'Yājñavalkya, all this what (there is) is acquired by day and night, all is subdued by day and night, by means of what does the sacrificer transcend day and night's reach?' By means of the Adhvaryu priest, by means of the eye, by means of the sun. Surely of the sacrifice the eye is the Adhvaryu. That which is this eye, it is this yonder sun. This is the Adhvaryu. This is liberation. This is transcendence.
5. (He) said: 'Yājñavalkya, all this what (there is) is acquired by the bright and dark fortnights, all is subdued by the bright and dark fortnights, by means of what does the sacrificer transcend the bright and dark fortnights' reach? By means of the Udgatṛ priest, by means of air, by means of prāṇa. Surely of the sacrifice, prāṇa is the Udgatṛ priest. That which is this prāṇa, it is this Vāyu. This is the Udgatṛ priest. This is liberation. This is transcendence.'
6. (He) said: 'Yājñavalkya, this intermediate region between heaven and earth which is without a commencement, by means of what approach does a sacrificer attain the heavenly world? By means of the Brahmā priest, by means of the mind, by means of the moon. Surely of the sacrifice, the mind is the Brahmā priest. That which is this mind it is the yonder moon.

This is Brahman. This is liberation. This is transcendence. The above regards liberation. Now regarding attainments.'

7. (He) said: 'Yājñavalkya today with how many Ṛg verses will the Hotṛ priest do this sacrifice?' 'Three' 'Which are those three?' 'The preparatory śloka, the oblational śloka accompanying the sacrifices and as the third the benedictory.' 'By means of them what does one win?' 'This, whatsoever which has prāṇa.'

8. (He) said: 'Yājñavalkya today with how many oblations will the Adhvaryu priest offer this sacrifice?' 'Three.' 'Which are those three?' 'Which when offered shine splendidly, which when offered make a loud noise, which when offered go down.' 'By means of these what does one win?' 'Which when offered shine splendidly, through these (one) wins the world of the deities only since the world of the deities shines bright as it were. Which when offered make a great noise, through these (one) wins the world of the ancestors, since the world of the ancestors is as if it is very noisy. Which when offered goes down, through these (one) wins the world of men, since this world is below, as it were.'

9. (He) said: 'Yājñavalkya, today by means of how many deities does the Brahmā priest (sitting) on the right, protect the sacrifice?' 'By means of one.' 'Which one is it?' 'The mind only. Certainly, the mind is infinite and infinite are the Viśvadevas. By means of this only he wins an infinite world.

10. (He) said: 'Yājñavalkya, today in this sacrifice how many hymns of praise will the Udgātṛ priest chant?' 'Three' 'Which are those three?' 'The preparatory śloka, the oblational śloka accompanying the sacrifices and as the third the benedictory.' 'Which are those which have regard to the self?' 'The preparatory śloka is the prāṇa only, the oblational śloka is the apāna only and the bendictory śloka is the vijāna only.' 'By the means of these, what does one

win?' 'By means of the preparatory one wins the world of the earth only, by means of the oblational one wins the world of the intermediate region between heaven and earth only, by means of the benedictory one wins the world of heaven only.' Then the Hotṛ priest Aśvala became quiet.

II

1. Now Jārakārava Ārtabhāga asked him, he said: 'Yājñavalkya, how many organs of apprehension, how many objects of organs of apprehension (are there)?' '(There are) eight organs of apprehension and eight objects.' 'These eight organs of apprehension and eight objects, which are these?'
2. The nose certainly is an organ of apprehension. It is seized by means of the apāna as it's object since by means of apāna does one smell odours.
3. Speech certainly is an organ of apprehension. It is seized by means of names as its object since by means of speech does one pronounce names.
4. The tongue certainly is an organ of apprehension. It is seized by means of taste as its object since by means of the tongue does one know taste.
5. The eye certainly is an organ of apprehension. It is seized by means of forms as its object since by means of the eye does one view forms.
6. The ear certainly is an organ of apprehension. It is seized by means of sound as its object since by means of the ear does one hear sounds.
7. The mind certainly is an organ of apprehension. It is seized by means of desire as its object since by means of the mind does one desire desires.
8. The hands certainly are an organ of apprehension. They are seized by means of action as their object since by means of the hands does one perform actions.

9. The skin certainly is an organ of apprehension. It is seized by means of touch as its object since by means of skin does one perceive touch. These are the eight organs of apprehension and the eight objects.

10. 'Yājñavalkya,' said (Ārtakhāga), '(here) all this is the food of death, which is that deity of which death is the food?' 'Fire surely is death. It is the food of water. (One who knows thus) overcomes reoccurring death.'

Yājñavalkya reaffirms that there is the death of death. Since there is the death of all, there will be no infinite regress in this concept. When the fetters that bind are destroyed, bondage is got rid off, liberation is possible. One who knows this conquers death.

11. 'Yājñavalkya,' said (he) where this (liberated) person dies, do his organs go away from him or do they not?' 'No.' Yājñavalkya said. 'They gather in him only. He (the body) swells up, he is bloated and the deceased lies bloated.'

The commentary points out that the aim of this passage is to state that for the liberated person, after the cessation of bondage such a person does not go anywhere.

12. 'Yājñavalkya,' said (he) 'where this (liberated) person dies, what does not leave him?' 'The name. Certainly, the name is unending and unending are the Viśvadevas. He by means of this (who knows thus) surely wins unending worlds.'

The commentary states that the name is eternal. 'The infinity of the name is its eternity.' (Swāmī Mādhavānanda 2018: 307)

13. 'Yājñavalkya,' said (Ārtabhāga), 'when of this dead person, the organ of speech is absorbed in fire, prāṇa in air, the eye in the sun, the mind in the moon, the ear in the directions, the body in the earth, the self in ether, the hairs on the body in

herbs, the hairs of the head in trees and blood and the seed in water, then of this person what becomes?' 'Dear Ārtabhāga, take my hand, the two of us only will know this. This is not to be discussed in an assembly (in public).' The two retired and discussed. Indeed, what the two spoke about was Karman only and what they praised was Karman only. Certainly, one becomes righteous by means of righteous acts, one becomes unrighteous by means of unrighteous acts. For this reason, Ārtabhāga of the line of Jaratkāru remained silent.

So far, a description of death in the form of grahs (organs) and atigrahs (objects) has been explained. Since this death too has its death, liberation is possible. The commentary describes liberation as the dissolution here only of the grahs and atigrahs, like the going out of a light. This verse seeks to clarify the nature of the cause of that death consisting in this bondage.

III

1. Now Bhujyu Lāhyāyani (grandson of Lahya) questioned him. 'Yājñavalkya,' (he) said, 'we were travelling in Madra as wandering mendicants observing a vow, and arrived at the house of Patañcala Kāpya. His daughter was possessed by a gandharva. We questioned him (the gandharva): "Who are you?" He said: "I am Sudhanvan, descended from Angiras." When we were questioning him regarding the borders of the worlds, to him we asked: "Where are the descendants of Parikṣit? Where are the descendants of Parikṣit?" And I ask you, Yājñavalkya, where are the descendants of Parikṣit? (speak) where are the descendants of Parikṣit?'

In this verse Bhujyu attempts to show the incredible nature of the meditation on identity with the universe, particular and general. The commentary also points out that he attempts to confuse his opponents thereby.

2. Yājñavalkya said: 'Surely, he (the gandharva) must have said to you that they went to the place where those who conduct the horse sacrifice go.' 'And where do those who conduct the horse sacrifice go?' 'Certainly, this world is equal to thirty-two times the space covered by the sun's chariot in a day surrounding it on all sides, covering twice the area is the earth. Surrounding it on all sides covering twice the area is the ocean. Now just as the edge of a razor, or the wing of a mosquito, that much is the opening between the ether (two halves of the cosmic shell). Indra, having assumed the form of a falcon, handed them over to Vāyu. Vāyu placed that in himself and proceeded to where performers of the horse sacrifice are.' Thus certainly did he (the gandharva) praise Vāyu only as it were. From that Vāyu only is the microcosm and Vāyu is the macrocosm. Who knows this thus overcomes reoccurring death. For this reason, Bhujya Lāhyāyani remained quiet.

The commentary points out that prāṇa is the inner self of all beings, mobile as well as immobile, yet it is also external to them. Thus it is said to be their diversity in forms relating to the body, the elements and deities. Air (prāṇa) is also the aggregate as one cosmic prāṇa.

IV

1. Then Uṣasta Cākrāyana questioned him. (He) said: 'Yājñavalkya, expound to me about the direct, perceptible Brahman which is the self of all.' 'This is your self within all.' 'Yājñavalkya, what is within all things?' 'Which by means of prāṇa is prāṇa, it is your self within all, which by means of apāna is apāna, it is your self within all; which by means of vyāna is vyāna, it is yourself within all; which by means of udāna is udāna, it is yourself, within all. It is yourself, within all.'

By using 'within all' is suggestive of all qualifications whatsoever. That which is direct used primarily, is immediate, unimpeded, and which is the limitless Brahman, that which is within all, the self of all—all these refer to the self.

2. Uṣasta Cākrāyana said: 'Just as one may say "a cow is such or a horse is such", this only has been shown thus. Expound to me precisely about the direct, perceptible Brahman which is the self of all.' 'This is your self, within all.' 'Yājñavalkya, what is within all things?' 'You cannot see the seer of viewing, you cannot hear the hearer of hearing, you cannot think the thinker of thinking, you cannot discern the discerner of discernment. Indeed, this is your self within all. Now anything else is afflicted.' For this reason, Uṣasta Cākrāyana remained quiet.

   The verse seeks to stress that witness of vision cannot be seen since that would amount to the penetrating of eternal vision by the act of ordinary vision. This latter act is affected by objects and reveals forms, yet it cannot see the inner self that pervades it. Similarly other organs cannot perceive the self. This is due to the very nature of the self.

V

1. Then Kahola Kauṣítakeya questioned him: 'Yājñavalkya,' (he) said, 'expound to me precisely about the direct, perceptible Brahman which is the self of all.' 'This is your self, within all.' 'Yājñavalkya, what is within all things?' 'It is that which surpassed hunger and thirst, grief and delusion, age and death. Having realized the self, indeed these Brāhmaṇas overcome the desire for sons, the desire for riches, the desire for worlds, adopt a wandering mendicant's life. Since that which is the desire for sons only is the desire for riches, is the desire for worlds, for both these are desires only. From

that, let a Brāhmaṇa, after gaining knowledge, let him seek to live by means of strength. Having gained knowledge and strength he becomes a sage. Having mastered both silence and its absence, non-silence, then he becomes a real Brāhmaṇa. Who is such a Brāhmaṇa? Whoever he is, he is such only. Now anything else is afflicted.' For this reason Kahola Kauṣítakeya remained quiet.

VI

1. Then Gārgi Vācaknavi questioned him. 'Yājñavalkya,' (she) said, 'when all this extends in all directions in water, in what indeed does water extend in all directions?' 'By means of air, Gārgi.' 'In what indeed does air extend in all directions?' 'In the world of the intermediate region between heaven and earth, Gārgi.' 'In what indeed does the world of the intermediate region between heaven and earth extend in all directions?' 'The world of the gandharvas, Gārgi.' 'In what indeed does the world of the gandharvas extend in all directions?' 'The world of the sun, Gārgi.' 'In what indeed does the world of the sun extend in all directions?' 'The world of the moon, Gārgi.' 'In what indeed does the world of the moon extend in all directions?' 'The world of the stars, Gārgi.' 'In what indeed does the world of the stars extend in all directions?' 'The world of the deities, Gārgi.' 'In what Indeed does the world of the deities extend in all directions?' 'The world of Indra, Gārgi.' 'In what indeed does the world of Indra extend in all directions?' 'The world of Prajāpati, Gārgi.' 'In what indeed does the world of Prajāpati extend in all directions?' 'The world of Brahmā, Gārgi.' 'In what indeed does the world of Brahmā extend in all directions?' He (Yājñavalkya) said: 'O Gārgi, do not question excessively lest your head fall down. Indeed, you are excessively questioning regarding a deity who is not known by means

of reasoning. O Gārgi, do not question excessively.' For this reason, Gārgi Vācaknavi remained quiet.

The preceding and following sections seek to explain the nature of the immediate and direct Brahman, the self within all. The aim is to guide the seeker to realize his own self, that which is within all and beyond all relative attributes, by taking up each external element and negating it.

VII

1. Then Uddālaka Āruni questioned him. (He) said: 'In Madra we resided in the house of Patañcala Kāpya while learning the scriptures regarding sacrifices. His wife was possessed by a gandharva. We questioned him (the gandharva): "Who are you?" He replied: "I am Kabandha Atharvana." To Patañcala Kāpya and those learning the scriptures regarding sacrifices he said: "Kāpya do you know that sūtra (thread) by means of which this world, the next world and all beings are united together?" Patañcala Kāpya said: "I know it not, illustrious sir." To Patañcala Kāpya and those learning the scriptures regarding sacrifices he said: "Kāpya do you know that inner controller which is within, who controls this world, and the next world and all worlds and all beings?" Patañcala Kāpya said: "I know it not, illustrious sir." To Patañcala Kāpya and those learning the scriptures regarding sacrifices he said: "Kāpya, he who knows that Sūtra and that inner controller, verily he is a knower of Brahman, he is a knower of the worlds, he is a knower of the deities, he is a knower of the Vedas, he is a knower of being, he is a knower of the self, he is a knower of all, he is a knower of all." To both of them he spoke. That I know. If you Yājñavalkya, without knowing that thread, that inner controller and still remove the cows meant for those who know Brahman, your head will fall down. "O Gautama,

I know that Sūtra and that inner controller." "Surely anyone may say, "I know, I know." Just as you know that you speak.'

This section seeks to describe the innermost entity of the world of Hiraṇyagarbha.

2. He said: 'Certainly, O Gautama, Vāyu is that sūtra. Indeed, it is by means of Vāyu, O Gautama, that this world and the next world and all beings are united together. From that, indeed O Gautama of a person who departs it is said that his limbs have loosened since they are united, O Gautama by Vāyu as a sūtra.' 'This is thus so, Yājñavalkya. Speak about the inner controller.'

The principle of Vāyu is termed as the sūtra. Vāyu is a subtle entity, like ether it supports the earth, the material of the subtle body, in which where the past actions and impressions of various beings, together as well as single, and whose external forms like waves of an ocean are the forty-nine Maruts. Vāyu is the sūtra, the thread that supports all. Thus, after death it is said that a man's limbs have been loosened.

3. (Yājñavalkya said): 'Who resides on the earth, yet is internal to the earth, that which the earth itself does not know, whose body is indeed the earth, who is the inner controller of the earth, this is your self, the inner controller (and) immortal.'

This verse is not directed at people on earth but who resides within the earth. The body and organs of the deity of the earth work or stop by the very presence of the lord as witness. Iśvara called Nārāyana controls the deity of the earth, directs her in the direction of her work from within, and is the internal ruler, a person's own immortal self.

4. 'Who resides in water, yet is internal to the water, that which the water does not know, whose body is indeed the water,

who is the inner controller of the water, this is your self, the inner controller and immortal.'

5. 'Who resides in fire, yet is internal to the fire, that which the fire does not know, whose body is indeed the fire, who is the inner controller of the fire, this is your self, the inner controller and immortal.'
6. 'Who resides in the intermediate region between heaven and earth, yet is internal to the intermediate region between heaven and earth, that which the intermediate region between heaven and earth does not know, whose body is indeed the intermediate region between heaven and earth, who is the inner controller of the intermediate region between heaven and earth, this is your self, the inner controller and immortal.'
7. 'Who resides in the air, yet is internal to the air, that which the air does not know, whose body is indeed the air, who is the inner controller of the air, this is your self, the inner controller and immortal.'
8. 'Who resides in heaven, yet is internal to heaven, that which heaven does not know, whose body is indeed heaven, who is the inner controller of heaven, this is your self, the inner controller and immortal.'
9. 'Who resides in the sun, yet is internal to the sun, that which the sun does not know, whose body is indeed the sun, who is the inner controller of the sun, this is your self, the inner controller and immortal.'
10. 'Who resides in the directions, yet is internal to the directions, that which the directions do not know, whose body are indeed the directions, who is the inner controller of the directions, this is your self, the inner controller and immortal.'
11. 'Who resides in moon and the stars, yet is internal to the moon and the stars, that which the moon and the stars does not know, whose body is indeed the moon and the stars, who

is the inner controller of the moon and the stars, this is your self, the inner controller and immortal.'

12. 'Who resides in the ether, yet is internal to the ether, that which the ether does not know, whose body is indeed the ether, who is the inner controller of the ether, this is your self, the inner controller and immortal.'
13. 'Who resides in the darkness, yet is internal to the darkness, that which the darkness does not know, whose body is indeed the darkness, who is the inner controller of the darkness, this is your self, the inner controller and immortal.'
14. 'Who resides in light, yet is internal to the light, that which the light does not know, whose body is indeed the light, who is the inner controller of the light, this is your self, the inner controller and immortal.'
15. 'Who resides in all beings, yet is internal to all beings, that which all beings do not know, whose body is indeed all beings, who is the inner controller of all beings, this is your self, the inner controller and immortal.'
16. 'Who resides in the prāṇa, yet is internal to the prāṇa, that which the prāṇa does not know, whose body is indeed prāṇa, who is the inner controller of all prāṇa, this is your self, the inner controller and immortal.'
17. 'Who resides in the organ of speech, yet is internal to the organ of speech, that which the organ of speech does not know, whose body is indeed the organ of speech, who is the inner controller of the organ of speech, this is your self, the inner controller and immortal.'
18. 'Who resides in the eye, yet is internal to the eye, that which the eye does not know, whose body is indeed the eye, who is the inner controller of the eye, this is your self, the inner controller and immortal.'
19. 'Who resides in the ear, yet is internal the ear, that which the ear does not know, whose body is indeed the ear, who

is the inner controller of the ear, this is your self, the inner controller and immortal.'

20. 'Who resides in the mind, yet is internal to the mind, that which the mind does not know, whose body is indeed the mind, who is the inner controller of the mind, this is your self, the inner controller and immortal.'
21. 'Who resides in the skin, yet is internal to the skin, that which the skin does not know, whose body is indeed the skin, who is the inner controller of the skin, this is your self, the inner controller and immortal.'
22. 'Who resides in the intellect, yet is internal to the intellect, that which the intellect does not know, whose body is indeed the intellect, who is the inner controller of the intellect, this is your self, the inner controller and immortal.'
23. 'Who resides in the seed, yet is internal to the seed, that which the seed does not know, whose body is indeed the seed, who is the inner controller of the seed, this is your self, the inner controller and immortal. Unseen yet the seer, unheard yet the hearer, unthought yet the thinker, unknown yet the knower. There is no seer other than this, there is no hearer other than this, there is no thinker other than this, there is no knower other than this. This is your self, the inner controller and immortal. Now anything else is afflicted. For this reason, Uddālaka Āruni remained silent.'

Now regarding the body. The deities of the earth and so on, with all their powers fail to see their internal ruler, who controls them. This is being explained. He is never perceived yet is himself the witness. He is never known but is the knower.

VIII

1. Then Vācaknavi spoke: 'Illustrious Brāhmaṇas, with your approval I will ask these two questions. If he will answer

these two questions of mine, then not anyone amongst you will defeat him at any time regarding the expounding of Brahman.

This section seeks to describe the unconditioned Brahman, devoid of attributes, immediate and direct.

2. She said: 'I indeed have two questions for you Yājñavalkya. Just as a strong son of the Kāśis or the Videhas, takes in his hands two sharp enemy penetrating arrows, and approaches nearby, thus only do I face you with two questions. Answer these two questions of mine.' 'Ask, O Gārgi.'

The analogy used is meant to convey that the questions are hard to answer.

3. She (Gārgi) said: 'Which rises above heaven, Yājñavalkya, which is below the earth, which is between heaven and earth and is these two, which people call that which was, is and will be, on what does that extend in all directions?'
4. He (Yājñavalkya) said: 'Which rises above heaven, which is below the earth, which is between heaven and earth and is these two, which people call that which was, is and will be, on ether does that extend in all directions.'
5. She said: 'Salutations be to you, O Yājñavalkya, who have answered my question. Preserve yourself for another.' 'Ask, O Gārgi.'
6. She (Gārgi) said: 'Which rises above heaven, Yājñavalkya, which is below the earth, which is between heaven and earth and is these two, which people call that which was, is and will be, on what does that extend in all directions?'
7. He (Yājñavalkya) said: 'Which rises above heaven, which is below the earth, which is between heaven and earth and is these two, which people call that which was, is and will be, in what does ether extend in all directions?'

Gārgi considered this question very difficult, impossible to answer. To her to be able to answer about the immutable Brahman by means of which the unmanifested ether was pervaded was almost impossible to answer logically. Yājñavalkya has to avoid the charges of non-comprehension if he cannot explain and 'contradiction' if he explains the unexplainable.

8. He said: 'O Gārgi, surely this is described as imperishable by the knowers of Brahman. It is neither corporeal nor subtle, neither small nor large, neither red nor oily, neither shade nor darkness, neither air nor ether, neither joined, without flavour, without odour, without eyes, without ears, without speech, without mind, non-luminous, without prāṇa, without a face. It is without measure, without interior or exterior. This does not eat anything and nothing eats this.

   Yājñavalkya seeks to avoid both these charges by referring to the 'knowers of Brahman'. Then the verse goes on to describe Brahman as being devoid of any attribute, as one with no second.

9. 'O Gārgi, surely in the rule of this imperishable, the sun and the moon are kept in their respective positions. O Gārgi, surely in the rule of this imperishable, heaven, and earth are kept in their respective positions. O Gārgi, surely in the rule of this imperishable, moments, short periods of time, days and nights, fortnights, months, seasons, years are kept in their respective positions. O Gārgi, surely in the rule of this imperishable, some rivers flow eastwards from white mountains, others flow to the west, and still others in different directions, are kept in their respective positions. O Gārgi, surely in the rule of this imperishable, men laud those who are generous, the gods, the sacrificer, and the ancestors are desirous of the Darvī offering.

The text seeks to negate the attributes of Brahman and indicate its existence. It brings forth inferential evidence in favour of the existence of Brahman. It asserts that the existence of Brahman can be inferred from the fixed order of the world.

10. 'Indeed, O Gārgi, whoever in this world not knowing this imperishable performs sacrifices, practises austerities, for many thousand years, of this he finds that it is transitory. O Gārgi, whoever departs from this world, not knowing this imperishable is to be pitied. Now O Gārgi, who in this world knows this imperishable departs from this world as a Brāhmaṇa.

    This is a very important verse. It highlights the crucial importance of knowing the imperishable if one seeks to escape the cycle of birth and rebirth. The ritualistic person enjoys the fruits of his rites. Then they are exhausted.

11. 'Surely, O Gārgi, this imperishable is that unseen seer, unheard hearer, unthought thinker, unknown knower. There is no other seer than this, there is no other hearer than this, there is no other thinker than this, there is no other knower than this. O Gārgi, by this very imperishable does ether extend in all directions.

    This immutable is the subject, omnipresent, eternal witness. There is no knower other than this. It is direct, immediate, it is beyond attributes, the self of all, that which pervades the (unmanifested) ether, the supreme goal, the supreme Brahman.

12. She said: 'Illustrious Brāhmaṇas you may consider it as bountiful that you can get off from him by means of a salutation to him. Certainly, amongst you all no one can defeat him in expounding Brahman.' For this reason, Gārgi Vācaknavi remained quiet.

IX

1. Then Vidagha Śākalyaḥ questioned him: 'O Yājñavalkya, how many gods are there?' He explained it by means of this nivid (invocation to the gods). 'That many as are indicated in the nivid relating to the Viśvadevas, three hundred and three and three thousand and three.' 'True,' said he. 'O Yājñavalkya, indeed how many gods are there?' 'Thirty-three' 'True,' said he. 'O Yājñavalkya, indeed how many gods are there?' 'Six,' 'True,' said he. 'O Yājñavalkya, indeed how many gods are there?' 'Three.' 'True,' said he. 'O Yājñavalkya, indeed how many gods are there?' 'Two.' 'True,' said he. 'O Yājñavalkya, indeed how many gods are there?' 'One and a half.' 'True,' said he. 'O Yājñavalkya, indeed how many gods are there?' 'One.' 'True,' said he. 'Which are those three hundred and three and three thousand and three?'

The nivid refers to a collection of verses stating the number of gods which are used to recite in the eulogistic hymns which are dedicated to the Viśvadevas.

2. (Yājñavalkya) said: 'These are manifestations of them only. Nevertheless, there are indeed thirty-three gods.' 'Which are these thirty-three?' 'The eight Vasus, the eleven Rudras, and twelve Ādityas, these amount to thirty-one and Indrā and Prajāpati constitute the thirty-three.'
3. 'Which are the Vasus?' 'Fire, the earth, and the air, and the intermediate region between heaven and earth, and the sun, heaven and the moon and stars. These are the Vasus. Since on these is all this put upon. From that they are known as Vasus.'
4. 'Which are the Rudras?' 'These ten organs in a person, with the self as the eleventh. When they go out from this mortal body, then they make them (his relations) cry. Since it is that

which makes them cry, from that they are called Rudras.'

5. 'Which are the Ādityas?' 'Certainly, of a year there are twelve months, these are the Ādityas, since these go taking away all this. Since they go taking away all this, from that they are called Ādityas.'
6. 'Which is Indra? Which is Prajāpati?' 'The thundercloud only is Indra, the sacrifice is Prajāpati.' 'Which is the thundercloud?' 'The thunderstorm.' 'Which is the sacrifice?' 'Sacrificial animals.'
7. 'Which are the six?' 'Fire and earth and air and the intermediate region between heaven and earth and the sun and heaven and these are the six since these six are all this.'
8. 'Which are the three gods?' 'These three worlds only, since all the gods are included in these.' 'Which are the two gods?' 'Food and prāṇa.' 'Which is the one and a half?' 'This which blows (air).'
9. 'Regarding that it is said, since as it were it is this only which blows, how then can it be one and a half? (The reply) because by means of him all this flourishes, it is one and a half.' 'Which is the one God?' 'It is prāṇa. He is Brahman. (They) call it that.'

Prāṇa is Brahman being vast and the sum of all deities. The deities are one and many. This infinite number is part of the limited number referred to in the nivid. These again are a part of the smaller number of deities right up to prāṇa. The prāṇa expands into these numbers right up to the infinite vastness. Thus prāṇa is one and infinite and also possesses various in-between numbers.

10. 'Whose abode is the earth only, whose world is fire, mind is light, he who knows such a person, who is the chief support of all souls, he certainly is a knower, Yājñavalkya.' 'Indeed, I know him, such a person, who is the chief support of all

souls, of whom you refer to. He is this person who is in this body only. Speak indeed, O Śākalya.' 'Who is his deity?' 'The immortal.' Said Yājñavalkya.

The purport here is to state that this God has for the body the earth, fire for the eyes, deliberates on issues and things by the mind, identifies with the earth and has a body and mind. Who knows this truly is a scholar.

11. 'Whose abode is desire only, whose world is the heart, mind is light, he who knows such a person, who is the chief support of all souls, he certainly is a knower, O Yājñavalkya.' 'Indeed, I know him, such a person, who is the chief support of all souls, of whom you refer to. He is this person who is identified with this desire only. Speak indeed, O Śākalya.' 'Who is his deity?' 'Women.' said Yājñavalkya.
12. 'Whose abode are forms only, whose world is the eye, mind is light, he who knows such a person, who is the chief support of all souls, he certainly is a knower, O Yājñavalkya.' 'Indeed, I know him, such a person, who is the chief support of all souls, of whom you refer to. He is this person who is in the sun only. Speak indeed, O Śākalya.' 'Who is his deity?' 'Truth.' said Yājñavalkya.
13. 'Whose abode is ether only, whose world is the ear, mind is light, he who knows such a person, who is the chief support of all souls, he certainly is a knower, O Yājñavalkya.' 'Indeed, I know him, such a person, who is the chief support of all souls, of whom you refer to. He is this person who is identified with the hearing and who is in the echo only. Speak indeed, O Śākalya.' 'Who is his deity?' 'The directions.' Said Yājñavalkya.
14. 'Whose abode is darkness only, whose world is the heart, mind is light, he who knows such a person, who is the chief support of all souls, he certainly is a knower, O Yājñavalkya.'

'Indeed, I know him, such a person, who is the chief support of all souls, of whom you refer to. He is this person who is identified with shadow (ignorance) only. Speak indeed, O Śākalya.' 'Who is his Deity?' 'Death.' Said Yājñavalkya.

15. 'Whose abode are forms only, whose world is the eye, mind is light, he who knows such a person, who is the chief support of all souls, he certainly is a knower, O Yājñavalkya.' 'Indeed, I know him, such a person, who is the chief support of all souls, of whom you refer to. He is this person who is in the mirror only. Speak indeed O Śākalya.' 'Who is his Deity?' 'The vital force.' Said Yājñavalkya.
16. 'Whose abode is water only, whose world is the heart, mind is light, he who knows such a person, who is the chief support of all souls, he certainly is a knower, O Yājñavalkya.' 'Indeed, I know him, such a person, who is the chief support of all souls, of whom you refer to. He is this person who is in the water only. Speak indeed, O Śākalya.' 'Who is his deity?' 'Varuna.' Said Yājñavalkya.
17. 'Whose abode is the seed only, whose world is the heart, mind is light, he who knows such a person, who is the chief support of all souls, he certainly is a knower, O Yājñavalkya.' 'Indeed, I know him, such a person, who is the chief support of all souls, of whom you refer to. He is this person who is identified with the son only. Speak indeed, O Śākalya.' 'Who is his deity?' 'Prajāpati.' Said Yājñavalkya.
18. 'Śākalya,' said Yājñavalkya, 'What! Have these Brāhmaṇas made you the means of extinguishing burning charcoal?'

The same prāṇa for the purposes of meditation has been shown in eight ways. Each god has been said to have eight dimensions, abode (general form), being (particular manifestation) and duty (cause), yet is just a form of prāṇa. Further the same prāṇa divided into five forms as per different quarters is unified at the mind.

19. 'Yājñavalkya,' said Śākalya, 'knowing what Brahman have you criticized these Brāhmaṇas (hailing from) Kuru and Pañcāla?' 'I know the directions with their deities and support.' 'If you know the directions with their deities and support?'

20. 'Which deity are you ought to be identified with in this eastern direction?' 'The sun deity.' 'It, the sun, on what is it established?' 'On the eye.' 'On what is the eye established?' 'On forms, since one sees forms with the eye.' 'On what are forms established?' 'On the heart.' said Yājñavalkya. 'Since one knows forms by means of the heart, on the heart only are forms established.' 'Indeed this is so, Yājñavalkya.'

The idea is that the sun is the deity in the east. The sun rests on the eye. The sun was produced by the eye. The eye rests on colour. Thus the eye, the sun, the east and all that live in the east are colours. Colours rest on the heart. Heart here is used to refer to intellect and manas together. What is meant is that a person remembers colours lying as impressions, through the heart, thus colours rest on the heart.

21. 'Which deity are you ought to be identified with in this southern direction?' 'The deity Yama.' 'He, Yama, on what is he established?' 'On gifts (to teachers).' 'On what are those gifts to teachers established?' 'On faith, since when a person has faith, a person offers gifts (to teachers). Thus it is on faith that gifts are established.' 'On what is faith established?' 'On the heart.' said Yājñavalkya. 'Since one knows faith by means of the heart, surely on the heart only is faith established.' 'Indeed this is so, Yājñavalkya.'

The commentary seeks to answer how Yama can be the effect of a sacrifice. Priests conduct the sacrifice, sacrificer redeems this from the priests and gains the south and (the favour) of Yama. Thus (the favour) of Yama is said to be the effect. The sacrifice rests on remuneration, which rests on faith. Faith is defined as faith in the Vedas accompanied by true devotion. Faith rests on the heart.

22. 'Which deity are you ought to be identified with in the western direction?' 'The deity Varuna.' 'He, Varuna, on what is he established?' 'On water.' 'On what is water established?' 'On seed.' 'On what is seed established?' 'On the heart. From that it is said of a newborn child who is similar (to his father) that he has emanated from his heart, he has been created from the heart as it were. Since only on the heart is seed established.' 'Indeed, this is so, Yājñavalkya.'

Varuṇa rests on water, which in turn rests on the seed. The seed rests on the heart. Thus when a newborn child is born, who resembles his father people say he has arisen from his father's heart.

23. 'Which deity are you ought to be identified with in the northern direction?' 'The deity Soma.' 'It, Soma, on what is he established?' 'On initiation.' 'On what is initiation established?' 'On truth.' From that it is said to one who is initiated, 'Speak the truth' since surely on truth only is initiation established.' 'On what is truth established?' 'On the heart.' Said Yājñavalkya 'Since, only by means of the heart does one know truth, thus it is on the heart that truth is established. 'Indeed, this is so Yājñavalkya.'

Here Soma can mean moon or creeper. Soma is said to rest on initiation which rests on the truth. Truth rests on the heart since one knows the truth through the heart.

24. 'Which deity are you ought to be identified with in this fixed direction?' 'The deity fire.' 'On what is fire established?' 'On the organ of speech.' 'On what is speech established?' 'On the heart.' 'On what is the heart established?'

The overhead direction is known as the fixed direction. The deity fire rests on speech. Speech rests on the heart.

All the directions are realized as the self. All are unified in the heart. The whole universe is from colour (form), name, and action. These are just modifications of the heart. Sākalya now asks about the heart.

25. 'O Ghost,' said Yājñavalkya, 'when you consider that this (heart) is elsewhere from us, if it were actually elsewhere from us, then dogs would eat this or birds would tear it to pieces.'

The idea is that the heart rests on the body and the body rests on the heart.

26. Śākalya said: 'In what are you and your self established?' (Yājñavalkya replied): 'In prāṇa (vital breath, in-breath).' 'In what is prāṇa established?' 'In apāna (out-breath).' 'And in what is apāna established?' 'In vyāna (diffused breath).' 'And in what is vyāna established?' 'In samāna (equalizing or middle breath). It the self is not this, not this. It is ungraspable for it is not grasped. It is incognizable since it cannot be cognized. This self is unyoked since it is not yoken. It is untrammelled, it does not suffer, it is not injured. There are eight abodes, eight worlds, eight deities, eight persons. I question you regarding that person who is known only by means of the Upaniṣads, who projects and withdraws these beings and also transcends them. If you cannot clearly speak to me regarding them your head will fall down.' Śākalya did not know him. His head fell down; and robbers carried away his bones assuming they were something different.

The idea here is that the body, mind, and the prāṇa (the breaths), work in a coordinated manner, are interdependent towards the aim of the individual self. Brahman, immediate and direct on which all these rest is now discussed. The self is 'not this, not this'. It cannot be perceived since it is beyond the character of an effect. Only what is different is perceived. The self not being gross is undecaying. Not being gross it is unattached and unfiltered. It is beyond, pain, injury, and bondage.

27. Then (Yājñavalkya) said: 'Illustrious Brāhmaṇas, who amongst you desires may question me. Or I may question him amongst you who so desires or I may question all of you.' These Brāhmaṇas did not dare.
28. With these verses he questioned them:
    1. Just as a large forest tree, so only is a person; his hairs are the leaves, the skin the outer bark.
    2. From his skin only does blood flow. (Similarly) sap (too flows) from the bark. From that blood issues from an injured person, just like sap from a tree that is hit.
    3. His flesh is its inner bark, his sinews are its inner bark. That is firm. His bones, which are within are the wood, and the marrow is created similar to the pith.
    4. When a tree is felled, it rises up from its root again in a new form; from which root does a man rise up after he is torn off by death?
    5. Do not say 'from the seed' since that is produced from what is living. Certainly, a tree rises from the seed. After its death that (the tree) surely rises again.'
    6. When they uproot a tree with its roots, it does not rise again, from which root does a man rise after he is torn off by death?
    7. He does not come into existence only when he is born; since who will bring him into existence again? Brahman is knowledge, bliss, the bestower of wealth, the ultimate abode of him, who stands firm in the knowledge of Brahman.

CHAPTER 4

I

1. Janaka, (king) of Videha, took his seat, when Yājñavalkya arrived. To him he said: 'Yājñavalkya, with what aim have you arrived? Do you wish for cattle or subtle questions?' 'Both only, O king.' (He) said:

   The usage of the word king here indicates that Janaka must have done the Vājapeya sacrifice. King also refers to one who rules territories by vassals who obey commands.

2. 'Let me hear that which anyone (among your teachers) has told you.' 'Jitvan Śailini has told me that "speech certainly is Brahman". Just as one who has a mother, one who has a father, one who has a teacher, ought to say, so said Śailini that speech certainly is Brahman, for what can one who cannot speak be?' 'But did he tell you its abode and support?' 'He did not tell me.' 'Indeed, this Brahman has one foot, O king.' 'Indeed, tell us Yājñavalkya.' 'Speech only is its abode, ether is its support. This ought to be meditated upon as intelligence.' 'What is this intelligence, Yājñavalkya?' 'It is speech only, O king,' said he. 'Indeed, by means of speech, O king, a friend is known. The Ṛg Veda, the Yajur Veda, the Sāma Veda, Atharvāṅgirasa, history, the Purāṇas, sciences, Upaniṣads, verses, aphorisms (sūtras), elucidations

and commentaries, (the result of) sacrifices, offerings, food and drink, and this world and the next world, and all beings are known by means of speech only, O king. Speech, O king, is the supreme Brahman certainly. Speech does not forsake him, all beings seek him, having become a deity he is merged in the deities, who knowing thus meditates on this.' 'I offer you one thousand cows with a bull as big as an elephant,' said Janaka of Videha. (In reply) Yājñavalkya said: 'My father considered that one ought not to accept (presents from a disciple) without properly instructing.'

What is being emphasized here is that meditating on the wrong notion of Brahman is fruitless. It produces no effect. The word abode is meant as a permanent resort.

3. 'That whatever has been said to you by anyone (among your teachers) let me hear.' 'Udaṅka Śaulkāyana has said to me that "prāṇa certainly is Brahman". Just as one who has a mother, one who has a father, one who has a teacher, ought to say, so said Śaulkāyana that prāṇa certainly is Brahman, for what can one be who does not have prāṇa?' 'But did he tell you its abode and support?' 'He did not tell me.' 'Indeed, this Brahman has one foot, O king.' 'Indeed tell us, Yājñavalkya.' 'Prāṇa only is its abode, ether is its support. This ought to be meditated upon as (what is) dear.' 'What is this dearness, Yājñavalkya?' 'It is prāṇa only, O king,' said Yājñavalkya. 'Indeed, for the sake of prāṇa one offers sacrifices for an unqualified person and one accepts presents from one who is not worthy. And for the sake of prāṇa only, O king, one becomes exposed to the threat of destruction wherever one may go. Prāṇa surely, O king, is the supreme Brahman. Prāṇa does not forsake him, all beings seek him, having become a deity he is merged in the deities, who knowing thus meditates on this.' 'I offer you one thousand cows with a bull as big as

an elephant,' said Janaka of Videha. (In reply) Yājñavalkya said: 'My father considered that one ought not to accept (presents from a disciple) without properly instructing.'

Prāṇa here refers to the deity Vāyu, as the organ of speech. For the sake of prāṇa are sacrifices performed. Prāṇa is dear. Prāṇa is the supreme Brahman.

4. 'That whatever has been said to you by anyone (among your teachers) let me hear.' 'Barku Vārṣna has said to me that "the eye certainly is Brahman". Just as one who has a mother, one who has a father, one who has a teacher, ought to say, so said Vārṣna that the eye certainly is Brahman, for what can one be who does not see?' 'But did he tell you its abode and support?' 'He did not tell me.' 'Indeed, this Brahman has one foot, O king.' 'Indeed, tell us, Yājñavalkya.' 'The eye only is its abode, ether is its support. This ought to be meditated upon as truth.' 'What is this truth, Yājñavalkya?' 'It is the eye only, O king.' Said Yājñavalkya. 'Indeed, if it is said to a person who sees by his own eyes, "Did you see?" and he answers, "I did see," then, that is true. The eye surely, O king, is the supreme Brahman. The eye does not forsake him, all beings seek him, having become a deity he is merged in the deities, who knowing thus meditates on this.' 'I offer you one thousand cows with a bull as big as an elephant,' said Janaka of Videha. (In reply) Yājñavalkya said: 'My father considered that one ought not to accept (presents from a disciple) without properly instructing.'
5. 'That whatever has been said to you by anyone (among your teachers) let me hear.' 'Gardhabhīvipīta Bhāradvāja has said to me that "the ear certainly is Brahman". Just as one who has a mother, one who has a father, one who has a teacher, ought to say, so said Bhāradvāja that the ear certainly is Brahman, for what can one be who cannot hear?' 'But did

he tell you its abode and support?' 'He did not tell me.' 'Indeed, this Brahman has one foot, O king.' 'Indeed, tell us Yājñavalkya.' 'The ear only is its abode, ether is its support. This ought to be meditated upon as unending.' 'What is this unending, Yājñavalkya?' 'It is the directions only, O king,' said Yājñavalkya. 'Therefore, O king, to whatever direction one may go to, a person never reaches its end since the directions are unending. The ear surely, O king, is the supreme Brahman. The ear does not forsake him, all beings seek him, having become a deity he is merged in the deities, who knowing thus meditates on this.' 'I offer you one thousand cows with a bull as big as an elephant,' said Janaka of Videha. (In reply) Yājñavalkya said: 'My father considered that one ought not to accept (presents from a disciple) without properly instructing.'

6. 'That whatever has been said to you by anyone (among your teachers) let me hear.' 'Satyakāma Jabala has said to me that "the mind certainly is Brahman". Just as one who has a mother, one who has a father, one who has a teacher, ought to say, so said Jabala that the mind certainly is Brahman, for what can one be without a mind?' 'But did he tell you its abode and support?' 'He did not tell me.' 'Indeed, this Brahman has one foot, O king.' 'Indeed, tell us, Yājñavalkya.' 'The mind only is its abode, ether is its support. This ought to be meditated upon as bliss.' 'What is this bliss, Yājñavalkya?' 'It is the mind only, O king,' said Yājñavalkya. 'Surely, by means of the mind, O king, a man woos a woman, of her a son resembling him is born and he is the source of bliss. The mind surely, O king, is the supreme Brahman. The mind does not forsake him, all beings seek him, having become a deity he is merged in the deities, who knowing thus meditates on this.' 'I offer you one thousand cows with a bull as big as an elephant,' said Janaka of Videha. (In reply) Yājñavalkya said:

‘My father considered that one ought not to accept (presents from a disciple) without properly instructing.’

7. ‘That whatever has been said to you by anyone (among your teachers) let me hear.’ ‘Vidagdha Śākalya has said to me that “the heart certainly is Brahman”. Just as one who has a mother, one who has a father, one who has a teacher, ought to say, so said Śākalya that the heart certainly is Brahman, for what can one be without a heart?’ ‘But did he tell you its abode and support?’ ‘He did not tell me.’ ‘Indeed, this Brahman has one foot, O king.’ ‘Indeed, tell us, Yājñavalkya.’ ‘The heart only is its abode, ether is its support. This ought to be meditated upon as stability.’ ‘What is this stability, Yājñavalkya?’ ‘It is the heart only, O king,’ said Yājñavalkya. ‘Surely the heart, O king, is the support of all beings since, O king, it is in the heart that all beings are established. The heart surely, O king, is the supreme Brahman. The heart does not forsake him, all beings seek him, having become a deity he is merged in the deities, who knowing thus meditates on this.’ ‘I offer you one thousand cows with a bull as big as an elephant,’ said Janaka of Videha. (In reply) Yājñavalkya said: ‘My father considered that one ought not to accept (presents from a disciple) without properly instructing.’

II

1. Janaka of Videha, approaching from his lounge said: ‘Salutations to you, Yājñavalkya, kindly instruct me.’ Yājñavalkya said: ‘Just as one desiring to go a long way, O king, ought to take a chariot or a ship, thus you have equipped yourself with the teachings of the Upaniṣads. Thus you are honoured and wealthy, and you have deeply studied the Vedas and been instructed in the Upaniṣads. Yet, where will you go when you are disjoined from this body?’ ‘Illustrious sir, I do not know where I shall go.’ ‘Then

surely that, where you will go I shall tell you.' 'Illustrious sir, please tell me.'

Yājñavalkya knew Brahman and its aspects, etc. Janaka prostrated before Yājñavalkya who stated that he would instruct Janaka.

2. 'Indeed this person who is in the right eye is Indha by name. Him surely, who is that Indha, is called Indra by people indirectly, for the deities are, as it appears, fond of indirect names and dislike that which is direct.

The being due to his splendour is known as Indra or Indha. Thus one attains the self called Vaiśvānara.

3. 'Now this Virāj (splendour) that is in the form of a person in the left eye is his wife. Their place of union is this ether within the heart. Now of these two, their food is this mass of blood, which is within the heart. Now of these two their covering is this which appears as it were, to be a net-like structure within the heart. Now of these two their path for moving is the nerve that rises upward from the heart. It is, as it were, like a hair partitioned a thousand times, thus are also the nerves of this (body) named Hitā which are established in the heart. It is by means of these that the essence of food passes when it moves. From that as it were only that (the self composed of Indra and Viraj) is an eater of subtler food than the gross food.

Viraj or matter is the wife of the self called Vaiśvānara. This couple becomes one in dreams. Further the food that nourishes the gross body is finer than the gross substances in the body that are eliminated but the food that sustains the subtle body is finer than that. The concept here is that Taijasa is nourished by finer food than the Vaiśvānara.

4. ‘Of this the eastern direction is the eastern prāṇa, the southern direction is the southern prāṇa, the western direction is the western prāṇa, the northern direction is the northern prāṇa, the rising direction is the prāṇa that is above, the direction below is the prāṇa that is below, and all the directions are all the prāṇas. It the self is not this, not this. It is ungraspable for it is not grasped. It is incognizable since it cannot be cognized. The self is unyoked since it is not yoked. It is untrammelled, it does not suffer, it is not injured.’ ‘Surely you have obtained the fearless, O Janaka,’ said Yājñavalkya. Janaka of Videha said: ‘Let the fearless reach you Yājñavalkya, illustrious sir, who has made us know the fearless, salutations be to you. This empire of Videha, as well as I am (at your behest).’

The import of this verse is that the seer identifies himself in stages with the prāṇa that comprises all. After withdrawing this prāṇa to the inner self is achieved the state of the witness. This is the transcendent stage spoken of as ‘not this, not this’.

III

1. Yājñavalkya approached Janaka of Videha. He (to himself) thought: ‘I shall not speak.’ However, once Janaka of Videha and Yājñavalkya had spoken at an Agnihotra sacrifice, Yājñavalkya had to him granted a boon. He chose the right to ask any question. To him Yājñavalkya granted this. So the king only first questioned him.
2. ‘Yājñavalkya, what light does this person have?’ he said. ‘The light of the sun, O king. It is by means of this light of the sun that a person sits, goes out, does work, and returns.’ ‘This is thus only, Yājñavalkya.’

The question here is whether the light is intrinsic or external. The answer is that the light is essentially different from the body.

3. ‘After the sun has set from this world, what light, indeed, does this person have?’ ‘The moon only is his light. It is by means of this light of the moon that a person sits, goes out, does work, and returns.’ ‘This is thus only, Yājñavalkya.’
4. ‘After the sun has set from this world, after the moon has set from this world, what light, indeed, does this person have?’ ‘Fire only is his light. It is by means of this light of fire that a person sits, goes out, does work, and returns.’ ‘This is thus only, Yājñavalkya.’
5. ‘After the sun has set from this world, Yājñavalkya, after the moon has set from this world, after the fire has ceased to burn, what light, indeed, does this person have?’ ‘Speech only is his light. It is by means of this light of speech that a person sits, goes out, does work, and returns. From that, O king, where even one’s own hand is not distinctly seen, even then where speech is uttered, one can approach there.’ ‘This is thus only, Yājñavalkya.’

   Speech here is used to indicate sound. By sound is its organ the ear stimulated, leading to discernment in the mind, by means of which can a person engage in external action. The verse seeks to explain how speech can be called a light.

6. ‘After the sun has set from this world, Yājñavalkya, after the moon has set from this world, after the fire has ceased to burn, and speech has ceased, what light, indeed, does this person have?’ ‘The self only is his light. It is by means of this light of the self that a person sits, goes out, does work, and returns.’

   In the waking state there is light external to the body. Yet in the states of dream and deep sleep, there is light. This is the light of the self. This light is different from the body and the organs, illumines them, yet is not illumined by anything else. This light is not perceived, being immaterial.

7. 'Who is the self?' 'This person which, consisting of intellect, is in the organs, the light which is within the heart. It, being the same, roams between the two worlds, as if thinking, as if wandering. It, having entered the dream state, goes beyond this world and the forms of death.'

Janaka cannot be certain if the self is one of the organs or something else. Thus the question: 'Who is this self?' The answer is the entity identified with the intellect. The self is wrongly identified with its limiting adjunct, the intellect, like the planet Rāhu with the sun and moon. All perception is due to association with the intellect. Like a gem imparts lustre to milk, so does the self impart lustre to the body and organs. The intellect, being transparent, reflects the intelligence of the self. Next is manas, which appropriates the reflection of the self by means of the intellect. Then the organs which come in contact with the manas, and then the body by means of the organs.

8. 'Certainly it, this person, while being born and assuming a body, gets connected to evils. When it departs while dying, it gives up these evils.'

This verse seeks to show that the self is distinct from the evils like the body and organs. Just as in this world a man moves between dream and waking states, so does he move between this world and the next by taking up different bodies and organs, continually till he attains freedom. Thus the self is distinct from the body and organs.

9. 'Surely of this person, there are two places, this and the next world. The third, the dream state, is at the junction (of these two). At this place of junction (between this and the next world), while staying, it sees both places, this world and the next world. Now, just as one obtains this place of the next world, having obtained this, one perceives both evil and bliss.

When it dreams, it takes away a little of this all-sustaining world, on its own it tears it apart and on its own creates it and dreams through its own splendour illumined by its own light. Here this person becomes self-luminous.'

The verse categorically affirms that a man is in one of two places, this world and the next world, i.e., this life in the present and the future life. The verse also points out that the dream state is not the next world but is at the junction of this world and the next.

10. 'In that state there are no chariots, no animals to be yoked to chariots, no roads. Yet he creates chariots, animals to be yoked to chariots, and roads. In that state there is no bliss, delight, extreme joy. Yet he creates bliss, delight, extreme joy. In that state there are no pools, lakes, rivers. Yet he creates pools, lakes, rivers, since he is the doer of creation.'

This verse talks to us about the dream state. The person creates the dream state from the world after putting the body aside. Impressions are caused or stimulated by the person's previous acts which then appear as objects in dream. These impressions are only modifications of the mind and have no independent existence or reality.

11. Regarding that there are these verses: by means of dream it makes the body inert. While it is awake it witnesses the sleeping (body). Having taken luminosity, it again comes to this place, the person made of gold, the single swan.

Objects in dream are revealed by means of the light of pure intelligence, the infinite being that goes between this world and the next, between dream and waking states.

12. 'Protecting the lesser nest by means of prāṇa, the immortal goes from the nest. The immortal achieves as much as he

wants wherever it may be, the person made of gold, the single swan.

13. In dream attaining diverse states, it creates many forms, as it were, to enjoy with women, or laughing or seeing what is terrifying.

14. 'Its play is seen (yet) it is not seen by anyone. People say that it should not be roused suddenly, for this is difficult to treat if this does not get back. Now some people say that the waking state is this (dream) state only, since, while awake, one sees these (objects) that one sees in a dream. (This is not so), since here in this dream state a person is self-illuminated.' Janaka said: 'I shall give you one thousand (cows), illustrious sir. Please instruct me further regarding liberation.'

The purport is to prove the existence of the self-luminous ātman. This transcends death, moves from world to world between waking and dream states and is eternal. Death is not its nature, thus allowing for the possibility of liberation.

15. 'Certainly, it this (self) in the state of serene sleep having delighted, having wandered, having seen good and evil, it again returns in the manner it came to the place from which it commenced, to dream. Whatever it sees there, it is unaffected by it, since this person is unattached.' 'This is thus only, Yājñavalkya. I shall give you one thousand (cows), illustrious sir. Please instruct me further regarding liberation.'

The state of deep sleep is the state of the highest serenity. A person being fatigued in the dream state enters the state of deep sleep. It is identified with dream. Neither death nor activity is the nature of the self. If either of these contentions was true, liberation would not be possible.

16. 'Certainly, it this (self) in the state of dream having delighted,

having wandered, having seen good and evil, it again returns in the manner it came to the place from which it commenced, to dream. Whatever it sees there, it is unaffected by it, since this person is unattached.' 'This is thus only, Yājñavalkya. I shall give you one thousand (cows), illustrious sir. Please instruct me further regarding liberation.'

The self is not affected by evils or contaminated by evils in both states, dream and waking.

17. 'Certainly, it this (self) in the state of waking having delighted, having wandered, having seen good and evil, it again returns in the manner it came to the place from which it commenced, to the state of dream (or dreamless sleep).'

The self is described as an infinite being, untouched by the waking state. The self is unaltered. The agency of the self is only due to limiting adjuncts and is not inherent in the self. This and the last verse stress the non-attachment of the self. The self is immortal, different from the attributes of the waking, dream, and deep sleep states.

18. 'Just as a large fish goes to both the banks of a river, eastern and western, thus does this self move along both these conditions, that of dream and waking.'

In the previous verse, the ātman is shown to be different from the body, etc. It transits the different states and is not the same as work and desire. The three states have been separately described. The aim is to prove the nature of the self as eternal, free, enlightened, and pure.

19. 'Just as a hawk or a falcon changing directions in the sky becomes tired, stretches its wings, and directs itself to its nest only, thus only does this person run towards the condition where no one desires any desire and no one sees any dream.'

Śruti passages also refer to the waking state as also being considered a dream. The commentary mentions that he has three abodes and also three dream states. (Ai. III.12)

The bird analogy is used to show that when, due to the activities of limiting adjuncts like the body, it gets fatigued, it enters its own self, where it is devoid of all such attributes.

20. 'Verily of this man are those nerves named hitā, which are as minute as a strand of hair split a thousand times and full of white, of blue, of yellow, of green, and of red (fluids). Now where, as it were he were being killed, being vanquished as it were, being chased by an elephant as it were, or he was falling into a well as it were, he mentally considers by means of ignorance whatever fears he has experienced in the waking state. Yet when he considers that he is a deity, as it were, that he is a king, as it were, or he thinks "I am this only, I am all". It is his highest world.'

What one sees in a dream is the result of past impressions based on ignorance. The elephant, etc., mentioned in this verse are created in a dream based on impressions arising from ignorance. The verse also explains the result of knowledge increasing and ignorance decreasing. When knowledge attains its zenith, ignorance is removed and one reaches the state of identity with all. When ignorance increases, there is identity with finite things, or as a separate entity. Ignorance represents the infinite as finite and makes the self appear limited. Desire arises from that which is thought to be separate. This spurs action. Liberation is not intrinsic to the self. Thus liberation from ignorance is attainable.

21. 'Verily this is his form which transcends craving, removed of evil, removed of fear. Just as a man in the embrace of his dear wife knows nothing internal or external, thus this person indeed in the embrace of the intelligent self knows

nothing internal or external. Certainly, that is his form, in which desires have been realized, in which the self is desired, in which he is free from desire and transcends grief.

Liberation, being described as identity with all, is being explained. This self is free completely from any form of desire, free from evil. Here evil refers to both merit and demerit. Since fear is caused by ignorance, the self is fearless. The ātman is that which reveals all, being the light which is pure intelligence.

22. 'Here (in this condition) a father is not a father, a mother is not a mother, the worlds are not worlds, deities are not deities, what is known is unknown, a thief is not a thief, a killer is not a killer, a devotee is no more a devotee, a hermit is no more a hermit. This is not affected by means of that which is evil, this is not affected by means of that which is virtuous since then the self has surpassed all the afflictions of the heart.'

The self-effulgent nature of the self in deep sleep is being reiterated. In this state, the self transcends all desires, actions, it being free from ignorance. Thus it is also beyond all relations. Thus relations in this state are said to not be relations; rites, worlds, actions, in fact all is transcended.

23. 'Certainly it does not see, yet indeed it does see even though it does not see since there cannot be any absence of viewing by the seer, since (the seer is) imperishable. But there is not a second separate entity, that which is another, for it to see.'

The vision of the witness is eternal. It is immortal. Thus in this state it sees. It is indescribable and ever luminous.

24. 'Certainly it does not smell, yet indeed it does smell even though it does not smell since there cannot be any absence of smelling by the smeller, since (the smeller is) imperishable.

But there is not a second separate entity, that which is another for it to smell.'

25. 'Certainly it does not taste, yet indeed it does taste even though it does not taste since there cannot be any absence of tasting by the taster, since (the taster is) imperishable. But there is not a second separate entity, that which is another for it to taste.'

26. 'Certainly it does not speak, yet indeed it does speak even though it does not speak since there cannot be any absence of speaking by the speaker, since (the speaker is) imperishable. But there is not a second separate entity, that which is another for it to speak to.'

27. 'Certainly it does not hear, yet indeed it does hear even though it does not hear since there cannot be any absence of hearing by the hearer, since (the hearer is) imperishable. But there is not a second separate entity, that which is another for it to hear.'

28. 'Certainly it does not think, yet indeed it does think even though it does not think since there cannot be any absence of thinking by the thinker, since (the thinker is) imperishable. But there is not a second separate entity, that which is another for it to think of.'

29. 'Certainly it does not touch, yet indeed it does touch even though it does not touch since there cannot be any absence of touching by the toucher, since (the toucher is) imperishable. But there is not a second separate entity, that which is another for it to touch.'

30. 'Certainly it does not know, yet indeed it does know even though it does not know since there cannot be any absence of knowing by the knower, since (the knower is) imperishable. But there is not a second separate entity, that which is another for it to know.'

The view that attributes such as vision have an existence apart from the self is erroneous. Further, Śruti texts speak of the self as being pure intelligence. The commentary uses the example of a naturally transparent crystal which assumes different colours by being in contact or near objects of different colours. Similarly, the self being pure intelligence appears to have powers of vision, etc. due to proximity with limiting adjuncts such as eyes, etc.

31. 'Certainly where there is a separate thing, as it were, then one may see the other, one may smell the other, one may taste the other, one may hear the other, one may think of the other, one may touch the other, one may know the other.'

In the state of deep sleep there is no other, thus no particulars are known. In the waking and dream states it appears due to ignorance that there is something else as different from the self. There is actually nothing different from the self.

32. 'Like water the seer becomes one, non-dual (Advaita). O king, this is the world of Brahman.' He (Yājñavalkya) expounded thus: 'This is the supreme goal, this is the supreme glory, this is the supreme world, this is the supreme bliss; all other beings live on a tiny fraction of this.'

In deep sleep there is no ignorance and therefore nothing separated from the self. Here the jivā is embraced by its own supreme self and is infinite, serene, without a second, and transparent like water. It is immortal and fearless. The commentary calls this the supreme attainment. All other attainments like taking a body, are due to ignorance and inferior to this. This identification with all is indeed the highest of all achievements.

33. 'Of men, he who is accomplished, wealthy, lords over others, is well endowed with every human enjoyment, of men this

is the supreme bliss. Now, one hundred times human bliss is one unit of bliss of the ancestors who have won their world. Now one hundred times the bliss of the ancestors who have won their world is one unit of bliss of the world of gandharvas. Now one hundred times this bliss of the world of gandharvas is one unit of the bliss of deities through action—those who attain divinity through action. Now one hundred times this bliss of deities through action is one unit of bliss of the deities by birth as well as one well versed in sacred learning, untainted and unaffected by desires. Now one hundred times this bliss of the deities by birth is one unit of the bliss of the world of Prajāpati as well as one well versed in sacred learning, untainted and unaffected by desires. Now one hundred times this bliss of the world of Prajāpati is one unit of the bliss of the world of Hiraṇyagarbha as well as one well versed in sacred learning, untainted and unaffected by desires. Now this only is the supreme bliss. This is the world of Brahma O king,' said Yājñavalkya. 'I shall give you one thousand (cows), illustrious sir. Please instruct me further regarding liberation.' At this Yājñavalkya grew apprehensive contemplating that this wise king would press him for all the ends (answers to his questions).

This verse seeks to outline the view or concept that all beings, whether men, or grass, or Hiraṇyagarbha, live on parts or fractions or particles of the supreme bliss. This verse attempts to portray this bliss as a whole through the means of the parts.

34. 'Certainly, it this (self) in the state of dream having delighted, having wandered, having seen good and evil, it again returns in the manner it came to the place from which it commenced, to the state of waking.'

This verse is the same as the first part of the Verse IV.3.16 which has been discussed.

35. 'Just as in the manner that a fully assembled cart moves along creaking, thus only this self in the body presided over by means of the intelligent self, when this passes away creaks (groans) as it rises (struggles) to breathe.

This verse and the next few verses describe the transmigration of the self. The analogy in the verse is used to show that the self will pass from one body to the next just as it comes to the waking state from the dream state.

The subtle body has the prāṇa for its main constituent. So when at death, when the prāṇa goes, the self also seems to go making a rattling noise. This occurs when breathing becomes difficult. The text shows that at the time of death, vital parts are denuded away, leading to loss of memory causing helplessness. Before this state of crisis, the commentary enjoins that a person practise the right means to ensure the appropriate stage is reached.

36. 'When it, this (the body), grows wizened (minute), is wizened by old age or disease, just as in the manner a mango or a fig or a peepul fruit is released (from its stalk), thus only this person completely frees itself from these limbs and again returns in the same way to particular bodies for the sake of prāṇa only.'

The aim of this and the last verse is to encourage the pursuit of renunciation. Many examples are cited to show that death is a constant in our lives so we must strive for liberation. The commentary further states that the entire universe, impelled by the jivā's work or karma, after his death, lays out another body for him repeatedly till he attains liberation.

37. 'Just as police officers, magistrates, and chiefs of villages wait for a king who is arriving with food, drink, and lodgings, saying, "Here he comes, here he comes," thus indeed for

him that knows, all beings wait, saying, "Here comes this Brahman, here this comes."'

38. 'Just as police officers, magistrates, and chiefs of villages congregate around a king wishing to set out, thus only do all the organs congregate around this self at the end (the time of death), as it rises (struggles) to breathe.'

IV

1. 'Where it, this self, becomes as if weak and bewildered, these organs come to it. It (the self) completely withdraws these particles of light and approaches the heart only. When this person in the eye turns away and returns then (the dying man) is unable to know colour.'

   It is stressed that actually the self does not become weak, but the body becomes weak. The words 'as it were' are emphasized in connection with it becoming weak and senseless at the time of death. Death is distinguished from the state of dream since in death the particles of light are completely withdrawn. The activities of the eye, etc. are stopped when the presiding deity of the eye, etc., turns away from the eye, etc.

2. 'He is one, he does not see, people say; he is one, he does not smell, people say; he is one, he does not taste, people say; he is one, he does not speak, people say; he is one, he does not hear, people say; he is one, he does not think, people say; he is one, he does not touch, people say; he is one, he does not know, people say.

   'The end of this heart gets illuminated and by means of this illumination the self departs either by means of the eye or by means of the head, or by means of other parts of the body. (When the self) departs the prāṇa accompanies it; (when the) prāṇa goes out all the organs accompany it. Then it (the self) becomes endowed with intelligence. That which has intelligence indeed passes on. Knowledge, actions, and past impressions accompany it.'

The organs get united with the subtle body of the dying man. Then it appears that he does not perceive. The presiding deities of the organs cease to work and the organs are joined in the heart. By means of the nerve end in the top of the heart, the individual self and the subtle body depart. It leaves the body as per its karma and knowledge. If it is to go to the sun, it will leave by the eye. If to the world of Hiraṇyagarbha, by the head. The commentary states that at the moment of death a man has a consciousness consisting of modifications of impressions due to his past karma. He goes to the body connected to this consciousness. Therefore, to have freedom of action at the time of death, right knowledge and merit should be acquired. One ought to follow the means to this as shown in the Upaniṣads.

3. 'Just as a leech in grass having gone to the end of the grass seizes another and withdraws there, thus only this self after having struck down this body, making it senseless, approaches a new body and draws itself there.'

The process of formation of the new body after death is touched upon.

4. 'Just as in the manner that a goldsmith takes a small piece of gold and moulds it into a fresher, better form, thus only this self after having struck down this body, making it senseless, creates another, fresher and better like that of the ancestors or the gandharvas, or the deities or of Prajāpati or of Hiraṇyagarbha or of other beings.'

The five elements are used again and again to make a new body.

5. 'Surely this self is Brahman, consisting of intelligence, consisting of mind, consisting of prāṇa, consisting of the eye,

consisting of the ear, consisting of earth, water, air, ether, fire, and consisting of what is other than fire, consisting of desire and the lack of desire, consisting of anger and the lack of anger, consisting of virtue and what is not virtuous, and consisting of all that, which is this. This explains what is intended to be said by saying (it) consists of this (perceived) and consists of that (informed). Just as one does, just as one acts, thus does one become. The doer of right becomes right, the doer of evil becomes evil. The virtuous are so by means of virtuous acts, evil by means of evil acts. Yet some say, this self consists of desire alone. Just as it desires so it becomes. What it wills, that is the action it does, that is the action it does, that it attains.

The self which transmigrates is the supreme self, Brahman, and is beyond thirst, etc. The Muṇḍaka Upaniṣad is alluded to where it is said the desire for objects causes for a person to be reborn in order to acquire these objects. Desire is the cause of transmigration.

6. Regarding that there is this verse:
'That being attached only with deeds, the subtle body goes where the mind is set. Attaining the end of whatever work it has done here, in this life, it comes again from that world to this world for work.'

Thus for one with desires. Now for one who has no desires, who is without desire, whose desires are extinguished, whose desires have been fulfilled, whose desire is the self, his prāṇa does not go out, being Brahman he merges in Brahman.

Desire is the cause of transmigration. One who knows Brahman and has eradicated his desires, his work produces no result. However, if one is attached to the results of work, one is born again. The desireless man does not transmigrate.

Desire leaves a person for whom all objects of desire are the self only. All objects are the self. He attains liberation and becomes Brahman. He merges in Brahman.

The Bhagavata Gita instructs in Niṣkām Karmayoga wherein it is enjoined that one should not be attached to the fruits of action. The Buddhists also state in the Four Noble truths that desire is the cause of suffering.

7. Regarding that there is this verse:
'When all the desires contained in his heart are renounced then the mortal becomes immortal, and realizes Brahman here (in this body).'
Just in the manner that the slough of a snake lies lifeless on an anthill, cast off, thus only this body lies. Now this bodiless, immortal, prāṇa is Brahman only, is luminosity indeed. 'I shall give you one thousand (cows), illustrious sir,' said Janaka of Videha.

In the absence of desire, a mortal becomes an immortal. A desire for anything other than the self constitutes ignorance. The liberated man on departing casts away his body, his tie to the mortal world, and he becomes immortal. Prāṇa implies that which lives.

8. Regarding that there is this verse:
'The subtle, widespread, ancient way has touched me, has been found by me only. By means of this, the illumined knowers of Brahman attain the world of heaven after being released (from this body).'

By saying 'has touched me', it is meant that liberation consisting in knowledge of Brahman has been achieved by me and has thus touched me.

9. 'Some say that on this there is white or blue or grey or green

or red. This was realized by a person who knows Brahman. By means of this a knower of Brahman, a doer of virtuous deeds, and a person of illumination also travel.'

The path of realization has no colour. The white and other colours referred to here indicate other parts, which are different from the knowledge of Brahman. These other parts indicate exits from different parts of the body. Transmigration is impossible when desire is exhausted when all objects of desire are known to be the self only.

10. 'Into blinding darkness enter those who meditate on ignorance. They who are enamored of knowledge enter into darkness greater than that.'

This is similar to a verse of the Īśa Upaniṣad (Īśa 9) which has been discussed previously.

11. 'Named unhappy, those worlds are enveloped in blinding darkness. To them, they, people who are ignorant and devoid of knowledge, go after departing.'
12. 'If by a person, the self is known as "this I am", then what desire, for whom, for the sake of which desire, will he cling to the body?'

The word 'if' is used to show that true self-knowledge is very rare. A person who realizes the self, for such a person there is nothing else to desire. For such a person all is the self.

13. 'Who has known and awakened the self which has penetrated this dangerous, impossible place (the body)? He is the maker of the universe since he is the maker of all, (all) is his world, he is the world only.'

The knower of the self is the maker of the universe. For the knower of the self is the maker of all. He is the self of all. One ought to meditate on one's own identity with the one and only supreme self.

14. 'Being here only, now we (have known) that (Brahman). If we do not, (we are) ignorant and the loss is great. Who knows that becomes immortal and others suffer only sorrow.'
15. 'When this is seen properly as the self, as God, as the lord of past and future, from that he does not wish to hide.'
16. 'From below which the year with its days revolves, on that the deities meditate as the light of all that is luminous, as immortal life.'
17. 'In which the five aggregates and ether are established, that only is known to be the self. Knowing that Brahman as immortal, I am immortal.'
18. 'They who have known the prāṇa of the prāṇa and the eye of the eye, and the ear of the ear and the mind of the mind, have realized Brahman eternal and foremost.'
19. 'By means of the mind only is it to be perceived. Here there is nothing diverse. He obtains death from death who as it were, sees diversity here.'
20. 'This is to be realized as one, alone, immeasurable, perpetual, and free from any taint. The self is superior from ether, unborn, infinite, and permanent.'

The self is to be realized as uniform pure intelligence. Brahman is unknowable. For to know there must be another, but in Brahman there is a unity of everything. Knowledge of Brahman entails the end of identification with what is external.

21. 'The intelligent seeker of Brahman after knowing him alone ought to strive at realization. May he not study too many words since that is just exhausting speech.'

Knowledge of Brahman that is strived for is intuitive. One should avoid too many words.

22. 'It surely, this infinite unborn self which is this, consisting of intellect and in the organs which is within this ether in the heart and in this lies the controller of everything, the lord of everything, the ruler of everything. It does not become greater by excellent work, nor does it become lesser at all by evil work. This is the lord of everything, this is the ruler of beings, this is the protector of beings. This is the bridge which keeps the different worlds apart. Him, the seekers of Brahman, aim to realize by means of reciting the Vedas, by means of sacrifices, by means of clarity, by means of religious austerity not leading to death. After knowing this only one becomes a sage. Seeking this world only monks give up their home. Surely since they knew this, the ancient knowers, people say did not wish for offspring, since they thought, "We who have obtained the self, (obtained) this world, of what use to us are offspring?" Overcoming the desire for sons, the desire for riches, the desire for worlds, they adopt a wandering mendicant's life, since that which is the desire for sons only is the desire for riches, is the desire for worlds, for both these are surely desires only. It the self is not this, not this. It is ungraspable for it is not grasped. It is incognizable since it cannot be cognized. The self is unyoked since it is not yoked. It is untrammelled. It does not suffer, it is not injured. Indeed (the knower) is not overcome by these. If for some reason he has done good or for some reason he has done evil, both these he overcomes. He is not afflicted by work done or not done.'

This verse seeks to show the applicability of the Vedas to the self as described here. Previously the topics of bondage and liberation were discussed. Liberation was explained in some detail.

23. 'That has been expressed in this hymn. This eternal glory of one who has realized Brahman is neither increased nor

decreased by work. One ought to know the nature of this only. Having known this a person is not afflicted by evil work. From that, one who knows thus controls his passions, is calm, free from desires, patient, focussed, sees the self in his own self only, sees everything in the self. Him, evil does not overcome, all evils (does he) overcome. Evil does not afflict him, (instead) all evil is burned by him. He becomes free from evil, taints, and doubts, and a true knower of Brahman. This is the world of Brahman O king. You have obtained it,' said Yājñavalkya. (Janaka of Videha replied), 'Illustrious sir, I give you Videha and with it myself also to serve you.'

The greatness attained by means of work is temporary. The greatness of a knower of Brahman is eternal. It is described as 'not this, not this'. It is attained by one who is beyond all desire. After attaining this state one is beyond being affected by evil actions, which include both good and evil, since to he who knows Brahman both are evil.

24. It, surely this infinite, unborn self, is the eater of food, the bestower of wealth. The person who knows thus obtains great wealth.
25. It, surely this infinite, unborn self who is undecaying, imperishable, immortal, fearless, is Brahman. Certainly, Brahman is beyond fear. A person who knows thus surely attains the fearless Brahman.

This verse sums up the central concepts regarding the self. The self is described as the fearless self which is the infinite, eternal Brahman. The crux is that the person who knows the self has been described previously as the fearless Brahman, such a person attains the fearless Brahman.

V

1. Now, it is said, Yājñavalkya had two wives, Maitreyī and Kātyāyanī. Of these two, Maitreyī spoke about Brahman, while Kātyāyanī was interested in mundane topics only. Now Yājñavalkya wished to prepare for another type of life.
2. 'Maitreyī,' said Yājñavalkya, 'indeed I am going to become an ascetic, (going) from this place, my dear. Well let me conclude your relationship with this Kātyāyanī.'
3. She (Maitreyī) said, 'Illustrious sir, even if the entire earth filled with wealth be mine, shall I become immortal by means of this?' 'No,' said Yājñavalkya, 'just as the life of those having plentiful means, so indeed would your life be. But of attaining immortality there is no hope by means of wealth.'
4. She (Maitreyī) said, 'What shall I do with this by means of which I shall not become immortal? Illustrious sir, speak to me of that alone which you know.'
5. He (Yājñavalkya) said, 'Verily you have been dear (always) to me, and now you have increased your dearness for me. My dear, if you wish, then I shall expound to you. However, while I expound, deeply meditate on it.'
6. He said, 'Surely, my dear, not for the sake of the husband does a husband become beloved; however; a husband is beloved for the sake of the self. Surely, my dear, not for the sake of the wife does a wife become beloved; however, a wife is beloved for the sake of the self. Surely, my dear, not for the sake of sons do sons become beloved; however, sons are beloved for the sake of the self. Surely, my dear, not for the sake of wealth does wealth become beloved; however, wealth is beloved for the sake of the self. Surely, my dear, not for the sake of Brāhmaṇa does a Brāhmaṇa become beloved; however, a Brāhmaṇa is beloved for the sake of the self. Surely, my dear, not for the sake of a Kṣatriya does a Kṣatriya become beloved; however, a Kṣatriya is beloved for the sake of the self. Surely, my dear, not for the sake

of the worlds do the worlds become beloved; however, the worlds are beloved for the sake of the self. Surely, my dear, not for the sake of the gods are gods beloved; however, the gods are beloved for the sake of the self. Surely, my dear, not for the sake of the Vedas are the Vedas beloved; however, the Vedas are beloved for the sake of the self. Surely, my dear, not for the sake of beings do beings become beloved; however, beings are beloved for the sake of the self. Surely, my dear, not for the sake of all is all beloved; however, all is beloved for the sake of the self. Certainly, O Maitreyī, it is the self that ought to be seen, ought to be heard, ought to be reflected on, and ought to be meditated upon. When, surely, my dear, the self is seen, heard, reflected upon and realized, then indeed all this is known.'

This verse is very similar to a previous verse (Br. 2.4.5). The self is realized by hearing from the teacher, based upon scripture, reflection by means of learning and meditation. There is nothing other than the self.

7. The Brāhmaṇa shuns him who knows the Brāhmaṇa as other than the self. The Kṣatriya shuns him who knows the Kṣatriya as other than the self. The world shuns him who knows the world as other than the self. The deities shun him who knows the deities as other than the self. The Vedas shun him who knows the Vedas as other than the self. Beings shun him who knows beings as other than the self. All shun him who knows all as other than the self. This Brāhmaṇa, this Kṣatriya, these worlds, these deities, these Vedas, these beings, all this is that which is the self.
8. Just as one is not able to grasp the external sounds of a drum being beaten, however, by grasping the drum or the beater of the drum only are the sounds grasped.
9. Just as one is not able to grasp the external sounds of a conch

being blown, however, by grasping the conch or the blower of the conch only are the sounds grasped.

10. Just as one is not able to grasp the external sounds of a vīnā being played, however, by grasping the vīnā or the player of the vīnā only are the sounds grasped.

11. Just as from a fire which arises from damp fuel, different kinds of smoke are produced, thus, my dear, the Ṛg Veda, the Yajur Veda, the Sāma Veda, Ātharvāṇgirasa, history, the Purāṇas, sciences, Upaniṣads, verses, aphorisms (sūtras), elucidations, commentaries, sacrifices, oblations in fire, food and drink, this world, the next world, and all beings are the breath of this great reality. From this are all these inspired.

This verse explicitly states that the worlds and all else are the breath of this great reality.

12. Just as the ocean is the one abode of all waters, thus the skin is the one abode of all kinds of touch, the nostrils are the one abode of all odours, thus the tongue is the one abode of all tastes, thus the eye is the one abode of all forms, thus the ear is the one abode of all sounds, thus the mind is the one abode of all volitions, thus the intellect is the one abode of all knowledge, thus the hands are the one abode of all actions, thus the organ of generation is the one abode of all enjoyment, thus the organ of excretion is the one abode of all excretions, thus the feet are the one abode of all walking, thus the organ of speech is the one abode of all the Vedas.

13. 'Just as a piece of rock salt does not have an inside or an outside, but is a uniform mass of taste, surely, thus, my dear, this self does not have an inside or an outside but is a uniform mass of consciousness only. From these elements does one arise and into these does one disappear. Once it departs there is no consciousness. My dear, this is what I speak,' said

Yājñavalkya.

When knowledge leads to the merging of all effects, the self alone remains, entire, pure intelligence, without that which is internal or external. It is compared to a lump of salt. The combination of elements with which it was previously associated being dissolved, so then, as per Yajñavalkya, after attaining knowledge does the particular consciousness dissolve.

14. She (Maitreyī) said, 'Here indeed, illustrious sir, you have caused me to be utterly confused. Verily I do not understand this (self).' He said, 'My dear, I am not stating anything confusing. Surely, this self is imperishable and indestructible.'
15. 'Since where there is duality as it were, there one views another, there one smells another, there one tastes another, there one speaks of another, there one hears another, there one thinks of another, there one knows another. However, where all has become the self only, then by means of whom and what should one view, then by means of whom and what should one smell, then by means of whom and what should one taste, then by means of whom and what should one speak, then by means of whom and what should one hear, then by means of whom and what should one think, then by means of whom and what should one touch, then by means of whom and what should one know? By means of which is all this is known, through what should one know that? It the self is not this, not this. It is ungraspable for it is not grasped. It is incognizable since it cannot be cognized. This self is unyoked since it is not yoken. It is untrammelled, it does not suffer, it is not injured. My dear, by means of what should one know the knower? So, O Maitreyī, the instruction has been granted to you. So much, indeed, my dear, regarding immortality. Having stated this, Yājñavalkya left.

The consistent theme of the four chapters of this Upaniṣad is that the self is the supreme Brahman. The means to attaining the self are diverse. It is to be arrived at by the process of 'not this, not this' and the renunciation of all. This verse discusses different concepts of the self.

VI

1. Now the lineage (of teachers): Pautimāsya (received this instruction) from Gaupavana, Gaupavana from (a different) Pautimāsya, (this) Pautimāsya from (a different) Gaupavana, (this) Gaupavana from Kauśika, Kauśika from Kauṇḍinya, Kauṇḍinya from Śāṇḍilya, Śāṇḍilya from Kauśika, and Gautama, Gautama
2. From Āgniveśya, Āgniveśya from Gārgya, Gārgya from (a different) Gārgya, (this) Gārgya from Gautama, Gautama from Saitava, Saitava from Pārāśaryāyana, Pārāśaryāyana from Gārgyāyaṇa, Gārgyāyaṇa from Uddālakāyana, Uddālakāyana from Jābālāyana, Jābālāyana from Mādhyandināyana, Mādhyandināyana from Saukarāyanṇa, Saukarāyanṇa from Kāsāyaṇa, Kāsāyaṇa from Sāyakāyana, Sāyakāyana from Kauśikāyani, Kauśikāyani
3. From Ghṛtakauśikāt, Ghṛtakauśikāt from Pārāśaryāyaṇa, Pārāśaryāyaṇa from Pārāśarya, Pārāśarya from Jātūkarṇya, Jātūkarṇya from Āsurāyaṇa and Yāska, Āsurāyaṇa from Iraivaṇi, Iraivaṇi from Aupajandhani, Aupajandhani from Āsuri, Āsuri from Bhāradvāja, Bhāradvāja from Ātreya, Ātreya from Māṇṭi, Māṇṭi from Gautama, Gautama from (a different) Gautama, (this) Gautama from Vātsya, Vātsya from Śāṇḍilya, Śāṇḍilya from Kaiśorya Kāpya, Kaiśorya Kāpya from Kumārahārita, Kumārahārita from Gālava, Gālava from Vidarbhīkauṇḍinya, he from Vatsnapāt Bābhrava, he from Pathin Saubhara, he from Ayāsya Āṅgirasa, he from Ābhūti Tvāṣṭra, he from Viśvarupa Tvāṣṭra, he from the two Aśvins,

the Aśvins from Dadhyac Ātharvana, he from Atharvan Daiva, he from Mṛtyu Prādhvaṁsana, he from Prādhvaṁsana, Prādhvaṁsana from Ekarṣi, Ekarṣi from Vipracitti, Vipracitti from Vyaṣṭi, Vyaṣṭi from Sanāru, Sanāru from Sanātana, Sanātana from Sanaga, Sanaga from Parameṣṭhin (Virāj), Parameṣṭhin from Brahmā/Brahman (Hiraṇyagarbha), Brahman is eternal. Salutations to Brahman.

CHAPTER 5

I

1. That is complete, this is complete. From completeness, completeness follows. Of the complete, if we remove what is complete, (then also) the complete alone is left. Aum is Brahman (that) is ether, the eternal ether, the ether containing air. So, indeed, stated the son of Kauravyāyanī. This is the knowledge that the seekers of Brahman have known. By means of this one knows that which is to be known.

The present chapter will throw light on some key meditations. Those meditations leading to many achievements eventually lead to liberation. The meditation on Aum is also strongly prescribed. By that is complete is meant that which has no limits and that which pervades all. That refers to the supreme Brahman. The supreme Brahman and the conditioned Brahman are both complete, infinite. The conditioned Brahman is complete in its real form as the supreme self. The differentiated Brahman proceeds from Brahman as its cause. The meaning of this verse is the same as the mantra in (1.4.10), namely, 'This (self) was indeed Brahman in the beginning. It knew only itself. Therefore it became all.'

II

1. Three types of Prajāpati's progeny: the deities, men, and demons, lived with Prajāpati their father as students of sacred learning. Having lived as Brahmacāris the deities said, 'Please speak to (teach) us.' He uttered to them the syllable 'Da', (and questioned), 'Have you understood?' They said, 'We have indeed understood, you said to us, "Control Yourselves."' (He) said, 'Indeed you have understood.'

This section is meant to enjoin the three disciplines including that of self control, etc.

2. Then to him the men said, 'Please speak to (teach) us.' He uttered to them the syllable 'Da', (and questioned), 'Have you understood?' They said, 'We have indeed understood, you said to us, "Donate."' (He) said, 'Indeed you have understood.'
3. Then to him the demons said, 'Please speak to (teach) us.' He uttered to them the syllable 'Da', (and questioned), 'Have you understood?' They said, 'We have indeed understood, you said to us, "Be merciful."' (He) said, 'Indeed you have understood.' This teaching only, this heavenly voice of thunder repeats as Da, Da, Da—control yourselves, be charitable, be merciful. One ought to learn these three—self control, making donations, and compassion.

The three disciplines of self-control, charity, and compassion are enjoined on three classes of beings, the deities, men, and Asuras.

III

1. This is Prajāpati which is the heart. This is Brahman, this is all. That, this has three syllables, Hṛ, Da, Yaṁ. One syllable is 'Hṛ'. He who knows thus to him his own people and others

bring (gifts). One syllable is 'Da'. He who knows thus, to him his own people and others give (their powers). One syllable is 'Ya'. He who knows thus goes to the world of heaven.

The verse states that Prajāpati is the heart, the intellect which is situated in the heart. The heart is identified with Prajāpati the protector of all beings. It is Brahman. The intellect is Brahman and it has been said in the third chapter that it is everything.

IV

1. This surely is that. This only was that, the true only. He who knows this great, adorable, firstborn as the Brahman the true, wins these worlds; and (his foe) is vanquished and becomes non-existent (for him) who knows this great adorable, firstborn as Brahman the true. Since truth is Brahman only.

The importance of the meditation on Brahman as Hṛdaya is stressed here. Since all these worlds are created by Satya-Brahman, the person who knows Satya-Brahman cognizes the worlds.

V

1. In the beginning this (the universe) was water only. That water created the true (or existing). The true is Brahman. Brahman (created) Prajāpati. Prajāpati (created) the deities. The deities meditated on truth alone. That (Satyam) consists of three syllables, Sa, Ti, Yam. One syllable is Sa, one syllable is Ti, and one syllable is Yam. The first and last syllables are truth, in the middle untruth. Thus untruth is covered on both sides by means of the truth; it shares in the nature of the truth only. Who knows thus, untruth does not harm.

This verse is dedicated to Satya-Brahman the firstborn. That he is the firstborn is being described. The water mentioned here refers to oblations which are relevant in the context of sacrifices such as the Agnihotra, these are by nature liquid and are thus referred to as water. At the initial stage there was only water. From this emerged Satya. Satya is Brahman. The three syllables of Satya, Sa, Ti, Ya are explained. Sa and Ya are beyond the scope or grip of death and are free. Ti is said to be untruth. This is so because the words 'mṛtya' and 'anṛta' (untruth) have 't' in them.

2. He, who is that truth is that yonder sun. This person who is in that orb and this person who is in the right eye, these two support each other. By means of his rays that is supported in this; by means of the prāṇa (vital breath), this one on the former. When he is about to depart he sees this orb clearly. These rays (then) do not come to him.

We now come to the different aspects of Satya-Brahman who is called the sun. Both the person in the right eye and the person in the orb are Satya-Brahman. They mutually support each other as described in this verse.

The period before death is also mentioned. This is in order to guide spiritual aspirants.

3. This person who is in this orb, of this 'Bhuḥ' is his head, since there is one head and there is this one syllable. 'Bhuvaḥ' is the arms, since there are two arms and these syllables are two. 'Ahar' (day) is his secret name. Who thus knows destroys evil and abandons it.

Bhūḥ, Bhuvaḥ, Svaḥ, known as the Vyāhṛtis are the limbs of he, the being in the solar orb.

4. This person who is in the right eye, of this 'Bhuḥ', is his head, since there is one head and there is this one syllable. 'Bhuvaḥ' is the arms, since there are two arms and these syllables are

two. 'Svaḥ' is the feet, since there are two feet and these syllables are two. 'Aham' (I) is his secret name. Who thus knows destroys evil and abandons it.

VI

1. This person consisting of mind is splendid by nature, is in the interior of the heart, similar to a grain of rice or barley in size. This, he is the lord of all, the ruler of all, and administers all this, whatever there is (in the universe).

This being is splendid because the mind reveals all and this being consists of mind. This being is the ruler of all, the entire universe. The commentary states that he who meditates on Brahman as identified with the mind attains identity with him.

VII

1. It is said that lightning is Brahman. Since it (lightning) dispels (darkness) it is called lightning. Who knows thus that lightning is Brahman dispels evils (arrayed in opposition to him) since lightning certainly is Brahman.

This verse continues to elucidate meditations on Satya-Brahman. Lightning dispels darkness. He who knows this dispels all evils.

VIII

1. A person ought to meditate on speech as a cow. Her four udders are the Svāhā sound, Vaṣaṭ sound, Hanta sound, and the Svadhā sound. The deities live on her two udders, the Svāhā sound, and the Vaṣaṭ sound. Men (live) on the Hanta sound and the ancestors (live) on the Svadhā sound. Prāṇa is her bull and the mind her calf.

Here is discussed another meditation on Brahman, namely

speech as Brahman. Speech is used to refer to the Vedas.

IX

1. Vaiśvānāra (the universal fire) which is this fire within a person by means of which eaten food is digested. Its sound is this which one hears thus by covering the ears. When it (the individual self) is about to depart, this sound is not heard.

This verse continues describing various types of meditation. It also describes an omen of death, namely, when the individual is about to depart, it no more hears this sound.

X

1. Certainly, when from this world a person departs he goes to the (deity) air. For him it makes an opening there (in his body) just like the hole of a chariot wheel. By means of this he approaches upwards and comes to the sun. For him it (air) makes an opening there (in his body) just like the hole of a tabor. By means of this he approaches upwards and comes to the moon. For him it (air) makes an opening there (in his body) just like the hole of a drum. By means of this he approaches upwards and comes to a world which has no fear and no cold. In this he lives eternally.

Here the aim of all meditations is being taken up. Such an evolved person reaches the world of Hiraṇyagarbha. Here he lives without privations and afflictions for countless years, constituting the lifetime of Hiraṇyagarbha.

XI

1. Certainly, this is the highest penance that a diseased person suffers. Who knows thus indeed wins the highest world. Certainly, this is the highest penance when people carry a

dead person to the forest. Who knows thus indeed wins the highest world. Certainly, this is the highest penance when on fire they lay a departed man. Who knows thus indeed wins the highest world.

Now is being enjoined austerity as a form of meditation. One is prescribed to not overly condemn or lose one's morale in the face of difficulties. Rather one ought to view it as an austerity.

XII

1. It is said by some that food is Brahman. That is not the case for surely food decomposes without prāṇa. It is said by some that prāṇa is Brahman. That is not the case for surely prāṇa dries up without food. Indeed, when these two deities become united, they reach their foremost state. Thus said Prātṛda to his father, 'Indeed, what honour can I do to a person who thus knows and indeed what evil can I do to such a person?' To him his father said (with a silencing gesture of) his hand, 'No, Prātṛda, on the contrary who can reach the foremost state by being united with these two?' To him he also said this, 'It is "Vi".' Certainly, food is 'Vi', since all these beings reside in food. It is 'Ram'. Certainly, prāṇa is Ram, since all these beings are happy in prāṇa. For who thus knows surely in him all beings reside, and all beings are happy.

This verse seeks to emphasize the relationship between prāṇa and anna, vital breath and food, as being mutually dependant. These two can only achieve their highest goal when they are united. Again, food is the abode of all beings. Prāṇa is where all beings are happy. A person is only happy when he has body and strength.

XIII

1. (One ought to meditate upon prāṇa as) the Uktha. Surely prāṇa is the Uktha since prāṇa causes all this to rise. From him who knows thus arises a son who is a knower of the Uktha and he wins union with or residence in the same world as the Uktha.
2. (One ought to meditate upon prāṇa as) the Yajus. Surely prāṇa is the Yajus since in prāṇa are all these beings joined. Indeed, for him who knows thus all beings are united for the sake of his pre-eminence and he wins union with or residence in the same world as the Yajus.
3. (One ought to meditate upon prāṇa as) the sāman. Surely, prāṇa is the sāman since in prāṇa do all these beings unite. Indeed, for him who knows thus all beings unite to ensure his pre-eminence and he wins union with or residence in the same world as the sāman.
4. (One ought to meditate upon prāṇa as) the Kṣatra. Surely, prāṇa is the Kṣatra since prāṇa indeed is the Kṣatra. This prāṇa protects the body from injuries. Indeed, who knows thus, obtains the Kṣatra which requires no protector and he wins union with or residence in the same world as the Kṣatra.

XIV

1. The earth, the intermediate region between heaven and earth, heaven, (these constitute) eight syllables. Eight syllables indeed is one foot (line) of the Gāyatrī. This (one foot) of this only is that. He who knows this foot of the Gāyatrī thus wins as much as the three worlds extend.

The foremost of metres, Gāyatrī is being discussed here. It is known as Gāyatrī since it protects the organs of the persons who recite it. This is a significant quality not shared by other metres. Gāyatrī is also said to be same as prāṇa, the soul of all metres. The meditation on Gāyatrī is crucial and strongly recommended.

2. Ṛcaḥ (verses), Yajūṃṣi (sacrificial formulas), Sāmāni (chants), (these constitute) eight syllables. Eight syllables is indeed one foot (line) of the Gāyatrī. This (one foot) of this only is that. He who knows this foot of the Gāyatrī thus wins as much as the threefold knowledge (represented by the Vedas) extend.

3. Prāṇa, apāna, and vyāna, (these constitute) eight syllables. Eight syllables indeed is one foot of the Gāyatrī. This (one foot) of this only is that. He who knows this foot of the Gāyatrī thus, wins as many creatures that breathe. Now of this only, the fourth, seen foot, rising above what is dark is this (sun) that blazes. Indeed, this fourth is that which is Turīya. It is (called) the seen foot, since it is as if this is seen. This is known as that which rises above darkness since it blazes higher and higher over all that is dark. He who knows this foot of the Gāyatrī thus blazes in that manner with splendour and fame.

The fourth seen foot is being described. Turīya stands generally for fourth. It is called seen foot to indicate the being in the solar orb, who is seen. Rajas stands for the universe which proceeds from activity.

4. This Gāyatrī is established on this fourth, seen foot which rises above darkness. That (again) is established on truth. Certainly, the eye is truth since the eye surely is truth. From that, if just now two disputants came stating, 'I saw,' and 'I heard,' we should have belief in him only who states, 'I saw.' Surely that truth is established in strength. Prāṇa surely is strength. That is established on prāṇa. From that it is said that strength is more vigorous than truth. Thus is the Gāyatrī established with regard to the self. Indeed, this Gāyatrī protected the Gayas. The Gayas are the prāṇas and this protects the prāṇas. It is named Gāyatrī since it protects the prāṇas. This Sāvitri (verse) which the teacher imparts to the

disciple is this only. To whomsoever it is imparted, his prāṇas are protected.

The crucially important fourth foot of Gāyatrī is being spoken of here. Previously the three feet consisting of the three Vedas, prāṇa, the three worlds were spoken of as resting on the fourth. The fourth foot, the sun is what the grass and subtle universe depend upon. The fourth foot rests on truth. Truth rests on the eye, since the eye is that by which the truth is demonstrated. Truth depends on strength. The Gāyatrī is prāṇa. Thus the universe depends on prāṇa.

5. That Sāvitri verse is imparted by some (to the disciple) as an anusṭubh metre, stating that speech is anusṭubh and we shall impart this speech. This should not be done. Gāyatrī is indeed Sāvitrī, one ought to impart this. Surely even if one who knows thus were to receive many gifts, this is not even enough for one foot of Gāyatrī.
6. He who accepts these three worlds complete (with wealth) will obtain (the fruits of knowing) this first foot of Gāyatrī only. Now he who accepts as much as the threefold knowledge (represented by the Vedas) extend, will obtain (the fruits of knowing) this second foot of Gāyatrī only. Now he who accepts as many creatures that breathe will obtain (the fruits of knowing) this third foot of Gāyatrī only. Now of this (the fruits of knowing), the fourth visible foot which rises above that what is dark, and is this (sun), which blazes, not anything is to be obtained. For how indeed could one accept such a gift?

The verse aims to illustrate the importance of knowledge of Gāyatrī. The situations mentioned here are hypothetical since there is no such donor or recipient. How can it be possible to accept a gift equivalent to the three worlds? Gāyatrī in its entirety ought to be properly meditated upon.

7. Of this (Gāyatrī) the worship. 'O Gāyatrī, thou art one-footed, two-footed, three-footed, four-footed, also without a foot since thou does not go about. Obeisance to you, the fourth seen foot which rises above darkness. May that (rival) never obtain that. Whom (a knower of Gāyatrī) may hate, (he should) state, 'For so and so may his desire not prosper.' Indeed, for him, the desire does not prosper for him with respect to he who thus offers salutations or (he may state), 'May I obtain that (desire of his).'

Gāyatrī can be achieved by meditating spiritual aspirants. In the unconditioned supreme form Gāyatrī has no feet since it is the self which is 'not this, not this'. The four feet mentioned above are from an apparent point of view.

8. Regarding this, indeed Janaka of Videha said to Buḍila Aśvatarāśvi, 'Indeed you termed yourself as one who knows Brahman, then how have you turned into an elephant carrying (me)?' 'Since, O king, I did not know its mouth,' said he. 'Its mouth is fire only. Certainly, if a lot of fuel is put into the fire the fire burns all of it. Thus only a knower of this, even if he were to commit many evils, he burns all that and becomes cleansed, pure, imperishable, and immortal.'

The verse continues to stress the importance of Gāyatrī. One identified with Gāyatrī is cleared of all sins.

XV

1. By means of a golden vessel is the face of the truth concealed. Remove that, O Pūṣan, so that for the sake of truth and virtue I may see it.

The first three verses of the section are the prayers of a man in his last stages of this life, who prays to the sun. The true face of the Satya-Brahman is concealed. The request is for this concealment to be removed so that this may be achieved. Various names are used to address the sun.

2. 'O Pūṣan, the solitary viewer, O controller, O Sūrya (sun), O progeny of Prajāpati, O multitude of rays, gather thy radiance so that I may see that which is your most propitious form. Whoever be that yonder person, that I am.'
3. 'May this enter into the immortal cosmic vital force and the body reduced to ashes (when one departs). O Aum, remember my actions, remember what has been done, remember my actions, remember what has been done.'
4. 'O Fire, lead us along the propitious path, so we may obtain prosperity. O God, thou knowest all our mental states. From us remove deceitful evil. In the highest degree we offer obeisance.'

Fire is prayed to so that the person may be led along the good, propitious northern path and not the southern part that leads to return. Repeated salutations are preferred, for we are not strong enough for anything else.

CHAPTER 6

I

1. 'Certainly who knows the most senior and most excellent becomes the most senior and most excellent amongst his community. Prāṇa, surely, is the most senior and most excellent. Who knows thus becomes the most senior and most excellent amongst his community and also among those he wishes to become.'

   The commentary takes up the question as to why Gāyatrī is prāṇa and not the organs. The answer is that the Gāyatrī is the most senior and excellent. The section explains how this is so. This chapter and the previous chapter deal with specific meditations, such as that on prāṇa, which have not been covered so far. The prāṇa functions before the other organs and the other organs work only after prāṇa starts its operations. How prāṇa is the most excellent will be shown in the next few verses. Further, the person who meditates on prāṇa in this form, himself becomes the most senior and excellent.

2. 'Certainly who knows the most pre-eminent becomes the most pre-eminent in his community. Speech surely is the most pre-eminent. Who knows thus becomes the most pre-eminent amongst his community and also among those he wishes to become.'

Results are achieved as per the meditation done. The result mentioned in this verse is as per the realization.

3. 'Certainly who knows the support is supported on smooth ground and is supported on rough ground. The eye surely is the support, since by means of the eye, a person is supported on smooth ground and on rough ground. Who knows thus is supported on smooth ground and is supported on rough ground.'
4. 'Certainly who knows prosperity for him is fulfilled whatever wish he seeks. The ear surely is prosperity since here are all the Vedas acquired. Who knows thus to him are fulfilled whatever wish he seeks.'
5. 'Certainly who knows the sanctuary becomes the sanctuary of his community and also the sanctuary of (other) people. The mind surely is the sanctuary. Who knows thus becomes the sanctuary of his community and also the sanctuary of (other) people.'
6. 'Certainly who knows procreation is endowed with progeny and animals. The seed surely is procreation. Who knows thus is endowed with progeny and with animals.'
7. They, the prāṇas approached Prajāpati contending about who excelled amongst them and stated: 'Who amongst us is the most pre-eminent?' He said, 'Surely, it which on departing, this body is considered to be worse off, certainly that is pre-eminent amongst you.'

   The aim of this verse appears to be to inculcate a sense of non-attachment to the body.

8. Speech left, it stayed away for a year and having returned said, 'How were you able to live without me?' (In reply) they said, 'Just as the mute, without speaking by means of the organ of speech, (but) breathing by means of prāṇa, seeing by means of the eye, hearing by means of the ear, knowing

by means of the mind, procreating by means of the seed. So have we lived. Speech entered (at this).'

Having been thus spoken to by Brahman, the organs one after the other set out to ascertain their abilities. One by one they realize that they are not pre-eminent.

9. The eye left, it stayed away for a year and having returned said, 'How were you able to live without me?' (In reply) they said, 'Just as the blind, not seeing by means of the eye, (but) breathing by means of prāṇa, speaking by means of the organ of speech, hearing by means of the ear, knowing by means of the mind, procreating by means of the seed. So have we lived. The eye entered (at this).'
10. The ear left, it stayed away for a year and having returned said, 'How were you able to live without me?' (In reply) they said, 'Just as the deaf, not hearing by means of the ear, (but) breathing by means of prāṇa, speaking by means of the organ of speech, seeing by means of the eye, knowing by means of the mind, procreating by means of the seed. So have we lived. The ear entered (at this).'
11. The mind left, it stayed away for a year and having returned said, 'How were you able to live without me?' (In reply) they said, 'Just as dullards, not knowing by means of the mind, (but) breathing by means of prāṇa, speaking by means of the organ of speech, seeing by means of the eye, hearing by means of the ear, procreating by means of the seed. So have we lived. The mind entered (at this).'
12. The seed (organ of procreation) left, it stayed away for a year and having returned said, 'How were you able to live without me?' (In reply) they said, 'Just as the impotent, not procreating by means of the seed, (but) breathing by means of prāṇa, speaking by means of the organ of speech, seeing by means of the eye, hearing by means of the ear, knowing

by means of the mind. So have we lived. The seed entered (at this).'

13. Then just as prāṇa was about to leave, in the manner that a large thoroughbred horse of Sind pulls at the pegs to which it is tied, thus did it pull out the vital breaths. They said, 'Illustrious sir, kindly do not leave, surely we will not be able to live without you.' 'Then for me make an offering.' 'Thus be it.'

The statements of persons should be tested; this is the import of the conversation in this section. Prāṇa is pre-eminent among the organs.

14. It, speech stated, 'In which I am pre-eminent, surely you are pre-eminent in that.' The eye, 'In which I am supported, surely you are supported in that.' The ear, 'In which I am prosperous, surely you are prosperous in that.' The mind, 'In which I am sheltered, surely you are sheltered in that.' The seed (organ of procreation), 'In which I am procreated, surely you are procreated in that.' 'Of this, myself, what will be my food? What will be my abode?' 'Whatever food which there is, even of dogs, worms, insects, and birds is your food, and water is your abode. Surely who knows the food of prāṇa thus, nothing is eaten or accepted that ought not to be eaten. From this, the wise, well-versed in the Vedas, sip a little water before they eat, and take a sip after they have eaten. (By) this indeed they think that they are ensuring prāṇa is not without an abode.'

The other organs all give attributes to prāṇa. All is the food of prāṇa.

II

1. Indeed Śvetaketu, grandson of Aruna, went to an assembly of the Pañcālas. He approached (the king) Pravāhaṇa, the son

of Jīvala, who was having (his servants) serve him. Seeing him, the king addressed him, stating, 'O youth!' He replied, 'Sir.' 'Have you been instructed by your father?' 'Yes,' he affirmed.

2. 'Do you know how these creatures take contrary paths after departing (death)?' 'No,' he (Śvetaketu) said. 'Do you know how these (creatures) return again to this world?' 'No,' he said. 'Do you know how that world is not filled thus with many (creatures) dying again and again?' He only said, 'No.' 'Do you know that oblation which is offered and water rises up and speaks becoming the voice of a person?' He only said, 'No.' 'Do you know by means of which way, either to the path of the deities or to the path of the ancestors, that by doing which creatures obtain either the way of the deities or the way of the ancestors?' Since we have heard the words of the sage, 'Two paths have I heard of, for men the path of the deities and the path of the ancestors. By means of these two paths the universe is joined, which is between the father (heaven) and the mother (earth)".' 'Of these I do not know even one,' he said.

3. Then to him the king gave an invitation to stay. The young boy disregarded the invitation and hurried away. To his father he came. To him, he said, 'Indeed, previously you have referred to me as well instructed.' 'How (did you feel embarrassed?) intelligent one?' 'That member of the princely class asked me five questions. Not even one of them do I know.' 'Which were these?' These (he stated) and repeated the first words.

4. He (the father) said, 'My son, you ought to know whatever I know, all that have I taught to you. Nevertheless, let us go there and live as students.' 'You only go.' He (Gautama) arrived at where Pravāhaṇa Jaivali was. For him (the king) brought a seat and had water brought and then made

respectful offerings for him. To him he said, 'Illustrious Gautama, we offer you a wish.'

5. He (Gautama) said, 'You have vowed this wish to me. Please tell me the words you spoke to the young man.'
6. The (king) said, 'Surely Gautama, that is counted among the divine wishes. Please ask (for something) regarding men.'
7. He (Gautama) said, 'It is known that I have plenty of gold, cattle and horses, maidservants, followers, and clothes. Do not be uncharitable to me regarding which is plentiful, unending and limitless.' 'Then surely, O Gautama, you ought to seek it by means of the prescribed manner.' 'I come to you (as a disciple).' Indeed the ancients approached a teacher merely by means of a declaration. Then Gautama resided (with the king) by announcing that he was a disciple.

Gautama rejects worldly boons and seeks knowledge.

8. He (the king) said, 'O Gautama, please do not take offence at us, just as your paternal grandfather did not. Prior to this, this knowledge has never resided with any Brāhmaṇa. However, I shall expound it to you, since when you speak thus who can refuse you?'
9. 'O Gautama that world is fire. Of this the sun only is fuel, the rays its smoke, the day its flame, the directions its cinder, the intermediate directions its sparks. In this fire, the deities put forward their faith. From that offering is caused King Soma.'

Here due to the nature of the answer to the questions asked, the fourth question is answered first. It is stated that the 'world is fire'. Here the aim is to explain results accruing to various sacrificial rites and to encourage meditation on the five fires. This is a means to obtaining the northern path.

10. 'O Gautama, Parjanya (the god of rain) is fire. Of this, the year only is fuel, the clouds are its smoke, the lightning its

flame, the thunder is its cinder, the sound of thunder its sparks. In this fire the deities present King Soma. From that offering is caused rain.'

The second fire is that of Parjanya. Parjanya is the deity associated with the materials of rain.

11. 'O Gautama, surely this world is fire. Of this the earth only is fuel, fire is its smoke, the night its flame, the moon its cinder, and the stars are the sparks. In this fire the deities present rain. From that offering is caused food.'

The third fire is the one pertaining to this world. The world here refers to the residing place of all creatures where are experienced the results of karma including its consequences, circumstances, and activities.

12. 'O Gautama, surely this person is fire. Of this, the open mouth only is fuel, prāṇa is its smoke, the world its flame, the eye its cinder, and the ear its sparks. In this fire the deities present food. From that offering is caused the seed.'

The person is fire. Procreation is the result of food.

13. 'O Gautama, surely the woman is fire. Of this, the organ of procreation only is the fuel, the hairs are its smoke, the vulva is the flame, the insertion is the cinder, the feeling of pleasure are the sparks. On this, in this fire the deities put forward the seed. From that offering a person is caused. He lives as long as (he) lives. Then at the time of death.'

The fourth fire was stated to be the person, woman is the fifth fire.

14. 'Then they take him away to the fire. Of this his fire only is the fire, the fuel is the fuel, the smoke its smoke, the flame its flame, the cinder its cinder, and the sparks its sparks. On this, in this fire, the deities put forward the person. From

that offering a person of radiant complexion is caused.'

15. 'Those who thus know this, who along with others (reside) in the forest and meditate with faith on the truth, they reach the light, from the light to the day, from the day to the fortnight of the waxing moon, from the fortnight of the waxing moon to the six months in which the sun travels northwards, from them to the world of the deities, from the world of the deities to the sun, from the sun to lightning. Then a person, created from (Hiraṇyagarbha's) mind comes to the region of lightning and leads them to the world of Brahmā. In these worlds of Brahmā they reside for many superlative years. For them, there is no return (to this world).'

The verse refers to those who know the five fires. Householders who do not know the meditation on the five fires or Satya-Brahman are born and reborn again and again. Those who know this meditation are freed from this cycle of birth and rebirth and reach the deity associated with the flame on the northern path.

16. Now those who by means of sacrifices, charity, and penance win worlds, they reach smoke (through fire of cremation), from smoke to the night, from the night to the fortnight of the waning moon, from the fortnight of the waning moon to the six months in which the sun travels southwards, from these above six months to the world of the ancestors, from the world of the ancestors to the moon. They become food on attaining the moon. There the deities eat (utilize) these, just in the manner that (priests) drink the bright Soma juice (stating as it were), 'increase, decrease'. When that, their (past deeds) are exhausted, then they reach this ether only. From ether to air, from air to rain, from rain to the earth. They become food on attaining the earth. Then again they are offered in the fire of a male, then again in the fire of a

female. Then they are born (and perform works) to rise up to (other) worlds. However, those who do not know these two paths become insects, moths, and all these creatures that bite.

The word smoke is used to designate the deity of smoke. The import of this verse is that ritualists who do not meditate and who do not know Brahman are reborn after enjoying the fruits of their action, until they know and attain the northern path.

Those who do not know the northern or southern path, do not meditate or even perform rites, for them the text and commentary state transmigratory existence is very painful and it is extremely difficult to escape from. The various questions asked are all answered in this section.

III

1. He who desires, 'I shall achieve greatness,' ought to do the following: on a propitious day of the fortnight of the waxing moon, during the northwards journey of the sun, he ought to undertake a vow relating to the Upasads for twelve days, having brought together in a bowl the wood of the udumbara tree or a cup, all the herbs and fruits, having swept and plastered (the ground), spread (the sacred kuśa grass), having kindled a fire, having purified the ghee in the correct way, under a constellation with a male name, having combined the offerings, and offer an oblation stating, 'O fire, I offer whatever portion to the deities under you, who being adverse, confound people's desires. May they be contented and satisfy me with every object of desire! Svāhā (hail). To that all accomplishing deity, who remains adverse clinging on to you thinking, "I support all," I offer this stream of ghee. Svāhā.'

Previously the results of meditation and rites have been

discussed. Meditation depends on nothing else. Rites presuppose wealth, divine and human. By greatness is meant here the attainment of wealth. The Mantha ceremony is described here in this regard.

2. 'To the most-senior hail, to the most excellent, hail.' (Stating this), offering an oblation in the fire, he ought to pour the remnants of the libation in the paste. 'To prāṇa hail, to the pre-eminent hail.' (Stating this), offering an oblation in the fire, he ought to pour the remnants of the libation in the paste. 'To the eyes, hail; to prosperity, hail.' (Stating this), offering an oblation in the fire, he ought to pour the remnants of the libation in the paste. 'To the ears, hail; to the abode, hail.' (Stating this), offering an oblation in the fire, he ought to pour the remnants of the libation in the paste. 'To the mind, hail; to the procreant, hail.' (Stating this), offering an oblation in the fire, he ought to pour the remnants of the libation in the paste. 'To the organ of generation, hail.' (Stating this), offering an oblation in the fire, he ought to pour the remnants of the libation in the paste.

   The words 'most-senior' and 'most excellent' mentioned are characteristics of prāṇa. This implies that those who know prāṇa alone can perform this ceremony.

3. 'To the fire, hail.' (Stating this), offering an oblation in the fire, he ought to pour the remnants of the libation in the paste. 'To the moon, hail.' (Stating this), offering an oblation in the fire, he ought to pour the remnants of the libation in the paste. 'To the earth, hail.' (Stating this), offering an oblation in the fire, he ought to pour the remnants of the libation in the paste. 'To the atmosphere, hail.' (Stating this), offering an oblation in the fire, he ought to pour the remnants of the libation in the paste. 'To the heaven, hail.' (Stating this), offering an oblation in the fire, he ought to pour the remnants of the libation in the paste.

'To the earth, atmosphere and heaven, hail.' (Stating this), offering an oblation in the fire, he ought to pour the remnants of the libation in the paste. 'To the Brāhmaṇa, hail.' (Stating this), offering an oblation in the fire, he ought to pour the remnants of the libation in the paste. 'To the Kṣatriya, hail.' (Stating this), offering an oblation in the fire, he ought to pour the remnants of the libation in the paste. 'To the past, hail.' (Stating this), offering an oblation in the fire, he ought to pour the remnants of the libation in the paste. 'To the future, hail.' (Stating this), offering an oblation in the fire, he ought to pour the remnants of the libation in the paste. 'To the universe, hail.' (Stating this), offering an oblation in the fire, he ought to pour the remnants of the libation in the paste. 'To all, hail.' (Stating this), offering an oblation in the fire, he ought to pour the remnants of the libation in the paste. 'To Prajāpati, hail.' (Stating this), offering an oblation in the fire, he ought to pour the remnants of the libation in the paste.

4. Then he touches this, stating, 'You are mobile, you are ablaze, you are complete, you are immovable, you are the one gathering place, you are the sound Hiṅ and are chanted, you are the Udgītha and are sung, you are the call for narration and are the response to this. You are radiant among the rain clouds, you are all-pervasive, you are the ruler. You are food, you are light. You are death. You are that in which everything merges.'
5. Then he lifts this (vessel), stating, 'You know all, we also know your greatness. Surely, he is the king, the lord, the sovereign. May that make me the king, lord, and sovereign.'
6. Then he drinks this, uttering the mantras: 'On that most worthy sun, the winds blow sweetly, the rivers are pouring honey, let the herbs be sweet to us. To the earth, hail. Let us meditate on the glory of the divine. Let the days and nights be sweet. Let the earth's dust be sweet. Let heaven our father

be propitious. To the atmosphere, hail. May he inspire our intellect. May the trees be sweet to us. Let the sun be sweet to us, let the cows be sweet to us. To heaven, hail.' Then he once again chants the whole Gāyatrī hymn and all the Madhumati verses (stating), 'May I be all this only.' To the earth, atmosphere, and heaven, hail. At the end, having had (the paste), washed his hands, he lies behind the fire with his head in the eastern direction. In the morning, he meditates on the sun with the following mantra: 'Of the directions you are the one lotus. Among men may I be the lotus.' Then he goes back just in this same way that he went out, sits behind the fire, and recites the lineage of gurus.

7. Uddālaka Āruṇi after expounding this to his disciple Vajasanena Yājñavalkya, said, 'Even if any one were to sprinkle this on a shrivelled-up stump, a branch would grow and leaves would appear.'
8. Vajasanena Yājñavalkya after expounding this very (topic) to his disciple Madhuka son of Paiṅgi, said, 'Even if any one were to sprinkle this on a shrivelled-up stump, a branch would grow and leaves would appear.'
9. Madhuka, son of Paiṅgi, after expounding this very (topic) to his disciple Cūla son of Bhagvitta, said, 'Even if any one were to sprinkle this on a shrivelled-up stump, a branch would grow and leaves would appear.'
10. Cūla, son of Bhagvitta, after expounding this very (topic) to his disciple Jānaki, son of Ayasthūṇa, said, 'Even if any one were to sprinkle this on a shrivelled-up stump, a branch would grow and leaves would appear.'
11. Jānaki, son of Ayasthūṇa, after expounding this very (topic) to his disciple Satyakāma, son of Jabāla, said, 'Even if any one were to sprinkle this on a shrivelled-up stump, a branch would grow and leaves would appear.'
12. Satyakāma, son of Jabāla, after expounding this very (topic)

to his disciples, said, 'Even if any one were to sprinkle this on a shrivelled-up stump, a branch would grow and leaves would appear. One ought not to expound to a person who is not a son or a disciple.'

13. 'Four things are of the wood of the udumbara tree. The sacrificial ladle is of the wood of the udumbara tree, the vessel is of the wood of the udumbara tree, the fuel is of the wood of the udumbara tree, and the two churning rods are of the wood of the udumbara tree. Cultivated grains ought to be of ten kinds, rice and barley, sesamum and beans, millet and panic seeds, wheat, lentils, pulses, and vetches. Having ground these, they should be soaked in curd, honey, and ghee and offered as an oblation.'

Four items associated with the sacrifice are made of fig wood. This has been spoken about in a previous passage. The text throws light on the species of grains which are also to be offered.

IV

1. 'Certainly of these beings, the earth is the essence. Of the earth, water (is the essence); of water, herbs (are the essence); of herbs, flowers (are the essence); of flowers, fruits (are the essence); of fruits, man (is the essence); and of man, the seed is the essence.'

This entire section is dedicated to obtaining a son with the desired good qualities who due to these qualities will achieve the worlds for himself and his father.

2. He (Prajāpati) thought, 'Well for him let me make a support. He created a woman. Having created the woman, he revered her. From that one should revere women. He reached out to the woman. By means of this they created progeny.'

The process of creating progeny is discussed here.

3. Her middle part is the altar, hairs the grass, skin the Soma press. The reproductive organs are the fire from the middle. Certainly, just as great as the world of one who conducts the Vājapeya sacrifice, (so great indeed is his world) who knowing thus procreates, such a person directs the good acts of the woman towards himself. However, he who not knowing this procreates, his good acts are directed by the woman to herself.
4. Indeed, knowing this, Uddālaka Āruni said, indeed knowing this Nāka Maudgalya said, indeed knowing this Kumārahārita said, 'Numerous men, wise men only by name, depart this world without acquiring any merits and impotent, namely, those who enter into sexual relations without knowing this. If asleep or awake a person spills the seed.'
5. Then he ought to touch it (or not) and along with that recite the mantra, 'Whatever seed of mine has spilled on earth, whatever seed has passed to the herbs, whatever has flowed to water, I once again claim this seed, let power come to me again. Let beauty come to me again. Let the fire and its altars be just in their appropriate place.' (After stating this) he may take it with his thumb and finger and place it on his breasts or eyebrows.
6. Now when a person sees himself in water (his reflection) he ought to recite this mantra: '(May the Gods grant) in me brilliance, power, fame, wealth, and merit.' Certainly, this is grace among women, since she has put on clean clothes. From that when she has put on clean clothes and is glorious, he ought to go to her and talk to her.
7. If she does not give in to his desire he should win her by means of gifts. If still she does not give in to his desire, he should persuade her by other means, excel over her by means of his power and glory and say, 'I excel over your glory.' She may feel her glory is challenged.

8. If she gives in to him, he should state, 'By means of power and glory, I grant you glory.' Indeed they both become glorious.
9. He who wishes thinking, let her fulfil my desires, after being intimate with her, he may recite, 'O, you who arise from every limb, you who have risen from the heart, thou are indeed the essence of the limbs. Of such a woman connected to me, distract her as if wounded by a poisonous arrow.'
10. Now, he who wishes, thinking, after having relations, 'May she not conceive,' after getting intimate, he may first inhale and then exhale, stating, 'By means of power with the seed, I reclaim the seed from you'. Then she may become without the seed.
11. Now, he who wishes, thinking, after having relations, 'May she conceive,' after getting intimate, he may first inhale and then exhale, stating, 'By means of power with the seed, I place the seed in you.' Indeed, she becomes pregnant.
12. Now whose wife has a lover and he wishes to harm him, he ought to light a fire in an unbaked earthen vessel, lay out tips of reed inversely, and offer these tips of reed placed in this manner, smeared with ghee, to the fire while staying the mantras, 'You have sacrificed in my blazing fire, I take away your prāṇa and apāṇa, you so and so.' 'You have sacrificed in my blazing fire, I take away your sons and cattle, you so and so.' 'You have sacrificed in my blazing fire, I take away your Vedic and Smṛti sanctioned rites, you so and so.' 'You have sacrificed in my blazing fire, I take away your dreams and hopes, you so and so.'

    The man, who is a scholar who thus knows, curses, departs from this world, powerless and without merit. From that one ought to not even wish to joke with the wife of a Vedic scholar who knows thus, since he who knows thus becomes far greater.

13. Now whose wife is undergoing menstrual periods, for three days she ought to drink from a bell metal shaped vessel. She may not be touched unnecessarily. At the conclusion of three nights, she may take a bath and put on fresh clothes. At this time, she may thresh rice.
14. He who wishes that his son be born with a fair complexion, that he be well-versed in one Veda and attain a full lifespan, they should have rice boiled with milk and should eat it dressed with ghee. Then they will be able to give birth to such a son.
15. Now, he who wishes that his son be born with a tawny or dark complexion, that he be well-versed in two Vedas and attain a full lifespan, they should have boiled rice mixed with curd and should eat it dressed with ghee. Then they will be able to give birth to such a son.
16. Now, he who wishes that his son be born with a dark complexion and red eyes, that he be well-versed in three Vedas and attain a full lifespan, they should have boiled rice cooked in water and should eat it dressed with ghee. Then they will be able to give birth to such a son.
17. Now, he who wishes that his daughter be born, who is a scholar and attain a full lifespan, they should have boiled rice cooked with sesamum and should eat it dressed with ghee. Then they will be able to give birth to such a daughter.
18. Now, he who wishes that his son be born, who is a famous scholar, participates in assemblies, a speaker of words that are desired to be heard, be well-versed in all the Vedas and attain a full lifespan, they should have boiled rice cooked with meat/the fleshy part of fruits. Then they will be able to give birth to such a son.
19. Now early in the morning, having made ghee as per the rules of Sthālīpāka, he takes the Sthālīpāka and offers the food, stating, 'To fire, hail; to Anumati, hail; to the splendid

sun, hail; to the creator which is true, hail.' After making the offering, he takes the remainder, eats a part of it, and gives the rest to his wife. Then he washes his hands, fills the water vessel, sprinkles his wife three times with the water, uttering the mantra, 'O Viśvāvasu, get up from here, seek another young woman, who is with her husband. I shall join my wife.'

Here the various things mentioned and the procedure detailed are in accordance with the Gṛha Sūtras.

20. He then approaches her, stating, 'I am ama (vital breath) and you are sā (speech), thou are speech, I am the vital force; I am the Sāman, you are the Ṛk; I am heaven, thou art the earth. Come, may we ardently strive together so we may give birth to a male child.'

The role of mantras is highlighted.

21. Then he prepares her, stating, 'O heaven and earth, spread yourself apart.' After being intimate with her, three times he ought to stroke her hair as the hair lies, stating, 'May Viṣṇu prepare the womb. May the forms be molded by Tvastṛ. May Prajāpati pour in. Let the seed be placed in you by Dhātṛ. Grant the seed, O Sinīvāli; O lady with the glorious looks, grant the seed. May the seed be placed by the two Aśvins coronated with lotus wreaths.'
22. The two Aśvins rub together two sticks made of gold to bring forth a fire. 'We request you that such a womb be produced during the tenth month. Just as the earth contains in its womb fire and just as heaven has in its womb rain, just as air has in its womb the quarters, thus I place a womb in you, so and so.'
23. When she is about to give birth, he ought to sprinkle her with water, stating, 'Just as the wind scatters a lotus pond

on all sides, thus may your foetus stir and emerge with its chorion. This fold of Indra has been put together along with a covering all around. O Indra, cause him to issue forth as the newborn.'

24. After (the son) is born, after preparing the fire, he ought to place the child in his lap, and mix together curd and ghee in a bell-metal vessel, he makes oblations repeatedly in the fire while reciting the mantra, 'In my own home, may I grow (as the sun) and may I nurture a thousand people. May the goddess of fortune, with progeny and cattle, never withdraw from his line, Svāha. Mentally I make an offering to you of my prāṇa, Svāha. In my actions, whatsoever I have done that is excessive, and whatsoever I have done which is insufficient, let the omniscient and benevolent Agni make it proper and good for us. Svāha.'

This verse explains, in considerable detail, the postnatal ceremony.

25. Then placing (his own mouth) near the child's right ear, he ought to repeat thrice, 'Speech, speech, speech.' Next, he should mix curd, honey, and ghee and then feed the child by means of a plain, gold (strip), uttering the mantras: 'I give to you the earth, I give to you the intermediate region between heaven and earth, I give to you heaven. I give to you all things, earth, the intermediate region between heaven and earth, and heaven.'

Speech and the three elements, their importance is emphasized.

26. Then his (the child's) name is given, stating, 'Thou art the Vedas.' That only becomes its secret name.
27. Then giving the child to the mother who breastfeeds the child, stating the mantra: 'Your breast is sustaining, fruitful, full of milk, bountiful, and generous, by means of which you

nurture deserving beings, O Saravatī, place it here, so that my child may be nourished from it.'

28. Then he addresses its mother, 'Thou are Ilā from the lineage of Mitra and Varuna. You are a heroine and have given birth to a hero. You who have given birth to a male child, may you be the mother of many sons.' Indeed, to such a son it is said, 'O, you have become greater than your father, O, you have become greater than your grandfather.' Surely he has attained the highest limit of wealth, fame, the splendour of knowing Brahman who takes birth as a son to a Brāhmaṇa who thus knows.

Obeisance is made to the mother. The divine mother.

V

1. Now the lineage of teachers: the son of Pautimāsī (received this) from the son of Kātyāyanī. He from the son of Gautamī, the son of Gautamī from the son of Bhāradvājī, the son of Bhāradvājī from the son of Pārāśari, he from the son of Aupasvastī, the son of Aupasvastī from the son of Pārāśari, he from the son of Kātyāyanī, the son of Kātyāyanī from the son of Kauśikī, he from the son of Ālambī and the son of Vaiyāghrapadī, the son of Vaiyāghrapadī from the son of Kāṇvi and the son of Kāpī, the son of Kāpī
2. From the son of Ātreyī, he from the son of Gautamī, the son of Gautamī from the son of Bhāradvājī, he from the son of Pārāśari, he from the son of Vātsī, he from the son of (a different) Pārāśari, he from the son of Vārkāruṇi, he from the son of (a different) Vārkāruṇi, he from the son of Ārtabhāgī, he from the son of Śauṅgī, he from the son of Sāṅkrtī, he from the son of Ālambāyanī, he from the son of Ālambī, he from the son of Jāyantī, he from the son of Māṇḍūkāyanī, he from the son of Māṇḍūkī, he from the son of Śāṇḍitī, he from

the son of Rāthītarī, he from the son of Bhālukī, he from the two sons of Krauñcikī, they from the son of Vaidabhṛtī, he from the son of Kārśakeyī, he from the son of Prācīayogī, he from the son of Sāñjīvī, he from the son of Prāśni, then Āsurivāsin, the son of Prāśni from Āsurāyaṇa, Āsurāyaṇa from Āsuri, Āsuri

3. From Yājñavalkya, Yājñavalkya from Uddālaka, Uddālaka, from Aruna, he from Upaveśi, Upaveśi from Kuśri, he from Vājaśravas, Vājaśravas from Jihvāvat, the son of Badhyoga, he from Asita, the son of Varṣagaṇa, he from Harita Kaśyapa, he from Śilpa Kaśyapa, this particular one from Kaśyapa, the son of Nidhruva, he from Vāc, Vāc from Ambhiṇī, Ambhiṇī from the sun. Indeed, these white Yajuses (sacrificial formulas) received from the sun are expounded on by Yājñvalkya Vājasaneya.
4. The lineage is the same extending to the son of Sāñjīvī. The son of Sāñjīvī from Māṇḍūkāyani, he from Māṇḍavya, he from Kautsa, he from Māhitthi, he from Vāmakakṣāyaṇa, he from Śāṇḍilya, he from Vātsya, he from Kuśri, Kuśri from Yājñavacas, the son of Rājastamba, he from Tura, the son of Kavaṣa, Kavaṣa from Prajāpati (Hiraṇyagarbha), Prajāpati from Brahman (the Vedas). Brahman is self-sustaining and eternal. Salutations to Brahman.

The Māṇḍūkya Upaniṣad

1. This syllable, that is Aum is all this. A clear explanation of this follows. The past, present, and future, all this is Aum. And whatsoever at all there is beyond the three periods of time is also Aum.

The Māṇḍūkya Upaniṣad and the Kārika are dedicated to the knowledge of Brahman. Realizing the meaning of Aum leads to realization of the reality of the self. The Upaniṣad states: 'Aum is Brahman.' The Praśna Upaniṣad enjoins the reader to meditate on the self as Aum. All is Aum. Whatever is within the realm of time, past, present, and future, is Aum, as also that which is beyond the realm of time.

2. All is indeed this Brahman. This self is Brahman. This self possesses four quarters.

All is Brahman. The self is Brahman. This verse contains one of the four mahāvākyas of the Upaniṣads, 'Ayam ātmā Brahma'. This is translated as 'this self is Brahman'. This verse states that all is Brahman. By reiterating that this self is Brahman it stresses the unity of the self and the universal principle. Śaṅkarācārya while commenting on this śloka points out that the self has four quarters similar to a Kārsā-paṇa coin, yet unlike a cow. The Kārsā-paṇa coin consists of sixteen units, four of which make a quarter.

3. Vaiśvānara, the first quarter, is located in the waking state, whose consciousness cognizes the external realm, who possesses seven limbs and nineteen mouths and enjoys gross objects.

The Vaiśvānarah quarter is expressed in the waking state. Its consciousnesses is apparently directed to objects other than itself (a view that is erroneous and is due to ignorance). Regarding the seven limbs, heaven is the head, the sun is the eye, air is the prāṇa, space is the central part, water the bladder, and the earth, the feet. The nineteen mouths refer to the five senses, the organs of action, five in number, the five vital breaths, the mind, faculty of intelligence, the ego and mind stuff. This is called Vaiśvānarah since it carries the world (Viśva) of beings. Since this is directed to objects, he cognizes things that are gross and corporeal.

4. Taijasa, the second quarter, located in the dream state, whose consciousness cognizes the internal realm, who possesses seven limbs and nineteen mouths and enjoys subtle, luminous objects.

   The taijasa quarter is expressed in the dream state. Due to avidyā, karma, and desire, the consciousness of the waking state leaves behind in the mind the impressions of external objects of the waking state. Compared to the other senses the mind is antaḥ (internal) and whose awareness is in accordance with the desire of that mind is known as antaḥ-prājñaḥ. This is known as taijasa since it witnesses the cognition that is objectless and luminous. The awareness in this realm is confined to impressions and is therefore subtle.

5. Deep sleep is the state where one who is sleeping does not see any dream and does not desire any desirable object. Prājña, the third quarter, is located in the sphere of deep sleep, who has become single, undifferentiated, who is a mass of consciousness, is blissful and indeed enjoys bliss, and whose mouth is consciousness.

   The third quarter is prājña expressed in the state of deep sleep. Sleep is a common aspect of the previous two states, namely, the waking and the dream states. Deep sleep is a feature of this state that distinguishes it from the other two. In this state the sleeping person does not see anything nor does he have any desires. A person in this state is assimilated singly as one, since just as the darkness of the night covers the (light of the) day, so the multitude of duality which are manifested due to modifications of the mind as the aforesaid states, become non-discernible in this state. This state is known as a mass of consciousness—prājñaghanaḥ. This is a state consisting of abundant bliss, since there is no misery due to modifications of the mind. The Yogasūtra of Patañjali also speaks of yoga being the state where there is cessation of fluctuations of consciousness (Feuerstein 1989: 26). Yet this is not bliss itself since the joy is not absolute. In this state he is known as Ānanda-Bhuk, an enjoyer of bliss and also cetomukaḥ since it is the gate leading to the two states of dream and waking. This is known as prājña since in this there is knowledge of past, future, and all objects. Of the three states, only this state possesses integrated consciousness.

6. Indeed, this is the ruler of all, this is all knowing, this is the controller within, this is the origin of all, and indeed this is the source and end of all.

   This prājña in its natural form is the ruler of all diverse beings. Again, this is the knower of all, having entered all beings it directs them. For this reason, he is the creator of the entire creation and is the cause of all. Thus, he is the origin and place of dissolution of all beings.

7. They think that the fourth quarter is that which does not cognize the internal realm, it does not cognize the external realm, nor what cognizes both the realms, nor is it a mass of cognition. It is neither cognitive nor non-cognitive, it is unseen without identifying marks, unthinkable, indescribable, it cannot be spoken of, ungraspable, its

essence is the knowledge of the single self, that into which the world is resolved, the peaceful, non-dual, Shivam, it is the self, it is that which should be known.

In his commentary Śaṅkarācārya points out that even though the characteristics of turīya are different to those of the self in the three states, turīya is not really different. Just as a rope is erroneously viewed as a snake, the self, even though it is one, is imagined in three different states to be possessed of various attributes. The self which appears to subsist in the three states is established as turīya just as in the manner of Tat Tvam Asi, that thou art, of the Chāndogya Upaniṣad. The instruments of valid knowledge in the case of turīya has no impact on turīya other than removing unwanted, superimposed attributes. Thus it is said, 'Duality ceases to exist after realization (Kārikā I.18) (Swāmī Gambhīrānanda 2003: 203).

It is prapañcopaśamam, that into which all phenomena have been resolved. The attributes of the first three states are negated and therefore this is unchanging, Advaitam, non-dual. The first three quarters are mere appearances. The self ought to be known as different from superimposed states.

8. That is the self which, with reference to the syllable (denoting it), is Aum. With reference to its elements (letters constituting Aum), the quarters are the elements and the elements are the quarters, namely 'a', 'u' and 'm'.

Here in this śloka, it is being explained what this syllable, Aum, is. The parts of the self are indeed the letters of Aum, namely, 'a', 'u', and 'm'.

9. Located in the waking state, Vaiśvānara is the letter 'a', the first element, so called either due to the root ap (obtaining) or due to being the first. A person who knows thus indeed acquires all he wishes and becomes the foremost.

He who is Vaiśvānara expressed in the waking state is the letter 'a'. It is the first letter of Aum. Just as the sound 'a' pervades all speech, Vaiśvānara pervades the entire universe. Again, just in the manner that letter called 'a' is first, so Vaiśvānara is also first. The person who knows this identity attains all desires and becomes the foremost.

10. Located in the dream state, taijasa is the the letter 'u', the second element. This is due to excellence or being intermediate. A person who knows thus, indeed, enhances the level of knowledge and he becomes same as all. There is none born in his family who does not know Brahman.

    He who is taijasa, expressed in the dream state is the letter 'u', the second letter of Aum. It is said that just as the letter 'u' excels the letter 'a', taijasa excels Vaiśvānara. In Aum the letter 'u' is between 'a' and 'm' and taijasa is between Vaiśvānara and prājña.

11. Located in the state of deep sleep, Prājña is the letter 'm', the third element. This is due to the root mi (measuring) or due to absorption. A person who knows thus measures all and absorbs all in himself.

    He who is prājña expressed in the state of deep sleep is the letter 'm'. By means of which similarity? The similarity due to measuring expressed here by the word 'miti'. Just as the vessel known as prastra is used to measure barley, similarly Vaiśvānara and taijasa are measured during their entry into and exit from prājña during cosmic dissolution and origination. Again, while pronouncing Aum, the letters 'a' and 'u' appear to get merged or absorbed in the letter 'm'. Thus also Vaiśvānara and taijasa appear to get absorbed into prājña during sleep. The person who knows this is able to measure and absorb all this, that is, he is able to know the reality of all this (the universe) and also by being able to absorb all this he becomes the self in its form as the cause of the world.

12. Turīya, the fourth, is without any element, beyond the conventional, that into which the physical universe resolves, propitious and non-dual, Aum is thus the self (ātman). A person who knows this enters the self by means of his own self.

    The fourth turīya has no letter. It is only the self. Due to the cessation of names and that which is nameable, which are themselves merely forms of speech and the mind, turīya is beyond the empirical. It is the negation of the phenomenal, auspicious, and the non-dual, Advaita form. Therefore, Aum possessed of the above three letters is the self only having three quarters. Who knows this by means of his own self enters the self. Such a knower of Brahman has entered the self by burning out the seed or impressions of the third state and is thus not reborn ever again. The commentary tells us that the syllable Aum when properly meditated upon becomes a resort to attaining Brahman even for those who are dull or of middle-level intelligence, as long as they are virtuous and know the commonalities of the above letters and elements.

The Muṇḍaka Upaniṣad

MUṆḌAKA 1

I

1. Brahmā, foremost among the deities, was the creator of the universe, the guardian of the world. He instructed his eldest son, Atharvā, in the knowledge of Brahman on which is established all knowledge.

   This verse is meant as a eulogy for Brahmavidyā, that is the vidyā of Brahman. This concerns the supreme self. This knowledge is imparted by Brahmā to his eldest son Atharvā. Brahmā exceeds the other deities, is foremost, the creator and protector.

2. The knowledge of Brahman which was expounded by Brahmā to Atharvā, and in an ancient era, Atharvā explained it to Aṅgiras. He passed it on to Satyavāha, son of Bhāradvāja. The son of Bhāradvāja transmitted it down to Aṅgiras, both higher and lesser (knowledge).

   This knowledge encompasses everything within the scope of higher (para) or lower (apara) knowledge.

3. Śaunaka, certainly a great householder, dutifully went near Aṅgiras and questioned, 'Illustrious sir, by which being known, everything becomes known?'

The question asked in this verse relates to the possibility of becoming omniscient. Is there a single cause of the world by knowing which one can know everything?

4. For him he said, 'Indeed there are two types of knowledge to be acquired, which knowers of Brahman have stated to be "the higher and the lower".'

There are two kinds of knowledge, the higher concerned with the supreme self and the lower, whose sphere is knowledge of virtue and vice as well as their means and ends.

5. There the non-supreme is the Ṛg Veda, the Yajur Veda, the Sāma Veda, the Atharva Veda, the rules of phonetics, rituals, grammar, etymology, metre, and astrology. Then the supreme is that by means of which the indestructible is attained.
6. That which is not seen, not grasped, without root, without features, with no eyes or ears, which does not have hands or feet, perpetual, pervading all material things, omnipresent, extremely subtle, that which is the undecaying origin of all elements which the discerning perceive everywhere.

This verse relates to the higher knowledge by which the indestructible is realized. That is beyond the sense organs, the organs of action. It is eternal and cannot be grasped. It is all-pervasive and extremely subtle. It is that indestructible which the wise view everywhere.

7. Just as a spider emits and pulls back (its threads), just as on the earth do herbs arise, just as from an existing person does hair (grow) on the head, thus so from the indestructible does the entire universe emanate.

From the indestructible whose characteristics have been discussed in the previous verse, which does not depend on anything else does the universe in its entirety originate.

8. By means of penance does Brahman expand. Food originates from that. From food prāṇa, (from that) mind, (from that) the existent (elements), (from that) the worlds, (from that) in the karmas, immortality.

This verse is elaborated in the commentary. By means of knowledge of creation does Brahman create the world. From this originates food. From this originates prāṇa or Hiraṇyagarbha. From this the cosmic mind. From this the five elements, the combination of the gross and subtle. From this the seven worlds such as the earth. Then the karmas and then immortality.

9. From that who is omniscient, always wise, where penance is comprised by knowledge, arises Brahmā (Hiraṇyagarbha), name-form and food.

II

1. That is this truth.
The karmas which the sages saw in the mantras are present in various ways in the three Vedas. Practise these perpetually, with a desire for the truth. This is your path leading to the world of good actions.

The mantras are Satyam, true, and are unerring in leading to the attainment of human ends. The duties enjoined in the Ṛg Veda, Yajur Veda, and Sāma Veda ought to be performed.

2. When the fire flares up after being borne on a sacrifice with a plentiful supply of fuel, then accompanied by faith, one ought to offer his oblations in the region between parts of ghee.

When the sacrificial fire is blazing, supported by sufficient fuel, then in the place between where oblations are offered, should one make oblations in honour of the deities. This is the path of karma which is towards attaining the results of karmas. Impediments do appear on this path.

3. It (the Agnihotra sacrifice) destroys seven worlds of his who performs the Agnihotra not followed by the Darśa (sacrifice of the new moon), the Paurṇamāsa (sacrifice of the full moon), nor the Cāturmāsya (sacrifice of the four months), nor the Āgrayaṇa (ritual performed during the harvest season), in the absence of guests, without proper offerings, without the Vaiṣvadeva rite (ceremonies to all deities) and not in the proper manner.

If the rites are not undertaken properly, it vitiates the fruits obtainable from the rite.

4. Fire is said to have seven tongues. These are enumerated as the black, formidable and expeditious as the mind and extremely red which is deeply the colour of smoke, the blazing spark, and the multiformed goddess.
5. These oblations in the form of rays of the sun take him and lead him to the (world) where the single lord of all deities presides, for who performs these rites, makes offerings, just at the correct time, when these (tongues) are shining.
6. Saying, 'Come, come,' to him, the brilliant offerings transport the sacrificer by means of rays of the sun, adoring him by uttering pleasant words. This is your virtuous world of Brahmā, attained by means of benevolent actions.

The point of this verse is to show that karma not connected with knowledge, only has limited results. It is motivated by desire, action, and ignorance. It then becomes a source of grief.

7. Fragile indeed are these rafts of the eighteen forms of sacrifice which are stated to be of lesser karma. The non-discerning who are elated in this as leading to that which is excellent, again endure old age and death.

Those that accomplish the sacrifice are eighteen in number—sixteen priests, the sacrifice, and his wife. Mere karma or karma devoid of knowledge is destroyed by this along with its fruit. The ignorant rejoice in this, stay in heaven for some time, and are then reborn.

8. Being in the middle of ignorance, thinking, 'We are indeed intelligent and wise,' fools faced with numerous troubles, ramble on just as the blind being led by the blind only.
9. Those foolish people existing amongst the many forms of ignorance think, 'We have attained the goal.' Since those in the midst of karma, who form attachment, do not know (what is true), by this they become afflicted by sorrow, are deprived (of heaven), and their worlds are emaciated.
10. Those misled people (who) think that rites and works of public good are the most excellent, do not know any other (path to liberation). Having experienced pleasure on the elevated realm of heaven, they return to this world or a lesser one.

The non-discriminating think that public works and sacrifices are the foremost means to achieve human objectives. Such people do not understand the knowledge of the self by means of which is the ultimate goal attained. Such people after enjoying the fruits of their karma in heaven enter the world again as humans or enter the world of beasts or hell as per their residual karma.

11. Those residing in the forest, while observing austerity, meditation, and faith, those who have subdued their passions, are learned and live the life as per the recommended stage of life, after being freed from dirt, go by means of the passage of the sun to where resides the immortal, undecaying Puruṣa.

On the other hand, forest-dwelling ascetics who meditate and do penance, are at peace with their senses controlled. Householders devoted to meditation are also freed from impurities. These persons move along the path of the sun, the northern path, to the world known as Satya, where resides the immortal Puruṣa.

12. After apprising the worlds attained by karma, a Brāhmaṇa may come to a state of renunciation. That (world) which is not affected, is not (attained) by means of what is affected. To know reality, he ought to go, carrying sacrificial fuel in his hands, to a teacher only who is learned in the Vedas and absorbed in Brahman.

A wise person who renounces the world, ought to turn away from the temporal world which is compared to a dream and a water bubble. These worlds are earned on the basis of merits and demerits based on ignorance and desire. Here the importance of renunciation is being stressed. The commentary describes universe as being constituted by products of action and therefore transient. Those in the quest for the eternal should be detached and should approach a suitably qualified teacher.

13. For him who has approached correctly, whose consciousness is tranquil, whose senses are under control, that enlightened person should expound the knowledge of Brahman by means of which one truly knows the indestructible, the real.

One should approach the teacher in the manner prescribed in the scriptures. The qualities of the good disciple are enumerated. After being correctly approached by a good disciple, it is then the duty of the teacher to save him from the realm of ignorance.

MUṆḌAKA 2

I

1. That is this truth.
   Just as from a well-lit fire sparks of similar form originate in their thousands, thus, dear one, various kinds of existing things originate from the indestructible and into it only does it return.

   This verse uses an analogy to explain that which is true and indestructible. Just as many sparks emanate from a fire thus also many types of creatures emanate from the indestructible. They are different due to different limiting adjuncts in the form of bodies. They originate from the indestructible and again merge into the indestructible at the time of dissolution.

2. The Puruṣa is brilliant and formless. He coexists with that which is internal and external, unborn without prāṇa, without mind. He is pure and higher than the higher indestructible (māyā).

   This verse speaks about the Puruṣa. The Puruṣa is all-pervasive, brilliant, transcendent, and without form. It is birthless and coexists with that which is internal or external. Since the Puruṣa is inborn it is immortal, ageless, and indestructible. To the ignorant the Puruṣa appears to be possessed of mind, senses, prāṇa, bodies, etc. Yet from its own standpoint it is without prāṇa or mind. All the different vital forces, organs, intellect are denied. Being without limiting adjuncts it is pure. It is higher than the unmanifested māyā. Māyā is the limiting adjunct of Brahman as name and form.

3. From this originate prāṇa, the mind, and all the sense organs (as well as) the sky, air, light, water, and that (which is) the support of all.

The Puruṣa is in fact the seed of origination for the prāṇa as well as for the mind and senses. In the main Puruṣa is devoid of prāṇa. Similarly, all the elements originate from Puruṣa.

The Virāt within the cosmic egg is born of Hiraṇyagarbha, who is the firstborn prāṇa. But Virāt too is born of Puruṣa.

4. Indeed, the inner self of all is this whose head is fire, two eyes are the sun and the moon, the directions are the two ears, the expressed Vedas are speech, air is the prāṇa, the entire universe is the heart, and of his two feet does the earth originate.

The Puruṣa is the one who sees, hears, thinks, knows, and is what is real in the sense of all. All beings are born from the Puruṣa.

5. From that (originates) fire of which the sun is the fuel, from the moon (proceeds) the clouds, (and from clouds) herbs on the earth. A man pours seed into the woman. From that person many progeny have emerged.
6. From that (originate) the Ṛg (verses), the Sāman (chants), the Yajuṣ (mantras), initiation, and all the sacrifices, ceremonies, and offerings, the year, the sacrificer, and the worlds where the moon purifies (everything) and where the sun (blazes).

The worlds mentioned in this verse are achieved by means of two paths, the southern path for those who have not attained knowledge and the northern path for those with knowledge.

7. From that (originate) the deities in various ways, the celestials, human beings, animals, birds, breathing in and out, rice and barley as well as penance, faith, truth, continence, and obedience to rules.
8. The seven sense organs are caused from him, (as are) the seven flames, their seven kinds of fuel, the seven types of oblations, these seven worlds in which the sense organs operate, which sense organs pervade the secret cavity (of the heart) and are placed in groups of seven.

The aim of these verses is to clearly state that from the supreme all-knowing Puruṣa, emerge karmas, the fruit of karmas, of those who have knowledge who sacrifice to the self as well as of ignorant people.

9. From this (is caused) the oceans and all the mountains, from this (is caused) all forms of rivers that flow, and from this (is caused) all herbs and their juices, by means of which, along with the elements, the inner self exists.

Therefore, all this emerges from the Puruṣa. Modifications have no independent reality and are therefore false. Only the Puruṣa is true.

10. Indeed the Puruṣa is all this, actions, penance. Who knows this supreme, undying Brahman, existing in the cavity of the heart, he, here in this world, dear one, cuts away the knot of ignorance.

There is nothing in the universe other than the Puruṣa. One who knows the Puruṣa attains realization. Karma, tapa, knowledge, the fruits of karma, all emanate from the Puruṣa.

They are the product of Brahman. One who realizes that he is the supreme, immortal Brahman existing in the cavity of the heart, he overcomes ignorance, destroys all the bondage of ignorance, here even while living.

II

1. It is apparent, placed near, known as moving in the secret cavity (in the heart), the great goal. Here, in this are established all that is mobile, breathes, and winks. Know this as real and non-real, which is to be wished for, the senior-most which surpasses the worldly knowledge of creatures.

   This Brahman in the cavity of the heart is being described. It is the greatest of all. It is that which is to be wished for. It is the highest and beyond the scope of ordinary knowledge.

2. That which is brilliant, minuter than minute, that in which are established all the worlds, and the dwellers of those worlds, that is this indestructible Brahman. It is this prāṇa. Indeed it is this speech and mind. That is this truth, that is immortal, that, dear one, is to be realized, realize it.

   Brahman is subtle, brilliant and indestructible. It is the support of all. It is the inner consciousness of all beings and senses in the universe. Elsewhere it is stated that it is the prāṇa of the prāṇa. (Br. IV.iv.18; Ke. I.2).

   Thus the disciple is called upon to fix the mind on the indestructible.

3. Holding the bow, the mighty weapon of the Upaniṣads, one ought to join to it an arrow sharpened by means of meditation. Drawing that, with the consciousness absorbed with the thought of Brahman, O dear one, strive for that indestructible Brahman as the target (goal).

After withdrawing all the organs from the objects and concentrating on Brahman alone as the indestructible, one should thus meditate.

4. Aum is the bow, surely the self is the arrow. Brahman is said to be the target of that. It is to be hit unerringly. Just as the arrow (becomes one with the target) a person ought to become one with it.

   Aum is the means for bringing the soul to the indestructible. The depiction of Aum leads to the self being fixed in the indestructible. The soul that has entered the body is the conditioned supreme self. The target of the soul is Brahman. A person without desires or attachment, whose senses are controlled, ought to strive to attain Brahman.

5. On which heaven, the earth, the intermediate region between heaven and earth, are strung along with the mind and all other vital breaths know him only as the one self. Discard any other assertions. Surely this is the bridge which takes a person to immortality.

   After knowing the self, the spiritual seeker is expected to give up lower knowledge as well as actions and their fruits. Knowledge of the self leads to immortality and liberation.

6. Where the nerves are brought together, just as the spokes on the hub of a chariot wheel, it this self moves within becoming manifold. Thus, one ought to concentrate on Aum thus as the self. May you, without hindrances, successfully cross to the other shore beyond darkness.
7. Who is omniscient, is always wise, who is this glory in the world, in the brilliant city of Brahman, this self is established within the space (in the heart).
8. Consisting of mind, the ruler of prāṇa and the body, established in food and present in the heart. The discerning,

by means of knowledge (of Brahman) clearly perceive (the self), the blissful form, immortal and radiant.

Heaven, earth, rivers, seas, seasons, etc., are all under the rule and sway of the self. The self is seated in the city of Brahman i.e., the lotus of the heart. The self is associated with various mental states being conditioned (apparently) by the mind. By means of knowledge gained from the scriptures and qualified teachers, after controlling all organs, renouncing all and being detached, the wise realize the self as existing everywhere including in oneself leading to bliss and immortality.

9. All problems are removed and all one's karmas are dissipated, the knot of the heart is severed, when this (self) is seen, both the higher and lower.

When both forms of knowledge are realized, the knot of the heart, ignorance and its consequences are destroyed, desires are dispelled. Then on the cessation of causes of the worldly stage one becomes free.

10. In the supreme vessel, consisting of gold, is Brahman, free from passions and partless. It is untainted and it is what illuminates light. That is which the knowers of the self realize.

Brahman is compared to a vessel or sheath since it is the place for realization, like a scabbard and sword. Brahman is the greatest, the self of all. The splendour and light of everything is due to their inner consciousness which is the same as Brahman. This is known to the wise people who know the self.

11. There the sun does not shine, nor does the moon, nor do the stars, nor these flashes of lightning. How can this fire (shine then)? All shines in accordance with him only. By means of his light does all this shine.

Brahman illuminates the sun. The sun does not illuminate Brahman. Similarly, the moon and stars. The universe shines due to Brahman. Brahman by its own nature is consciousness light.

12. Certainly, this Brahman is immortal. Brahman is the beginning, Brahman is the end. Brahman is on the right and on the left. It stretches out above and below. Surely this world is Brahman, the senior-most.

MUṆḌAKA 3

I

1. Two birds closely associated, with similar names, cling to one tree. Of these two, one bird eats a berry full of taste and the other looks on, not eating.

   The analogy is used to explain the difference between the wise and the ignorant as well as between God and individual souls. The ignorant clings to the tree of the subtle body enjoying the fruits of action and going through various experiences. Iśvara is by nature wise, pure, and has māyā as his limiting adjunct. He is the controller of the enjoyed and the enjoyer.

2. On the same tree, a soul remains submerged (in worldly affairs) and is grief-stricken, worried due to its powerlessness. When it sees the other, the lord that is adored and his greatness, the person is liberated from sorrow.

   The individual soul who under the weight of ignorance identifies with the body, appears as if sunken amidst worldly troubles, desires, and afflictions. However, when such a soul is shown the path of yoga, practises good conduct, controls his organs, meditates, then he sees the supreme lord, the self of all, beyond grief and death. Then he is liberated from grief and he attains the end of all desires.

3. When the seer sees the radiant creator, the lord, the origin of Brahmā, then being illumined, dispelling virtue and vice, being free from taint, one achieves supreme sameness (with the lord).

The truly enlightened seer, having been freed from bondage, suffering, and taint, achieves the supreme non-dual sameness.

4. Certainly, this prāṇa is that which shines in all beings. Knowing this the wise do not speak excessively. Disporting in the self, rejoicing in the self, engaged in work, this one is the senior-most amongst those who know Brahman.

In the commentary it is stated that the prāṇa of all vital forces shines through all beings. Such a person does not speak excessively. For when one realizes that all is the self and there is nothing else, then what need for excessive speech? Such a person has his enjoyment in the self alone. He is drawn to spiritual practices.

5. This self surely is attainable by means of the truth, penance, by means of complete knowledge, by perpetual Brahmacarya. (The self is) within the body, consisting of light, radiant, which can be seen by ascetics whose deficiencies have been removed.

The self can be attained by means of the truth and abjuring the untruth, penance, knowledge. The radiant self can be attained by ascetics through truth, penance, and complete knowledge.

6. Truth alone is victorious and not falsehood. By means of truth is accomplished the path to the gods, by means of which seers who are free from desire ascend to where exists that supreme reservoir of truth.
7. That is great and divine and its form cannot be thought. It is subtler than the subtle, radiant, still further away than what

is far, yet that is here and near. Indeed, it is seen as seated here in this body in the cavity (in the heart).

Brahman is unattainable for the ignorant. Yet it is close at hand for the wise enlightened few, since it is the self. Yogis perceive it as located in the cavity of the heart. The ignorant cannot perceive it here.

8. It is not grasped by means of the eye or even by means of speech nor by means of any other senses; nor is it attained by penance or karma. (When) one's being is purified by the favour of knowledge, thus by him, when the mind is calm in meditation can be seen the indivisible self.

This cannot be known by the senses. The commentary mentions the analogy of a mirror. Just as a stained mirror or ruffled water cannot accurately reflect objects, so the intellect blemished by impurities of attachment cannot perceive the self. However, one who is pure, follows the path of the truth, has senses withdrawn from objects, is engrossed in meditation, such a person is fit to see Brahman.

9. This subtle self is to be realized by means of the consciousness in which the senses have entered in five forms. The senses and consciousness of all creatures are pervaded by the self. When this (the mind) is purified then the self blazes forth.

The subtle self maybe known via pure intelligence. A pure intellect devoid of attachment, grief, etc., reveals itself, its own reality.

10. Whichever worlds a pure being mentally wishes for and whichever desire he aspires for, such worlds and such desires he obtains. From that, one who aspires for prosperity ought to worship the knower of the self.

The person of pure intellect attains any world he wishes to, as well as any object. Therefore one who desires objects and prosperity ought to revere a knower of the self.

II

1. He knows this most exalted place of Brahman, where this universe is established, and is pure and radiant. The wise who worship this person, being free from desire, transcend this seed (the cycle of birth and rebirth).

   Those who are free from desire, who aspire for liberation, a person who knows the self as if it is the ultimate reality, such a person transcends the human condition.

2. Who desires what is desirable, brooding about these desires, he is born in various places along with these desires. Yet of one whose desires are fully satisfied, and who has control over oneself, here only do all his desires completely dissolve.
3. This self is not obtained by study nor by means of intelligence nor by repeated hearing. This self indeed which one seeks to achieve is obtainable by means of this fact of seeking. The self then reveals its own nature.

   The act of sincerely seeking the self is a means to attain the self. With knowledge ignorance is dispelled and the self is revealed. Spiritual disciplines are a significant help to the prayer for attaining the self.

4. This self is not obtained by one devoid of strength, nor by delusion nor by incorrect penance. Yet, he who strives, through these means, if he be wise, this self of his, enters the sanctuary of Brahman.

   Spiritual disciplines are being emphasized here, namely strength, lack of delusion, correct penance. A discerning man following the above who strives diligently for the self enters Brahman.

5. Having achieved this the sages are contented with their knowledge, established in the self, unswayed by passions, serene, having obtained the all-pervading self anywhere, those discerning persons, attentive, indeed enter into all.

   The discerning enlightened ones who have realized Brahman as their own selves, such persons are always deeply engrossed in meditation, even at the time of passing. Just as space confined in a pot is freed after breaking of the pot, so such persons are free of the limiting adjuncts based on ignorance. They enter into all.

6. Those who have completely ascertained the meaning of Vedanta knowledge, who by striving along the path of yoga, of sanyāsa, have purified their being, they, in the worlds of Brahmā, at the time of departure, being identified with supreme immortality, all attain supreme liberation.

   For such liberated persons the time of death is the true departure. They are liberated and attain Brahman. They do not follow any path. The attainment of Brahman is not limited to space.

7. The fifteen parts go to (the elements) on which they are established and all deities into their respective deities. The karmas and the self consisting of intelligence all become single in the supreme imperishable being.

   This verse describes how the constituents of a person resolve into their own basis at the time of liberation. They merge in their causes.

8. Just as rivers ending in the ocean, giving up name and form, thus the wise liberated of name and form attain the divine Puruṣa, that is better than the best.

Name and form are created due to ignorance. The wise, becoming free of ignorance and therefore name and form, attain the divine Puruṣa.

9. Surely the person who knows that supreme Brahman becomes Brahman only. No one will be born in his line who does not know Brahman. He overcomes grief, he overcomes sin. He is free from the knots of the heart and attains immortality.

   He who truly knows that he is Brahman, inevitably attains Brahman. No being can be an obstacle in his path for he is their self. Even in this birth he goes beyond grief, merit, and demerit. He becomes immortal.

10. To them only should one expound the knowledge of Brahman who perform rites, are well versed in the scriptures, who wish to attain Brahman, who with faith, by themselves, sacrifice to the fire known as ekaṛsi and by whom the vow of carrying fire on the head has been undertaken as per rules. The vow of holding fire on the head is a Vedic vow known to those who follow the Atharva Veda.
11. That is this truth. The sage Aṅgiras spoke of it in ancient times. This should not be perused by one who has not performed the vow. Obeisance to the supreme sage. Obeisance to the supreme sage.

    This knowledge ought to be imparted to one who seeks the ultimate, one who is desirous for liberation, and approaches a qualified teacher in the correct manner. However, knowledge is clear to one who has fulfilled the necessary vows.

Select Bibliography

Apte, VamanShivram, *The Student's Sanskrit-English Dictionary*, Delhi: Parimal Publications, 2020.

Chatterjee, Satishchandra and Datta, Dhirendra Mohan, *An Introduction to Indian Philosophy*, Delhi: Motilal Banarsidass, 2016.

Feuerstein, Georg, *The Yoga-sūtra of Patañjali*, Noida: Simon & Schuster, 1989.

Gambhīrānanda, Swāmī, *Eight Upaniṣads, Volume one*, Kolkata: Advaita Ashrama, 2006.

Gambhīrānanda, Swāmī, *Eight Upaniṣads, Volume two*, Kolkata: Advaita Ashrama, 2006.

Hiriyanna, Mysore, *Outlines of Indian Philosophy*, Delhi: Motilal Banarasidass, 2000.

Madhavananda, Swāmī, *The Bṛhadāraṇyaka Upaniṣad.* Kolkata: Advaita Ashrama, 2018.

Mahadevan, T. M. P., *Sankaracharya*, New Delhi: National Book Trust, 2017.

Nikhilananda, Swami, *Vedānta-sāra of Sadānanda*, Kolkata: Advaita Ashrama, 2020.

Olivelle, Patrick, *Upaniṣads*, Oxford: Oxford University Press, 2008.

Potter, Karl H., *Presuppositions of India's Philosophies*, New Delhi: Motilal Banarsidass, 2024.

Radhakrishnan, Sarvepalli, *The Principal Upaniṣads*, Noida, London: HarperCollins Publishers, 2019.

Roebuck, Valerie J., *The Upaniṣads*, Gurugram: Penguin Books India, 2000

Sastri, S. Sitarama, *Upanishads and Sri Sankara's Commentary* (Vol. 1), Delhi: Alpha Editions, 2020.

Sastri, S. Sitarama, *The Upanishads and Sri Sankara's Commentary* (Vol. 2), London: Forgotten Books, 2018.

Sharma, Chandradhar, *A Critical Survey of Indian Philosophy*, Delhi: Motilal Banarsidass, 2013.

Swāhānanda, Swāmī, *The Chāndogya Upaniṣad*. Chennai: Adhyaksha, 2009.

Tripathy, Preeti, *Indian Religions: Tradition, History and Culture*, Delhi: Axis Publications, 2010.

Bronkhorst, Johannes, *Greater Magadha: Studies in the Culture of Early India*, Leiden: Brill, 2007.

Index